The Villa and The Vortex

Also published by Handheld Press

The Villa and The Vortex

Supernatural Stories, 1916–1924

by Elinor Mordaunt

edited by Melissa Edmundson

Handheld Classic 22

This edition published in 2021 by Handheld Press
72 Warminster Road, Bath BA2 6RU, United Kingdom.
www.handheldpress.co.uk

ISBN 978-1-912766-42-0

1 2 3 4 5 6 7 8 9 0

Series design by Nadja Guggi and typeset in Adobe Caslon Pro
and Open Sans.

Printed and bound in Great Britain by Short Run Press, Exeter.

Contents

Acknowledgements

I would like to express my gratitude to Kate Macdonald of Handheld Press, for commissioning me to curate the stories in this book.

I also wish to thank Jeff Makala for his feedback on the introduction and his editorial assistance.

And my gratitude, as always, goes to Murray, Maggie, Kitsey, and Remy for their furry support.

Melissa Edmundson

Melissa Edmundson is Lecturer in British Literature at Clemson University and specializes in nineteenth and early twentieth-century British women writers, with a particular interest in women's supernatural fiction. She is the editor of a critical edition of Alice Perrin's *East of Suez* (1901), published by Victorian Secrets in 2011, and author of *Women's Ghost Literature in Nineteenth-Century Britain* (University of Wales Press, 2013) and *Women's Colonial Gothic Writing, 1850–1930: Haunted Empire* (Palgrave Macmillan, 2018). Her other work includes essays on the First World War ghost stories of H. D. Everett and haunted objects in the supernatural fiction of Margery Lawrence, as well as a chapter on women writers and ghost stories for *The Routledge Handbook to the Ghost Story*. She has also edited *Avenging Angels: Ghost Stories by Victorian Women Writers*, published by Victorian Secrets in 2018. Her Handheld Press titles include *Women's Weird: Strange Stories by Women, 1890–1940* (2019) and *Women's Weird 2: More Strange Stories by Women, 1891–1937* (2020).

Introduction

BY MELISSA EDMUNDSON

> 'I seem to have lived so many lives, died so many deaths;
> been in so many different countries, among such diverse
> people, becoming for the time being part of themselves,
> that there are times when I feel like a disembodied spirit;
> just floating about seeing and not being seen.'

— Elinor Mordaunt, *Sinabada*

Elinor Mordaunt lived an eventful life, a life that would have fitted well into the plot of one of her many novels. She was an independent, free-spirited woman, travelling the world, and visiting North and South America, Africa, Asia, and Australia. She lost a fiancé early in life, escaped from one abusive husband, separated from another, and raised a son entirely on her own. She survived malaria, the zeppelin attacks on London during the First World War, and the 1918–19 Spanish flu. Amidst this life of adventure, Mordaunt was constantly gathering material for her writing. From the beginning of the twentieth century until the early 1940s she published best-selling novels with leading London publishing houses, as well as collections of short fiction, travel literature, works for children, and numerous pieces for magazines and newspapers. Her writing was compared by reviewers to that of Algernon Blackwood, H G Wells, and Joseph Conrad, and her work was reviewed favourably alongside publications by Blackwood and James Joyce. Both Virginia Woolf and Katherine Mansfield reviewed her work.

Throughout her career as a professional writer, Mordaunt also excelled at the supernatural story. From her earliest published collection in 1914, she included supernatural and weird themes, and each collection that followed incorporated at least one strange tale. Many of these stories involve Mordaunt's fascination with the sea and sailing, while others concern themselves with life in the back streets and alleyways of London. Her characters likewise come from all walks of life and reflect Mordaunt's lifelong interest in and observation of people. Across her work, no two of her strange tales are alike. There are non-supernatural stories of obsession and revenge that lean towards the Gothic and Weird, while a few stories could now be described as science fiction. In these collections, there are inventive reimaginings of haunted houses, 'ghosts' of people not yet dead, prehistoric beings, monsters that inhabit dreams, witches that come straight out of a folk horror tradition, mermaids, cursed plays, and deranged scientists.

Elinor Mordaunt is responsible for an eclectic and wide-ranging output of supernatural fiction that rivals the best writing by her contemporaries. Yet in the decades following her death in 1942, Mordaunt was neglected and largely forgotten as an author, her work omitted from the subsequent anthologies that helped to ensure the reputations of fellow writers. Her otherworldly creations have lost none of their potency and still have the power to shock, to impress us with their originality and inventiveness. This major voice within the supernatural genre has been neglected for far too long, and it is time that her work returned to a wider audience.

Life and works

Elinor Mordaunt was born Evelyn May Clowes on 7 May 1872 at Cotgrave, near Nottingham, to St John Legh Clowes and Elizabeth Caroline Bingham Clowes, and had six brothers and a sister. The family moved to Charlton Park, Cheltenham, Gloucestershire, when she was five and later lived in Oxfordshire. Mordaunt was allowed a great deal of freedom in her youth and said in her autobiography that 'there was certainly nothing Victorian about my upbringing' (Mordaunt 1938, 29). She described her early education as 'perfectly futile' (35), as the family changed governesses quite often and with each new one her education seemed to start over again. She remembered that Cassell's threepenny book series of classic works was a revelation in her self-education, and she constantly carried one in her pocket. Her mother would read Thomas Hardy's novels aloud to the family, and she would enact Shakespeare plays with her friends. When she was around eighteen, Mordaunt's family sent her to London for a couple of months to study painting, but she was happy to return to the country, riding horses and spending time outdoors.

In her twenties, Mordaunt began a courtship with William Banks Wright, who made his money in South Africa by farming and speculating in gold. She accepted his proposal of marriage, and intended to return to South Africa with him, but the marriage was delayed because of her father's stroke, and Wright departed without her, planning to return to Britain in six months. He died suddenly of fever while leading an expedition along the Zambezi River near Bulawayo.

Around 1897, still mourning the loss of Wright, Mordaunt went to Mauritius with a cousin's family and shortly after married Maurice Wiehe, a sugar planter. The marriage was unhappy from the beginning, and Mordaunt states in her autobiography that Wiehe only married her with the idea of obtaining some professional position by connecting himself to her family. At one point, he even offered her 'as a stake' when playing cards (76). The marriage resulted in two stillborn children, but Mordaunt said, 'One effect it had upon me was that it started me writing' (74). Suffering from malaria and pregnant once again, Mordaunt left Mauritius – and her husband – two and a half years later. She spent three months at her family's home in England but, still desperate for a change and feeling miserable and depressed, decided to sail for Australia. She recalled, 'One might have thought my life had ended in the mid-twenties. Nothing of the sort, it was beginning again, but upon a completely different plane. I was at last getting hold of it and knew what I wanted' (80).

Shortly after arriving in Melbourne in 1903, with £30 to her name, Mordaunt gave birth to her son, Godfrey Weston Wiehe. Taking advantage of the gift she had for drawing and painting, she sewed blouses and cushions, painted fabrics, parasols, and advertisements and eventually ran a small embroidery design business. She said, 'I remember everything by line and colour, the curve of a road, the fine lines of a person's face, the expression etched upon it when this or that was said. [...] I gather it all up and use it in my stories' (40, 41).

She took an editorial post at a woman's monthly magazine at £2 a week, which made it possible for her to move out of her two-room residence in Melbourne and into a small cottage outside the city. She wrote articles on cooking, managed the advice columns, and wrote short stories, but was later fired with only a week's notice because the printers could not read her writing. Luckily, Mordaunt's first book, *The Garden of Contentment* (1902), a series of fictional letters written from England which she began while living in Mauritius, was receiving good reviews, and Charles Bogue Luffman, the principal of Burnley College (a horticultural school in Melbourne) put her in touch with a man who wanted to redesign his garden, agreeing to pay her £200 to complete the project.

She then accepted an offer from Luffman to live with him and supervise the female students at the college. Mordaunt valued his friendship, but he began to be possessive and, as Mordaunt was uninterested in a romantic relationship, the two parted ways. She left the college with five shillings and returned to rented rooms and her painting and home design work. She eventually took commissions for several design projects. Her health was constantly bad, however, and after her fourth trip to the hospital, her friends urged her to travel back to England.

In 1908, Mordaunt returned to England and lived for a short time at her parents' home while making money selling short stories to magazines and writing children's stories under the name 'John Heron'. Shortly after her arrival, *Rosemary: That's for Remembrance*

(1909) was published in Melbourne and London, and her first travel book *On the Wallaby through Victoria* (1911), writing as 'E M Clowes', was published by William Heinemann. During this time she also began writing fairy tales, and an illustrated collection of fairy stories for children, *Shoe and Stocking Stories*, was published in 1915. She moved to London after being hired by the weekly paper *Black and White* and worked there until it ceased publication in 1912.

Luckily for Mordaunt, her publishing career was about to take off. *A Ship of Solace* (1911), based on her journey from Britain to Australia, was accepted by William Heinemann, who told Mordaunt upon their first meeting, 'You've got genius' (147). Heinemann paid her £30 for the novel, which enabled her to open a bank account. She published several books with Heinemann, and used her newfound success to reinvent herself, legally changing her name to 'Evelyn May Mordaunt'.

By 1933 Mordaunt had published books with Heinemann, Cassell, Methuen, Hutchinson, Martin Secker and Michael Joseph. Her novel *Mrs Van Kleek*, published by Secker in 1933, was later adapted into a play. With this success and financial stability, Mordaunt moved to Greenwich, and around 1920 to St John's Wood. After her son had finished college and moved to Kenya Mordaunt was dreading another English winter which would wreak havoc on her health. In 1923 she approached the foreign editor at the *Daily News* with a plan to sail from Marseilles to Tahiti, over the course of a month, on cargo ships and sailing boats. The paper agreed to pay for a series of articles, at £20 each, related to her travels. From Marseilles, she traveled to Martinique, Guadeloupe, through the Panama Canal, and on to Tahiti. She declared, 'I loved the life at Tahiti. I know it is mostly spoilt by dissolute and idle white people, but one can keep clear of them' (237). From Tahiti, she sailed to the Samoan Islands and on to Fiji, New Zealand, Brisbane, and then on to Papua New Guinea where she stayed for a few months. There she was proclaimed 'Sinabada', meaning 'Lady King', and only after her departure did she discover an article written in a French paper saying that she 'was the only woman ever known to have reigned as monarch over sixty cannibal islands' (262). Mordaunt eventually described these travels in *The Venture Book* and *The Further Venture Book*, both published in 1926. After returning to Brisbane, she booked passage on a Dutch cargo boat headed to Indonesia (then the Dutch East Indies). From there, the trip took her to Bali, Java, Sumatra, Ceylon, Bombay, and then to Kenya to visit her son, now married. More years of travel in the Americas followed.

In 1931 Mordaunt's novel *Gin and Bitters* was published pseudonymously by 'A Riposte' with the subtitle 'A Novel about a Novelist who writes Novels about other Novelists'. It was a satirical response to Somerset Maugham's best-selling *roman à clef Cakes and Ale* (1930), whose two main characters many read as unflattering representations of Thomas Hardy and Hugh Walpole. Mordaunt was close friends with Florence Dugdale Hardy and most likely wrote her satire out of retaliation for Maugham's portrayal of the recently deceased Hardy. Her book caused a scandal when Maugham discovered who had written it and that it was to be published in the UK by Martin Secker under the title *Full Circle*. Maugham sued Mordaunt for libel and Secker was forced to withdraw the book from publication and destroy the remaining stock before the case reached court.[1]

Mordaunt was happiest when traveling, and her personal demons always seemed to resurface when she returned to England. She wrote in her autobiography of feeling unsettled at this point in her life, saying, 'I seemed indeed to be forever battling in a sea with a strong underpull' (346). One adverse effect of traveling so much meant that 'though I had friends all over the world, I had no great or intimate friends; too many people had died, and I had nothing and nobody to tie me anywhere' (346–47). She remarked 'It is, indeed, evident that from the very first the fates planned for me to walk alone and to possess nothing that I have not earned; and once in possession they snatch what I have away from me as quickly as possible' (Mordaunt 1938, 347).

After being separated from her husband for over thirty years, Mordaunt advertised for information about him. Hearing nothing, she presumed he was dead, and assumed that she was free to remarry.[2] In 1933, she married Robert Rawnsley Bowles (1865–1947), and in late 1933 the couple sailed from England to Sydney. Mordaunt devoted only a few lines to this relationship in her autobiography, cryptically saying, 'Later on I did, ridiculously enough, fall really in love and married a man several years older than myself, but it began and ended in tragedy' (347). On her arrival at San Pedro, California, in December 1936, Mordaunt is recorded as a widow on the passenger lists.

During the late 1930s, Mordaunt resided in Chelsea, London, and her final years continued to be productive despite lingering health problems. She died at the Radcliffe Infirmary, Oxford, on 25 June 1942.

The art of the short story

Elinor Mordaunt was dedicated to the short story form and consistently published short fiction collections amongst her novels. The first, *The Island* (1914), was based on her time on Mauritius. This was followed by *Before Midnight* (1917), *Old Wine in New Bottles* (1919), *Short Shipments* (1922), *People, Houses & Ships* (1924), *And Then–?: Tales of Land and Sea* (1927), *Traveller's Pack* (1933), and *Death It Is and Other Stories* (1939). *The Tales of Elinor Mordaunt* (1934) contains thirty-eight of her stories drawn from previous collections.

To her, these stories represented an important part of her output as a writer, and she found the writing process both frustrating and therapeutic. In *Sinabada*, she remarked:

> one unalterably good point in writing books and stories [...] is that one can look back upon one's own silly life, which falls in blocks of years like the slices of a cut cake, almost as dispassionately as one looks back upon one's last novel. Almost I say, for there is an inmost core of

oneself so deeply wounded by it all that one dare not so much as touch it with a thought; the only way is to live on the top of things. (347–48)

In 'How to Write Short Stories', published in 1924, Mordaunt, writing from personal experience, declared that 'melancholy alone breeds good work. Nobody can express big things until they have gone through soul-stirring experiences'. In the article, she also repeated what to her was an integral part of the creative process: that good writing must come from within the author's own experiences. She said, 'I have given up the idea that you have to wait for inspiration. Some of the stories I write have been simmering in my mind for many years before they find expression' (Mordaunt 1924, 13). When asked how to write a short story, she stressed the importance of discipline and advised, 'You should write your stories without ceasing if you want to succeed, sparing nothing in the way of trouble, grudging nothing in the way of serious mental outlay' (Mordaunt 1924). Writing was a way of life, but it was also serious and time-consuming work.

Her work was consistently mentioned in major periodicals of the time and received mostly positive reviews. Given this literary fame which she sustained through a forty-year career, it is perplexing to consider how and why her work is now virtually forgotten. In his article, 'How *Not* to Write Novels' for the *Derby Daily Telegraph* on 26 October 1929, W Pett Ridge listed some common pitfalls in fiction writing, and praised Mordaunt, along with John Galsworthy, Arnold Bennett, and W B Maxwell for their ability to write about ordinary, everyday characters. R Brimley Johnson in *Some Contemporary Novelists (Women)* (1920) commended the 'severe aloofness and grim humour' of Mordaunt's writing, as well as her ability to draw distinct characters (Johnson 1920, 47). As a 'dissector of souls', she 'has a cool, penetrating, gift for emotional analysis and a dramatic instinct for composition' (59). Johnson compared Mordaunt's work in her own time to that of the Brontë sisters: 'Like them, she is not quite in line with the main developments of her age. She, too, has in her a certain violence of phrase and thought, an almost savage intensity that approaches the melodramatic' (59–60). Yet when discussing her *Before Midnight* (1914), Johnson regressed to the regrettable opinion that Mordaunt was not 'very successful in the short story where, indeed, women have seldom excelled' (57). As dismissive as this statement is, it gives readers a clue as to why Mordaunt's work is so underrepresented in discussions of short fiction from the early twentieth century: women's writing just didn't matter for many critics, especially in Mordaunt's time, but also in the decades following her death. Additionally, some reviewers did not know what to do with Mordaunt's writing. It was either too melodramatic or too unflinching.

However, her supernatural stories were favourably compared to the work of Algernon Blackwood and H G Wells, who were then considered two of the masters of the Weird tale. *Punch*'s review of *Before Midnight* noted the 'psychic (though not always ghostly) character' of the stories, which on the whole are 'original and impressive' (Anon, *Punch* 1917) and concluded that 'all lovers of the occult' will find the collection worthwhile reading. Indeed, *Before Midnight* is one of Mordaunt's most supernaturally-themed collections, including 'The Weakening Point' and 'The Country-side,' along with 'Pan', 'The Vision', and 'Parentage'. *The Illustrated London News* highlighted how the stories departed from the more realistic themes in her earlier novels, saying that Mordaunt 'lean[ed] towards the mystical and the occult' to excellent effect in the collection (Anon, *Illustrated London News* 1917). The *New Statesman* review drew particular attention to 'The Country-side,' calling it 'a really terrifying study in modern witchcraft', and remarking that the story's 'combination of every-day things with the things of occult and ancient horror is in a high degree effective'. The reviewer concluded by saying that the 'collection stands head-and-shoulders above most volumes of short stories' (Anon, *New Statesman* 1917).

Reviews for later collections also tended to highlight her supernatural stories. For instance, Edwin Muir's review of *People, Houses & Ships* for *The Nation & The Athenaeum* noted 'Her best stories are those about houses' and singled out 'Four Wallpapers', 'in which the horror is not laid on, but is part of the scheme' (Muir 1924). The *Bookman*'s review of *Short Shipments* specifically mentioned the 'eerie beauty' of 'The Fountain' and the 'weird history' of 'Hodge', concluding, 'All who can appreciate good writing will find great pleasure in this book' (Anon, *Bookman* 1922). H C Harwood's review in the *Outlook* likewise called attention to 'Hodge,' remarking, 'It is in the shocker that her success is most evident' (Harwood 1922). The *Spectator* called 'Hodge' 'the most horrifying' story in the collection before declaring that 'People with strong nerves may pass an exciting couple of hours over the volume' (Anon, *Spectator* 1922, 533).

W L Courtney, writing for the *Daily Telegraph*, proclaimed that the stories in *Before Midnight* were 'so good that I can think of no better compliment than to say that they are worthy to be read side by side with Mr Blackwood's' (Courtney 1917). C S Evans echoed Courtney and other reviewers in recognizing Mordaunt's ability to draw sympathetic, human characters:

> [The other stories in *Before Midnight*] are all more than usually interesting, because they approach the subject from the human side. Miss Mordaunt's people are breathing human folk, even those most sensitive people who experience the lure of the unknown, and not merely abstractions created to carry out an idea. (Evans 1917)

The *Saturday Review* was even more complimentary: 'She challenges Mr Wells in the laboratory, Mr Burke in Limehouse, Mr Conrad at sea' (Anon, *Saturday Review* 1922, 422).

Other reviews focused on Mordaunt's ability to vary her subject matter, the vigorous quality of her writing, and her ability to hold a reader's attention. The review of *And Then–?* in the *Bookman* applauded her 'relentless grasp of human nature in its fundamental weakness and strength' (Anon, *Bookman* 1928). This 'relentless', at times fatalistic, quality in Mordaunt's writing is remarked upon in several reviews, with the reviewers ultimately finding her hard-edged style appealing. In August 1914, the *Bookman* reviewed *The Island* alongside James Joyce's *Dubliners*, and commended Mordaunt for a 'very powerful' collection, saying of the stories, 'If they were less powerful they might be much more pleasant to read, but then they would have failed of their purpose' (Pugh 1914). There is indeed a relentless bleakness to Mordaunt's supernatural fiction that blends perfectly with the supernatural entities that appear in the pages of these collections.

The stories

Although she remained doubtful about the existence of an afterlife, Mordaunt occasionally mentioned in her autobiography her encounters with the supernatural. These include the premonitions she had throughout her life and the ghostly tales and local legends that were told to her as a child. One particular story was about witches' charms and how to use snails to heal warts, something she would later incorporate into her own tale of witchcraft, 'The Country-side.' During her time in Papua New Guinea, she recalled seeing a Napoleonic sailor cross a path in front of her, 'the only authentic ghost of my life' (Mordaunt 1938, 285). Mordaunt's short stories showcase a variety of otherworldly, supernatural entities as she drew inspiration from folklore, myth, legend, and history.

One quality that sets Mordaunt's supernatural stories apart from many other contemporary strange/ghostly tales is their length, with some at the length of a novella. Mordaunt excelled at these longer stories, using the space to more fully develop individual characters and to explore their motives and fears, their secret desires and obsessions, their rise and inevitable downfalls.

The first story in this volume, 'The Weakening Point,' is an example of a prophetic dream narrative with a very similar plot to John Buchan's story 'Basilissa', which was published in *Blackwood's* in 1914 and later developed into his 1926 novel *The Dancing Floor*. However, unlike Buchan's story, there is no happy ending and the impending doom of the recurring dream never abates. Bond Challice struggles with an ominous dream every year on his birthday, to such an extent that his life becomes paralyzed by fear. Challice remarks, 'I've never read anything adequate about fear. I've never heard anyone say anything that's any use about it – that gives one any idea of what it really is' (21). And indeed, the story is as much about Challice facing his fear as it is about meeting the monster in his dreams. In many ways, the two things are one.

There are also definite, yet subtle, class and societal tensions in the story. Like the monster in his dream, Bond Challice seems to live in progressively smaller rooms, as the expectations that accompany his role as aristocrat and heir to the Challice estate give him constant anxiety. He fails at being a soldier, leaves Cambridge, loses his fiancée, fails at everything. Bond doesn't seem to 'fit' anywhere. To Bond's father, 'It appeared to him inexplicable that he and his wife, normal as they were, should have produced anything so abnormal as Bond had grown to be' (35). Challice's loyal friend Patterson is asked by Bond's mother to help her son, not thinking about the inconvenience to him or the financial strains he is put under at the repeated requests. The narrator also notes that Bond had access to help that others not of his class would not have: 'If he had been a poor man he would have been in a lunatic asylum with an infinitesimal chance of ever getting well again – permeated with the very atmosphere of madness' (34). The real point of fear in this story is not the impending death symbolized by the imagined monster, but the reality of a life wasted.

'The Country-side' is a tale of witchcraft tinged with folk horror. The locals and their traditions are seen from the perspective of

Margaret Wister, the rector's wife and an outsider. Coming from the city, she represents a threat to the inhabitants of the isolated village and must carefully manoeuvre within the village's rigid social structures. Her status as a marginal character puts her in contact with another outsider, Mrs Orpin, the local wise woman whom many fear as a witch in league with the devil. Yet it is through Mrs Orpin that Margaret is able to make her husband confess his less-than-religious habits. Indeed, by the narrative's end, Mordaunt manages to craft a tale both of a woman's suffering and of womanly power, as the rector and his Christian faith are literally overpowered by a group of women practicing folk magic.

With the relentless loneliness and isolation of the rural setting, Margaret is haunted well before her encounter with Mrs Orpin. The tension gradually builds as the battle between the old ways and the new – folk magic and Christian religion – reaches a climax. Yet, as with her other stories, Mordaunt is careful never to lose the human element. The cultural conflicts between urban and rural, old and new religion, and traditional and modern ways of thinking are encapsulated in the literal battle over Margaret's soul in the final pages as the traditional Welsh belief in sin eating provides one of the most effective shock endings in all of Mordaunt's short fiction.

'The Vortex' is a story of creative obsession. In many ways, Lawrence Kestervon is reminiscent of Bond Challice; he is a lost soul who has failed so often in life that he has little left to lose. And herein lies the problem. Kestervon becomes fixated on making his latest play a success, but to what cost? Mordaunt explores what happens when someone puts their heart and soul into the creative process and considers what can happen when that 'soul' is pure evil. Once again, imagination and reality are combined to create an uneasy sense of something being not quite right. The actors and actresses in the play feel this uneasiness but are powerless to prevent themselves (and their real lives) from being taken over by their not-so-fictional characters.

At the beginning of 'The Fountain,' an epigraph by the sixth-century Welsh poet Taliesin gives a clue to the story's folkloric influences. The story reflects the ancient Druidic belief in the transmigration of souls and individuals reborn into different forms. It also draws upon the legend of the *gwenhidwy* (or *gwenhudwy*), a mermaid originating in Welsh folklore. The aptly named Sylvia Colquhoun embodies the natural world around her and exists as a liminal figure throughout the story. She never fully fits into the extravagant, society world of her husband, who further isolates Sylvia due to his philandering and numerous affairs, including one with Sylvia's supposed friend. This sense of liminality is closely linked to the supernatural elements of the story. At one point the narrator describes how Sylvia exists as an elemental entity as well as a woman:

> while to some it seemed like a shadowy plume of water, to others it bore the aspect of a woman, ethereal as mist. 'Both!' cried one hussy, brazen with fear, asserting what must have seemed, to her own limited intelligence, an impossibility. 'Both at once! Not altogether a woman, nor altogether water.' (174)

Harry Colquhoun likewise says, 'People can't be *things*; there's animate and inanimate nature. Oh, hang it all, running water is animate enough, but ... Well, I learnt it all at school, but I can't put it into words; you know what I mean – water's not like – well, human beings' (179).

In the story, death is, chillingly, not a place for rest or peace, and Sylvia remains a victim. Even in death, she is not able to completely transcend her corporeal form or her suffering. Her husband gradually comes to realize this and believes that she is being driven to haunt him by ancient, powerful forces beyond her control, forces that, he believes, are punishing him for his mistreatment of his wife. He, in turn, knows these forces demand a sacrifice. Speaking to Herries near the end of the story, Colquhoun wonders about the power of this 'pagan belief', asking, 'Can a lot of people believing in a thing *make*, create it?' (192). The answer to this question lies at the heart of Mordaunt's story of loneliness and retribution.

The title character in 'Hodge' is one of Mordaunt's most inventive supernatural creations. As a being from prehistory, he is a natural part of the landscape. He is not necessarily out of place, but is otherworldly in the sense that he is not supposed to exist in modern times. When the Fane siblings uncover Hodge, they also expose his behaviour that does not fit with their modern sensibilities. Consequently, Hodge cannot be allowed to fully exist in their world; he belongs to the place but not to the time. This idea connects to the spectral qualities of Hodge within the narrative, as the narrator comments, 'for all its new-found life, it was as far away as any ghost'. Like a ghost, Hodge, after his 'rebirth' into a world he remembers but now cannot fathom, is forced to exist on the periphery, not able to fully become a part of the living world around him. 'Hodge', much like 'The Fountain' and 'The Landlady', provides an intriguing examination of protagonists that are very much between worlds. These characters' liminality places them in a metaphorical no man's land as each story explores how perpetual loneliness and being out of one's natural environment can lead to a ghostly existence. In these stories, Mordaunt seems to suggest that there is no way out of this spiritual conundrum. We can become trapped in isolation and loneliness. It is perhaps no surprise, given this predicament, that each of the supernatural characters in this particular grouping of stories are also some of Mordaunt's most sympathetic portrayals.

'"Luz"' blends the weird tale with science fiction as an unhinged man of science seeks to push the borders of the possible, while at the same time falling victim to hubris that leads directly to a downfall, very much in the tradition of Mary Shelley's Victor Frankenstein. Even before the horrifying events that conclude the story, Mordaunt describes the disorientation caused by a dense fog. The familiar streets and landmarks of London become unknowable to the narrator as she loses her way and becomes increasingly scared and confused. The disorientation also makes her more vulnerable to the mysterious blind man who offers her help. As with 'The Weakening Point', this story contains a meditation on the nature of fear. The narrator realizes that she is scared of fear itself:

> Maybe my fear was all the wilder in that it was concerned with nothing definite. I did not even think of death. In truth, I did not fear *anything* – 'to fear', that is the verb, carrying a different, and, for me at least, a less dreadful meaning. It was Fear itself which had me in its grip, stark, unreasoning – 'shrill, hair-bristling Fear'. (203)

The sense of something present, something not defined but there nonetheless, pervades this claustrophobic tale of obsession and science gone wrong.

'The Landlady' is a reflection on our emotional connections with certain places and how a shared experience of a place can bring us together. It is also about the power of memory and how memories can make the past seem more real and tangible. In the opening paragraph, the narrator asks, 'Why should there not be ghosts of the living as well as of the dead? Why – come to that – should not the word stand, simply and solely, for the true ego of any one of us?' (216). The story certainly pushes the boundaries of what – or who – constitutes a 'ghost', as another character declares, 'She's not a ghost, I tell you, at least not in the ordinary way' (224). The story also interrogates meanings of 'house' and 'home' and notions of dwelling and possessing. Later, Miss Champneys says about returning to her 'real' home, 'It will be like going to heaven'. But as with the other stories in this collection, the notion of heaven is complicated by the end of the story and represents not so much a release as an imprisonment, an unfulfilled move to another house that is not her true home. The past may be another country, but in Mordaunt's story, it is also home.

'Four Wallpapers' is a classic haunted house tale. Mordaunt inventively plays with time as, through the concept of layered wallpapers, readers experience, or 'view', the haunting from 'last' to 'first'. In this story, Mordaunt once again effectively uses first-person narration to give an immediacy and directness to events. We see the ghosts through the eyes of the narrator, and as with previous stories, the past (and past indiscretions) resurface to affect the living. The descriptions of the ghosts and their movement through the wallpapered room is strikingly original, in many ways anticipating how ghosts would appear visually on film. As in 'The Villa,' the house comes alive with troubled energy, and we see apparitions pass in and out of view. The wallpaper is very much like skin – strip it off and it reveals the sinews and bones (the inner workings) of a troubled house that has refused for many years to be a home.

'The Villa' concerns generational haunting and a curse that backfires on a young couple looking for the perfect home. It is based on Mordaunt's trip to Ragusa (in present-day Croatia) in 1914. In *Sinabada*, she recalled visiting the house that would provide inspiration for the story: 'I loved the Ombla so that I thought I would like to live forever on the sunny side of it, and went all round a huge old house which was for sale with a little landing-stage to the river' (Mordaunt 1938, 170). What makes the story so unsettling is the fact that the villa takes revenge not only on the young couple who directly wish ill of its original owner, but also continues to revenge itself on subsequent inhabitants who had nothing to do with the original curse. By dwelling in the villa, they become susceptible to its anger at being robbed of its 'rightful' owner. Mordaunt describes the villa as a sentient being: hating, revenging, waiting. It seemingly sleeps until the next unfortunate enters its doors and falls under its control.

With each generation of the Steven family, its vengeance intensifies. The birth of Daisy Steven's daughter, as well as the subsequent birth of her granddaughter, are each immediately followed by a death. These births are a physical representation of lingering trauma and loss and are marked by previous episodes of violence directly caused by the malign influence of the villa. Though gone, lost mothers haunt the text. The villa preys on the granddaughter of Archie and Daisy Steven, who suffers from terrible dreams associated with a place she has never seen. The sins of the fathers and mothers are visited upon the children, and their children after them, in a seemingly never-ending cycle of sorrow, grief, and forced expiation. Indeed, a feeling of loss pervades the story. The narrator imagines to herself:

> Somehow or other I have missed the lightheartedness of that intermediate generation. Perhaps it did not go deep enough, was never really there at all – think of the secret, brooding sense of wrong, the truly primitive suspicions and fear and passion, which must have possessed my father, despite his veneer of modernity and gaiety, to lead to such an end. And wondering over this brings one to that other wonder as to what my mother *really* thought, to affect me as I was affected; though it may have been nothing more than the fact that I was conceived and passed the months before my birth in that accursed Villa. How melodramatic it looks when one writes it, and yet that is what it was. (294)

The ending of Mordaunt's story and the ultimate fate of the villa leaves readers with an intriguing question: can intense hatred be perpetually sustained, or does it eventually wear itself out?

✖

In *Writing a New World: Two Centuries of Australian Women Writers* (1988), Dale Spender includes a brief mention of Mordaunt's work in a chapter titled 'The Supporting Cast.' She says, 'it would be helpful if her work were to be more thoroughly examined for the possible place it might provide the author in women's literary history' (Spender 1988, 193). Sadly, Spender's book was published over thirty years ago, and Mordaunt's writing is still very much underacknowledged. Though this present collection contains a selection of Mordaunt's best supernatural tales, it is by no means comprehensive. Supernatural/Weird stories appear in every collection of short fiction she published from 1914–1939, meaning that she contributed to the genre of supernatural fiction for a quarter of a century. Yet it is difficult to find Mordaunt's name included in anthologies along with the other 'greats' of the supernatural genre. It is my sincere hope that this present volume of Elinor Mordaunt's supernatural fiction will allow her work to take its place within women's literary history and within the tradition of supernatural fiction.

Notes

1   Responding to a notice in *The New York Times* on 7 May 1931 that the British rights to the novel were being held up, Mordaunt wrote a letter published in *The New York Times* on 14 May 1931, claiming: 'Neither Somerset Maugham nor his friends have approached me in any way in regard to the English rights; nor have I heard anything from Hugh Walpole, which is not surprising, as I am totally unacquainted with him' (Mordaunt 1931). For more on this dispute, see Raymond Toole Stott's *A Bibliography of the Works of W Somerset Maugham* (1973), 226; Ted Morgan's *Maugham* (1980), 338–342; and Samuel J Rogal's *A William Somerset Maugham Encyclopedia* (1997), 68.

2   Records show that a Maurice W Wiehe, born in Mauritius in 1864, died in Southwark, London, in 1951 at age 86. Available electoral records show that he was living in St Pancras, London, in 1937–1939 and 1948.

Works Cited

Anon, review of *Before Midnight*, *New Statesman*, 17 March 1917, 570.

Anon, review of *Before Midnight*, *Punch*, 21 March 1917, 188.

Anon, review of *Before Midnight*, *The Illustrated London News*, 14 April 1917, 444.

Anon, review of *Short Shipments*, *Saturday Review*, 22 April 1922, 422–423.

Anon, review of *Short Shipments*, *Spectator*, 29 April 1922, 532–533.

Anon, review of *Short Shipments*, *Bookman*, October 1922, 6.

Anon, review of *And Then–?*, *Bookman*, April 1928, 64.

Courtney, W L, review of *Before Midnight*, *Saturday Review*, 31 March 1917, ix.

Evans, C S, 'The Lure of the Unknown,' *Bookman*, May 1917, 52.

Harwood, H C, review of *Short Shipments*, *Outlook*, 15 April 1922, 303.

Johnson, R Brimley, *Some Contemporary Novelists (Women)* (London: Leonard Parsons, 1920).

Mordaunt, Elinor, 'How to Write Short Stories,' *Daily News* (Perth), 19 January 1924, 13.

—, 'Letters to the Editor,' *The New York Times*, 14 May 1931, 21.

—, *Sinabada* (New York: The Greystone Press, 1938).

Muir, Edwin, review of *People, Houses & Ships*, *The Nation & The Athenaeum*, 20 December 1924, 447.

Pugh, Edwin, review of *The Island*, *Bookman*, August 1914, 220.

Ridge, W Pett, 'How *Not* to Write Novels,' *Derby Daily Telegraph*, 26 October 1929, 6.

Spender, Dale, *Writing a New World: Two Centuries of Australian Women Writers* (London: Pandora, 1988)

Publication dates

Unless otherwise noted, the present texts are based on *The Tales of Elinor Mordaunt*, published by Martin Secker in 1934.

'The Weakening Point' was originally published in the 16 January 1916 issue of *The Illustrated Sunday Magazine*. It was included in Mordaunt's collection *Before Midnight* (Cassell 1917) and *The Tales of Elinor Mordaunt*.

'The Country-side' was published in *Before Midnight* and *Tales of Elinor Mordaunt*.

'The Vortex' was published in Mordaunt's *Old Wine in New Bottles* (Hutchinson 1919) and later in *Tales of Elinor Mordaunt* (Hutchinson 1922).

'The Fountain' was originally published in the June 1921 issue of *Hutchinson's Magazine*. It later appeared in *Short Shipments* and *Tales of Elinor Mordaunt*. 'The Fountain' was also included in *A Muster of Ghosts* (1924), edited by Bohun Lynch.

'"Luz"' was published in *Short Shipments* and *Tales of Elinor Mordaunt*.

'The Landlady' was originally published in the August 1923 issue of *Hutchinson's Magazine*. It later appeared in Mordaunt's collection *People, Houses & Ships* (Hutchinson 1924) and *Tales of Elinor Mordaunt*.

'Four Wallpapers' was published in *People, Houses & Ships*. The present text is based on this edition.

'The Villa' was published in *People, Houses & Ships* and *Tales of Elinor Mordaunt*.

Obvious typographical errors and inconsistencies have been silently corrected, and some punctuation has been modernised where it would not affect meaning. American spellings have been rendered into British English.

1 The Weakening Point (1916)

The boy had been born soon after midnight, on the twenty-fourth of June – happily born to expectant and happy young parents – the very crown of their love, heir to great estates and all the spacious beauties of Challice Court. No baby in the world could have been more eagerly desired, dreamt over, planned for.

His mother was so pretty, a fair, slender girl, with just those same wonderful grey-blue eyes which the boy inherited; his father such a sure specimen of the soldier, early developed into the country squire. A little Georgian, a little inclined to solidity in mind and body, but for all that a very upright, kind-hearted English gentleman without an enemy in the world. No wonder it seemed impossible to believe that anything but good could come of their mating, while the state of life into which the boy was born – the quiet, well-ordered life at Challice – with ample space and air and leisure, its all exquisite cleanliness – appeared to be so much part of the eternal fitness of things that there was no placing the curious shadow which lay across the young life.

Looking back, it seemed as if there had never been any dark corners in the family history. Through century after century the Challices had passed on their name, like an untarnished shield, free from the breath of any scandal; while the same quiet, dignified women – so much of a type that they, too, might have belonged to one unbroken race – had ruled over their household, brought up their children, ministered among their poor, from one generation to another: for through all time no Challice had ever been guilty of anything like a *mésalliance*.

And Challice itself. What an inheritance! The church with its square, squat tower, the village, the scattered hamlets, climbing the rolling Downs and dipping to the sea; for mile upon mile of the Downs was Challice property: so secure that it seemed as if the very clouds which topped them – bent to them, raced across them – were more a part of Challice ownership and less of God's than the rest of the sky.

Then nearer home, more intimate, there was the Park, an endless land of romance to little Bond Challice. There were the great trees, with twisted trunks all gnarled and split, the long velvety shadows mantling the deer at twilight; the little streams and oozy dips with the tall, hollow-stemmed hemlocks – which made such pipes – and the masses glow of marsh mallows; the squirrels' caches among the hollows of the beech roots; the wise old pike – which still lurked in those fishponds whence the monks of Challice had drawn their fasts – or feasts. All alike dear to the boy, who left his daisy-chains for a pony at the age of three, fighting against the leading rein, with Osborn – the stud groom – who had been a jockey and won more than one race for old Bond Challice, young Bond's grandfather. For it had always been like that, a Bond and then a Jervis, then another Bond. The custom was so fixed that before his birth the boy's father and mother had only discussed the question of feminine names, in case the longed-for baby should – by any mischance – prove to be a girl.

Picture the old house, red-bricked and peaceful, with that great vine across the south end, which the only alien bride – a beauty with an historic name – had brought with her from Italy, when she gave up her own high-sounding title for the nobler one of plain Mrs Challice. Picture it thus, set round with the wide park, the woods, coppices, hangers, spinneys – and, above all, the mothering Downs. It was like nothing so much as one of those naïve, mellow pictures of the Christ

Child in the arms of the Virgin: smiling too, for the place seemed to gather and hold all the sunshine of years. Its mullioned windows twinkled with it: even amid the snow its warm walls looked sun-browned. Indoors everything shone: the polished oak panelling, the pewter and silver, the weapons upon the walls of the great centre hall with its far-away beams, while over all was the scent of beeswax and lavender and pot-pourri.

In the walled garden – which lay smiling, full in the sun's eye – all the paths were edged knee high with rosemary, against which little Bond loved to brush himself in his tunic days. There was a round pond in the middle of it with goldfish, and there were peacocks, blue and white. Bond always knew that the white were the ghosts of the blue which had died, and come back to pace the grassy paths and smooth lawns which no peacock could help loving. Not that the thought frightened him. His whole world revolved round him so smoothly and sweetly; it was so beautiful, so fragrant, and, above all, so secure. Once indeed a hawk dropped sheer from the blue and took one of his yellow bantam chicks almost from under his very eyes. But that was all of horror which he knew – apart from his birthnights. And after all, there was so much blue sky, and there had been only that one hawk, as there was that one night of terror in the whole of every year – while years were long in those days.

When Bond grew older he began to question his mother as to how it had all begun.

On the anniversary of his first birthday, Mrs Challice told him, he had cried so violently that the nurse had come running to her in a panic. And that showed how bad it must have been, for like all nurses she distrusted mothers and the judgment of mothers. On his third birthnight it had been the same; while on the fourth he had scrambled out of his cot, run to her room and flung himself upon her bed, lain clinging to her till morning, sobbing passionately, trembling from head to foot, the dear, soft little body drenched with sweat.

Still one can forget a lot in a year, and somehow Mrs Challice, engrossed as she was in the child, missed the curious sequence of these nights of terror; till, on the morning after he topped his fifth year, nurse remarked what a pity it was that Master Bond was always so upset on the night before his birthday – spoiling all his pleasure in parties and presents.

Before Bond's sixth birthday the mother had begun to connect things up and had the child to sleep with her. Thus she saw it all through. The uneasy startings and twitchings, the swelling rise and climax of his terror – when he awoke and clung round her neck shrieking.

'It's coming, it's coming! Send it away, Mummy – Oh, Mummy, Mummy! Send it away, send it away – do send it away!'

He had lain trembling without sleep all the rest of the night, and at daybreak Mrs Challice sent for the doctor who prescribed a soothing draught and perfect quiet. Not that this last injunction was needed, for the strong, restless boy was limp, inert and apathetic for days to come.

Gradually, however, he won back his old self, and they all began to forget – till the spring wore round to summer once more.

On Bond's seventh birthday both his parents were abroad. They had been hurrying home, for the thought of that dream had got on Mrs Challice's nerves – when Jervis contracted malaria in Florence, which delayed them so that they did not get back till nearly three weeks later than they had originally intended.

But the nurse had written, telling them that Master Bond had dreamt 'as usual'. She had persuaded the housekeeper to sleep with her for the night – somehow it seemed to Mrs

Challice as monstrous that her son's agony should be regarded as inevitable, prepared for. He had been more frightened than ever before – there was no quieting him, said the nurse; while he did not seem to pick up after it as he had always done before – 'the precious lamb'.

However, there did not look much wrong with 'the precious lamb' three weeks later when he raced down the drive to meet them: his yellow curls blowing back from his forehead, his bare brown legs flying, his mouth wide open, shouting 'Mummy, Mummy, Mummy, Daddy', – three 'Mummy's' for every 'Daddy'. Indeed, he looked so well that Mrs Challice's fears were lulled. He seemed such a real boy, so strong and straight and fearless; so completely normal, so full of life and the joy of life.

A week or two before the next birthday, however, she began to grow anxious again: watched him with a brooding air, worried over him unceasingly, and finally took him up to see a great brain specialist, who laughed at the very sight of the lad; pinched his cheek and declared that there did not look to be much wrong there; and finally sounded his lungs and heart and tested the contraction of the pupils of the eyes, all with the tolerantly amused air of a man who is pandering to a wealthy woman's fancy. As for the dreams, most children dreamt; nightmare was a question of digestion, and the fact that the dreams came on the boy's birthnight merely a matter of coincidence. He could – and did – cite many cases which were every bit as curious. Things happened like that; then they got on a person's nerves, were watched, almost waited for. The only piece of real advice that he gave Mrs Challice was to be careful that her own nerves did not react on her son.

Exactly two years and three days later he received a telegram from a doctor in Charlsford – the Challices' nearest town – asking him to come down at once and see a child who was suffering from some curious brain trouble.

The great man had a crowded day in front of him when he received the message. It was after five o'clock before he could reach Waterloo, and just on seven when his train steamed into Charlsford, where he found Doctor Watson waiting on the platform.

The Challices' carriage – with the shining bays that Bond loved – was there; and as the two doctors drove away together the local man expounded some of the particulars of the case.

'You will remember the boy – his mother tells me she took him to see you. A splendid little fellow – at most times perfectly normal – no hereditary weakness – no trace of disease – not in the least nervous or over highly strung. I attended his mother when he was born – the whole thing went as smoothly as possible. I can't imagine any prenatal complications – I confess the whole thing beats me. But there it is. Each birthnight the boy has a dream – almost like a sort of seizure – which obsesses him with terror. A brain storm – if one can believe in such things. Every year since he was a tiny little chap – he's just ten now – they have sent for me; and each time the reaction seems slower in coming. One would imagine that there must be some cerebral irritation, but –' Here he launched forth into scientific speculations and theories, breaking off every moment or so to give the great man time to air his own opinion. But Sir James could afford to be silent, he was thinking and listening, turning all that the other man said rather slowly over in his own mind: and it was only when the carriage was actually turning in at the lodge gates that he broke silence.

'I think I remember them. A charming couple – mother and child. About as healthy and normal as anyone could well be. You don't mean to say that you've brought me all this distance because of that child's dreams?'

'I think when you see the boy you will realize why I took such a step.' Doctor Watson's tone was stiff, for out of an immense weariness the great man had spoken irritably. 'I acknowledge the whole thing is beyond me, and the truth is I'm afraid of the poor little chap's reason giving way,' he added, and said no more. He would let things be, he thought; Sir James could draw his own conclusions when he saw the patient; he did not fancy that – in the end – he would be blamed for over anxiety. He was right; for the moment that the specialist's eyes lighted on the child, he realized that here was a case which no sensible man would have dared to treat lightly.

Little Bond Challice was propped up in bed; he dare not lie down for fear of sleeping. His great blue eyes were wild with the terror of sleep; while it was heartbreaking to see the way that – in his fear – he fought with heart and soul against the narcotic which the great man gave him – twice as powerful a dose as any country practitioner would have ventured on – and the fashion in which he clung to his mother, his boyish strength already greater than hers, his fine young body rigid with agony, his muscular brown hands bruising her slim arms.

But at last it was over, and the boy slept. It was a close June evening; but even this was not hot enough to account for the sweat which was thick on Sir James Barton's forehead, for the agony of the child had been terrible to see.

The two doctors ate their belated dinner together, with all the dead and gone Challices gazing calmly down upon them from their gold frames – not a simper, not a sign of nerves or weakness in any one of the high-bred faces – while Jervis Challice talked to them of the boy, the centre and summit of his whole life.

After a while Mrs Challice joined them. She had had no sleep the night before, all that day she had scarcely left her boy's side; but she was as quiet and steady eyed, as exquisitely dainty, as much the great lady as she had ever been.

They were both, husband and wife alike, people to whom

one could speak openly. Between them they went over the boy's family history, discussed the question of their own health; the whole disposal of the nine months before he was born; the first few months of his infancy.

But at the end of it all Sir James was no wiser than he had been before, for there was nothing, absolutely nothing, upon which he felt he could lay a finger and say, 'It was there that the rift began.' Or even – more doubtfully – 'It *might* have been there.'

Just as they were leaving Mrs Challice put a book into his hands.

'I thought it might be of some help – some use – to you,' she said, looking at him with grave, clear eyes, out of which all the blue seemed to have been momentarily wiped away.

In the midnight express, racing back to town, and later when he ought to have been asleep, the great specialist pored over the little book which his new patient's mother had given him. It was a diary began on the first day when she guessed that she might become a mother; and carried on – without a single break – up to the twenty-third of June, ten years earlier: while through it all there was evidence of a great pride, of love and that high courage which meets a danger as though it were a sacrament – and not one single word of doubt or fear.

When Sir James went down to Challice again a week later the boy was better, though listless and dispirited; sitting on the sunny terrace with a litter of young puppies upon his knees, gazing out over his wide inheritance with a strangely wistful, questioning look.

It was during this visit Mr and Mrs Challice agreed to the doctor's proposal that their son should he sent to school. And it was on his way there, a month later, that the specialist again saw him, to find himself almost laughing at his own fears.

The boy was perfectly all right. No one could have looked

less like one troubled with nerves of any sort. There was nothing of the mollycoddle about him either, and it was plain enough that he was wild to be at school, out of leading-strings, away among boys of his own age.

They left him there over that twenty-fourth of June – though God only knows what Mrs Challice suffered during that night, or what the boy suffered waiting for the horror. Though they guessed something of it a few days later, sitting by his bedside while he raved his way through a fierce attack of brain fever.

They took him away after that, and he was at home with a tutor for nearly three years. Then he was sent to Eton, where no one, excepting the headmaster – and that only through Sir James Barton himself – knew why young Challice always went away just before the one great day of the year, returning when there were only two or three weeks left to the term.

At this time he was willing to talk to his mother about what they both called 'It'. But as he got older, and his boyish reticence grew, he seemed to find it more and more difficult to speak of, while it was evident that he faced his trial with an ever-increasing dread.

The strange thing about it was that it was all so vague. His fear was so inexplicable, so out of proportion to anything he ever saw. Perhaps that was it. Had it been more real, more definite, it might have been easier to grapple with; but it was merely a great shadowy form, too far away for there to be any particular reason for the terror with which it inspired the boy: that wild, unreasoning panic which some people – whose susceptibilities hark back through the ages – feel for the dark, for wide open spaces, for the untamable quality which still lurks in all the cat tribe, for anything which touches them in the middle of the back. It must have indeed been something like that, for – as the boy willingly acknowledged – there was absolutely nothing in the shape itself to account for his terror. Though, of course, there was always the inevitable progress of the thing to be reckoned with.

Anything which persists, which appears at regular intervals, which approaches nearer and is still incomprehensible, is likely to affect even the strongest nerves. And perhaps it was the steady sequence of the dreams which frightened Bond more than anything else. The scene was always the same. He saw the monster at the end of a long vista of brilliantly lighted rooms, but each year the number of rooms which lay between them became one less. Inversely, as the shape grew nearer it seemed to become slightly smaller, though no plainer and no less terrible – rather it was as if the fearfulness of it concentrated to something more poignant each year.

If it had ever skipped a room, had retreated, had even rushed at him, he felt that he could have endured it better; it was this steady progress which helped to make it all so unendurable.

All the Challices had been soldiers; and, almost as a matter of course, young Bond went to Sandhurst.

He arrived there at the beginning of the autumn term: he was liked and respected, but he made no intimate friends. No man with a secret in his life finds it easy to do that; for the wiser among his acquaintances – those whom he would naturally choose – realize that he is holding something back from them. But despite all this, and a certain lack of geniality, Bond was such a good rider and excellent shot, so well-bred and good-looking, so much the born soldier, that he was respected by all, excepting a few of the smaller and more jealous-minded who declared that he gave himself airs. For there is nothing which angers the vulgar-minded so much as reserve.

Much against his will, urged on to it by his mother, Bond managed to get a few days' leave at the time of his birthday.

But his whole heart was in his work, and he went back *just* too soon, before his nerves – horribly shaken as they were – had properly regained their balance.

Sir James Barton – who had grown to love the gallant Challice couple and their son – had always said: 'When he reaches maturity, finishes with his growing-pains, he may be able to throw the whole thing off. Meanwhile the danger lies in anything happening to upset him, to deepen the impression of his dream by making him feel in any way apart from others.'

It was precisely this 'upset' which – appearing in the most unexpected form – was responsible for young Challice relinquishing, once and for all, a soldier's career.

He funked in the riding-school. For a boy who had been brought up astride a horse such a thing seems sufficiently incredible to be regarded as a sort of joke. But to young Challice it was a real tragedy, for it struck at the very root of his self-respect, was the beginning of much that came after. Everyone else was ready to gloss it over, laugh it off, but Bond himself knew better. He had funked once, he might funk again, a man like that was no use for fighting.

He showed a real courage in renouncing the ideal of his life, in going to Cambridge and settling down steadily to work for the Bar. But once there he went to pieces. The thought of his mother's agonized pity, of his father's hopeless attempt at understanding, haunted him. He was always afraid that he was going to be afraid again. The boy who had been so wild with excitement at the mere thought of mixing with his fellows, so eagerly sociable, now kept apart from other men, wondering how much they had heard, breaking through his reserve only when – at some supper or dinner-party – he had taken enough wine to make him forget, feel more like his old self.

During his last year he made a friend. A curiously quiet, clumsy fellow, with badly cut clothes, overhanging brows, unkempt shock of hair, and an old briar pipe, which – lighted or unlighted – was for ever between his teeth, whether he was poring over the books – which so inevitably collected round him that he seemed to spin them out of himself as a caterpillar does with its cocoon – or striding mile upon mile across the flat country, on one of those interminable walks in which young Bond Challice dropped into the habit of accompanying him.

Patterson was of a different class from his friend. His father was a hard-worked Methodist parson, his grandfather had been a silk spinner in North Staffordshire, his grandmother a mill girl. He himself spoke with the broad Midland burr, when he spoke at all – which was seldom. Though his silence was occasionally broken by an outpouring of speech which had in it something of real oratory. Usually he spoke from one side of his mouth only, gripping his pipe in the other; but at times like these he would take it out and hold it in his hand, waving it in the air as he spoke.

Curiously enough Patterson was the only person with whom Bond felt absolutely at ease; perhaps because nothing surprised him. For he realized that there was no end to the intricacies of human nature and the further and deeper intricacies of the spirit.

It was at the beginning of the Michaelmas term that they first made definite friends, started their walks together. And to young Bond Challice the memory of Patterson was for ever mingled with the scent and rustle of dying leaves, the light veils of mist which hung across the fields – thickened to something of the texture of a girl's scarf above the streams – the feeling of a rough coat collar, wet beneath his chin; the stench of sheep and turnips in the open fields, the sweeping cry of the pee-wits above the freshly turned furrows.

In after years he never thought of Patterson as belonging to the spring or summer, though their friendship ran on, uninterruptedly, through the year which followed; while with this one friend – and with him alone – he discussed 'the Dream' – for at this time he could not speak of it to anyone else, not even to his mother.

Patterson took it quite gravely. He never even thought of brushing it away with the useless advice as to not thinking or speaking of it. For he believed that it was best to have everything brought out into the open, thoroughly well aired. He didn't say much, but he let Bond talk, and that was the best thing he could do, while he took it every bit as seriously as his friend; so that there was no longer any need to put it on one side with a half-nervous laugh. Indeed, it was Patterson and not Bond who said – when it first came to be discussed between them – 'I don't see that there is anything to laugh at.' It was also Patterson who made the suggestion – the first of its kind which anyone had ever ventured on – that they should definitely prepare for the dream: endeavouring to circumvent it by keeping young Challice awake all night.

A few days before the birthnight they both managed to get a couple of nights' leave of absence and went down to Challice Court; for, as Patterson said, 'It isn't fair to keep your people out of it.'

Patterson and his briar pipe seemed oddly out of place in Bond's home, while the Challices themselves were clearly puzzled by their son's new friend. After a couple of days, however, they, too, found themselves telling him everything, confiding in him, appealing to him as they had never confided in or appealed to anyone in the whole of their lives; while as to the man himself, from the first moment he would have lain down and allowed Mrs Challice to walk over him. For she was like nothing that he had ever known before; the very sight of her slender white hands laid so quietly in her lap entranced him, accustomed as he was to his own women's eternal busyness with knitting-needles or sewing.

Bond made one stipulation. Patterson, and Patterson alone, was to watch with him that night – for he had grown terribly afraid of showing any weakness in front of his people.

They sat it out in the boy's own den, hung round with all the paraphernalia of sport. The day had been cold and wet, very unlike June, and a little fire was lighted in the grate, serving alike for warmth and for keeping hot the coffee with which they proposed to ensure wakefulness.

Bond had felt certain that he would not sleep; and with Patterson to keep him company it would be easy enough to keep the enemy at bay, he had even laughed at the precaution of the coffee.

Towards twelve o'clock, however, it was as if he had been drugged. He even entreated the other man to let him sleep; swore at him, wearily and pettishly, when he took him by the arm and forced him to tramp up and down the room.

Towards two o'clock it seemed hopeless to go on fighting the enemy in that warm room, amid the sleeping household. And Patterson dragged his charge out of doors, up hill and down dale, till – from atop the swelling breast of the Downs – they saw the sun rising across the sea.

By that time Bond had passed the desire to sleep. It seemed that he had at last scotched his bogey. He was wild with excitement and triumph as they tramped back to Challice, and insisted that they should have out their horses and ride till it was time to race home and get a bath in readiness for breakfast – though Patterson hated riding, sat like a sack, looked each moment as though he was going to tumble off, but somehow managed to stick on, the pipe still between his teeth.

At breakfast-time that morning, when Bond took his mother in his arms and hugged her in his old, exuberant boyish fashion, she did a surprising thing for a woman of her calibre; she went up to Patterson and kissed him good morning also – exactly as if he had been a second son.

Bond was in the seventh heaven. The spell was broken; he went back to Cambridge and worked and played like a young Titan.

'What a good chap that fellow Challice is' – 'Ripping good sort, Challice – never knew he had so much in him, always thought he was a bit of a stick.'

That was the general verdict. He was borne high on the wave of popular enthusiasm: was in constant demand: started hunting again the following winter; went to dances, flirted, lived to the full; and finally fell in love with the sister of one of his newer friends, the only daughter of a famous judge: proposed and was accepted – to the delight of everyone, for Doris Cartwright was exactly the sort of bride that a Challice was expected to choose.

The young couple spent the Easter vacation at Challice Court. Bond was still confident, but his buoyancy was beginning to ebb. Time was drawing in, and the thought of the dream grew upon him once more.

Then, though Doris was very sweet, very loyal, and very much in love, she expected a great deal from him, more than she would have done from any other man; while she had none of that passionate pity, that half-maternal passion, which makes so many of the best and strongest women devote themselves to the weakest – or even worst – of the opposite sex. It would have been absolutely impossible for Bond to speak of the dream to Doris, who never dreamed at all; and somehow in the exuberance of life he had let Patterson – who was spending his holidays with his own people – slip a little away from him; while Mr and Mrs Challice – believing that the dreams were at an end, as he himself had done – thought it wiser not to mention the matter. Thus the boy was driven back upon himself; all the more so by the feeling that he must appear, and really ought to be, completely happy.

When Bond got back to Cambridge he found a letter from Patterson telling him that his father had died, and that he was now responsible for his mother and two younger sisters; all of which obliged him to give up every thought of a literary career – on which he had set his heart – and accept the position in a silk mill – with the far-off possibility of a junior partnership – which had been offered him by one of his relations.

Young Challice wrote begging his friend to let him do something which would, at any rate, enable him to finish his career at Cambridge. But it was of no use. Apart from himself Patterson had now three people to provide for, and it was impossible to allow Bond to shoulder such a burden, merely on the pretence of keeping his special confidant near to him.

'I am just as close to you as I ever have been, or ever could be,' wrote Patterson. 'I can't say I will come to you if anything happens, for my time is not my own. But you can always reach me in a few hours. What would separate us spiritually – and, therefore, irrevocably – would be the fact that I failed in my desire to depend upon myself, or to support those who now depend upon me.'

Bond wrote and argued the point; all the more hotly because he realized that Patterson was right. He even travelled up to Edge and saw his friend in his own home, with his mother, in her deep widow's weeds – large boned, slow moving, curiously masculine in appearance, so exactly like her son, and yet withal so completely maternal – and his two sisters, Bertha – a raw-boned girl of seventeen, already at work as a warehouse clerk in one of the mills – and little Emmie, the cripple, as long-nosed, round-backed and bright-eyed as a shrew mouse, and indeed it was always by that name, 'Mouse', that she was known.

He had high tea with the Pattersons; sat and talked to them, was entertained to the very limit of their resources, and saw – for the first time – what a perfectly self-respecting life can be like, stripped bare of every luxury – even the beer and baccy, the freedom from obligation, the door-to-door gossip of the working-class; while, at the same time, he realized the bitterness of being unable to do anything for the man he loved – with Challice and its suites of empty rooms, with all that his father and mother, as well as himself, were only too eager to offer.

It is a lesson which youth is slow to learn, which can only come to us all by bitter experience. This spiritual boundary to human endeavour, this inability to help those who are most worth the helping; this indomitable pride which at once makes a friend what he is, and places us gently – with all our clumsy, well-meant efforts – on one side.

Young Challice went back to Cambridge saddened, and yet in a way strengthened. There was Patterson, only a bare year older than himself, fighting for dear life. And there was he, with everything he could possibly need or desire, obsessed by a mere dream.

He would not go home for that twenty-fourth of June. He had made up his mind to see the thing out alone. But on the twenty-third his nerves suddenly failed him; he was overcome with the primitive desire to run – he didn't mind where so long as it involved some movement.

Without even asking for leave of absence he packed a small bag and took himself off up to London; then – as it was still early in the day – he went on to Reading – simply because it meant a drive across town from one station to another, a direct journey, and an ultimate arrival in an unknown place, where nobody would recognize him. He did not even go to an hotel; he took a room – in a furnished lodging such as he had never before known – and there battled through his agony alone.

He stayed there three days.

The room he occupied was papered in khaki colour, with bunches of dark brown daisies at intervals. Sometimes they seemed to run diagonally, sometimes they formed lozenges, sometimes they lay in vertical lines across his vision; but they were always pushing themselves forward, making themselves felt. The heavy curtains, with their frowning canopy, were a variant of the same colour; while the carpet was thick with dust; all the furniture far too big for the room – excepting the equipment of the washing-stand, which was ludicrously small – the huge bed a thing of alternate, and apparently irreconcilable, quarries and morasses.

On two mornings the maid-of-all-work left a milk jug full of hot water outside the bedroom door. But it was not touched, neither did the lodger give any signs of life till – on the third day – the landlady, fearing the scandal of a suicide, sent her husband to batter at the door.

But Bond was not dead. He answered their knocking quite calmly, with a request for tea and toast, and himself opened the door to take in the tray.

He was unshaven and haggard, with bloodshot eyes. But the landlady, who took him his tea, reported to the little group of friends – which had gathered in her kitchen – that he seemed quiet and reasonable enough; rather to their disappointment, having hoped for and prognosticated every sort of horror.

'Likely enough it's only the drink,' said one. 'You'll find his room full up with empty bottles when he leaves, mark my words,' added another. For drink, though an everyday affair in comparison with suicide, was better than nothing.

But there were no bottles – either full or empty – to be

found in the first floor front when the mysterious lodger left; while to the landlady's certain knowledge nothing in the way of food or drink – beyond that one portion of tea and toast – had gone into the room during the whole three days.

Bond did not at once return to Cambridge. Forgetting to write and tell anyone where he was, overwhelmed by his own thoughts, he went up to town and took a room at an hotel where he had never stayed before – never even heard of anyone staying. From this he wandered round the streets; went to his club; stared about him – scarcely seeming to realize what people said when they spoke to him: ate little, drank a good deal, and hardly slept at all till, at last, he swam – by an inspiration, as he would have said – into the heavenly haven of morphia.

A fortnight later he drifted back to Cambridge. He looked so ill, his position and his people were so well known, that much might have been forgiven him. Almost any sort of lie would have sufficed.

But young Challice made no attempt to defend himself, even by the most transparent excuse: showed so plainly that he did not care what happened, that he was sent down, and went back to Challice.

His mother was in despair. He did nothing. He would not ride or fish, or interest himself in the place. It was no use asking people to stay, for he was merely rude to them, and that made his father angry; while he was irritable and restless to such a degree that there seemed nothing of the old Bond left.

Doris Cartwright was abroad. They were both so young that it had been agreed to put the wedding off for at least a year.

Mrs Challice proposed that the girl should be sent for; but 'For God's sake spare me that' was all she got in answer to this suggestion.

Then – without telling her son – she sent a letter to Patterson begging him to write and suggest a visit, telling him something of the condition into which Bond had sunk.

Without a moment's hesitation Patterson complied with her request, though it meant a sacrifice of time and money, of which Mrs Challice never even dreamt. Both seemed to come natural to her, were as much part of her life as food and air. She could, of course, understand 'the poor people' running short of those commodities – which they might have misused if they had them – but she could not realize the condition of a man with a good coat to his back and no money in the bank and no leisure.

Bond gave the invitation grudgingly. He had got into the state where he found going down hill easier than climbing up; for, after all, what was the use of topping a hill to be rolled back afresh each year?

But gradually Patterson's individuality began to tell upon him. They smoked together; went walks together, tramping for miles over the short frost-bitten grass of the Downs – for by this time it was near upon Christmas. Finally Patterson's friendly silence drew the other man on to talk, and at last – quite suddenly – he began to speak of the dream.

They had been walking home through the gathering twilight when Bond slipped and twisted his ankle.

It had frozen for days. But that afternoon, quite suddenly, a thaw had set in. Bond was tired – he was not half so good a walker as he had been the year before – and was walking carelessly, with dragging feet, when he slipped on the side of a sharp dip. Patterson caught him by the arm, but he did not fall; indeed, he scarcely seemed to have hurt himself, though he limped a little for the rest of the way home. But at dinner his left ankle showed a distorted shape through his silk sock, and for a couple of days he was obliged to keep it up on a sofa.

He did not miss much, for the thaw had really set in, and

with it a heavy persistent rain. Patterson indulged himself in one long tramp each day; for the rest of the time he sat by his friend's side, while they talked or read or played chess.

It was by the firelight one evening, as he lay on the sofa smoking – while Patterson sprawled his long length over a low basket chair, with the wire-haired terrier across his knee – that Bond began.

'Pat, do you remember that dream of mine?'

'Yes.'

'Well, you know this last June – I meant to keep awake again. But I couldn't. I wanted – more still – to sleep; and I wanted – well, to see what happened. A day or two before the thing had begun to drive me. I couldn't keep quiet, stick at anything. You know how one sometimes gets the fidgets in one leg; well, I got the fidgets all over me – body and mind. The end of it was I went off to Reading.'

Patterson glanced up at him curiously, his pipe still in his mouth. 'Why Reading?'

'Oh, I don't know – there was no reason in anything. I began to do things – go to places – and then stopped, wondering if it was really I who was there – I felt as if I was going dotty. And all the time, through it all, there was only one idea: being in an awful funk – and yet wanting to know where "It" had got to. I've never read anything adequate about fear. I've never heard anyone say anything that's any use about it – that gives one any idea of what it really is. I suppose they're all frightened of people thinking that they speak from personal experience.'

'It's that sort of standardizing of right and wrong which does more to prevent progress than anything else in the world,' remarked Patterson, out of the corner of his mouth.

'Well, it's beyond me. It's a sort of sweating hell. It pricks out in pins and needles all over the back of one's hands, and up one's arms. It makes one feel as if one had no inside, and one's eyes were on fire. But it's more than that. It's as if everything you are, or had been – all the centre of your life, all that you've inherited, all that race and civilization and reason have given you – was being torn up by the roots. And yet it's got a frightful sort of fascination about it. It's as if you were – I can't explain – but you know those old pictures of the Last Judgment? Well, it's as if one was all of that *in* oneself; and yet standing aside, swaying and sick – utterly rotten – emptied! Absolutely unable to go away and take one's eyes off the damned thing.'

'I wouldn't think too much about that part of it if I were you, Challice.'

'Well, that's how it takes me.'

'Stick to the concrete fact of funk – and the dream; and try to beat it at that.'

'I can't – I'm always wanting to know – I can hardly wait for this year to pass. Though some day I shall die of it – it will sound pretty, won't it – as an end to all the Challices? I look at all those old fellows in the church – stone figures, so stiff and straight with their crossed legs – and wonder what they would have thought of it.' Bond paused, swung round into the corner of the sofa, and put his bandaged foot up on a chair; then leant forward gazing into the fire, his chin on his hand.

For a moment or so neither spoke. Then he began again. 'You know we thought we had beaten it last June. Well, that – that time at Reading –' he hesitated, glancing up at Patterson who nodded. 'Well – it had missed a room.'

'You mean it was two rooms nearer than it had been the year before?'

'Yes.'

'Well, my dear fellow, it's got to be beaten somehow. Or it will beat you.'

'Yes – I suppose so.' Bond spoke slowly, staring into the fire.

'But I don't know that I want –'

'Want what?' Patterson spoke sharply. For the inevitability of the thing, the way in which the other man seemed to be knuckling down under it, scared him.

'Want it to – go – altogether. It may be a sort of warning – an omen of the future. There must be some meaning, some reason in it.'

'Look here, Challice, we can't afford to worry about the future – we don't want omens and warnings. We want every day as it comes, clear cut and complete, if we mean to keep sane. Was it Jefferies who said "Eternity is now?" No day that's coming will ever be any more important than this day – which is here with us, at this very moment.'

'It's easy to talk. But isn't there something engineers call "the weakening point" in all they do? Which, for no reason whatever, is incapable of bearing the strain that's put upon it – which there's no guarding against, providing for; which splits up their best work – nullifies every possible precaution and calculation. That's what it's come to with me. Look here, I'm twenty-two now. That means that I've had twenty-two of those dreams, that it's twenty-two rooms nearer than it was at the beginning – for I suppose the same thing happened when I was too much of a kid to realize what frightened me. It's knocked me over again and again, but I've always managed to bob up somehow. Last time it was you who dragged me up by the hair of my head. But you see it did no real good – the thing came on – just the same. *It* doesn't care. Nothing will do any good, nothing will stop it. And now I've reached "the weakening point". There's no more rebound left in me – somehow the spring's gone wrong. Besides – well, there's something else.'

'Better have it all now we're about it.' Patterson's voice was cool, but his deep-set, light coloured eyes were fixed on his friend with the desperate expression of a dog – which realizes its master's sorrow, and is yet powerless to help. The inarticulate anguish of one who feels, to his very heart's core, the truth of those tragic words of the Koran: 'Wherein one soul shall not make satisfaction for another.'

'Well, I'm twenty-two now,' went on Bond, in the slow, halting manner in which one speaks of something which is difficult, delving out words to express what one knows is beyond all expression. 'Twenty-two rooms have closed up behind. I know – I know by those that remain. And now –' He got up and limped with dragging foot across the hearthrug – where he stood with one arm leaning on the mantelshelf, his back to the other man. 'Well, there are only five left. That's the truth. Put that in your pipe and smoke it.'

There was a few moments' silence between the two; for the life of him Patterson could think of nothing to say. Then young Challice flung round and repeated – almost angrily – 'Five – do you realize what that means?'

The other man faced him bravely: 'Not what you think, anyhow.'

'What *I* think – and what *you* think too – if you'd pluck enough to own it. The end.'

'The end of what?'

'As much of me as is bound up with it – life or reason – the Lord only knows.' Bond shrugged his shoulders as he limped back to the sofa and lifted his bandaged foot with one hand to a chair. 'But, anyhow, there's an end.'

'Of *it*.'

'Of both of us. We're inseparable – I know that. But, anyhow, an end of some sort – when I'm twenty-seven. Thank God there's no prolonging it! It can't come any further – unless I go on building more rooms.'

'It will vanish – die out.'

Young Challice shook his head obstinately. 'It won't do that – unless it takes me with it. Why can't you realize that I know, that there's something in me which knows?' he added angrily.

'Look here, Challice, you're letting yourself believe the worst – letting it beat you. You'll go on feeling like that till you won't be able to stand up against it.'

'I've stood up against it all this time. I'm sick and tired of the fight. I'm not like those old crusading Johnnies. The race was young then – I'm at the end of it; weakened, drawn fine. They conquered all the enemies for me.'

'Excepting yourself.'

Bond's smooth, flaxen head was still bent, he was rolling over one of the dogs in the hearth with his sound foot. But now he raised his eyes, without lifting his head, and looked at his friend curiously – 'Excepting myself.' He repeated the words slowly. His eyes were sunken deep, his cheeks and temples hollow: there was the splendid frame of the man with all his youth and breeding; but it struck Patterson that he looked as if something was eating him away. He was like a fine fruit, mined to a mere hectic crust by some invading insect.

In another moment or so he spoke again, more gently than before.

'Do you know, Pat – that last time it struck me – the thing's growing so much smaller.'

'It will die out – vanish.'

'You keep on repeating that – I tell you I know it will last as long as I do. But this growing smaller – it's strange. It's so near, it's almost familiar – and yet I can't place it. It's not a man, or an animal – or a ghost – it's nothing that one can put into words. And yet – curiously enough – I am conscious of a horrible sense of fellowship for it. Loathsome as it is, I want – yes, that's what it's come to – I want to see it again, more than I want anything else in the world.'

A few days after this talk Patterson went back to Edge – very reluctantly, but it was impossible for him to stay away any longer. He left the Challices somewhat happier. It seemed as if Bond meant to pull himself together. He was going abroad directly Christmas was over, and intended to travel. One thing he promised – that wherever he might be he would communicate with his friend shortly before the twenty-fourth of June, and that they would spend the birthday together.

It was all very carefully settled. For once Patterson swallowed his pride enough to talk things over fairly and clearly with the Challices. And it was arranged that they should meet all expenses incurred by the trip, while his two sisters should spend their time, during his absence, at Challice Court, and so slacken the strain on his home resources.

Never, during the whole course of their friendship, had Patterson made such a sacrifice, for he was a man with whom it was a real agony to accept any favour. Through it all the one salve to his raw feeling was found in the thought of his elder sister's enjoyment, of her pleasure in the comfort of the great house, the easily swinging carriages, the wide sun-steeped gardens. He liked to picture it all. To wonder what the Mouse would think of the deer in the park, the paraphernalia of late dinner; the morning tea – set as if for a party – silver teapot and all – brought to her as she lay deep among the swelling pillows of a Challice bed; the quiet and ease, the well-being; and above all the curious inhumanity, the mutual suspicion which divided the household, keeping Mr and Mrs Challice – kind as they were – completely apart from all the hopes and fears, the emotions, the loves and hates, of the colony of well-trained servants who lived and moved and had their being beneath the same roof. It was so different from the rough familiarity and affection of the one maid-of-all-work at Edge that he looked forward with some amusement to hearing the Mouse's opinions, which were always quite clear-cut and decisive, however misguided they might be.

The two girls had their visit to Challice Court. It would have been sheer wanton cruelty to deprive them of that after all the planning and saving, the dress-making, the contriving, the hopes and fears which had occupied them for months beforehand. But the two friends did not spend that twenty-fourth of June together; for the simple reason that no one knew precisely where Bond was to be found.

He had written fairly often during the early part of the spring. And when the birthday week arrived, and there had been no news for close on two months, Patterson went off to Munich, from whence the latest letter had been sent, on the off-chance of finding his friend there.

But his quest was fruitless; for Challice had left his last address nearly six weeks earlier, and nowhere was it possible to get any news of him.

Early in July Mrs Challice wrote to say that she had heard from her son that he was staying in some place on the Adriatic Coast, and seemed to be well.

Patterson had been obsessed by his anxiety for his friend; all through that long journey to Munich, the hopeless seeking and questioning, the desperate pursuit of what seemed like possible clues; the weary dispirited journey home again, with nothing to show for all his time and trouble.

Quite naturally – for he was human – the news that his friend was safe and well irritated him. At first the relief was such that he felt like a man who rises to the surface of the water, and is at last able to draw breath after a long immersion. Then it seemed to him that Bond might at least have written to his mother, who with her woman's imagining of every sort of possible evil had worn herself out with anxiety.

After all this stress of feeling some reaction was inevitable, and for the time being Patterson put Bond Challice completely out of his thoughts. He had battled through the birthnight alone with, apparently, no ill consequence. It was plain sailing now, for another year anyhow.

The uncle who had given Patterson employment died suddenly that year; Bertha got married, his mother had a long illness; there was a strike among the mill people. All the responsibility of everything seemed to fall upon the young man's heavy stooping shoulders, and with characteristic thoroughness he set himself to meeting and solving the problems of each day as it came.

It was over three years since he had seen Bond, when he received a letter, most urgently written, from Mrs Challice telling him that her son was ill with fever in Rome, that her husband was laid up with a bad attack of gout, and that she could not leave him.

'You are the only person I can depend upon,' she wrote. 'I know that you will go to my boy, whatever it may cost you.'

It cost Patterson a great deal that could not be calculated in mere money, for he had lately fallen in love, was struggling in his inarticulate way to put what he felt into words, at the same time to save, to better his position. But still, Mrs Challice was right in saying that she could depend upon him. For he had no sooner read her letter than he went straight upstairs and – half mechanically – began to pack his bag, at the same time issuing instructions to the Mouse as to what was to be done during his absence.

Bond was very ill. It was not only the fever, he had a racking cough, he was ravaged by dissipation. There was a girl with him – his engagement to Doris Cartwright had been broken off long before – a hectic creature with a shrill, wild laugh which nearly drove Patterson mad.

It seemed that she and young Challice practised table-turning, spiritualism, crystal-gazing together; even a milder sort of Black Magic: viewed everything through a shifting, rainbow woof of fantasy and emotion; saw visions, dreams, were for ever astrain for symbols.

'That's what's made us such friends,' she explained one day, sitting on the balcony of the hotel, while Bond slumbered fitfully in the room behind them. 'We both see things – we're like sensitive plates to all sorts of impressions that no one else even guesses at. You know how a dog stiffens and growls when it realizes anything uncanny. Bond and I are like that. Other people see with their eyes, hear with the ears, but we see and hear and feel with our spines – with every pore of our skins. Other people love with their hearts, with their passions; but we love with a sort of hate, an incalculable, devouring curiosity.'

'Love! You don't even know the meaning of the word,' snapped Patterson, from out of one corner of his mouth. And then – though they had been talking in whispers so as not to disturb their patient – the girl laughed: one of those harsh, discordant laughs which was provoked by any sign of feeling in others.

'She's like Coleridge's "Nightmare Life in Death"!' thought Patterson. And he was right, for her heavy, reddish-gold hair, thick white skin and red lips were curiously unprepossessing to any normally healthy-minded person. The very sight of her long white fingers with their pointed nails sickened him.

Directly Bond began to mend he, too, grew tired of her, as he grew tired of everything; paid her off with a quite brutal frankness, and persuaded Patterson to go on to the Riviera with him.

'I don't deserve it after the way I've behaved to you,' he said. 'I don't deserve much of anybody. But I want you to stay with me over – over – you know what. I shan't bother you much more – anyhow, there's only once after this. And – well, it's been pretty bad these last few years.'

That was the only reference he ever made to the dream, to the fact that two more rooms had been passed since their last meeting. But Patterson believed that he was always thinking of it, of the past or future. Certain it was that he seemed increasingly ill at ease in the present.

His moods were for ever changing; he became more and more difficult to deal with. Sometimes he would not go out for days. Then he took a fancy for motoring, and sent all the way to Milan for a motor of a particular make which he fancied, and drove it himself. But, as far as Patterson was concerned, there was no pleasure in these drives. For Bond was alternately overcome with fear of what might happen – reducing the speed to a mere crawl, sweating and trembling if a child ran across the road, many yards ahead – or utterly reckless, indulging in a wild debauch of danger, as careless of others as he was of himself.

When they were bathing together one day, a series of tiny red marks on his arms aroused the other man's suspicion, explained something of these moods. But nothing could be done; the doctor whom Patterson called in – on the pretence that Mr Challice had caught a fresh chill – was as helpless as he was.

The struggle, the restlessness, the hopelessness – the blank periods of depression which marked those next few weeks, could never be forgotten. The two friends wandered about from one place to another – always starting off at a moment's notice – and finally made their way into Switzerland. Again and again Challice ordered Patterson to be gone, taunted him with the fact that he was supplying the funds; insulted and abused him. Then wept and clung to him, entreating that he should not be left alone: shaking off with disgust all the rag-tag and bob-tail which in some moods he collected round him.

The glare of the sun and snow seemed to eat into Patterson's brain. He had worked terribly hard during the last few years; his eyes troubled him so that his sight seemed to become distorted, and he felt that it would need very little more to push him forward on to the borderland of insanity, where young Challice was so plainly hovering. Indeed, it took him all his strength of will to stick to it during those first weeks in June; not to turn tail and ignominiously fly – back to the solid, unemotional, everyday life of the Midlands, through every phase of which he could have found his way blindfold.

The night of the twenty-fourth they slept in two rooms which opened out of each other. Patterson had begged Bond to let them again try the plan of keeping awake, but he would not listen to it.

'The *thing* may have gone back a room, or it mayn't have moved on. If I missed this time I should be sure that there was only the one room left – I must see it out. I could never keep sane through another year without knowing. It's better to be sure of the very worst than to face such uncertainty,' he said.

'Make up your mind to keep awake both times,' urged Patterson. 'Then it will be over and done with – you'll be free of it.'

'Do you think that would stop it – that or anything else in heaven or earth? I believe it's a law to itself. I don't believe that anything could touch it. Do you remember us talking of "the weakening point"? Well, I've found out something else since then – the "point of inevitability". I sometimes wonder if God Himself gets scared, setting things rolling and not being able to stop them. For it's all beyond our power, I'm certain of that.'

'It's got nothing to do with God' – Patterson spoke sharply, for his own helplessness angered him. 'It's yourself and no one but yourself who's got to beat this thing.'

Bond stared at his friend curiously. The grey-blue eyes, which had made him so like his mother, were bloodshot now, and he had an unpleasant trick of glancing at his fellows sideways and then averting them. It was the first time for weeks that he had looked Patterson full in the face.

'You said something like that before. As if it was myself – or an essence of myself.'

'Well, I half believe it is. You project it. You wait for it and watch.'

'Then if it's myself it's inevitable,' Bond spoke with a species of sullen satisfaction, as though glad to prove that he was right. 'It will go on with me to the end – there's no more getting away from it than from one's own shadow. What's the good of talking? You go round and round in a ring, you defeat yourself, you know nothing of it. It is *I* who know.'

He was right. It was no good talking. Patterson felt that also, for Challice had got to that most fatal point in any malady where he regarded his own knowledge of it as unique.

That night of the twenty-fourth was radiantly still and clear. As Patterson went out into the little hanging balcony, just before eleven o'clock, and stood there smoking, he felt that it was good to be alive – uplifted upon, bathed in the clean air.

Bond had already gone to bed. All that day he had been restless. By the time evening came he was in a fever. It seemed to Patterson that he was like a man who is all eagerness for the worst: to have it over and done with. Like the Childe Roland, in Browning's poem, with:

> Neither pride
> Nor hope rekindling at the end descried,
> So much as gladness that some end should be.

He had been so overstrung that it had appeared impossible he should ever sleep again. But – though it was less than half an hour since they had said good night – Patterson, passing through the other man's room on his way to his own, saw that he was sleeping heavily; while it seemed that there must have been some unguessed-at weight in the clear air; for, despite all his determination to keep awake, Patterson also slept, almost before his head touched the pillow.

He had a curious and disturbing dream. It seemed that all the forces which held the world firmly together, along with the power that arched the sky above it, were displaced, and that the mountains came marching down across the wide valley over which he had gazed an hour or so before; while he realized them now as people – or rather giants – of an immense stature with wise, kind faces. But their kindness mattered not at all to him, for they were so big, and he was so small, that they trod him under foot, without even seeing him, without stumbling or being put out of step by him.

Still the inexplicable happened, as it does in dreams, and though he was crushed he was not dead. Directly the mountains had passed him – bearing steadily onward – there came the sea, which seemed like the 'chariot of Israel and the horsemen thereof', while those who held the reins, and guided them, saw him as little as the men who were the mountains had done, but swept over him and so on their way, leaving him lying there spent and breathless.

Lastly, it seemed as if the sky – which had the face of a negro – was bending to him, toppling for a fall; while the only other person left alive in the world – excepting himself – was someone unseen who laughed, with that same shrill, mocking laughter of the red-haired girl who had been with them in Rome.

It was this laughter which spurred him on to struggle to a sitting position, with the idea of escape – though he did not know where he could run or what he could do. Till finally he awoke himself with his efforts, and realized that the laughter was real and not only a part of his dream; though, likely enough, the author of it.

Trembling and sweating, Patterson fumbled for a light and went into the next room, where he found that it was Bond, who – crouched upon the bare boards, in one corner of his room – was laughing so wildly that all the other people along that corridor opened their doors and peered out with frightened faces.

It was a month later when Patterson got back to England. Even then Challice was not with him, though he had left him much better, and safe enough in the charge of a doctor and two nurses who were accustomed to 'nervous cases'. If he had been a poor man he would have been in a lunatic asylum with an infinitesimal chance of ever getting well again – permeated with the very atmosphere of madness.

Patterson went straight to Challice Court to make his report. He had not seen Mrs Challice for more than three years, and he was shocked at the change in her. She was like some delicate plant which has been left in the open for too long and is wilted by the frost.

She was wild to go to her boy, but Patterson made her understand that Bond was far better – anyhow for the present – with none of his own people near.

For the first time during all the years which he had known them, he had a really intimate talk with Mr Challice, who – despite his liking for and real gratitude towards his son's friend – had always held a little apart from him; showing that awkward sense of distance between them which women – with their more fluid temperament, suiting itself to different levels – find it easier to ignore.

The florid, kindly man was broken. It appeared to him inexplicable that he and his wife, normal as they were, should have produced anything so abnormal as Bond had grown to be.

To Patterson, on the contrary, it seemed so evident that there was some impish force in nature, which was always to be expected in the most unexpected places, that he had grown to look for it.

It was like the 'weakening point', it was like Bond's 'point of inevitability'. To say such or such a thing could not happen seemed certain to attract it. It was bred by incongruities, was ever ready to give the most unsuspicious people the lie to their faces.

Long ago Patterson had arrived at the idea that one had only to go on long enough regarding oneself or one's race as immune from any special sin or failing, to be suddenly confronted with it. For the probable progresses in a circle – wide enough it may be – away from the improbable, and meets it again. Far back – before the Challices were Challices – nature must have run wild in them. They were swept by impulses and passions, seethed in that yeast which goes to the making of man, subject to fears and superstitions, as yet unbound by the swaddling bands of religion. They ran wild and naked. They dreaded the dark, the sense of an enemy behind them; they were one with the wind and the clouds and the rank, teeming earth; knew many things, subtle, illusive and fearful, which had long since been pressed out of them by the sheer weight of a more precise knowledge. Like the wild beasts they had hunted in their dreams; felt the spirits which are in the wind, the drawing kinship of running water.

Out of all this they had built up the House of Challice, through generation after generation of order; growing ever fewer in number – like a plant which is pinched to bring each flower to perfection. For ever pushing onwards and upwards – as it seemed to them. In reality moving in a circle. Till at last

– as man who is lost in the bush, proud of his progress, finds himself back at the place from which he started – they reached the climax in Bond, who – the last of them all, the only one left of the name – dipped again to the wild inexplicable terror of the Unknown.

Patterson had long made a study of this universal circling, was for ever on the lookout for it. But to Mr Challice it was inexplicable beyond all words. No one individual in all the known history of their race had ever been very different from another was the argument which he put forward again and again. Sufficient reason in itself, as it seemed to Patterson, for the swing round, the mocking laugh, the sounding smack of Fate.

He had learnt a good deal about Bond's later career from his ravings while he lay ill in Rome. Even more from his female companion's stripping of her own soul; for much that she said of herself, she said of him also. There seemed, indeed, little enough in life which Bond Challice – young as he was – had not touched: turned inside out and flung away from him with nausea or weariness. But now Patterson learnt even more from the boy's father, who told him of the gambling and other debts which he had paid; of the wild debauches of spending into which his son had seemed to delight in flinging himself. Indeed, one would think that he had hesitated at nothing, denied himself no whim of the moment; the more fantastic his desire the more eager he had seemed to gratify it.

'If it had been hunting or racing – or even cards among his own class – I could have stood it,' Mr Challice declared. 'But I went over to see him in Paris once – things had got beyond bearing. I'm a rich man, but no income would stand it. It was robbing the place, robbing the people, breaking his mother's heart. And by God, Patterson! If you could have seen the crew I found him among. It was like nothing so much as the turning up of a flat stone – a lot of weedy, white-faced decadents, stupid with absinthe. What's to be done with the boy? I've tried my best – we've all tried.'

'It's that dream – he's obsessed by it – he's always wanting to get at it, or away from it.'

The old man gave a gesture of despair. 'A Challice – the last of all the Challices – to go to hell for a dream!' He hesitated a moment or two, then reached across the table, poured himself out a glass of port wine, and held it up to the light from mere force of habit: 'There'll be no more of us either – the boy's done for himself. You remember Miss Cartwright? There was a horrible scene here the last time Bond was home – it must have been about the end of June. He insulted – abused her – here – here in this very room at his own table! The girl he was to marry! And then burst out crying with his head on the table – like a woman! By God, I wonder I didn't kill him. The only one that's left! And how we've worshipped him – my wife and I. We thought there was never any child like him. He was so plucky, so handsome! He used to come out hunting with me when he was only seven – and ride. Let me tell you this: there was nothing he wouldn't ride! What's come to the boy? God knows he's had everything a man could have. We thought too much of him – that's it. And now what is he? Good God! It's too awful to think of!'

'He may be better when he comes back, he may be different – he's been very ill.' It was all Patterson could find to say to a man whose life, apart from this sorrow, had been so smooth, so serene. Who believed in the permanent stability of race as he believed in his God; regarded his own place in the world – with a great pride but with no vanity at all – as being unchangeable, untouchable.

Two months later Bond returned to his home. He was supposed to be quite well again, though he still had a valet who was part nurse-attendant. A man with an immovable yellowish face, shaped like a coffin, whom they all disliked and tried to ignore; for it seemed to them as though he was a sort of symbol of Bond's weakness. All the same, Bond did not require any guarding or any watching; he was very quiet, and quite reasonable, gentle with everyone; while the only difficulty in dealing with him arose from the fact that he never seemed to want to do anything. If they left him alone he would sit for hours without moving, looking straight in front of him; lost in a sort of empty dream. On the brightest summer mornings – when the whole of the outside world seemed to be calling, when all of youth was abroad – he would remain in this twilight attitude of a very old man with folded hands. He shrank from going out of doors; it seemed as if the bright light tired him, set him all on edge; he was more peaceful when the green shutters were half drawn in the rooms.

Sometimes his father or mother would persuade him to go out with them. Then Mrs Challice would stop to speak to some cottager, or gather a few flowers, and Bond would slip away home, where she would find him on her return, sitting idle in a darkened room. It was the same with his father. He would try to interest the boy in some cottages which were being built, in the young pheasants, in the new plantation, and Bond would answer 'Yes' or 'No' to all he said. But the moment that the old man turned his attention to a woodman or keeper he would be off – silent as a hare through a furrow – back to the shelter of four walls; away from the open places which oppressed, almost terrified him.

Both Mr and Mrs Challice were used to being serenely busy. All through the day they had innumerable letters to write; the responsibilities of a great house, of a large estate and many dependents made demands on their time. Then there were the gardens and the kennels, the stables to see to, and numberless social duties to discharge. In the evening Mrs Challice would sit with folded hands – for she disliked fidgeting with useless trifles – but never during the hours of daylight. Bond, on the contrary, who was young, with all those woods to shoot through, all those horses to ride; with the little world – which was to be his own – all around him, sat thus from morning to night. He never even read a book or a paper – he would pick them up and lay them down again, staring in front of him. If he spoke he left his sentences unfinished.

Doris Cartwright, softened by time, only remembering how much she loved him, wrote a tender, womanly letter; she was willing to let bygones be bygones; to face the future afresh by his side, if only she could help him.

Bond was still Challice enough to realize the sacrifice of pride entailed in such a letter, and his heart warmed to his old love. He half thought of begging her to come to him. Then he thought he would write and thank her for her kind letter; tell her – which was true enough – that the mainspring of his life was broken, that he was past helping. Vaguely enough he outlined this letter again and again in his own mind, till it began to seem like the ghost of a letter which had really been written. When he did realize that he had got no farther than thinking over it, he felt – with relief – that it was best to let things be. Doris could not think any worse of him than she must do already. And, anyhow, it was too late now to repair his fault.

Summer slid into autumn, autumn gave place to winter, and the hunting season began. There was a meet and hunt breakfast at Challice Court, during which Bond sat in the window of his own room and stared down at the hounds and horses in the courtyard below him – wondering that such a sight had ever stirred him, that he had ever thought it worth while to do anything.

Patterson was to come to them for Christmas, but his mother died during the first week in December, and he was unable to get away from Edge. In the early spring the Challices went abroad for a while – father, mother and son. By this time Bond's silence and inertia had infected them also. They could think of nothing to talk about. The rest of the world – the people coming and going in the great hotels – seemed to have become detached and far away. The pictures, the buildings, the scenery left them untouched, and blank, and they were glad to get back to Challice Court early in April. There, at least, was the daily routine, the sense of obligation to help keep them going.

During the second week in June, Patterson put all his own affairs on one side and came to them, bringing with him the Mouse, who would otherwise have been left alone. For his sweetheart, resenting his silence and delay, had married someone else to show Patterson that she did not care for him.

The atmosphere of the house seemed to clear, to grow more bracing with their advent. The Mouse, who could never marry or bear children, appeared to have concentrated all the forces of life in her distorted little body. The small, bright eyes under the overhanging brows were alight with eager interest in everything. She was so matter of fact that she seemed to be for ever straightening out other people's tangled skeins, while there was something so ordinary and familiar and comfortable about her that she settled down in Challice Court as though she belonged there; everyone took her for granted; while both brother and sister brought a breath from the workaday business world into the rarefied atmosphere of Challice Court, at once more crude and more robust.

They loved to be out of doors and they took Bond with them. The Mouse could not walk far, and that gave them a good excuse for driving; without appearing to notice that – by this time – Bond could not walk far either.

He was so quiet and reasonable that again Patterson put forward his suggestion as to keeping awake all through the dream night. But on this point Bond was firm, he would not even listen to the reason which the other man put forward.

'I should die,' he said quite calmly. 'It would reach the last room and I should just go out. Keeping awake now would be like going to sleep at the end of a battle – ruining it all. I must see it through, you can't keep me awake! You've no right to keep me awake.' Quite suddenly he seemed to grow excited. 'Why, man, it's what I've been waiting for all this time!'

That night Mrs Challice and the Mouse sat up together in the boudoir which was on the same floor as Bond's room, and Mr Challice went to bed – for even then he refused to face the reality of the dream – while Patterson sat and read in the little sitting-room which opened out of his friend's bedroom.

He was not overcome with sleep as he had been before. Rather he felt very wide awake, his brain was crystal clear. All his faculties seemed to run with a strange smoothness. It was as if his entire being was like some machine which has been freshly oiled and set in order.

The house was absolutely still. Somewhere in the garden a nightingale was singing; the air was laden with the dew-drenched scent of a border of white tobacco flower which lay beneath the window, the sky serene – without a cloud. It seemed to Patterson as if the whole world was bathed in peace.

Out of the silence of the house – which had gone to sleep at so much the same time for centuries, that it seemed impossible to keep it stirring – a distant clock struck twelve. Then, one by one, told off the quarters.

One o'clock sounded – a quarter-past, half-past, a quarter to two.

The memory of why he was waiting there came back to Patterson, or rather he forced it on himself. He felt that he ought to be anxious, he ought to be frightened – and he was neither. For a few minutes he had a sense of self-reproach.

Then the conviction grew upon him that things had been taken out of his hands, that there was something going on which was altogether beneficent, with which it would be a sort of sacrilege to interfere.

Just after the clock struck two he thought he heard his own name, and ran into the next room. But Bond was still sleeping – though he must have changed his position, for he was lying on his back with his arms outspread upon the counterpane, instead of curled round on his side as he had been an hour before.

Patterson had not waited to strike a light; but the moonlight was in the room, and he could see him quite clearly lying very still, very much at rest. For a few minutes he stood there looking at him, still with that sense of peace. And then – at the sound of a light knocking – he turned to the door, outside which he found Mrs Challice, with the Mouse clinging to her arm.

'I came – I thought I heard Bond call me,' she said. She was panting a little from the haste which she had made, but it was plain that she was neither frightened nor disturbed, and it seemed to Patterson that there was the same peace in both of them which he found in himself.

The next moment Mr Challice came along the corridor in his dressing-gown, with a candle in his hand.

'What is it?' he asked. 'Does the boy want me?'

'No, sir, he's asleep.'

'But I heard him call me.' The old man spoke testily. Anything unusual irritated him; the very fact of all four being gathered together there, in the small hours of the morning, made him feel ill at ease, out of gear.

'What are you all doing here? There must be something wrong!'

'I thought I heard him, too,' answered Mrs Challice. And for a moment or two they hung listening with the door ajar between them. That mysterious, sly, half-open door, the very look of which has such a curious effect upon the sensitive, that many find themselves unable to sit quiet, to find any ease in a room with it.

It was Patterson who pushed the door a little wider.

'Look,' he whispered, and they all peered in. Bond had not stirred. Something in the immovability of his hands, laid out upon the white counterpane, must have struck them as strange, for without a word they all crept forward a little nearer.

Mr Challice had been holding his candle back so that the light should not strike upon the sleeper's eyes. But now he raised it and bent forward.

The boy was dead. He was smiling; the beautiful, clear-cut Challice face wore a look of ineffable peace. Something in the way in which his hands were thrown out upon the bed suggested that he had raised his arms to meet, or greet, something which was coming to him; something which – in that last moment – brought him a joy that he had never known before.

2 The Country-side (1917)

Religion is an ordered superstition. In its modern forms – more particularly in that form taken by the English Church – it has become so ordered, so barren, so free from imagination and emotion, that it is like a plant which has been over-pruned, with no luxuriance of growth, with little beauty; circled by a high fence which may keep out evil, which does keep out light; utterly alien to that garden of roses and herbs, of peace, of perfume and splendour which it might be, which it sometimes has been, despite its many parasites, its over-luxuriant growth, and piercing thorns.

But, still, the root of all religions lies about what we – in connection with our own beliefs – call 'faith', and – in connection with other people's beliefs – 'delusion'.

It is all one and the same thing: all superstition, or the supposition regarding things which must for ever remain outside our exact understanding.

There is an idea that no vine grows such fine grapes as that which is planted over some source of corruption: and it does not do to dig too deeply around the far-stretching roots of our faith. For there are things there of which it is not pleasant to think, from the story of the two sons of Rizpah, and the five sons of Michal, who were delivered up by David to be hanged in the first days of barley harvest, that the famine might be stayed from the land – in itself the outcome of a far older belief in the legend of Tammuz or Adonis – to the witch-burning of a later day.

All this preamble is intended to lead your mind, somewhat gradually, to the story of Margaret Wister, and is mainly written in the endeavour to impress upon you that nothing is so strange as to be impossible; that those early roots of our Christian faith are still instinct with a sinister life. Also, maybe, to prepare the way a little, for if I had by saying that Mrs Wister, wife of the Reverend Robert Wister, the rector of a prosperous, squire-ridden English country parish, practised witchcraft, this story might be put on one side, with the tolerant and half tender smile which we accord to fairy tales or such-like remnants of a past youth.

The Wisters had been married for seven years, the first five years of their life together being passed in a poor and overcrowded South London parish, where the husband was at first junior and then senior curate.

Mrs Wister had been a governess. She was only twenty-three when she married; but there was nothing girlish about her. For six years she had been obliged to set an example of decorum – often to girls but little younger than herself – shut away from all tentative love-makings by which a woman learns so much regarding the transitory nature of human passions; from all harmless gaieties and natural exuberances either of taste or feeling.

She took life very seriously. She had never had any practice in making a fool of herself over trifles – and that in itself is a bad thing – because she could not afford to take any risks. Thus all her growth, both religious and intellectual, was inward; while deep beneath all else – absolutely untouched until the Reverend Robert Wister crossed her path – lay a deep well of passion, as primitive as that which animated the breast of any cave-dwelling woman.

She was a small creature, slender yet rounded, with a clear white skin, red lips – the upper a little too thin, the lower a trifle too full – very fair hair, thick and fine and straight, and deep hazel eyes.

She would have made a charming little ballerina, with her blonde hair over her ears, and all white tulle and roses. In this she would have had plenty of outlet for her nature, and things would never have got to that point where they happened as they did happen.

People used to say that it was a thousand pities she had no child, that she would make an exquisite, a Madonna-like mother. That, too, might – indeed, probably would – have changed the whole aspect of affairs; for it would have given her something else on which to concentrate, apart from the Reverend Robert. And this, after all, was what she most needed.

Those first years of married life in London were very happy, despite the grime and degradation which lay all around them.

They were neither of them particularly spiritually minded or sensitive, so far as the outside world was concerned. There was a great deal of very evident work to be done, and they were both continually busy – with boys' clubs, and women's clubs, with evening classes, with relief measures and clinical centres. They had little time to think, to analyze themselves or their work, in which religion had got as far away as possible from its old roots of superstition, of fear, and self-searching – stripped very bare, disinfected and fumigated as it were.

Margaret Wister proved an excellent helpmate. Her destiny had arranged for her the role of a childless, hard-worked clergyman's wife, and very admirably she fitted the part – looked it, too, with her exquisitely smooth, fair head and quiet ways.

Robert Wister was a bigly made, muscular man, who had been captain of the football team at his private school, had won his blue at Oxford, and showed himself a good oar, good shot, and good all-round athlete.

As curate of St Cuthbert's he had had no time for sport, even if the rector had approved of it; but he had an enormous amount of very hard work, for the most part among a rough, unscrupulous, and masculine element: while more than once he had been driven to use his fists in a fashion which gave him more kudos than the most spiritually minded and eloquent sermon which it was possible for any cleric to preach.

He had a naïve idea that he could write, fancied himself as an intellectual; while his wife, who was in reality far more clever than he was, took him at his own valuation! For though all her outside energies were given up to her husband's work, the whole in-driven passion of her nature was for the man himself; was, indeed, an obsession which was kept wholesome by a regular life and plenty of work; but which might – in times of idleness and ease, under the influence of imagination, beauty, or fear – gather to something corroding, cancer-like. For Margaret Wister was one of those people whose greatest safeguard lies in the perpetual demands of the commonplace.

She honestly believed her husband – that big, hearty animal, slow-thinking, obtuse, and a trifle bumptious, with all the dominant instincts of the old English squire – seignorial rights and all – to be something of a genius, fretting continually against the petty demands on his time, which, as she took it, were almost akin to the robbing of posterity.

When at last, after five years of married life, her husband's cousin, Lord Leyton – who had never appeared to so much as remember their existence – found himself with a comfortable living in Sussex thrown upon his hands, and – not quite knowing what to do with it, too lazy to bother himself – offered it to Robert Wister, Margaret's first thought was that at last Robert would have leisure to do 'his own work', as she called it.

They had been so driven. Though they were always working along the same lines they were but little together, hardly ever alone. When they went to bed at night they were too tired out – by the endless succession of duties, the evening classes, the entertainments and meetings – to talk; while Robert dropped to sleep the moment his head touched the pillow.

But Margaret his wife – who, for all her quiet exterior, was far more highly wrought – would often find it difficult to settle off, and lie for quite a long time, thinking over her day's work, planning for her husband, and watching him as he lay asleep; brooding, almost gloating, over the one thing in the world which was really hers – with due deference to the Almighty – for there was no shutter in the room, and the high lamp in the street outside flooded the room with light, showing him asleep, with his fine curly head on the pillow at her side.

Had she but known it, it was the happiest time of her life. If there were only some guide near us all, to cry halt when we reach the summit of our joy, to say, 'Pause here, do not waste time looking back, do not try to rush forward, for there is nothing better to come', how different life might be! But there is no one, and, like the rest of her fellow-creatures, Margaret Wister looked to the future to be better than the present; to add to her sum of happiness by giving her Robert a chance of showing what he really could do.

They arrived at their new home in late September. The little village – every garden crammed with dahlias and Michaelmas daisies, every wall mantled with Virginia creeper – lay glowing in the afternoon sunshine, hazy with autumn mist, all set round with cornfields, like a watercolour drawing in a golden mount, framed by the sweeping side of the Southern Downs.

The air was full of the good scent of autumn leaves and wood-smoke, and Robert Wister sniffed it appreciatively.

'By Jove!' he said, 'but it smells good. It smells like home.' As the cab turned in at the rectory gate his eyes moved towards the sweep of woodland which lay to the north of the downs, overhung by a whirling host of rooks.

'I suppose those are some of Leyton's coverts. I hear he's awfully keen about his pheasants; I only hope he'll give me some shooting. Though, after all, there's nothing to compare with a day over the stubble after the partridges, with a good dog or two.' His face glowed, as he stood with outstretched hand to help his wife from the cab; then he took her in his arms and kissed her, rather boisterously, on the steps of her new home, right in front of the trim, be-capped and aproned parlourmaid.

'May it bring us both luck, eh, dear?' he said, meaning, as Margaret well knew, the advent of that child for which he had never ceased to long.

Margaret Wister had one of those pale, clear skins which seldom change colour; but she was a little embarrassed at the thought of all that his words implied.

'I did not know that you ever shot,' she said, more by way of diverting the girl's mind from any guess at his possible meaning than for any other reason.

'Oh, there're lots of things you don't know about me yet,' he answered, laughing. And then he turned to the waiting girl.

'You're Mary, I suppose? Lady Leyton wrote and told us all sorts of nice things about you. Get those rugs in, will you? And then – what about tea – eh, Margaret?'

Mary's report to cook, later on over the kitchen tea, was to the effect that Master seemed real nice and friendly, but the new Missus a stuck-up, cold thing. 'You never saw anything more pretty than the way as he behaved to 'er, helping 'er out of the cab an' all, just as if they was only just married. An' she without as much as a smile on 'er face.'

This was the first note of antagonism which met Mrs Wister, right on the steps of her new home.

Mary was a good, honest, and thoroughly well-trained servant, so was the cook; but they did not understand her and she did not understand them.

In London Margaret had a wild gutter-snipe of a girl, who had adored her; declared that she was more like an angel than a woman; stole her pocket-handkerchiefs, wore her stockings, and spent a good part of her wages in making her fantastic presents. She would race up the stone stairs from the basement, directly she heard her come in, take off her boots for her, and tell her all the news of the day – regardless of the dinner, half in or half out of the oven, boiling over anyhow.

Then there was also an old woman, who sometimes came in to help, and called the curate's wife 'ducky'.

But now it seemed to her that the two stereotyped servants, which the importance of the living and the size of the rectory demanded, were joined together against her. Their cold looks, their very docility, were like a sort of secret contempt, a conspiracy of two against one. She was not bred to it, could not get used to it; while her experiences as a governess had left her with a secret distrust and fear of the servant class.

It was the same in the village: she was antagonized by the very respect of the people. She never seemed to get to know them any better. They curtsied to her when they met her, or pulled their forelocks; if she suggested going into their houses they made her welcome with the fine courtesy of the English rustic, dusting the best chair for her to sit upon.

That seemed to Margaret an emblem of what she got of their real life: everything arranged and made tidy for her. They allowed her only the skin of their troubles; the bitterness, the passion, the root of it all they kept from her, though they took her charity. Of their inner joys, of their loves and hates, she knew nothing, excepting so much as was told by the occasional advent of an unwanted child.

At first she believed them to be of a pastoral innocence. Then things came to her notice which showed that some of them were possessed by a cunning beyond anything she had met with in the slums, a grossness almost Saturnalian in its abandon and excess.

She saw them in sickness and health; but she never knew

them any better. It was as if there was something between their spirit and hers which was as thick and impenetrable as the many layers of coarse clothing which lay 'twixt her eyes and their private person – bodies subject to the same uses as her own, skins which, unroughened by hard work and weather, might well show every bit as fine and white.

As it was, she saw nothing beyond the ruddy or yellowish-brown faces, the expression of stolid indifference and respect.

Looking back, it seemed to her that the souls of the people in London – to whom she and Robert had been used to minister – were naked as the lights over the stalls in the New Cut on a Saturday night, flaming with iniquity, blown hither and thither with every wind of desire or greed, naked and unashamed. And yet by their very openness, by the fierceness of their flame, less fearful than these creatures of smouldering, silent passions, of deeply buried loves and hates, among whom her new life was cast.

The distant downs were open and wind-swept, but all round the rectory there were trees.

The leaves fell slowly that year; there was no sudden frost to nip them from their stems. The first part of the winter was very mild and damp, and they lay in heaps beneath the trees. It seemed to Margaret Wister that they smelt of death.

Even the country people realized that there was something which was not wholesome in the weather – 'unseasonable' they called it.

It was difficult to find anything to do. The two servants were competent; none of the villagers seemed very poor; the girls were all out at service, the old people lived with their married sons and daughters, there were hardly any sick folk. If anyone was really ill, soup and port wine were sent from the Hall; if a girl was known to have gone wrong she was obliged to remain away, or else her parents, if they wished to have her with them, must leave.

The whole place belonged to Lord Leyton.

When he was expected to come into residence the drives were swept, all the edges of the one road through the village cleared of weeds.

No one seemed to know what became of the weeds or the dead leaves, they were simply swept away out of sight.

It was the same with all which was unseemly in human nature.

Everything on Lord Leyton's estate must be just so. There must be nothing left about which could offend the eye. Loose morals and loose scraps of paper alike – the great thing was that they should be out of sight.

It was difficult to get books; there was no lending or public library anywhere near. Margaret had thought that they would now buy books and magazines, which they had never before been able to afford. But, though their income was so much larger there seemed to be no margin. The way in which they must live, the things expected of them, appeared as inexorable as the laws of the Medes and Persians.

Then Robert's expenses increased in a number of ways. Lord Leyton did ask him to shoot as he had hoped, and that necessitated a change of dress – a pepper-and-salt coat, breeches, and gaiters. He had been used to wear his clerical dress on all occasions. Now when they dined out he expressed himself as being adverse to parading his profession, and bought himself a suit of ordinary evening clothes, asserting his apartness from the ordinary layman merely by the fact that he wore a black tie, where they wore white, and said grace before dinner.

He had never been a teetotaller; had often, even in Deptford, taken a glass of beer with his midday meal. But at Christmas Lord Leyton sent him a case of Madeira, which he got into the way of enjoying after dinner each night; for in the country everyone dined late. When it was finished he missed it, so that he got more. 'Dinner's merely a meal without a glass of wine', was what he said, and quoted St Paul.

There were no evening classes, excepting during the season when he was preparing young people for Confirmation, and later on, when he started a night school for young men. Nobody ever dropped in. They never went out, unless it were to dine, and Robert dropped into the habit of going to sleep after dinner each night; while, to Margaret's ears, the quiet had a sort of sound of its own, more nerve-racking than any roar and rattle of traffic.

Every evening that they were both at home the same thing happened. Robert would say that he must go and do some work, and tell Mary to light the study fire. Then he would go in there, and sit down in front of the fire with his pipe in his mouth to think out his plans. But that was as far as it ever got. Even his sermons had to be prepared in the mornings, and often when there happened to be a Meet anywhere near on a Saturday, or his cousin or one of the farmers offered him some shooting, he contented himself with reading over an old one.

No wonder he was sleepy at night, for he was out the best part of the day. The want of light and air in London had bleached him, the constant nervous strain had kept him thin, his hands had been white, he looked almost ascetic.

Now he grew florid; despite all the exercise he took he put on flesh. His voice was louder, more hearty. He smelt of the open air, of animals.

At times Margaret was conscious – despite all her passionate, craving love, her adoration – of a certain feeling of repulsion towards her husband.

He had never before been used to snore; now he snored as he slept – heavily.

He had been bred in the country, was of the country. For years his instincts had lain dormant; but now he realized that he was in his right place, living a life native to himself, and was intensely happy, wanted nothing more.

Every day it seemed as though the blood ran redder in his veins; but as he bloomed his wife waxed whiter; even her lips lost their colour, grew thinner and more pinched.

'A poor peaky bit o' goods the rector's wife be, fur sure; an' 'im such a fine gentleman an' all.'

'A tight-mouthed, bad-tempered 'un: with looks as 'ud turn the milk sour.'

This was the general trend of opinion in the village, and it hit to the bone; for she seemed to realize every shade of their feeling towards her.

She did not know what to talk to them about. Robert knew, and they liked him in their inarticulate, grudging way. It was the same with the gentry: bridge and sport, politics – a Toryism as rigid and one-sided as the beliefs which led to the Inquisition – servants and doles; round and round the same little circle.

Margaret – in her rather ill-fitting, not quite low enough evening dress – was dumb when she came out to dinner among the other women, who stood by the fire with their shimmering skirts raised, their satin-shod feet stretched out to the blaze. The only person who ever really attempted to talk to her on these occasions was the woman who, in all country house parties, is to be found winding wool after dinner, sitting rather on the edge of her chair and wearing a dull dress trimmed with priceless old Honiton.

Sometimes the idea came over Robert that his wife was not happy in the life which suited him so well. At first he was anxious, but as he himself sank deeper into it a sense of exasperation grew upon him.

What did she want? She could not expect to get on unless she made some sort of effort to adapt herself. The thought of the book which she had expected him to write rubbed like a sore place between them.

One day he was going out rabbit-shooting with one of the tenant farmers. It was a lovely morning, with a promise of spring in the air, though it was still only the first month of the new year.

He came to breakfast dressed in breeches and gaiters. Directly the meal was over he took his gun, filled his pockets with cartridges, and whistled to his dogs. When he first came to the parish someone had given him a red setter as a sort of watch-dog, and lately he had bought a bitch with the idea of breeding. Sometimes it seemed to Margaret that all his talk was of animals, their pedigrees, their possible offsprings; he had never discussed sex in regard to human beings; but now it was as though some hidden vein of sensuality came out in the way in which he talked of the dumb creatures he had gathered round him.

She had hardly spoken all breakfast time. Robert thought that she was sulking because he was going shooting again for the third day running; for he never even guessed at the corroding loneliness which nearly drove her mad.

Just as he was going out Mary came running across the hall with a packet of sandwiches for him to put in his pocket.

He had not intended to say good-bye to his wife; but as he thanked the girl, almost with effusion, he half turned and happened to notice her standing in the dining-room doorway, looking at him wistfully.

'Mary remembers everything,' he said gauchely, as though to explain his friendliness.

'It was I who ordered them for you,' answered Margaret, so stiffly that he was angry. 'Surely she can't be jealous of her own servant,' he thought. Then he realized how pale she was, with bluish shadows about her eyes, and softened to her.

'You look wretched, Meg; chilled to the bone.'

'I seem to be always cold now.'

'You should go out more: give your circulation a chance.'

'There's nowhere to go.'

'Well, why not come to-day and help me with the sandwiches? I'm sure there are plenty.' He patted his bulging pocket, laughing, for he felt ready to be in a good humour with everyone.

Margaret hesitated; she was famished for his company, and yet she felt that he did not really want her; she did not understand country things, was frightened of the cows, dreaded the sight of bloodshed, the sound of a gun. She never forgot the day when she had gone out after the hounds in the governess cart, with Lord Leyton's children and the governess, and actually been in at the death. She felt as though she were petrified, turned to stone.

'Well, Mrs Wister, what do you think of fox-hunting?' one of the neighbouring squires had asked her, pushing his sweating horse up almost against the splash-board of the cart.

Her answer was so low that he had not caught it – the children were all talking at once, wild with excitement and glee – and he leant forward over his horse's neck, bellowing a loud-voiced, 'What?'

At that moment there had been a sudden break in the flow of the talk, and they had all caught little Mrs Wister's answer, low as it was spoken from between tightly closed white lips:

'I – I think it's devilish!'

'By Jove! the mischief a woman like that can do in a place! Socialist, crank, damned dangerous!' That was the general verdict. Everyone warned Leyton against her; she would be putting things into the working people's heads, they said, not in the least realizing that the working class mistrusted her as much as they did.

Of course, the thing came to Robert's ears, and he was very

angry about it. He had already had a few days' hunting, and hoped for more. He rode well, belonged to a county family, and the men who liked him – as they liked everyone who was the same as themselves – were willing to give him an occasional mount; if only his wife did not spoil everything by what he called her 'silly, hysterical folly'.

For the first time it came into his head that he had married beneath him.

Nothing could reconcile Margaret to all the killing which went on. To her mind the country seemed like a sort of shambles. If it had been the poor who killed for food, she would not have minded so much, but they seemed to have little share in the carnage apart from an occasional bout of poaching.

If her husband had asked her to accompany him on any other sort of expedition, she would have accepted with alacrity. Even now the memory of the two lonely days she passed – of the long hours which stretched out in front of her – filled her with dismay. The lengthening days seemed to bring nothing save an increased number of hours; for the rector was out of doors almost from dawn till dusk.

'I have accounts to do, and some letters to write; and then there are the church flowers,' she said, hesitating.

'Well, join us at lunch. We are going to have it in the New Barn – you know, in that big field of Hargreaves', just below Hyde Wood. And look here, if you do come – and it will do you no end of good – you might as well bring some cake to help out the feast!'

As Margaret Wister walked through the fields that day she was conscious of feeling happier, more light-hearted, than she had done for months. It seemed as though, with the promise of spring, some dark, stifling curtain were lifted from her heart and mind.

She really had no conscientious objection to country life,

or even to the shedding of blood, for she herself ate meat at least once every day. The horror she felt for much in which her husband delighted was purely involuntary. Now, in this happier frame of mind, she tried to reason herself out of it. If one lived in the country one must adapt one's self to the usages of country life.

But her very first step in among the damp, half-dead undergrowth of the wood brought it all back to her – with the scream of a rabbit beneath a weasel's teeth, the distressed fluttering and scolding of a little flock of small birds, which led her eye to a hawk, hung motionless against the blue sky, high overhead.

All the rest of the way she was trembling and straining for the sound of a shot. But none came.

As she opened the gate and stepped into the field at the far side of the wood, close against the big barn – hoary and with nothing new about it but its name – she almost ran into a little group of men. There were Hargreaves, and a youth of eighteen, son of a local land agent; a couple of other farmers, two rough-looking working men – who did not seem quite like labourers – and her husband, who was on his knees, with his coat off and one arm up a hole. There was also a girl, buxom and weather-beaten, in a rough tweed dress, her reddish-brown head uncovered.

Robert looked up and nodded, while the others raised their caps and the girl – whom she knew to be Hargreaves' daughter – stared.

'Hallo Meg, that's right.' The rector had been kneeling with his spare hand spread out flat against the red, clayey bank above him. Now he raised it and wiped it across his forehead: 'I say, but I'm hot – the little beggar!'

'Let me have a try, sir,' put in a farmer, while one of the hangers-on pushed forward officiously with a spade.

'No, no, it's so close you might hurt it. I touched it a moment ago – lucky it's muzzled. Wait a moment, I believe I've got it now.' He lay flat on his stomach against the bank, with his face laid cheek downwards upon it, his eyes glancing sideways – bright and a little bloodshot – straining his arm still farther up into the hole. Margaret could see the muscles swell on the bare strip which showed between the rough earth and his tightly rolled sleeve.

'That's it!' He drew himself sharply back upon his heels, and gave a vindictive shake to the struggling, yellowish-tinted creature which he held in his hand. 'Ugh! you little beast!' he said.

His face was ugly; Margaret saw his grasp tighten round the writhing animal; for a moment she thought that he was going to kill it.

Then he tossed it over to the girl, who had sat down on the grass and was busy over something.

'Here you are, Miss Hargreaves, here's your pet.'

Margaret moved a few steps, and stood looking down at her – shaking a little – anxious to get the impression of her husband's face from before her eyes.

Trixie Hargeaves was holding the creature, which Robert had thrown to her, upright on her knee, with one hand round its neck and the other busied over the scrap of string which served as a muzzle. A similar animal, of a sable brown colour, nosed round on her lap. By her side lay a hessian bag which heaved as though there was something alive in it.

Margaret looked down at the animals with distaste. A pungent, sour smell hung about them; they looked meanly wicked, with their sharply pointed noses and red eyes.

'What are those?' she asked.

'Ferrets,' the girl answered, without looking up.

'What horrible-looking things!'

'I don't know about that; they're right enough, they can't help their looks.' Trixie's voice was sulky; she enjoyed being the only woman among a group of men. Besides, what did the rector's wife want there, with her superior, sneering ways?

'You're Miss Hargreaves, are you not? I think I've seen you at church.' Margaret tried to speak pleasantly, while she watched the girl's capable brown hands poke the writhing beasts into the bag, back among their fellows. She had no wish to spoil sport, was ashamed of the antipathy which she felt.

But it was all no good. The lunch passed miserably; they were all glad when she went – even Robert, she knew that as she walked home. Though he had tried to make jokes, to discuss the day's sport, he was as awkward as a small boy disturbed among his fellows by some grown-up person of whom he is a little afraid.

Margaret was hot and sore. She had almost hated him as he had glanced up at her sideways from the bank, his face smeared with clay. But now it cut her to the heart to feel that he looked upon her as a bar to his pleasure.

The gulf between them widened and widened. Sometimes she scorned him so bitterly that her contempt was written plain for anyone to see upon her white face. Sometimes their apartness hurt her so that it was like a physical agony, which she felt must kill her unless some relief could be found.

Once, towards the autumn, they had a week's holiday, and – with some sad thought of getting back what they had for ever lost – they decided to spend it in London.

They went down to the parish where they had lived for so long. Only a year had passed; but already the people had changed or forgotten them. The rector was away on his summer holiday.

It was a stifling September day, the pavement burnt their unaccustomed feet. 'My God, to think that I ever lived in such a place!' exclaimed Robert. His hand was at his round clerical collar. It was horrible to think of being obliged to wear such a thing, day in, day out – symbolical of all the drab monotony of South London.

Margaret hated it as much as he did. It seemed as though there was nothing she cared for left in life.

After three days of London they went to the sea. They could not go home because they were not expected, the servants were having a holiday. In the old days they would have gone, anyhow; and Robert would have built up the fire, and Margaret would have cooked chops, or scrambled eggs – very badly. But they would have been happy and gay, even over the washing up of the dishes; delighted with the feeling of having the place to themselves.

One could not do that sort of thing in the country, where everything was arranged and set; where even the very cows and trees seemed to know what was expected of them; where all which was out of the way must be sly and covert.

Robert Wister hunted pretty regularly that winter. There was no reason why he should not; it did not cost him anything beyond the occasional keep of a borrowed horse. The parish was so small that there was but little to do, and the people liked a sporting parson; they were proud of a man who mixed with the gentry, shared their pleasures. Besides, it prevented him from poking overmuch into their affairs.

He was very seldom at home; when he was he slept, or attended to the dogs, which he now bred for profit. He was intimate with people – spoke of them by their Christian names – whom Margaret did not even know by sight. 'Oh, they're not your sort – not clever enough for you,' he would say when she asked about them; suggested that they should be invited to dinner.

Among all the villagers, the only one who interested Margaret was an old woman who lived at the edge of one of the large blocks of woodland, with a son who seemed half an imbecile – earning his living by cutting faggots and occasionally trimming hedges. And after all that was not so much interest as a sort of fascination.

The old woman was bedridden. Day in, day out, she lay under the patchwork quilt which had been part of her wedding dower; close beneath the roof in the one bedroom of the tree-encompassed house.

The roof was so sloping that she could hardly have sat quite upright even had she been able to. Margaret never knew whether she could sit up or get out of bed, what was the matter with her.

The son cooked for her and did the work downstairs; but it seemed as though she must get up to do her own room, to make the bed and wash herself – though no one ever saw her do it, for she would have no neighbour in to help her.

The son earned the living, kept the home together for both of them – a bent and distorted creature with shambling legs, whom she treated like a child, scolded and raved at. Neighbours said that sometimes when Jabe was a little the worse for drink – and half a pint of beer was enough to go to his weak head – she would rise up out of her bed and beat him unmercifully with an ash stick, which always stood in one corner of her room, and with which, in years past, she had been wont, to help herself about. Everyone knew that he slept in her room across the foot of her bed, for she declared that as long as she lived she would keep him under her own eye. There was no knowing what would be going on if she left him down there alone, with the shameless hussies that were about in these days. Though it may have been that the old woman was really quite helpless, afraid of being left alone. It was no use questioning Jabe; his answer was always the same – given with an apprehensive glance round, as though the old woman might suddenly appear at his elbow:

'I'm sure I dunno; her does what her thinks best ter do.'

There was nothing obsequious about old Mrs Orpin. She was shrilly abusive, proud and intolerant: the people looked on her as a witch. Indeed, they declared that was why she kept her bed. Did she put her nose out of doors the devil would get her.

At times some sorely tried house-mother would climb the steep stairs, emboldened by exasperation, to complain that the cow would not let down her milk, or the butter come in the churn. On these occasions the old hag's triumphant answer was always the same:

'I knowed it, I knowed it.'

They went to her for sore eyes, for the reclaiming of errant husbands, and she swelled with pride. There was never any queen on her throne as arrogant, as self-satisfied.

Sometimes they would find her in a boasting mood, when she would brag to them of things which they spent their lives in hiding.

'I was a real gay 'un in my time, I was. Eh, but the body and souls 'o the men! – I knew 'em inside an' outside, I did. An' my own body, too, and the ways of it; that's what made me master o' 'em. You'll only master them as you beats in knowledgeableness. An' you poor slumikin' things, you don't know naught, you're like the hares in the furrow, fruz in; sent all zany-like by men's passions an' strong ways. Why, if Jabe there once got his will on me he'd kill me; times in an' times out he's wanted to; only he dursn't. Keep 'em under from the first. That's the only way with the likes of them. Sons or lovers.'

Margaret tackled her about her supposed powers, of which she had heard something, though not much.

'Why do you want to pretend that you know things which are past human knowledge? Can cure diseases, sorrows, of the nature of which you are completely ignorant?' she inquired impatiently. 'In the old days you'd have been taken for a witch.'

The old woman kept her head bent, plucking with claw-like fingers at the edge of the patchwork counterpane; for days after Margaret could visualize the pieces which formed that particular part of it – a pink cotton powdered with tiny black specks, a triangular scrap of rosebud chintz, a bit of brown calico.

'How dust thee know as how I ain't?' she demanded sulkily.

'What do you mean?'

'Who told you as all the witches was dead, burned, and such-like?'

'What nonsense! You don't mean to say that you think you can pretend to me?'

'What is it as ye're calling pretence?' The old hag glanced up, her blear eyes alight with malice. 'There's things as I could tell you, my fine madam, as 'ud set that cold blood o' yours on the boil; an' there's no mistake about that, neither.'

'So you say. But as you either won't or can't talk sensibly to-day I'd better go,' answered Margaret lightly, and walked out of the place determined that she would never go near it again: 'unless the old thing is really ill', she added to herself, with a feeling as though she were keeping a sort of loophole open for herself.

The very next week news came to her in a roundabout way that Jabe could hardly drag himself to his work; complained of being up night after night with his mother, who was 'main bad'. No one would go near her except for their own ends, and it seemed to Margaret that now her duty was plain.

The old hag passed no remark in regard to the sudden termination of Mrs Wister's last visit; but held herself aloof, with the air of someone who was engrossed in matters of far greater importance than those which were likely to circle round one small, fair-haired woman.

Margaret offered to read to her. But here she met with a distinct rebuff, for Mrs Orpin merely gazed over her head and remarked that she was 'a-scholared' herself.

It was early in January. Through the one tiny window Margaret Wister could see that the sky was already crimson, though it was not yet four o'clock.

In London the lights would be pricking out one by one; the red and yellow lamps on the taxis flashing like fireflies, the very 'buses radiant with a sort of life which at night time seemed all their own; quite apart from the human beings with whom they consorted.

Here there was nothing – a few rooks flying home to roost, and thin strips of snow lying in the bare furrows of the plough, that was all.

She had moved to the window and stood looking out. 'You have quite a nice view of the sunset here,' she remarked idly for something to say.

There was no answer. She stood with her back to the old woman. After a moment or two a feeling came over her as though someone was standing close at her back, so close that she actually pulled herself together, fearful of being touched. Though all the time she told herself that it was nonsense, that old Mrs Orpin could not rise from her bed, or if she had done so she would have heard her.

She determined that she would not let her nerves overcome her, even to the extent of turning round to look, and went on talking of indifferent subjects: the prospect of finer weather, the forthcoming Primrose League Festival.

Still the old woman did not speak. And at last, as though something drew her – overcome by that mysterious fear of some terror close behind her, which we have all known as children, she turned.

Mrs Orpin was still in her bed, but she seemed to be sitting a little more upright, and was gazing at her with that curious intensity which one sees in a cat watching a hole, with half-closed eyes, the pupils drawn to a pin-point.

'There ain't any wise women these days, ain't there?' she began suddenly. 'Well now, thee hearken to me, and I'll tell thee.'

She caught at the ends of Margaret's fur boa with her hand, and peered up in her face as she spoke. 'Jabe brought me a white bowl o' water a night or so back to wash mesen in. There was things in it as I seed,' here she nodded mysteriously. 'To other folks a bowl o' water's just a bowl o' water; it ain't anything more, that 'ull tell yer. Other folks 'ud a' seen the white bottom o' the bowl; but this is what I seed. There was a big old barn up agin it; an' at one side o' the barn was a stack o' hay with a truss, or maybe two, took out o' it. I told Jabe what it was as I did see – the owd barn and the rick, an' a little gate out o' the wood close alongside o' it, and the hedge just about begun to be cut an' layered, running towards where the sun sets, away from the gate – it ain't no good sayin' east nor west to Jabe, he's that soft. "Lord bless us, Mither," seys 'ee, "if that ain't the New Barn, rick an' all, along which I be workin'." Now hearken thee here, missus; there weren't any rick o' no sort alongside that ther barn when I was out last – ten years and more back.'

Margaret laughed; a sense of relief came over her. She did not know what she had expected, but certainly nothing so simple or harmless as this.

'That was very strange,' she said; 'but one does have those sort of inward visions sometimes. Perhaps Jabe had told you that he was working there and of the new rick, and you'd forgotten it.'

The old woman took her hand away and tossed her head haughtily. 'I don't waste my time talkin' ter Jabe. I'm not one as holds with chit-chattin', chit-chattin' with one's childer as though they was one's equals,' she remarked; while Margaret was amused to see how angry she was at not being taken seriously.

'You seem to keep Jabe in fine order.' Margaret was still smiling. 'But, after all, he's not a child. Some day he may revolt, and then what will you do? Now I must go. I hope –'

All the time she had been speaking the old woman's eyes had been fixed on her with an expression of impatient scorn. It was almost as though she said, in as many words, 'Oh, do be quick and have done with all that silly talk of things you know nothing about.' Now she broke in as though her patience was at an end.

'Thee counts as how I know no more nor other folk,' she said, grasping her visitor's wrist, holding it with a clutch which felt like steel. 'Well, hearken thee here now. There's a hussy, round and brown and plump as a ripe pippin, an' there's a chap as she meets come Tuesdays an' Fridays a'twixt the owd barn an' the rick. You go an' see if I'm not telling you the truth. No one ever comes a-nigh me, no one never tells me naught, but I knows – I knows.'

'Really, Mrs Orpin, I've something better to do than to spend my time tracking the village girls and their sweethearts. And I think that you –'

With a wild laugh the old creature flung her visitor's hand away from her, and, crossing her arms over her breast, rocked herself to and fro in a paroxysm of mirth. 'The village girls and their sweethearts! That's good, that's fine! Let me tell thee this, my fine lady. It ain't only the village wenches as plays the harlot, an' it ain't only the village chaps as –'

The rest of the words were lost, for Margaret was already half-way down the narrow stairway, nursing her bruised wrist, in a tumult of indignation and disgust.

People had said far worse things to her in the old days on the Thames-side: unutterable, unrepeatable things, which she had taken as part of the day's work, almost as the natural mode of expression from such people. She had rebuked it, never let it pass; but that had been as a matter of duty, she had been outside it all – and it had left her untouched, unshaken.

But something in old Mrs Orpin's words, or perhaps more in the abominable insinuation of her expression, shook her so that the whole thing seemed to be photographed on her mind, and throughout the remainder of that day – and indeed for many, many days afterwards – she could see her, hear her shrill laugh, her cracked voice.

That evening at dinner she spoke of it to her husband. 'That old Mrs Orpin's mad; she ought to be shut up, she and that wretched, imbecile son of hers.'

The rector raised his head. His jaw seemed to have grown heavier, all the fine lines of his face were lost in something that was more than flesh, a sort of inward coarsening. He was surprised at his wife's tone, for she was usually tolerant to the point of indifference.

'Oh, they're all right. Jabe isn't really an idiot; he's only a bit off; he gets through his work well enough.'

'He must be either wanting or a perfect fool, to let that old mother of his bully him as she does. Abominable old creature! She tries to make out that she's a sort of witch – furious if anyone doubts her. It would serve her right to be treated as she would have been a century or two back – burnt at the stake. I should be glad to hear of it – it would be a good thing – an example to others,' pursued Mrs Wister, amazed at the sound of her own voice, shrill and vindictive, at the feelings which were stirred up within her as she spoke.

Her husband stared, his mouth dropping open a little in a way she had not known it do before. Sometimes it seemed as though he were getting as animal as the people around him, 'whose talk is of oxen'.

'A woman like that poisons the very air. She has got some

sordid story of a vision which she declared she had seen in a basin of water. I simply wouldn't listen to her. I came away and left her shrieking.'

'What sort of a vision?' asked the rector heavily. He had just filled himself a second glass of wine and held it up to the light as he spoke.

'Something about that barn – you know the place they call the New Barn, where I came and had lunch with you one day. She actually wanted me to go and see whether some story of a couple, whom she declares to be in the habit of meeting there, is true or not.' Margaret laughed. 'If would be a dignified thing for the parson's wife to spend her time –' Her voice trailed off.

The rector's head was bent over the fruit on his plate, his whole attention seemingly engrossed by the orange which he was peeling.

'All those old women are hopeless gossips,' he said, after a pause, during which the mental vision of old Mrs Orpin – with which his wife's mind had been occupied all that day – was displaced by something as vivid and far more disquieting, far more personal: the expression – was it of fear or guilt? – furtive and sly, and in some odd way wholly rustic, which had flashed across her husband's face in that moment before he dropped his eyes from hers to his plate.

Even then she seemed numbed, frozen, so that she could not grasp any meaning in, any reason for her uneasiness, was only conscious, during the remainder of the dinner-hour, of a sense of chill such as one might have when summer suddenly gives place to winter, windy and wet, with falling leaves and leaden sky.

Almost the moment she was in bed she dropped asleep, as heavily as though she had been drugged.

But towards three o'clock she awoke suddenly, with a mind that was crystal clear. She saw again the scene that had been set before her as she joined the shooting party outside the New Barn; the bent head of a girl, russet tinted, while at the same moment came the thought of those two evenings, Tuesday and Friday, the evenings upon which – all that past winter – the rector had held a young men's class, that had seemed to grow longer and longer as time went on.

All sorts of other hitherto unconsidered trifles rose to her mind. She remembered how her husband had always been talking of the Hargreaves, at one time, and then ceased to mention them; the expression of the girl when she had met her, and greeted her, tried to get into friendly conversation, one day not so very long ago; the young man who had come running with a forgotten book which Robert had left in the class-room one Friday night; his surprise at finding that Mr Wister had not yet arrived. 'He left early a'cause he said as 'ow he was expectin' some'un to come an' see him on business; I made sure as he'd be here by now,' he had insisted, tiresomely enough as it seemed to Margaret, who had been in the hall and heard him ring.

Even then she would not definitely face the thought which was at the back of her mind; she seemed to be always holding herself away from it in agonized fear, as one may try to hold the rest of one's body back from the seat of some intolerable pain.

From spring the weather had leapt back to winter, while the length of the days made their dreariness only the more apparent. Margaret stayed indoors for several days, shivering over the fire. It seemed that she had taken some chill, both outward and inward, which had the effect of almost stupefying her.

She was so palpably ill that it gave her an excuse – for which she was thankful – to keep away from her husband; to relax something of her normal ways of life.

One afternoon, sitting wrapped in a sort of dreamy stupor,

she allowed the fire to go out, and rang to have it remade.

It was the cook who answered the bell, and brought paper and sticks to relight it, for the parlourmaid was having her afternoon off duty.

She was a fat, rather untidy-looking girl, more human and get-at-able than Mary.

A sense of utter, desolate loneliness had hung over Margaret all that day, and, thankful for any human companionship, she began to talk to the girl.

After a moment or two, noticing that the thick, red hands – busy over the reluctant fire, picking up morsels of charred stick from the hearth and replacing them beneath the coals – were scarred with warts, she asked the girl what she had done for them.

Up to now Emmie had been shy and difficult, stuffed full as she was with Mary's tales of their mistress's stand-off ways; but on this question of the warts it seemed that Mrs Wister had touched some point where she was so surcharged with morbid interest and excitement that she would have talked to anyone.

'I'd been to Rose, the chemist, and I don't know what not; everyone as I'd seen had been telling me something different what to do. But it wasn't a scrap of good – though you wouldn't believe the shillin's as I've spent on it, Marm, no you wouldn't. I'm sure I was ashamed for anyone to look at my hands, an' all of a tremble I've been on a Sunday when I've brought in the tea, for fear that you or the Master should mention them. But now they ain't nothing to what they used to be, not since last full moon.'

'Why since last full moon?'

'Well, Marm – it seems that silly, I'm sure you wouldn't never credit it – I laughed myself when it was told to me. But it were true enough, gospel true – and – well, my hands aren't the same as they was a couple o' weeks back, everyone notices it. Being engaged an' all makes a girl feel a thing like that; an' my young man couldn't bear them, that's the fact.'

'But what did you do?'

The fire had been obstinate and slow to take light, Emmie had been feeding it stick by stick, while it seemed as though her tongue kept time to the movement of her hands. But now she sat back on her heels, while her face grew slowly crimson as she adjusted the fire-irons. She had been a fool to talk like that! What would Mary say to her if she heard of it? To the missus too, of all people.

'Well, Marm, it's like this; one gets talking and hearing things. I don't generally set much store by what the people about here say, they're that countrified an' ignorant. But when a girl's worried, as I was about them there warts, it seems as though she would catch at anything; an' I went to see the old woman – because they was all on at me, more for a sort of a lark than anything else. Though I wouldn't go again not if I was ever so; the place itself with them there dark trees all round it gave me the shivers – an' as for the old woman herself, she was like one of those witches as you read of in books' – once again the girl warmed to her recital, her eyes round with importance. 'When she took hold of my hand to look at my warts a shiver went through me, all over, from head to foot. I thought I'd got my death, I told Mary so when I came home that evening. I was that chilled through and through I was obliged to ask her to make me a cup o' tea. An 'orrible old woman I call her, with those wild eyes, fit to bore you through an' through like a gimlet. I wouldn't not a' done anything she told me, and so I said to Mary. But Tom has seemed to be getting real nasty about my warts – an' after all there wasn't any real harm in what she was on at me to do; an' so I did it.'

'Did what?' To her own ears Margaret's voice had a curiously flat sound.

'Well, it seemed that silly, Marm, I don't know what you'll say, an' nasty too. She told me to get a snail at the full o' the moon an' rub it on the warts; and then to take it and put it on the spike of a blackthorn. An' then – or so she said – as the snail withered away my warts it 'ud wither away with 'em. Horrid it seemed, an' I didn't believe, no, not for a minute, as how it 'ud come true; though she kept on sayin' "I know it, I know it," artful like, you know, Marm. But the old woman was right, there's a many as has quite gone away, an' the rest is dying off, you can see for yourself, Marm.'

The girl stretched out a red hand, and Margaret, taking it in her own, regarded it gravely, with that intense scrutiny which one often gives to a thing of which one is only half aware.

Emmie had spoken the truth, the horrid things were still there in plenty, but they were shrunken and withered, and there were still more marks where others had been.

'What old woman was it?' The question was a mere waste of breath. Of course she knew what old woman it was; but it seemed as though someone quite outside herself put it, with the idea, as it were, of verifying something, driving something home.

'Orpin was the name, Mrs Orpin. She's got a son as is a luny, or so I've been told, for I wasn't never one to mix myself with other people.' Emmie's voice was prim, it seemed as though she were again repenting of her outspokenness, taking refuge in the stiff gentility of the well-trained servant. 'A horrid old woman I call her, I wouldn't go anear her again, not if I was ever so. Though I must say this, she did speak the truth, and it's my opinion you'll excuse me saying so, Marm – that there's nothing that dreadful old woman don't know – there's a look in her eye. There, Marm, I think it will burn nicely now, and shall I fetch the tea up, please, Marm?'

In love or hate or fear, it always seems that a certain point of intensity is reached when the person most concerned is distinguished by the word 'the'.

To Margaret Wister, old Mrs Orpin had grown to be 'The old woman'. Anyone who was country-bred would have taken her more naturally, for the real rustic mind – despite all its gorming wonder over anything new – is close to the primitive; deep rooted in all that is ancient and uncouth; at one with a sort of horror which is absolutely apart from the horrors of the town. So much so that country crimes, country loves and hates have their own distinctive manifestations.

Your true rustic is suckled on spells, incarnations, and superstitions. The worship of Odin and Thor is somewhere deep ingrained in his nature. The strange influence of the moon, the portents which are to be found in the movements of animals, the sacred influence of the quicken, or bunch of ash keys, the power which lies in the three names of Jehovah, Alpha and Omega, written upon a fair sheet of paper and sealed with red wax.

The country woman turns her money in her pocket when she hears the cuckoo for the first time, when she sees the new moon. The town woman goes her way untouched, laughs or shudders at the superstitions which are an integral part of the everyday life of a shepherd or plough-herd.

Orpin – the very name held in it a tang of something ominous to Margaret Wister's mind. Why did the woman obsess her so? Sometimes it seemed as though her brain, her heart, and mind were so many photographic plates on which the picture of that old hag was the only thing to register itself, with, somewhere in the background – like the so-called 'ghost photos' in which one is taken over the other – a man, heavy jowled, with something at once sly and appealing in his sidelong glance, and a girl, with wind-roughened head, bent over a lapful of small-eyed, narrow beasts, supple as snakes.

One thing she made up her mind that she would not do – revisit the cottage in the wood.

And yet her walks seemed to be for ever taking her that way. There seemed, on more mature thoughts, a thousand reasons why she should go, if only to confute afresh all that the old hag had said – or worse, left unsaid.

Her very feet were in league against her, to take her there.

Meanwhile the whole week seemed to concentrate itself down to two sharp points of anguish – those hours of Tuesday and Friday when Robert might or might not be still at his class.

She could not have borne to go to the New Barn and see for herself who, if anyone, met there, betwixt it and the towering bulk of the rick. If she had gone, and seen what she was sure – somewhere at the back of her mind, though she would not put the thought to words – that she would see, it would have killed her; her avoidance of it was as instinctive as the avoidance of any certain death well can be.

But one night she did find herself outside the school house where the class was held. There was only one dim light in it, and that went out just as she reached the gate.

Next moment the schoolmaster emerged, locking the door behind him.

As he crossed the yard Margaret spoke to him: 'Has Mr Wister gone yet, Mr Bryce?'

'Yes, oh yes, some time ago.' The man poked his head forward, peering at her through the darkness. 'Who is it? Oh, Mrs Wister. I'm sure I beg your pardon,' he added, raising his hat as he spoke; 'but it's so difficult to see when one first comes out of the light. I stayed behind correcting some of the work. I can't understand how you didn't meet him – but perhaps he went the short way home through the fields. I remember he did seem rather pressed for time. Dear, dear, I am sorry that you should have had all that walk for nothing.'

'It doesn't matter in the least. I wanted some fresh air, and I thought I would look in and see if he was still here.' It seemed to Margaret as though someone else repeated these words; speaking with clear-cut decision, in a thin voice from somewhere infinitely far away.

She heard the schoolmaster offer his escort to somebody – she supposed that it was the person who had been speaking. She heard the same voice protest that it was most kind, but quite unnecessary; heard it say good-night, and then left it – or went with it – she could not tell which.

Anyhow, it was silent during all that chill, scurrying passage across the fields back to the rectory; when the very touch of the wind against her cheek scared her, and the grass and bushes at the roadside seemed alive with terror.

One thing was certain. Neither that strange voice nor her own asked whether the rector was at home when Mary opened the door in answer to her ring.

She went upstairs and laid on her bed, pulling the eiderdown over her, turning her face to the wall for the sake of an even greater darkness than the curtained room afforded.

Presently Robert came in; she heard him go to his room and wash his hands; then he came and stood by her bed, apologizing for being late, asking if she was ill, what he could do for her; if she would come down, or have her dinner upstairs; standing awkwardly at her side, without once touching her or bending over her.

She did not reply, because it seemed as though there was nothing to say; as though, indeed, there were no words left in her. And after a while he went away.

Later on she got undressed and crept into bed; slept all that night without stirring, a sleep which was as heavy as death.

When she got down next morning Robert had finished

his breakfast, and gone off to some board meeting or other, to which it seemed Lord Leyton was to drive him; or such was the information volunteered by Mary, as she brought in fresh tea.

Margaret scarcely listened. It didn't seem to matter to her where Robert had gone, or said he had gone. The sun was streaming in through the windows of the dining-room. She could let him go in the daylight; it was in the evening or on dark, misty days that the close-growing woods and enfolding downs appeared like whispering walls set round some sinister and wordless scene.

But at that moment all she thought of was the necessity – though she did not know why there was any necessity – of waiting till it was at least half-past ten before making her way to the cottage in the wood.

She had no idea why she was going, what she would find to say when she got there. Once up the narrow, dark stairs, however, standing by old Mrs Orpin's bedside, she realized that it was not necessary to attempt any explanation; that she was in the presence of a superior and uncanny knowledge.

For a moment or so the eyes of the two women held each other: Margaret Wister's clear hazel, heavily ringed with dark shadows; Mrs Orpin's red-rimmed, alive with triumph.

Margaret's gaze was the first to falter, for the thought of guilt in the man she loved made her feel ashamed. Perhaps she could have borne anything better than this thing which she knew of, though she would not acknowledge it; there were intellectual sins – sins of ambition and pride or of a fine sort of rage. But the hiding away, the petty lies and pretences, the degradation of such sins of the flesh were beyond her comprehension.

Once again she turned and walked over to the window, while the old woman's eyes followed her.

It was a March day, the wind was sweeping the clouds, wisp-like trails of white gossamer, across the sky; shadows mimicked in the racing light and shade which swept over the still, bare field. There was a madder-tinted flush on the woods where the young buds were swelling; the swallows had come. It seemed as if everything was alive and moving, gathering itself together for a new lease of life. 'And here am I,' thought Margaret Wister, 'dull and heavy as a snake with an unsloughed skin – futile, utterly useless. I, who am – after all – the one thing which makes a sin of what Robert chooses to do. The real reason of damnation, the condition of heaven or hell.'

'Look 'ee here, Missus.' The old woman's tone was peremptory, and the rector's wife turned as though she were somehow bound to obey. Mrs Orpin had turned down the hem of her sheet, and spread out a white handkerchief, upon which was laid something which looked like a piece of dried bracken.

'Look 'ee here, an' listen to me, now as you know that old Mother Orpin ain't the cheat as 'ee took 'er for. I gathered this 'ere sprig o' male fern, on a St John's Eve, eight or ten years back, when I had the full use of me legs. I cut 'un with a silver knife, as I had off my owd Missus – for it maun never be as much as touched with iron – an' I laid a fine white nappy under it, for the seed maun not be let fall to the ground, nor be touched by hand – neither one nor the other. When I cut 'un I says – as them as know 'ud tell 'ee maun be said: "God greet thee, noble sprig. With God the Father I seek thee; with God the Son I find thee; with the Holy Ghost I break thee. I abjures thee, stalk an' leaf, by the power of the Mightiest that thou shows me what I orders"' – the ancient formula, used throughout unremembered ages, rolled smoothly off the old woman's tongue, terminating with the final appeal to the Blessed Virgin and the Trinity.

'Silence! Silence!' cried Mrs Wister. 'I refuse to listen to such blasphemy.' She was sure that she said it; that she heard her own voice repeat the words. But the next moment she began to doubt the testimony of her senses, for old Mrs Orpin went on as imperturbably as though she had heard nothing: 'I took 'un to the church one day when the 'oomen as was cleaning there had left the door open, an' I laid 'un on the altar an' said "Our Father" over 'un. An' now here it be. Lay out thy kerchief on the bed – woman.'

For the life of her Margaret could not have said why she obeyed; but the fact remains that she took her small white handkerchief from her bag and spread it out on the bed, when the old woman lifted hers carefully by each corner and emptied the dried fern-leaf into it.

'Guard it as thee would guard thine own heart,' she said. 'In two weeks' time that there young son o' Maester Hargreaves is agoin' to be wed. Then is the time to track them as is faithless to their marriage beds. If so be as ye're too mealy-minded to go watch as I bid yer, hark yer here now, Missus, yer'll take that there bit o' fern with yer when yer goes to the marryin', for it 'ull be in this 'ere church an' both you and the Reverant will be bidden to the feast as follows. Them there Hargreaves are purse-proud devils; there ain't nothing from a marryin' to a buryin' as they won't make show on – an' you'll lay it, sly-like so that there's none to see yer do it, under the cloth a'neath the place where yer man'll be sittin'.

'If so hap he's been all as he should by rights a' been to thee, there's no harm done. But if so be he's guilty – an' I know what I know – he'll turn as pale as death, shakin' from head to foot so as he maun get up – all swayin' as though he was drunken, an' be gone from o' the room.

'Then thee comes to me, an' I'll tell thee what ter do to the hussy as has stole 'un from yer – with the lust o' the eye an' all the wanton ways o' she.'

Without a word Margaret Wister gathered up her handkerchief by the four corners, twisted them together, and thrust it into the bosom of her dress.

Never once did her eyes meet those of Mrs Orpin. Even as she went down the dark stairs she kept them bent. All the way home, through the woods, where the catkins hung upon the hazels and the wood mercury was green beneath her feet, she never once raised them.

The last time she had seen old Mrs Orpin she had told herself that she would have nothing more to do with her; been full of smarting pride and scorn, drawing back within herself as though from some polluting touch.

But it seemed as though by this time she was beaten, drawn in, made one with all the primitive passions – smouldering and sullen, all the slow-working, subtle ways of primitive men and women.

When she got home she went up to her room, hunted out a little bit of silk – choosing, with a sort of bitter, perverted sentiment, a scrap of trimming from her wedding dress – and made a little bag into which she put the morsel of dried fern, hanging it by a cord round her neck, wondering all the while if it was really she – Margaret Wister – who was doing this thing.

There was a childish rhyme which she remembered, running somehow thus:

> If this be I,
> As I should hope it be,
> I've a little dog at home
> And he'll know me.
>
> If it be I
> He'll wag his little tail.
> But if it be not
> He'll loudly bark and wail.

A true little rhyme – pregnant with a knowledge, more than half forgotten – of the faithful love of a dog, which can recognize and lament over the very shadow of its master.

But as for Margaret, she had not even a dog to recognize the real her, the integral ego. Slow tears came into her eyes at the thought of her own loneliness. It seemed as if there, alone, she was capable of human feeling; for the rest she was like a creature driven by some hateful force, against which she was powerless.

The invitation to the wedding arrived two days later, and she accepted it. Her husband watched her as she opened the letter – it seemed as though he was always watching her now. He would pretend to go out, noisily slamming the front door; then he would creep back and, opening the door of the room where she was sitting very gently, peer in as though to make sure that she was still there, after which, if she did not look up, he would slip away without a word.

Whenever Margaret lifted her eyes – and she seemed to do so less and less often, with a conscious effort as though she were actually raising some weight – he seemed to be watching her, as if wondering how much she knew.

If either of them could have spoken openly; if he could have challenged her, or she accused him, it might have cleared the air; but they had both got beyond that.

At night the rector slept heavily. He had taken to drinking port at dinner instead of Madeira, and his one glass had given place to two, then three. But Margaret could not sleep; it was only at night that her brain appeared capable of working. During the day she seemed to be in a state of stupefaction, as though she were drugged, but at night her teeming brain raced her pulses.

The day of young Hargreaves' wedding arrived, a soft and brooding spring day which made itself felt in every limb, in the cooing of wood-doves among the trees, the press of green shoots through the moist ground; seeming to draw and pinch the human heart in its progress with the almost intolerable agony of all useless, unwanted things.

Margaret wore a silk dress of brownish-green – autumnal, like her mood – and a small round hat with a bent brim across her eyes. She was always – had been, even at her poorest – scrupulously dainty about her person; but on this particular day she felt as though she were somehow preparing for a sacrifice, in which clean raiment and purification were part of the recognized ritual.

Her husband commented on her appearance, his eyes sliding – past her face – from the brown feather on her hat to the pointed bronze shoe, with its steel buckle. 'My word! but you are a swell!' he said. 'You'll astonish the Hargreaves; they're very simple people, you know. I'm afraid that you'll find them rough, be shocked. They may get a little lively. Weddings in the country are the occasions for all sorts of jollification – a little too much liquor – loose speech. You'll find it best to slip away early.'

It was evident that he did not want her to go, but could not find any reason for an open objection. He was looking extraordinarily well in his florid, Georgian way – it would have been difficult for anyone to recognize the rather ascetic young curate of St Cuthbert's in the deep-chested, robust man with his almost oppressive air of animal vitality.

The back of his neck had grown red, with deep lines across it. When he laughed he threw back his head and opened his mouth wide. It sometimes seemed to Margaret that when he was near her he took all the air, left her scarcely enough for her shallow breathing.

The wedding itself was like a prelude to a play, in which she sat down, knelt, rose to her feet as though taking the part of some meaningless super.

But anyhow it was all meaningless – people made vows, and then they broke them. In the whole arrangement there seemed to be some grotesque – almost ludicrous – confusion between the flesh and the spirit. People were always glossing things over; why did they not face them out, make up their minds once for all which was the strongest? Then how ridiculous it was to use the same formula for any two people – herself and Robert, for instance. The oaths which had been intended to bind her were quite superficial; she had one mate, and she would never want another, even if he died; had he never come into her life it is more than probable that there never would have been anyone else. But for Robert there must always be someone; even in the old days she had never thought of him remaining a widower supposing she died first – he would need someone to look after him, that was the way in which she had put it to herself.

She wondered now if he had taken her share of the vows as well as his own, whether it would have kept him faithful to her; if anything would keep young Hargreaves – with that loose, sensual mouth – faithful to the rabbit-faced, narrow-chested slip of a girl with whom he was now kneeling before the altar.

Farmer Hargreaves gave Margaret his arm out of the church, and through the two or three meadows that lay between it and the house; while she heard herself talking to him – of the wedding, of his new daughter-in-law, of the weather, of the crops. He was flattered and pleased; people had said the parson's wife was stuck up, but he found her uncommonly pleasant, and almost pretty, though peaky-looking, not a patch on his girl, in her pink-flounced gown.

'Thee ought to get a bit more colour in thy cheeks living here in this fine air; but I misdoubts as thou don't get out an' about in the fresh air enough. Look at the rector now;

uncommon well he looks, not like the same man as he did when he comed here. But I maun say this, he took to country life, from the first go off, like a duck to water.'

'I never had much colour,' answered Margaret, 'but for all that I'm never ill.'

'Well, and there are some like that. I'd a mare once that always looked as though her were on the road to die; creepin' aben her work for all the world like a sniggle. When she was gotten with foal I an' my missus 'ud spend half our time cockering her up; until we found out that there weren't nothing, in reason, nor yet out, 'ud down her. Why I tell thee straight, missus, her'd get through as much work as any two of the others, without turning a hair; an' there wasn't any mare as I ever had as 'ud throw a better foal – with less trouble neither.'

He talked on till they reached the house. Then the men dispersed, and all the other women, excepting an old dame who was hovering about the ready-set table, went upstairs to take off their hats. Only Margaret remained behind: 'I'm afraid I shall not be able to stay very long – it is scarcely worth while,' she said; and sat herself down on the wide old sofa by the window, to wait till they came back.

It was Miss Hargreaves who had asked her whether she would like to go upstairs; sulkily, as though Mrs Wister's very existence grieved her. Her face was flushed with health and fresh air, her full lips crimson.

'What a pretty frock you have got on,' said Margaret, who wished no harm to the girl; it was no good blaming her, even if the fern should reveal all that she suspected was true. She belonged to the country – the lush, fertile country. And Robert, too, he belonged to it. What wonder if they had been caught in its seductive toils? It was what the country was full of, seemed to be made for; the propagation of each after its own kind; every beast and bird, and insect and flower, was busied over it – multiplying and killing, that was the whole sum of country life.

Her eyes strayed to the skirt of the girl's dress, for flounces had only just come into fashion again, and this was flounced from waist to hem.

This, indeed, was her only thought. But as she looked up her eyes met those of Trixie Hargreaves – full – for the first time; large and blue and heavy-lidded, suffused with a sort of defiant shame.

The dress was well planned; the girl so generously built that it was hardly possible for anyone to suspect anything. Her parents might see her every day for weeks to come, and yet not notice the faint-growing difference in her form.

But Mrs Wister knew, rather than saw, or else even the girl's look would have told her nothing.

As she sat alone on the settee, with the soft spring air – laden with the scent of grape hyacinths – creeping in through the open window, she tried to think things out. There were other men in the world; hanging about the farm, even during the short walk from church she had seen two strapping young farmers on either side of Trixie, competing for her smiles.

The women in the room above were moving about, setting themselves to rights; from somewhere at the back of the house came the sound of water splashing and men's voices, mingled with laughter.

The old woman came and went. Once Margaret saw her husband peer round the corner of the open door.

She knew that there was not much time left to do what she had to do. But she was overcome by a curious sort of languor. It would be done, because it was ordained and set, by some implacable and aloof power of which she understood nothing. There was no need for her to fret or hurry, the chance would come.

She was right there; it came to her clear with none of her

contriving. For presently the farmer's voice sounded from the back kitchen: 'Best to get the ale drawn now, eh, Mrs Gullet?'

The old woman went to the dresser and took down a large jug then moved over to the fireplace for the cellar key, which hung on a nail against the jamb. There was the sound of drawing corks in the distance, and more laughter.

The bridegroom came swaggering into the big kitchen, to smirk at himself, and set his tie straight in the glass above the mantelshelf; while someone shouted an Elizabethan witticism after him, which he returned in kind – with the embellishment of a meaningless oath. He did not realize that there was anyone, save the old woman – who did not count – in the room, until he caught sight of Margaret in the glass, upon which he retreated with a crimson face.

The old woman was grumbling because none of the other women came downstairs to give her a hand; the cellar stairs were steep, and she had rheumatism that bad she misdoubted she had been hit by an 'elf' shot – on her way home the night before. It wouldn't be a lucky marriage she knew that. For the butter had never come in the churn – not as it should do – from the first day the couple was 'church-bawled'. As for that there girl Trixie she had one rue-bargain already. Girls weren't what they were when she was young, a flighty, feather-brained lot.

'What is a rue-bargain?' asked Margaret idly. Still she did not feel hurried, the time would be given her.

The old woman, half-way out of the door, turned and stared in surprise at her ignorance. 'To be bawled in church for sure an' then not to come up to the scratch. She were to a' been married at the New Year – Miss Yes-an'-No. If I'd been her mother I'd a' walloped 'er – saving yer presence, Marm – for throwing over as nice a young chap as never was, all in a moment like that. His house full o' furniture, bought an' all; makin' 'im look that foolish like it's little wonder as 'ee went off to the States to be out on it all! Well, here am I keeping yon with my talking, an the beer to be drawed an' all. One as didn't know the Hargreaves as I knows 'em, wouldn't think to find them giving beer at a wedding. But that's their way; that's for the relations, that is; with t'owd chap tippin' them the wink to say as how they prefers it to the sherry wine – of which they bain't but four bottle, though don't thee tell nobody as I told yer.'

The old woman grumbled her way to the top of the cellar steps, which were just outside the door, and so down them; her voice growing fainter at every step.

'Whistle, Polly, whistle,' roared an hilarious voice from the back kitchen, to be followed by a thin, far-away fluttering whistle, which showed that – whatever old Mrs Gullet might be doing – she had not got her mouth to the tap of the beer barrel.

Margaret had been to rustic weddings before, she knew that the parson sat on the left-hand of the bride – with the bridegroom to the right; and, after a moment or so of fumbling at her breast, she got up, moved across the room, lifted the edge of the table-cloth, and slipped the fern beneath it.

Then she sat down again on the settee – her hands folded on her lap, in a manner which was symbolical. The whole affair had been taken out of them. If Robert was guilty there remained only one thing to be done, to put herself, her barren, useless self, out of the way so that he might legalize the child which Trixie Hargreaves would bear to him; while if he were not guilty no harm would be done. Presently the women came down the stairs, laughing and whispering, with the bride in their midst. Mrs Hargreaves – a close-lipped, secretive-looking woman – lingered by the door to waylay old Mrs Gullet as she came panting up the steps; giving her some last instructions. Then she crossed over to the window to apologize to Mrs Wister for having kept her so long waiting, with her eyes glancing sideways at the table, counting the places to see that they were rightly set, for at the last moment a couple of uninvited cousins had joined the party.

Then the men came in with shining hair and red faces. Mrs Hargreaves sniffed the air as though she thought that she smelt whisky, reprimanded her husband in a sharp aside, and then, smiling, bade her guests be seated.

Her glance was chill as it swept Trixie, in the pink frock, and Margaret wondered if, after all, she did know, or guess, or whether it was merely the antagonism so common between mother and daughter.

They all stood while the rector said grace, and then they sat down, while Farmer Hargreaves began to carve the cold turkey. There were fowls at the other end of the table; there were cold pork and beef, jellies and custards and blancmanges.

No one spoke much. The young men and women looked at each other shyly, the elders were busy with their food. Mrs Hargreaves' anxious glance went up and down the table. They would be better when liquor had loosened their tongues. Only the host made jokes as he carved; told stories of his own wedding, laughing at them freely.

Margaret and her husband were at the opposite ends of the table, she could look straight down it at him.

She saw the farmer heap a plate and pass it down to him: 'Cum on then, Paerson,' she heard him say, 'I know as thee be a fine trencher-man.'

Robert's face was flushed, his eyes bright, it was evident that he had already had something to drink.

The young bridegroom reached across his bride and poured him out a glass of sherry.

'Here you are, Paerson, wet yer whistle afore yer start,' he spoke familiarly, almost – as it seemed to Margaret – contemptuously.

The rector had just raised his knife and fork; but now he put them down, and taking the glass in his hand rose to his feet.

Every scrap of colour had gone out of his face as suddenly as though a cloth had been wiped over it. The wine in the glass which he held slopped over the edge, showing how his hand shook.

The murmured attempt at conversation ceased, every face was turned in the same direction – pale and flushed, long and round, all alike with the chins dropping a little, mouths open, eyes staring.

'I – I – I have come here –' began the rector. What was happening? Was he going to propose the health of the bride and bridegroom, forgetting that the feast was scarcely begun? The women appeared frightened; but the men glanced sideways at each other and grinned. Margaret felt a foot brush past her gown as one youth kicked another under the table.

The bride was shrinking sideways; for the rector trembled so that it almost seemed as though he might fall upon her.

'I rise to – to –' he began again; upon which young Hargreaves stretched an arm round, behind his newly-made wife, and tweaked him by the coat.

'Sit thee down, Paerson; 'tain't time fur that yet awhile. Thee mun –'

He broke off as Robert Wister turned and stared at him, the glass in his hand held at such an angle that the last drop of wine was spilled on the cloth; while the next moment the glass itself dropped from his hand, and with a glance round the table, his white face drawn and piteous with a sort of childish horror and dismay, he turned and hurried out of the room.

'He's a bit upset. Maybe it's a touch of the liver, or summat – hurrin' on an empty stomach an' all.' The kindly farmer had his hand on Margaret's arm, as though trying to reassure her, while the rest of the company looked awkward and self-conscious, as though something in the incident reflected on them personally.

To Margaret it seemed that for the moment all her senses, which had been for so long half-numbed, were doubled. For she saw and heard all this, though at the same time her entire attention seemed to be engrossed by Trixie Hargreaves.

She had watched Robert's piteous self-betrayal with her full-lipped mouth tight shut instead of half open, as were the others. It seemed as though her blooming face had grown suddenly old, drawn, and anxious.

As he rushed from the room she had half risen to her feet, the knuckles of her hands showing white as she pressed them on the table. For a moment she hesitated thus, and then sank back on to her chair, without even glancing in the direction of her mother, who eyed her steadily.

The company picked up their knives and forks.

'I don't think I ever smelt anything like those grape hyacinths, Mr Hargreaves,' said Margaret. 'The perfume which came through the window while I was waiting down here was beyond words. And those yellow things, like large cowslips – what do you call them?'

Everyone stared at her with an air of shocked amazement. But she had started the conversation, and for a few moments it went on, accompanied by the rattle of knives and forks.

Then, during a sudden pause, came a sound which struck them all silent – the heart-rending sound of a man sobbing.

At this Trixie was out of her chair in a moment. Her mother caught at her dress as she passed – one of those flying frills of rose-pink; but she tore it almost savagely from her hand and was gone.

In a moment every eye was turned to Margaret, and realizing that there was something expected of her – something which she must do – she laid her napkin on the table and pushed back her chair.

'You will excuse me, I hope, Mrs Hargreaves; my husband is subject to these heart attacks; they are terribly painful at the time, but there is no real need for anxiety. We have – there are remedies.'

As she left the room they all turned their heads from side to side and stared at each other. 'Well I never! Did you ever see the like of that now? Heartless!'

Out from the large kitchen there was an anteroom; then a passage flagged with red bricks, which led to the porch, where Mrs Wister found her husband sitting, with his head leaning against the woodwork at the side.

Trixie Hargreaves stood by him, with one knee on the seat, so that his shoulder rested against her. She had one arm round his neck, and with the other hand, holding a white handkerchief, she wiped his forehead.

'There, there!' she was saying. 'There – now you'll be all right, my dear love, my man.'

Margaret could see that his shoulders shook. It was as if he were retching violently, though no sound came apart from an occasional sob, which seemed as though it would tear his chest.

Trixie raised her eyes and looked at her, with no sign of antagonism. It was as though Robert were a great child regarding whom their one concern was to find the best thing to do.

After a moment Margaret turned and went down the passage to where she had guessed, by the sound of running water, the back kitchen might be found. Here she drew a cup of water, and returning, handed it to Trixie, who held it to Robert's lips.

At first he seemed to choke over it; then he took a long draught, and drew himself a little upright, while the girl again wiped his brow, smoothing back his damp hair. Centuries ago, back in Deptford, Margaret had been used to run her fingers through it and kiss it while he slept; someone had once said that all men with curly hair were weak, but she had never really thought whether Robert was, or was not, weak; he was far too near and dear for any analysis.

Presently he raised his head and looked at his wife as she stood leaning against the opposite side of the porch; then up at Trixie, his lips trembling.

'I don't know what happened,' he said; 'I felt so ill suddenly – deadly sick – and frightened – horribly frightened, as though I was going to die.' He looked at Margaret; it seemed as though he wanted to work upon her pity to excuse him something.

'I hope that I didn't make a scene, upset people. I never felt so awful in my life. I was obliged to come out into the air, and Miss Hargreaves –'

'Yes, I know,' said Margaret; at which they both looked up, and for a moment their glances held. Those of the other two troubled, half defiant and half shamed; hers cold and sad, like that of a creature from another world.

It was the wife who spoke first – rather hurriedly, for fear that they should attempt any excuse or explanation. 'I think, Robert, for all our sakes, that the best thing will be for you to come home with me now, and for Miss Hargreaves to go back to her father's guests. She can say that I was so stupefied that I did not know what to do; that it was a good thing that there was someone with their wits about them, etc. Then, if she will come – it will seem only natural, as you were her father's guest – up to the rectory this evening, she will be able to see how you are after your – your attack.'

They acquiesced in this; it seemed as though she had taken the lead so decisively that there was no choice save to do as she told them.

Together they got Robert to his feet, and Margaret made him lean upon her with one arm round her shoulder, while Trixie stood for a moment with his hand in hers, her face raised. With a woman's greater abandonment to love she would have kissed him there, in front of his wife, had he given any sign of wishing it.

But he did not, and after a pause she turned round and went into the house without a word, while Mrs Wister braced herself to her husband's weight.

'Come,' she said; 'we must get home as best we can.'

All the way back to the rectory he talked of the attack which had overcome him, wondering what it could be, saying that he must stay in bed and send Mary for the doctor, set his affairs in order. 'It was so sudden – so utterly unaccountable,' he kept saying. 'I had done nothing, taken nothing, which could have possibly upset me.'

It was very evident that he feared she might suspect him of having drunk too much, or of God only knows what else; that he looked on her as a possible judge, to be feared and almost hated.

Directly they got home – and after they had gone a little way he moved more easily, seemed refreshed by the air – she made him lie down on the sofa in the study; he would not go to bed, after all; and she knew why – that he wished to be sure of seeing Trixie when she called that evening. Then she sent for the doctor, for it seemed to her that it would be best to make the fact of his indisposition as public as possible.

When the doctor did come there seemed little that he could say. The rector's heart appeared somewhat quicker in its beat, his pulse fuller than it should be. He was manifestly very shaken, but as neither he nor Mrs Wister would acknowledge that he had received any sort of shock – though the doctor himself suspected something of the nature of a violent quarrel – there was nothing for him to say, beyond speaking of the effect that the sudden spell of spring heat was having upon all his patients.

To Margaret it seemed as though she were putting

everything into order, getting things into train, as it were; that the story of her life was moving to an end with the smooth inevitability of a Greek tragedy. She held no key to what that end might be; had no idea of what was coming next. But of this she was certain: it was all ordered, prepared, would be carried out decently, with dignity. For it is only people who fight against Fate who make an ugly, clashing confusion of their lives. For the others there are deep, agonizing wounds, both of mind and body, but there is at least the dignity of beauty and silence.

She was still in that curiously receptive state, sure that she only had to wait to be shown the way. And here she was right, for it was pointed out to her clearly, without any effort on her part, emanating, in this case, from the doctor when she was seeing him off in the hall.

'You're looking very seedy yourself, Mrs Wister – as if you were in need of a change, or a little feeding up. It does not do to let oneself get too run down; one loses all power of rebound. If anything happens, any slight illness, a cold or anything, it takes hold and is difficult to cure.'

'I think I'm all right. Perhaps a little run down.'

The doctor put out a soft, plump hand and clasped her wrist. 'Your pulse is a bit uncertain, I should say your nerves were out of order. Now, how have you been sleeping?'

Here it was – the thing which she had been waiting for. She took her chance calmly. 'I've not been sleeping well for some time. I think, though it sounds a ridiculous thing to say, that the silence gets on my nerves. If you could let me have something that would start me off again, I believe I should be all right. Perhaps I've got it into my head that I can't sleep,' she added with a little laugh.

'I will send you something – a few powders – when I send your husband's medicine. I will make them very mild, and you can take one every night for a week. I dare say that will put you right again. But I would get away if I were you; nothing will do you – both of you, indeed – so much good as a thorough change.'

'I will try and persuade Robert. About the medicine, now, doctor, I would like him to have a dose as soon as possible.'

'Yes, that's right. I'm going home now, and I will make it up and send it straight round to you.'

'And the powders? It would be a pity to give your lad two journeys.'

'And the powders. I won't forget. Though, mind you, Mrs Wister, a fortnight at Margate – or, if you object to that, Broadstairs – would do you far more good than any of my physic.'

The afternoon dragged on its way with a heavy quiet. The wind had dropped, the blue sky and clouds were alike lost; it seemed as though the whole of nature were overhung by a heavy curtain of grey which muffled colour and speech and sound, so that they touched the senses with a dull obscurity.

Robert Wister felt oppressed, almost suffocated. He was so used to being out of doors that it made him restless to be too long within four walls. Yet he realized that he was an invalid – that he had behaved at the wedding that day in a manner which could only be excused by ill-health. That it would be scarcely seemly for him to go out and about.

Every now and then he got up and stared out of the window like a disconsolate child; the mayfly were out – they lasted such a short time, and it was just the evening for fishing. But directly he heard his wife coming he ran back to the sofa, and lay there with closed eyes.

Soon after five the medicine came from the doctor. Margaret undid the parcel in the hall, and brought his to him. 'It's the best time to take it now you've just had your tea,' she said.

The rector drank it off obediently, with a glance at the tray which stood by his side. 'I was not able to eat anything,' he said, observing, with a sense of resentment, that his wife seemed in nowise touched, engrossed in herself.

'I don't think you'll want anything more at present,' she said; 'I'm going to lie down a little and rest; I have slept badly for the last few nights.'

A sense of relief came over Robert. He would now be able to get up, to move about the house, to behave like a normal being. Though with this came a sense of resentment against her for her heartlessness.

Though he was better now he certainly had been very ill indeed; was frightened of illness as all normally healthy people are.

Once again Mary was out; Emmie was somewhere in the back regions; the house was almost abnormally quiet.

After a while he moved into the dining-room and mixed himself a whisky and soda; then into the drawing-room.

There was a photograph of himself as he had appeared in the St Cuthbert's days, in a silver frame upon Margaret's writing-table, and he stood staring at it for a moment or two – rather contemptuously. Then he moved back into his study and took up a book.

But he had lost the habit of reading; and after a while he threw it on one side, and picked up a sporting paper.

The time seemed interminable. At last Emmie appeared with the lamp. And then – after another long pause – came to say that dinner was ready; asking what she was to do. For she had taken Mrs Wister her hot water and found her lying on her bed asleep, did not know whether to waken her or not.

'No, no, don't disturb her; she has had bad nights lately – so she tells me. Just keep some soup hot, and she can have it when she stirs.'

Robert was conscious of a little glow of self-appreciation as he spoke; he was seeing to his wife's comfort like a good husband. He *was* a good husband, as long as she did not know anything to the contrary.

He dawdled over his dinner and his three glasses of port, which seemed to put new life into him. That was what Margaret needed; there was nothing like port for toning up the system.

He had almost given up the thought of seeing Trixie that night. Though the desire for her swelled up in him so that he half thought of walking towards the farm, hanging about a little in hopes of seeing her.

But it was only an idle thought; for he knew well enough that, particularly just now, he must do nothing to endanger his reputation. He was conscious of a sense almost of resentment against Trixie, along with his craving to see her, to be near her. For somehow he thought that if it had not been for her things would not have happened as they did; not being profound enough to realize that he was so ripe for such happenings that – at the beginning – any woman would have done equally well.

At half-past nine – when he had long given her up – Trixie arrived, and all speculation was lost in his delight at the mere sight of her; his feeling that here at last was someone to 'be nice' to him – as he himself would have expressed it.

She was all flushed with hurrying through the night air, wrapped from head to foot in an old ulster. But for all her colour she was nervous and depressed. The excuse which she had given for her late visit to Emmie, who opened the door to her, was that her father and mother were anxious to know if Mr Wister was any better; though, as a matter of fact, they had gone to bed early and believed her to be in her room, already asleep.

When she was shown into the study she had not a word to say of her father. It was all of her mother that she spoke: 'She suspects something, I know she does; she watches me all the time – that's her way. Oh, it's horrible! I've always been open, not minded what people said or thought of me; but now I seem to be for ever lying – and I'm sure I don't know what Tom' – Tom was the newly-married brother – 'thinks of it all. I wouldn't mind if we could go away together, openly.'

'We can't – you know we can't. You must remember my –' he was going to say 'my cloth', and then, suddenly ashamed, changed the word to 'profession'.

'I know, I know; though any outsider would think it 'ud be the sort of profession that 'ud make one have to be open. And it isn't only that – there's your wife. I thought from what you told me that she was as cold as a stone, didn't care for you. But she's not like that, anyhow where you're concerned. I don't know, but looking at her to-day I felt that she half worshipped you, would die for you. Besides, she's a lady, one of your own sort. I wouldn't – even if anything happened – make you as good a sort of wife, as the world counts it, as she does. Though you tell me that you never did love her – not as you love me.' There was something almost of entreaty in the girl's voice, as though she wanted him to reassure her in some way. 'I don't know what to do.' She spread her arms out on the study table and dropped her head upon them, with a little moan: 'I've felt rather proud of it, thought it was rather grand till to-day. But now I'm frightened. Even if she found out and divorced you – if we were able to marry – things would never seem right. Not for my people, I mean – they're that old-fashioned; not for me either, for the matter of that; I don't believe I'd ever feel we were really married; though God knows I love you so that I'd go through fire for you.'

The rector moved over to the mantelpiece; picked up his pipe, filled it, and rammed the tobacco down with his little finger. He did not know what to say; for it was a curious fact that though both his wife and Trixie Hargreaves believed he would marry her if possible, he himself had no such idea. Or if it came to him, it was with a sense of shrinking, of something which, at the worst, he might be driven to. In his passion for the girl herself there was nothing permanent or domestic. He realized this clearly, as men – even the stupidest of them – do realize such things, which, with all her quicker intelligence, a woman is slow to grasp.

Now, because he really did not know what to do or say, Robert Wister took refuge in a caress; and moving across the room put one hand on Trixie's hair; then slid it round under her chin, raised her face, and kissed her on the lips. 'It will all come right, dear. I know I have done wrong, horribly wrong. But things right themselves somehow, one must' – he was going to say, 'put one's trust in God,' he had said it so often, but again he changed his words – 'try not to lose one's self-control, get flurried. After all' – suddenly his face grew flushed, boyish, honest – 'why are we told to be fruitful and multiply – eyes and ears and imagination, all alike fed up with sex, from the time we are kids at school – tied and bound as we are? What is a marriage without children? It isn't half a marriage. If we had been given children I'd never have as much as looked at another woman,' he added. And now he spoke the truth; not one child – wistful and quiet as only children so often are – would have satisfied him, but a nursery full of boisterous growing girls and boys, a sort of tally-hoing pack.

'Then – then we wouldn't have had our love,' said Trixie, with the element of simplicity which is in all primitive women.

'No, we wouldn't have had our love,' agreed Robert Wister; perhaps rather lukewarmly, for she glanced up at him with a sort of fierceness.

'Well, by God, that's been worth something!' she breathed; and caught at his hand, would have said more but for a sudden tumult in the hall.

It was Mary's voice shrilly raised. It seemed as though she

were making her way through the hall from the kitchen; throwing back her words as she went to someone who still remained there. 'I will tell him; I've to tell him. It's my duty, I say; an' oh dear, oh dear, I wonder why I ever –'

Robert Wister moved again to the fireplace; and Trixie sat up straight, smoothing out the gloves which she had been in too great a hurry to put on. 'Well, I suppose I ought to be going,' she was beginning in a mincing voice, when – with a perfunctory knock – the study door was pushed open, and the parlourmaid burst into the room, still wearing her hat and coat.

Her face was patched in crimson and white, as though haste and fear had struggled for mastery. For some moments it seemed as though she had exhausted all her words in her transit through the hall, or else her panting breath half choked her.

Again Trixie Hargreaves murmured something about going, and rose from her chair. At which a stream of words broke forth from the other woman, shaken by some overwhelming fear out of all her set ways. For Mary was a thoroughly good servant, very regular in her ways. Always on her day out she was back at ten; and put on her cap and apron to come and ask her master and mistress if there was anything else they needed, to wish them good night. In the face of all this her disarray was the more noticeable – even if it had been unaccompanied by an incoherent flow of speech. 'Oh, sir, I don't know what you'll say to me – I don't know whatever took me to go and do such a thing – but Emmie had been; it was Emmie as told me that the old woman was that cunning and creepy-like. But I'll never forget it, no, not if I live to be a hundred! She dared me to do it. An' I did it. Oh dear, oh dear!' Here the girl broke off in a shuddering, hysterical sob.

'Did what?' inquired the rector.

'Went to see that there old Mrs Orpin. I don't care what

folks say about there being no devil – saving your presence, sir – they wouldn't say it if they'd seen that dreadful old woman as I did. She was in 'er bed; and she had a great white enamel basin o' water on 'er knee, and she was stirring it round with her finger. I meant to ask her about my friend, you know, sir, Ben Hawkins's son, for he's gone off to a job in Bristol, and there's never any knowing –' She paused for a moment, her face was sombre, she had her own troubles, and there was never any knowing.

Then the more recent happenings took possession of her again. 'You wouldn't wonder that I was upset if you could have seen her, sir, and the way she carried on – laughing and all!'

Again she shuddered; for the first time in her life she realized that a laugh could be terrible, absolutely devoid of merriment or derision.

'Well, there's nothing in that to be so very frightened about, a silly old woman who plays on the credulity of you silly girls. You deserve everything you get, if you will go tampering with such folly.'

He spoke pompously; it seemed to give him a sort of strength to find someone to rebuke.

Mary took out her handkerchief and put it to her eyes, then began to twist it round and round in her fingers: 'It wasn't about myself, sir, I'm in such an upset. It's what she said about you and the mistress – terrible things! O' death and – and all sorts of wickedness – I told Emmie it was my plain duty to tell you of it – then, just as I was making off, she called after me. About the mistress, sir, she said as how she had come to this place all fresh an' fair, but as how the black ox had trodden on her foot since then –'

'The black ox? But what in the world –' Robert Wister was beginning, when Trixie broke in:

'I know, it's a country saying – it means she's had trouble.'

Mary turned and stared at her. They were all standing in a rough triangle, overcome by a sort of creeping fear out of all proportion to the things of which the girl was telling them.

'She said: "Get thee along home, girl, there's one that is coming to join us to-night, and if a hare crosses your path on the way you will know that it's the truth I'm speakin' an' that you've met her half way. When you get back, if you find her gone" – those were her very words, as I stand here, sir – "if you find her gone, put a saucer of salt on her breast".'

'But this is sheer balderdash!' broke in the rector. He glanced from his terror-stricken parlourmaid to Trixie Hargreaves, and saw to his surprise that she had taken on that strange mottled paleness which some naturally high-coloured people show in moments of great agitation.

'Oh, oh,' she said, 'don't' – and put both her hands over her ears, as though she wished to shut out the sound of Robert Wister's robust voice. 'It's what they do here – in the country – for – for the sin eater.' Her voice sank to the merest whisper on the last words.

'The what?' – the rector stared at her with drooping jaw. There was something uncanny, horrible in the whole thing.

'Yes, you're right.' It was Mary who spoke, turning to Trixie as she did so – drawing her apart, as it were – so that the matter now hung between the two women. 'That's what she said of the mistress. She has suffered for the sins of others, now let them others eat her sin, which it is they as have druv her to.'

'Yes, yes, I know – and I?' breathed Trixie.

'I came home. I came by the field against the wood. I was all moithered with fear, or I wouldn't have come that way. And just before I got to the gate – oh, my God, how it frightened me! My God! My God!' She crossed her hands over her breast, and rocked herself to and fro in an agony of hysterical fear. The correct and well-trained parlourmaid, out of whose veins no training in the whole world, even among the best families, could wholly eradicate the deep well-spring of rustic superstition and fear – 'When I was just nigh the gate a great hare ran under it, and clean across my feet. An' I knew that the – that the missus was –'

'Why, your mistress is upstairs lying on her bed asleep. I never heard such nonsense! I –' The rector's words broke off into a great burst of rather too high-pitched laughter.

It had been a trying day, things had worked upon him, and after all he was an invalid, in the doctor's hands. It was no wonder his nerves had been stretched taut by Mary's incredible tale. But now – this was too much – bordering on the grotesque. Did the fool of a girl mean that it was his wife, Margaret Wister, who was careering about the fields at night in the form of a hare? 'Marthas', they called them, 'Marthas'. He laughed again. 'She was tired out, she didn't even come down to dinner. I think perhaps she was over-anxious' – he was going to say 'over-anxious about me', which seemed a sane and wifely failing, when he realized that he was out of it – that the two women were gazing at each other with their very souls in their eyes.

It was Mary who moved first, and she turned and ran, with her hat all on one side, her best skirt gathered up around her knees; while – 'No, no, no!' cried Trixie, and followed her – as though the rector were not in the room, as though the house were her own.

'What would Margaret think?' That was his one thought as he knocked the ashes out of his pipe, and filled it again, with shaking hands.

He half moved across the room as though to follow them, then came back. After all there was nothing he could do, it was best to let the women have it out among themselves, he was thinking, when there came the sound of a long-drawn, wailing cry from the upper storey.

He heard Emmie run up the stairs two steps at a time – then there came another cry; then a long silence.

He stood in the middle of the room with his unlighted pipe in his hand. What did it all mean – what was going on up there? It seemed as if he were rooted to the spot like a man in a dream, or did not dare to go upstairs to see what was wrong. Though all his faculties seemed tearing themselves to tatters in their effort to see, to hear, to guess.

A moment or two later Emmie came running down the stairs – with her apron up to her face, blubbering unrestrainedly – and bolted into the dining-room.

By some supreme effort the rector tore his feet from his study carpet, and met her in the doorway as she returned.

'What – what?' he began, loudly, truculently; then glanced down at what she carried in her hand.

A small white glass salt-cellar.

3 The Vortex (1919)

CAST

JAMES MEADE ... Sir Vincent Fair
MRS MEADE ... Violet Madden
CHARLES WYNNE ... Humphrey St John
CLARE HARGREAVES ... Beatrice Atherton
GRIBBLE – A MANSERVANT ... Augustus King
FRENCH MAID ... Kitty le Strange (wife of Humphrey St
John)
DOCTOR, SERVANTS, AND HARRY BRAIDE, taking a
small part as Miss Hargreaves' chauffeur, who tells the story.

AUTHOR
LAWRENCE KESTERVON

Is it possible for the actors and actresses in a play to become so obsessed by it, so worked upon by the frenzied ardour of the author, that they lose their real characteristics and become part of it? I think so, and it is upon this that I base my conviction.

In 1887, that is, Lawrence Kestervon was seventeen years of age, he won a small scholarship for English composition.

This scholarship was intended to help promising lads to get through Cambridge. But Lawrence's father, a bank manager, had been struck down at a comparatively early age by a paralytic seizure and there was nothing but his small pension for the family to live on. It took Mrs Kestervon all her time to wait upon her husband. She spoon-fed him like a child, a by no means amenable one; so that young Kestervon's ideas of home were forever associated with a futile and furious man – bloodshot eyes and drawn face – throwing about everything he could lay hands on, shouting abuse at a meek, trembling woman, so nerve-ridden that she was in a perpetual state of dropping, spilling, breaking what he called for: weeping, oh yes, always weeping, in a silent, half-hearted manner. Then there was his sister Annie, with her high cheek-bones – so like her father's – flushed scarlet, declaring shrilly that such a home was enough to send any girl to the dogs! She proved it, too, for she always did what she said, did Anne ….

Such was the beginning and end of home life for Lawrence Kestervon. His father died when he was eighteen. Annie had already dropped out of the family circle, gone Heaven only knew where. His mother, worn down to a sort of apathy, went to live with a widowed sister in the north of England. It was cheaper than trying to make a home for Lawrence, and always, always, everything had hung upon that; the need for economy, shaving life down to the bare bone.

Lawrence did not care much one way or another; if parents do not love their children their children do not love them. Is it likely that they should? Truth to tell, Mrs Kestervon's decision fitted in with the boy's own wishes. There was no sense of chill at his heart, for it burnt with something more potent than affection – something which was at once home, friendship, love, father, mother, food, warmth, shelter – and this was ambition. That scholarship had set him all aflame to tread the paths of literature; never, for one moment, to rest content with the level plains, the broad highways, but to make straight, whatever the cost, for those hilltops which catch the sun no matter in which direction it may turn.

He had already spent two-thirds of the sum allotted to him by his scholarship, or rather it had been engulfed in the family morass commonly termed 'general expenses'. Fifty pounds remained; he was perfectly certain that he could live for one year on fifty pounds, and by that time his future would be assured.

By dint of denying himself everything which makes life tolerable he did live on it and wrote a play. He took a whole year over it, writing and rewriting it – half-starved, baked and frozen by turns in an attic – until the play was as intricate, involved, soulless as those geometrical puzzles which we find at the end of magazines.

To do the boy Lawrence justice, he had the astuteness to realize what was bad, the courage to destroy it. That year's work went into the fire.

After this he descended from his attic to the basement cellar – not merely symbolically, but literally: struggled through an attack of rheumatic fever, which affected him more or less for life; started to write advertisements, got a few odd paragraphs into a few equally odd and almost unknown papers, supplied the footnotes to comic pictures; wrote verses, mostly for religious periodicals, at a shilling a verse. Then he went back to his attic; descending after a few years to the more reputable middle of the house, and bought, at twenty-three, the first new suit which he had possessed since he was eighteen. *That*, after all, had been one of his father's sheared down for him. At thirty-five he found himself in a state of comparative affluence; that is, he was making about as much as the girl who stamped and addressed the refusal slips of his more serious efforts.

After this he steadily climbed upwards, but in such a small way that he never dared to look back and see how small a distance he had travelled. He had two rooms instead of one, he afforded himself an occasional meal at a cheap Italian café; once even he left London for a fortnight on the Yorkshire moors ...

He would have repeated this extravagance, for it opened his eyes to a world of beauty and delight of which he had heretofore scarcely dreamed.

'If only I could do this every year,' he thought to himself,

'I might really write something worth doing.' He formed, indeed, a plan for spending six months of each year in London, making enough by any sort of hack work to last him over the next six, and then retiring to Yorkshire to work at that *magnum opus* which had never quite ceased to simmer in his brain.

The Yorkshire trip was, however, never to be repeated. Perhaps it had awakened him to new possibilities in life, quickened him to beauty of another kind, or perhaps it merely strengthened him physically, awakened his latent manhood. But whatever the reason it was about this time that he first began to notice women as individuals – apart from their obviously comic or possibly tragic histories, and fell in love with the sister of one of the clerks in a magazine editor's office.

It is certain, from what he told me, that Iris Hames was beautiful, with that calculating air of dignity and innocence, that clear, creamy paleness consistent with perfect health, which is the dower of so many London girls. But it is equally certain that her brain and heart alike were empty of everything save a perpetual, petty scheming for new possessions, sensations, tastes: that in her was to be found a replica of the daughter of the horse-leech with her cry of 'Give, give.' Iris, however, did not say 'give'; but 'I wouldn't mind if I had –'

Always, ever since the days of that scholarship, Kestervon's trend had been in the direction of tragedy. He felt, realized tragedy; saw it in half the faces which he looked upon; deduced it from scraps of conversation in 'bus or underground, from the baldest notices of police-court processes in the daily papers. The upper crust of life might show gay and cheerful; but underneath it all lay unplumbed depths of hopelessness, misery, cruelty. All the same, it seemed to him that the only way in which he could make money was by a bald chronicling of the obvious: short paragraphs on fires and financial affairs; or serio-comic sketches and stories, connected, for the most part, with over-stout wives, jealous husbands, interfering mothers-in-law. Always he wondered drearily whether any so-called humorous writers were themselves amused by what they wrote; or merely contemptuous of the inanity and futility of the public for which they catered, sophistically aware of the ease with which loud laughter may be drawn from empty minds ...

During the period of his engagement he did very little work except in the comic line. He made more money by that than by anything else, and money had now – for the first time, despite all his poverty – become the chief desire of life, apart from Iris herself. In honest truth he had never before realized what poverty really meant; the feeling of meanness and inferiority which it engenders; the annoyance of not being able to spend, to give, to make a splash; the anguish implied in the fear of not 'making good'.

He moved from Kennington to West Kensington so as to be nearer his betrothed. 'It is much quieter here and you will be able to write better', that was what she said. But she was wrong. The whole atmosphere of the place depressed him. It was much more expensive, and Iris made perpetual demands upon his time.

He had never before gone about with a woman, and he could not have imagined how much it cost. It seemed that they could not venture anywhere without getting caught in a shower of rain and having to return home in a taxi; that Iris was always hungry, in need of chocolates, or tea, or fruit. Then there was that question of taking a flat, of furnishing it ... It was impossible to believe how many things were absolutely necessary to the setting of love until he went over the long lists with his betrothed, and she explained how important each item really was.

At the end of two years of feverish misery and more feverish joy, the engagement was broken off. Iris had worshipped him for what she called his 'romantic appearance'. Just when she was beginning to grow tired of his economy, which seemed like meanness, and the little time he appeared to be able to spare for her and her amusement, some friend spoke of him as 'that seedy old thing', and this was the end. He *was* seedy-looking, he was years older than she was, and where was the good of life unless you got some fun out of it?

To Lawrence Kestervon his dismissal came with the suddenness of a mortal blow. He had gone on working for Iris Hames as he had once worked for art, for the fulfilment of his ambitions: slowly, doggedly, perpetually, like some spider spinning in the dark, using up the very material of life itself.

He had never really suffered before, but now he suffered horribly. It seemed as though love had awakened him to life, and at the same time had made him more sensitive to pain. He pictured Iris in the arms of another lover, and it was hell; he looked forward over the long stretch of barren life which might yet remain to him, and it seemed worse than death.

He left West Kensington and returned to his old haunts in Kennington. He could not bear the drawing-room floor because it was too smug – faintly reminiscent of Edith Grove; the attic was too light, and he shrank from light like a wounded animal. Thus it was that he crept back to his damp basement room and seized upon paper and pen as some men might seize upon drugs. Freed from all desire to make money – the little cash which he had saved for the making of a home assured him of a livelihood for far longer than he could imagine himself as desiring to live – he produced another play.

He did not in the least mind what became of the thing, using his capacity for work as a bereaved mother uses poppy heads to her aching breast. He did not care whether it was ever finished; he ceased to hesitate between what would pay and what he felt to be real art, but poured into it the savage misery and resentment of a soul robbed of all that it ever believed itself to possess. The play was an amazing production, the sort of thing an English manager and English public goes mad over once in ten years, during some short interval or so when they are sated with burlesque.

Kestervon had gained one advantage from his engagement to Iris Hames: a passing acquaintance with the stage – for she had a sister in a beauty chorus – and a knowledge of the existence of such people as theatrical and literary agents.

It was through one of these that his play came to be placed with an actor-manager who knew a good thing when he saw it, and who had capital to risk on the work of an unknown man.

The cast was one of the very best. It seemed indeed that Kestervon was made now that he cared so little! Beatrice Atherton assumed the chief woman's part, and that alone was enough to make the success of almost anything; Sir Vincent Fair himself was the injured husband; then there was Violet Madden as the wife; Humphrey St John, as 'Charles Wynne', the lover; and Augustus King in the part of 'Gribble', the manservant and the villain of the piece. If any one character could be so called; for it seemed as though Fate made fools of all alike. Though it is certain that I went home after each rehearsal in half a mind to dismiss all my servants for fear that one of them might prove to be a secret, second 'Gribble', 'Gribble' as Kestervon willed my friend into showing him.

And yet how King had grumbled over the smallness of the part when it was allotted to him!

The plot of the story was commonplace enough; a wife with ideas of her own; another woman; a husband; a suspected lover, and that villainous so wrongly called domestic Gribble.

It was the things Kestervon made them say which told; the

amazing perversities of feeling which they betrayed. 'Meade', the husband, loved his wife, and yet at the same time he was mad for another woman, eating his soul out for her. 'Meade', as drawn by Kestervon, reminded me of nothing so much as a black panther they once had in the London Zoo, which, if it could get nothing else to feed upon and was within sight of prey it could not reach, devoured its own flesh. 'Meade' was a good fellow in the main, victimized by his own passions; wanting all sorts of things and never quite certain what he wanted most. One might almost have said that Fair's 'Meade' was the villain, and not 'Charles Wynne'. Though I knew, we all knew, that that was not the way Kestervon intended it to be taken …

'Meade' could not bear the idea of his wife belonging to another man: and yet he was unable to rid himself of the thought that, if he were able to prove that fact, he would be free to win the other woman.

As to 'Charles Wynne' – Humphrey St John – he made love to 'Mrs Meade' because he was in the habit of making love to any attractive woman he came across; while she accepted his advances for the mere sake of convincing her husband that she had, in modern jargon, a 'right to live her own life'.

Of course the thing ended in tragedy – what else could you expect with Kestervon let loose, as it were, for the first time?

The husband watches his wife; he follows her, dogs her, torn between jealousy and hope, egged on by his detestable servant, until he actually counts upon seeing her incriminate herself. He comes home one night, finds that she is not there, and follows her to 'Charles Wynne's' rooms. There he perceives a woman, wrapped in a long, loose cloak, standing with her back to him, both hands on 'Wynne's' shoulders, her lips raised to his, and believes it is his wife. Overcome with sheer primitive rage, he shoots her; only to find as she swings round, facing him in her death agony, that it is the other woman, 'Clare Hargreaves', presented by Beatrice Atherton, the woman whom he himself had thought to put in his wife's place, the woman who was in reality 'Wynne's' passionately devoted and faithful mistress – whom he has killed.

The wife's part was rather colourless, though Violet Madden made it live as few other actresses could have done. For the rest the whole interest of the play was centred in the eternal triangle of one woman and two men – Beatrice Atherton, Vincent Fair and St John – with Augustus King as Gribble diffusing suspicion as some plants diffuse a poisonous breath ...

The rehearsals went on for a long time. Again and again the production of the play was retarded because of a series of tiresome accidents to one or another of the company. Everything went wrong which could possibly go wrong, but no one ever thought of letting the thing drop. They could not have done so, by that time, however much they wished. Even Fair, who you would have thought was pretty much his own master, could not let go of it, for the simple reason that Kestervon and his damnable story held them. From the very first rehearsal I don't believe that the thing was clear out of the head of any one of them, down to the meanest scene-shifter, for one single moment. I can only feel thankful that the public never had a sight of it – for God only knows how many homes it might not have broken up before it ran its wicked course.

At first everyone thought Kestervon rather a nuisance, he was so immensely in earnest, behaving as though there never had been, never would be any other play. For his success seemed to have, at last, brought him back to life in a new and unfamiliar way.

I remember Fair saying that he wished he could afford to refuse all plays by living authors. And indeed one could not wonder, for Kestervon haunted the theatre, attended every rehearsal, had his own ideas upon the way in which everything ought to be done, the interpretation of pretty well every word. For, like most intensely shy and reserved men, there was no holding him once he got the bit between his teeth, no quieting him, no putting him down. It seemed as though his success had at last lit a fire within him: a fire which respected nothing, spared nothing …

He behaved as though the actors had no private duties or affections, no being apart from *his* play. At first everyone, very naturally, resented this attitude. Then, one by one, they began to give in to it with that half-laugh which shows the realization of weakness. They ended by declaring that, after all, he was the only person who could show them how to 'take' the parts he had set for them.

If you know anything of actors and actresses you will realize how extraordinary was this attitude. It was most extraordinary of all in the case of Sir Vincent Fair, who was, in his own way, a very great man, with a strong notion of his own importance. I have an immense admiration for Fair, but it is certain that he thinks it is he and not Shakespeare who created the character of 'Hamlet'. It was thus doubly strange to watch him influenced – surrendering to the wishes of Lawrence Kestervon. For it is certain that Kestervon changed his whole attitude towards the interpretation of 'Meade's' 'character'. He altered Beatrice Atherton's reading of *her* part, he altered St John; above all, he modified Augustus King, who had conceived of 'Gribble' as a funny man. He forced him to bring out the devilish innuendoes contained in every one of 'Gribble's' rather pointless jokes. And that was not all. In forcing everyone else to realize it he literally turned King inside out. He reincarnated him, as 'Gribble' himself.

Yes, that was it, he deprived him of his own identity and put the identity of that sneaking scoundrel in its place.

Why, even in the early days, when there had been

comparatively few rehearsals, I was walking down the Strand, and happening to see a man edging along the pavement, neat, smug, furtive – so furtive that a policeman followed him with a careful eye – I thought to myself:

'There's a fellow just like that "Gribble"!' and hurrying to overtake him out of sheer curiosity, found to my amazement – my horror, nothing less – that it *was* Augustus King. Augustus King, usually so buoyant and debonair, walking the pavement with his hands in his pockets, his head thrown back as though the whole of London belonged to him! Augustus King! one of the frankest and best-liked men on the English stage ...

As the rehearsals went on the atmosphere was overcharged, as though one of the worst thunderstorms ever known was due to burst next moment ...

Everybody felt it, the very stage-carpenters and scene-shifters. For Fair was irritable in a way he had never been before, and his temper, combined with Kestervon's exactions, was enough to try the strongest nerves.

Lady Fair, who so often used to come to rehearsal and sit in the stalls – watching, but saying nothing until she found herself alone with her husband – Lady Fair, whose opinion was, Sir Vincent said, worth hundreds a year to him, actually spoke to me on the subject. It was one day when her husband, having ordered a scene to be taken over again – Kestervon's suggestion, this! – had asked me to see if she would not like to go across to the Savoy for a cup of tea.

She refused, saying that she would rather stay and see the thing through, and I sat down by her side. We all liked Fair's wife, though strangers thought her cold, and perhaps she was in general rather detached and aloof. But she was one of the fairest-minded people I ever met, a rare quality in her sex. It seemed as though she saw all round every question, was determined to give everybody a patient hearing; while many a down-in-the-world actor or actress has owed more than they could ever express to Laura Fair. It was odd how her married name suited her!

She had a well-cut, rather colourless face, and beautiful blue eyes. She was always quietly and very elegantly dressed, with every line true.

She must have been a good deal upset before she could have spoken as she did. As I have said, she never discussed her husband's affairs with anyone. Still, I was one of their very oldest friends, and she, like everyone else, I suppose, felt an occasional need for outside sympathy.

'I hate this play,' she said.' I wish Vincent had never taken it. I wish he would give it up even now!'

'You don't think it's good?'

'Oh, yes, I think it's – well, "good" isn't the word – wonderful, powerful, clever – inhumanly clever! But all the same I think it's a bad play in itself. A morally bad play, I mean.'

'You feel that Kestervon –' I hesitated.

'Oh, I think that Mr Kestervon's all right, poor man! Vincent brought him to dinner one night, and I felt very, very sorry for him. He struck me as the sort of man who had never known anything but the hard side of life, never been mothered. But there are – oh, well, you know there are such things as typhoid carriers. I think there is a germ of something terrible – evil – in this play; that Mr Kestervon was weak, lonely, non-resistant when he wrote it – and somehow or other he caught the infection and is transmitting it, generating it, spreading it. He can't help himself. Look at him now, he's like a man in high fever.'

I followed the direction of Laura Fair's eyes.

Kestervon was facing us, speaking quickly, excitedly, with much gesture. Fair was standing with one hand to his chin – doubtful, sombre as 'Meade' himself, though the rehearsal was, for the moment, at a standstill. He was looking at

Violet Madden too, just – well, just as 'Meade' might have looked at his wife, angry, suspicious, and yet half-gloating. Miss Madden herself – 'Mrs Meade' – seemed to be taking no notice of anyone; though I saw her slip her hand behind her back, and allow it to lie for just one moment in that of St John – 'Charles Wynne' – who stood behind her. The auditorium of the theatre was in darkness, and I suppose she and everyone else took it for granted that Lady Fair and I had gone out to tea.

Yet it was impossible that she should not have seen what I saw, for she had trained herself to help her husband by a fine keenness of perception. For all that her voice went on quite smoothly, almost without a break.

'If one could take his temperature now one would probably find it above a hundred! He will kill himself if it goes on,' she said. Remember we were still talking of Kestervon. Then she added, with such bitterness and passion as I could never have believed her capable of: 'Well, I only hope he will – for the sake of everyone concerned.'

I was surprised. I do not know what I was about to answer, when my attention was diverted by something even more amazing.

The scene, the 'Meades'' drawing-room, was just roughly put together. The painted wall cloth on the right did not quite touch the floor and someone was actually lying flat, peering under it close behind 'Wynne' and 'Mrs Meade'.

The folly of the action struck me most; for the back of the stage was still quite open, and anyone who had not a perfect mania for peeping and prying could see all that was going on without any difficulty. Imagine then my surprise, my disgust, when a moment later I saw this Peeping Tom rise from his lowly position, brush the dust carefully away from his trousers, glancing furtively this way and that, and realized that it was actually Augustus King! …

I do not know what Lady Fair and I talked about after that; I was too dazed, and in a way frightened. But I do remember that there was no more actual rehearsing; while just before Vincent joined us King drew him aside and stood for a moment or two whispering in his ear: whispered! though all the rest of the players had dispersed!

The more I thought over what I had seen the more puzzled I felt. I gave up the Augustus King part of it in despair; but St John – 'Charles Wynne' – had lately been married. His wife was the girl who took the French maid's part, and they were supposed to be tremendously in love. He and Violet Madden had always seemed rather to dislike each other. I remember what he said when the parts were distributed: 'After all, I'm glad I've only got to *pretend* to make love to her.'

Then why *pretend* to make love to her, or rather allow himself to be made love to, when the actual scene was in abeyance?

A few days after this I found little Mrs St John – 'Kitty le Strange' to the theatrical world – crying in a quiet corner among the wings. We were friends; but, anyhow, she was so angry that she would have confided in a scene-shifter …

'Look at my husband and that Atherton woman,' she said; 'only look at them! It makes me sick, that's what it does.'

I did look, thoroughly puzzled; for he and Beatrice Atherton were standing aside talking together, looking into each other's eyes in a way which was unmistakable.

'It's all very well, it's a different thing when he really *is* acting, when the play is really on, but *now*! Just look! He flirts with Miss Madden too; he flirts with everyone, just like that beastly "Wynne" man! One would think that he was possessed by something beastly, inherent in the play – the rotter himself.'

For a moment she was silent, dabbing at her eyes, then she

broke out again: 'That devilish Kestervon has got them all on a string, does what he likes with them!'

After this Lady Fair attended all the rehearsals. I had never known her to be so constant, and I fancy that she was anxious and oppressed, as we all were, though less nerve-ridden and harried than the rest of us.

She herself had been on the stage for a very short time, but left it for good on her marriage. She had always spoken of her efforts in that direction with a little laugh, as though she herself had no opinion of them; I was more than surprised to hear her break out one afternoon, just at that part where 'Meade' is hovering between his real affection for and duty to his wife, and his infatuation for the other woman. 'If only I had the part instead of that stick Violet Madden, I could have held him; I know I could have held him!'

It seemed as though she, too, were being drawn into the vortex of horror formed by this diabolical play, made part of it. Even now I remember how, in the love scenes between 'Meade' and 'Clare Hargreaves', my cheeks burned, and how I felt shamed that she should be witness to them. Though again and again we had watched, criticized, laughed over, her husband's love-making, which she declared to be the weakest part of his acting.

A few days later, the rehearsal being over, we went to Sir Vincent's dressing-room to fetch him. He had been called away for a moment and we waited there.

The revolver with which 'Meade' was supposed to shoot his wife lay upon his dressing-table. Lady Fair took it in her hand and turned it round and round absently, listening for her husband's step …

Stage revolvers are, in actual performances, charged with 'blanks'; at rehearsals they are not charged at all: we had both seen Vincent Fair holding the weapon in his hand at this rehearsal, making a feint of using it. What put it into my head that the thing might be loaded I am unable to say; on the face of it the idea was ludicrous. And yet a wave of cold sweat came over me as I realized Laura Fair's careless handling.

'Mind! Mind!' I cried, so sharply that my own voice startled me. I can see, even now, the amazed look in her large blue eyes as I caught her wrist hard and took the revolver from her hand. She was so sure that there could be no danger; that such things never were loaded ...

Never, I say. I wonder whose face was the whitest, hers or mine, as I extracted the half-dozen cartridges, and slipped them into my pocket; for it was plain that even she recognized the blunt grey noses.

She showed her uneasiness plainly by her next remark, for she is not the sort of woman from whom one expects inane half-truths.

'Vincent is too dreadfully careless!'

As though any man could have fully loaded a stage revolver out of sheer absent-mindedness!

She wrote to me after this and begged me to do all I could to stop the play. She might as well have asked me to check the incoming tide.

I could do nothing, nobody could do anything. As for Kestervon, he was like a creature possessed – and possessing.

I have never given you any idea of his personal appearance, have I? Well, he was tall, with rather high shoulders, so that his head seemed a trifle sunk between them; he had odd light eyes set in immense dark caves; the mouth and long thin nose of a fanatic. His arms were too long, giving him an ungainly appearance, but he had beautiful hands. The very first day I met him I had noticed and admired them. Now I began to hate the very sight of them; for he used his hands as though he were a conductor, without a baton.

Conducting – what?

Well, these people, all of them more or less my friends. He was using his will like the bunch of threads by which the operator of a marionette show animates the puppets.

And it was not only their movements, their speech, that he mastered: somehow or other the virus had gone far deeper than that: for every man and woman in that play was as restless, as unhappy, as evilly disposed, as suspicious as the people whom they were supposed to represent.

Kitty le Strange, St John's wife, once the jolliest, frankest little creature, had sealed herself up into some tight-lipped, altogether odious collaboration with Augustus King. But no, what am I saying? Augustus King had ceased to exist, there is no other word for it. She, the French maid, was one with 'Gribble', the embodied essence of all foul-mouthed, foul-minded, peeping, prying menials since the world began.

Kitty peeped and peered and whispered too; was, in real life as in the play, hand and glove with 'Gribble'. I saw them with their heads together one afternoon in a little teashop I used to frequent. And that man, who used to be one of my best pals, hid his face with one hand when I entered, while she bent so low over the menu that I could see nothing more than the white of a sidelong eye.

As to St John, he did not seem to mind what his wife did, or whom she took up with. By now he was flirting with Violet Madden – 'Mrs Meade' – so desperately that I did not know what to make of it.

Fair was deceived too. It seems a ridiculous thing to say, but he was more jealous of Miss Madden, as his stage wife, than he had ever been of Laura.

Laura! Such miles above any other woman I ever met!

Later on I became obsessed, gradually but none the less surely, with the idea that both he and St John (the 'Charles Wynne' of the play) were both desperately in love with Miss

Atherton. Though 'love' is too good a word for the fury of passionate desire which possessed them; which changed Vincent Fair's kind, self-satisfied face into something that only too plainly bore the mark of the beast.

I believe that among no half-dozen people in the world could there have been found a more miserable tangle of unhappy hate, no less unhappy love, evil suspicions, jealousies …

The only person who seemed happy was Kestervon; and happiness was not exactly the word to express it. In his every glance and gesture he showed an overwhelming, loathsome joy in his own freshly-discovered power.

From a quiet, almost morose man he had become obtrusive in his need for an auditor. It was at this time that I learnt something of his youth, of Iris Hames, for he talked incessantly. It was more often of his play, of the people in it, than of his real life, that he talked. Often enough it seemed to me that he was mad; and that in some awful way madness had become contagious. It was only by continually reminding myself of my own identity that I could keep clear of the contagion.

The play had been advertised for weeks now: the announcements of it flamed out at me in immense posters from every hoarding. Goodness knows I ought to have got used to the idea of it. And yet – though I knew as well as anyone when the date was at last fixed – the words 'To-night' struck through me like a rapier. 'To-night'. 'To-night'. Oddly enough, despite all my apprehension, far away at the back of my mind had lain a secret conviction that Kestervon's play would have but an abortive bringing forth; sans audience, sans applause …

Vincent Fair did not believe in rehearsing up to the last moment, and in general gave his company a three days' rest before the actual production of a new play. But now, for no reason whatever, as it seemed, he called a rehearsal for the last afternoon. Not that it would have needed much calling, or so one might have thought; for every member of the cast had been hanging about the theatre during the whole of that morning and the day preceding it.

And yet, at two o'clock, the time fixed for the rehearsal, there was not a single one of the cast present, apart from Violet Madden, Kitty le Strange, red-eyed and sullen, and one or two of the minor characters, while, oddly enough, Kestervon was missing for the first time on record.

We waited until half-past two. It was to be a full-dress rehearsal and everything was ready. Still no one else appeared. Violet Madden, sitting on a chair almost in the middle of the stage – not fidgeting, but with folded hands – had, I thought, an expression upon her face of mingled expectancy and triumph. It was the look of a martyr who rather enjoys martyrdom.

Kitty, leaning against the support of one of the wings, glanced at her sideways with bent head, tapping her foot, twitching all over; on wires as it seemed …

The scene-shifters and prompters stood ready.

We were all waiting, and yet I could take my oath that it was for something quite different from that quiet opening in the 'Meades" drawing-room which we had grown so used to in rehearsals.

Then Lady Fair fluttered up the centre aisle of the stalls and beckoned to me. I say 'fluttered' because her face showed so wan and detached in the dim light and her walk was so hurried and uncertain that it reminded me of a white moth with half-folded wings.

She held a scrap of paper in her hand as she leaned towards me over the rails of the orchestra.

'Harry, you must come with me – at once! Something dreadful is happening! Go round the other way; don't say anything to anyone, I will wait outside … Quick – oh, quick!'

She jerked out the words and had turned away before I gathered my senses for a word. Outside the entrance of the theatre I found her waiting in a taxi.

'Twenty-five, Filsham Road, Maida Vale,' she said, 'tell him to drive quickly, for God's sake tell him to make haste! Tell him it's a matter of life or death.'

As I seated myself she saw me glance towards the scrap of paper which she still held, and smoothed it out upon her knee so that I might read what was written there – 25, Filsham Road, Maida Vale – a typed address, no name, no message.

'"Gribble" gave it to me.'

Only afterwards it struck me how odd it was she should say 'Gribble' when Augustus King was as much her friend as mine; but it only shows how completely we were all 'engulfed', as it were. 'He said it might interest me, that there was no time to be lost,' she went on. 'He laughed – Harry, it's awful when he laughs! There's something dreadful at the back of all his jokes nowadays.'

For a moment or so she was silent; then she broke out again. 'Tell that man to hurry, we shall never get there. I'm sure he's taken the wrong turn! Why go all up Oxford Street? There must be a shorter way! Ask him if he's certain that he knows where it is – *Filsham Road*.'

Almost before the words were out of her mouth she was on her feet leaning over me, confusing the man with questions and directions. Laura Fair, so self-contained and controlled! …

Filsham Road is one of those interminable thoroughfares of north-west London, where the number you want is inevitably at the opposite end to that by which you enter it.

When we saw the name on the corner house we thought we were already there; then found that there were what seemed like miles to traverse before we reached number twenty-five.

I don't know what we had expected in the way of mystery, but what we found provided something like an anti-climax to our fears.

A shop – a corset shop!

I was wondering who we were to ask for, what we were to say, as I helped Laura Fair out of the taxi and told the man to wait.

But with that wonderful faculty which a woman has of collecting herself, of gathering some sort of hasty composure like a garment around her, she spoke to the girl behind the counter.

'I want to see the gentleman who is lodging on the first floor,' she said, with her usual quiet dignity.

Months later, when she was once more able to speak of the affair, she told me that she had noticed the curtains at the drawing-room windows, and realized that they did not correspond with the rest of the house.

The girl answered very civilly that the entrance was by the side door, and would we be pleased to ring? …

We went to the side door; but there was no need to ring, for it was open. The stairs – there was no hall – edged the wall of the shop just in front of us …

Even then, lacking my companion's clear intuition, I wondered what would happen supposing we walked into the apartments of some total stranger? What was it she expected to find?

As she set her foot upon the first step, all petty doubt was at an end, for the sound of a shot rang echoing through the flimsy house.

Odd I should remember that the strip of oilcloth running up the stairs was white, with crimson flowers, green leaves, and yet retain no idea of how we reached the first floor landing! All I know is that I found myself facing in at the open door of the drawing-room, and saw Laura Fair clinging to her husband, who still held a smoking revolver in his hand, and was staring straight in front of him with blank, grey face; while Humphrey St John knelt, bending over the body of a woman who lay on the floor, with a stain, as red as the rose-decked carpet, spreading across the bodice of her white dress.

I suppose I still kept some outward semblance of self-possession, for I remember that I knelt on the floor facing St John; opened the front of Miss Atherton's dress – for of course it was she who lay there! – and felt her heart, which St John had apparently never even thought of doing. He was gazing at her like a man in some anguished dream, as if he wondered what in the world they were both doing there …

She was not dead, and a moment later, when Lady Fair fetched some water out of the adjoining bedroom and moistened her hair and forehead, she opened her eyes; then closed them again with a little moan.

Laura Fair had put St John gently on one side when she bent over the woman; and he had sunk into a chair; stared from one to another; desperate enough, but even more puzzled.

The girl from the shop below appeared in the open doorway with bleached face.

'Will you go and find a doctor, there has been an accident,' said Lady Fair, glancing up at her, and murmuring something which sounded like 'Just over the way,' the girl vanished.

Laura Fair's eyes met mine, and I knew of what she was thinking.

'What are we to tell him when he comes? St John – Fair – you must pull yourselves together! What are we to tell the doctor?' I asked.

At this St John's wavering eyes fixed themselves, not on me, but on Vincent Fair, with a look of dazed uncertainty. 'We were rehearsing – it was an accident. I –'

'But these rooms,' I put in. 'Do they belong to you?'

'Yes, I took them – a week ago.'

'To meet her – Miss Atherton here?'

'I suppose so,' he spoke doubtfully, as though he did not know why he had taken them, and was trying to remember. Then, quite suddenly, his whole face began to twitch.

'Good God – there's Kitty, what about Kitty? My God, I had forgotten! … Kitty! … Laura! …'

Laura Fair came to the rescue, as I knew she would.

'The doctor's the first difficulty, Humphrey. We must *all* say the same thing. Tell the doctor that we were rehearsing. Give me that.'

She moved to her husband's side, took the revolver from his hand, and opening it, coolly extracted the remaining cartridges and put them in her own handbag.

'It was an accident, remember – an *accident*. He'll have to understand that it must be kept out of the papers. It will be all right, if –' she glanced at Miss Atherton, and seemed to change what she had been about to say – 'It has only grazed the shoulder; she'll be all right. We've got to try not to make things worse than they are. Anyhow, thank Heaven, this is the end of that terrible play – of all of this.'

'Laura, you don't think – you know … It wasn't me – it was – my God, I don't know what it was! But you – you – you knew, all the time –'

Fair spoke stammeringly; he was deathly white, his face was drawn, but in an odd way purged of all traces of guilty passion.

'Know! Of course I know! It wasn't you – it was none of you, my friends – my dearest, my best friends,' cried Laura Fair. 'If I didn't know that, would I be here now, speaking like this, trying to help you?'

She broke off at the sound of a man's step upon the stairs. It was the doctor, with the white-faced girl from the shop, and another woman peering over his shoulder. He gave an odd, half-surprised glance at Miss Atherton, whom we had lifted on to a sofa.

'This – this is the patient? I had half thought –' he said.

Then he turned to me in a puzzled way – perhaps he thought I looked the calmest, most matter of fact person in the room. 'There's someone sitting on your doorstep … something wrong down there … Now, let me see –'

He bent over Miss Atherton and I went downstairs.

It was Lawrence Kestervon who sat upon the doorstep. He held one hand raised, flourishing it about, as though manipulating the antics of a bunch of marionettes. With the other hand he beat time. He was laughing, his wide, light grey eyes were all alight with childish, mad glee …

Bending over him, one hand upon his shoulder, was Augustus King. Thank goodness, it was the *real* Augustus King, as I realized the moment he raised himself and looked straight into my eyes with his own frank blue ones.

'I followed him,' he said. 'I saw him in the Edgware Road and thought something was wrong. He's, he's – oh, I say, Harry, old chap, look here, he's –' he touched his own forehead significantly.

One must be hardened indeed to call a man mad to his own face, though poor Kestervon would not have cared, could not have known …

'And not only him, but something … something …' went on King. 'Look here, Harry, there's been something damned odd about the whole thing. He had us like – like that!' he added, and pointed to the raised hand, the twitching fingers – 'had me, had all of us – well, just on a string!'

4 Hodge (1921)

People are accustomed to think of Somerset as a county of deep, bosky bays, sunny coves, woods, moorlands. The very name conjures up a set picture in their mind's eye, as certain Christian names have a knack of doing – we all know the 'Bobs', 'Marys', 'Lucys' of this world.

But Hemerton was in itself sufficient to blur this bland illusion of Somerset. It lay a mile and a half back from the sea, counting it at full tide; at low tide the sly, smooth waters, unbroken by a single rock, slipped away for another mile or more across a dreary ooze of black mud.

The village lay pasted flat upon the marsh, with no trees worthy of the name in sight: a few twisted blackthorn bushes, a few split willows, one wreck of a giant blighted ash in the Rectory gardens, and that was all.

For months on end the place swam in vapours. There were wonderful effects of sunrise and sunset, veils of crimson and gold, of every shade of blue and purple. At times the grey sea-lavender was like silver, the wet, black mud gleaming like dark opals; while at high summer there was purple willow-strife spilled thick along the ditches, giving the strange place a transitory air of warm-blooded life; but for the most part it was all as aloof and detached as a sleep-walker.

The birds fitted the place as a verger fits his quiet and dusky church: herons and waders of all kinds; wild-crying curlew; and here and there a hawk, hanging motionless high overhead.

There were scarcely fifty houses in Hemerton, and these were all alike, flat and brown and grey; where there had been plaster it was flaked and ashen. The very church stooped, as though shamed to a sort of poor-relation pose by the immense indifference of the mist-veiled sky – the drooping lids on a scornful face – for even at midday, in midsummer, the heavens were never quite clear, quite blue, but still veiled and apart.

The Rectory was a two-storeyed building, low at that, and patched with damp: small, with a narrow-chested air, tiny windows, a thin, grudging doorway, blistered paint, which gave it a leprous air; and just that one tree, with its pale, curled leaves in summer, its jangling keys in winter.

It was amazing to find that any creature so warmly vital as the Rector's daughter, Rhoda Fane, had been begotten, born, reared in such a place; spent her entire life there, apart from two years of school at Clifton, and six months in Brussels, cut short by her mother's death.

She was like a beech wood in September: ruddy, crisp, fragrant. Her hair, dark-brown, with copper lights, was so springing with life that it seemed more inclined to grow up than hang down; her face was almost round, her wide, brown eyes frank and eager. She was as good as any man with her leaping-pole: broad-shouldered, deep-breasted, with a soft, deep contralto voice.

Her only brother was four years younger than herself. Funds had run low, drained away by their mother's illness, before it was time for him to go to school; he was too delicate for the second-best, roughing it among lads of a lower class, and so he was kept at home, taught by his father: a thin trickle of distilled classics and wavering mathematics; a good deal of history, no geography.

He, in startling contrast to his sister, was a true child of the marshes: thin light hair, vellum-white, peaked face, pale grey eyes beneath an overhanging brow, large transparent ears: narrow-chested, long-armed, stooping, so that he seemed almost a hunchback.

In all ways he was the shadow of Rhoda, followed her everywhere; and as there is no shadow without the sun, so it seemed that he could scarcely have existed apart from her. Small as he already was, he almost pulled himself out of life while she was away at school; and after a bare week from home she would get back to find him with the best part of his substance peeled from him, white as a willow-wand.

Different as these two were, they were passionately attached to each other. The Rector was a kind father when he drew himself out of the morass of melancholy and disillusion into which he had fallen since his wife died, wilting away with damp and discontent, and sheer loathing of the soil in which it had been his misfortune to plant her. But still, at the best, he was a parent, and so apart, while there were no neighbours, no playfellows.

Once or twice Rhoda's school-friends came to stay at the Rectory, and for the first day or so it seemed delightful to talk of dress, of a gayer world, possible lovers. But after a very little while they began to pall upon her: they understood nothing of what was her one absorbing interest – the natural life of the place in which she lived: were discontented, disdainful of the marshland, hated the mud, feared the fogs, shivered in the damp. Apart from all this, Hector was madly jealous; hated them.

Hector! No, I was wrong when I spoke as though names gave a uniform impression of places or people: in this case the boy's name expressed him as little as the slow, luscious, sweet 'Summerzetshire' expressed Hemerton, its mud and marshes.

Anyhow, the brother and sister were sufficient to each other, for they shared a never-failing, or even diminishing, interest – and what more can any two people wish for? – a passionate absorption in, a minute knowledge of, the wild life of the marshland; its legends and folk-lore; its habits and calls; the mating seasons and manners of the birds; the place and habit of every wild flower; the way of the wind with the sky, and all it portends; the changing seasons, seemingly so uneven from year to year, and yet working out so much the same in the end: balancing, mild early in the winter and cold later, or *vice versa*; a tardy summer and a sunny autumn; a snowless winter and an extra wet spring to make up for it.

They could not have said how they first came to hear of the Forest: they had always talked of it. To Hector, at least, it was so vivid that he seemed to have actually struggled through its immense depths, swung in its hanging creepers, smelt its sickly-sweet orchids, breathed its hot, damp air – so far real to both alike that they would find themselves saying, 'Do you remember?' in speaking of paths that they had never traversed.

Provisionally they had fixed their Forest at the Miocene Period. Or, rather, this is what it came to: the boy ceasing to protest against the winged monsters, the rhinoceros, the long-jawed mastodon which fascinated the girl's imagination; though there was one impassioned scene when he flamed out over his clear remembrance of a sabre-toothed tiger, putting all those others – stupid, hulking brutes! – out of court by many thousands of years.

'They couldn't have been there, couldn't – not with us and with "It" – I saw it, I tell you – I tell you I saw it!' His pale face flamed, his eyes were as bright as steel. 'The mastodon! That's nothing – nothing! But the sabre-toothed tiger – I tell you I saw it. What are you grinning at now? – in our Forest – ours, mind you! – I saw it!'

'Oh, indeed, indeed!' Suddenly, because the day was so hot, because they were bored, because she was unwittingly impressed, as always, by her brother's heat of conviction, Rhoda's serene temper was gone. 'And did you see yourself?

and what were you doing there, may I ask – *you*! Silly infant, don't you know that there weren't any men then? Phew! Everyone knows that – everyone. You and your old tiger!'

There was mockery in her laugh as she took him by the lapels of his coat; shook him.

Then, next moment, when he turned aside, sullen and pale, his brows in a pent-house above his eyes, she was filled with contrition. The rotten, thundery day had set her all on edge; it was a shame to tease him like this; and, after all, how often had she herself remembered back? Though there was a difference, and she knew it, a sense of fantasy, pretending; while Hector was as jealous of every detail of their Forest as a long-banished exile over every cherished memory of his own land.

And yet – perhaps because it *had* never meant so much to her as it did to her brother; perhaps because he had never definitely stood out against her before – she was persistent in her determination to have the Forest just as she wished: to get her brother to state his views clearly, then to refute them by the clear light of well-authenticated research; that was the way.

And, of course, there *were* no men contemporary with that wretched tiger: he knew that; he must know.

Lolling under their one tree, in the steamy, early afternoon, she coaxed him back to the subject, and was beaten upon it, as the half-hearted always are.

He was so amazingly clear about the whole thing ... Why, it might have happened yesterday!

He had been up in the trees, slinking along – not the hunting man, but the hunted – watchful, furtive; a picker-up of what other beasts had slain and taken their fill of: more watchful than usual because he had already come across a carcass left by the long-toothed terror, all the blood sucked out of it. Swinging from bough to bough by his hands – which, even when he stood upright, as upright as possible, dangled far below his knees – he had actually seen it: seen its gleaming tusks, its shining eyes; seen it and fled, wild with terror.

Was it likely that he could ever forget it? 'It and its beastly teeth!' he added; then fell silent, brooding; while even Rhoda was awed to silence.

It was that very evening that they found their Forest, or, rather, a part of it.

Something in the day – the sort of day when one feels that anything might, something *must*, happen; the intense heat; the veiled, metallic sky; the still, thunder-laden air; their incipient quarrel – had made the boy restless; while Rhoda would have done anything in the world to make up for that sort of gulf which she had seemed to open between them by her mockery.

The Rector had gone off to a farm three miles away; told them that he would not be back to tea until after five. At the time it had not seemed to matter, but gradually the idea of being chained close to the house for goodness knows how long became unendurable.

'After five! Why, it might as well be midnight,' as Hector said.

It seemed as though he must have known they were going to find something; had infected Rhoda with his own unrest; for, after a glass of milk at four, they started off, away to the sea, running and walking by turns, inexplicably hurried. They had meant to bathe, but for once their memories were at fault; and they found that the tide was out, a mere rim of molten lead on the far edge of the horizon.

They were both tired, but they could not rest. They cut inland for a bit, then out again; crossing the mud-flats until the mud oozed above their boots and drove them back again.

They must have wandered about a long time, for the light – although it did not actually go – became illusive; the air freshened with that salty scent which tells of a flowing tide.

Hector insisted that they ought to wait until it was full in and have their bathe by moonlight; but, as Rhoda pointed out, that would mean no supper, dawdling about for hours. After some time they compromised: they would go out and meet the tide; see what it was like.

Almost at the water's edge they found It – their Forest.

There it was, buried like a fly in amber: twisted trunks and boughs, matted creepers, all ash-grey and black.

How far it stretched up and down the shore they could not have said, the time was too short, the sea too near for any exploration, but not far, they thought, or they must have discovered it before. 'Nothing more than a fold out of the old world, squeezed up to the surface'; that was what they agreed upon.

They divided and ran in opposite directions – 'Just to try and find out,' as Rhoda said. But after a few yards, a couple of dozen, maybe, they called back to each other that they had lost it.

The darkness was gathering, the water almost to their feet; they were bitterly disappointed, but anyhow there was to-morrow, many 'to-morrows'.

All that evening they talked of nothing else. 'It's been there for thousands and tens of thousands of years! It will be there to-morrow,' they said.

It was towards two o'clock in the morning that Hector, restless with excitement and fear, padded into his sister's room; found her sleeping – stupidly sleeping – with the moonlight full upon her, and shook her awake; unreasonably angry, as wakeful people always are with the sleepers.

'Suppose we never find it again! Oh, Rhoda, supposing we never find it again!'

'Find what?'

'The Forest, you idiot! – our Forest.'

'Hector, don't be silly. Go back to bed; you'll get cold. Of course we'll find it.'

'Why of course? I've been thinking and thinking and thinking. There wasn't a tree or bush or landmark of any sort: we had pottered about all over the shop: supposing we've lost it for ever? Oh, supposing, Rhoda, Rhoda! What sillies we were! Why didn't we stay there, camp opposite to it until the tide went out? I feel it in my bones – we'll never find it again – never – never – never! There might have been skulls, all sorts of things – long teeth – tigers' teeth! And now we've lost it. It's no good talking – we've lost it; I know we've lost it – after all these years! After thousands and thousands and thousands of years of remembering!'

The boy's forehead was glistening with sweat; the tears were running down his face, white as bone in the moonlight. Rhoda drew him into her bed, comforted him as best she could, very sleepy, and unperturbed – for, of course, they would find it. How could they help finding it? And after a while he fell asleep, still moaning and crying, searching for a lost path through his dreams.

He was right in his foreboding. They did not find it. Perhaps the tide had been out further than usual: they had walked farther than they thought; they had dreamt the whole thing; the light had deceived them – impossible to say.

At first, in the broad light of day, even Hector was incredulous of their misfortune. Then, as the completeness of their loss grew upon them, they became desperate – possessed by that terrible restlessness of the searcher after lost things. Day after day they would come back from the sea worn out, utterly hopeless; declaring that here was the end of the whole thing; sick at the very thought of the secret mud, the long black shore.

They gave it up. They would never go near 'the rotten thing' again.

Then, a few hours later, the thought of the freshly-receding tide began to work like madness in their veins, and they would be out and away.

It was easier for Rhoda; for she was of those who 'sleep o' nights'; easier until she found that her brother slipped off on moonlight nights while she slumbered: coming back at all hours, haggard and worn to fainting-point.

He stooped more than ever: his brow was more overhung, furrowed with horizontal lines. Sometimes, furious with herself for her sleepiness, Rhoda would awake, jump out of bed and run to the window in the fresh dawn, to see the boy dragging himself home, old as the ages, his hands hanging loose to his knees.

At last the breaking-point came. He was very ill: after a long convalescence money was collected from numerous relations, family treasures were sold, and he was sent away to school.

He came back for his holidays a changed creature, talking of footer, then of cricket; of boys and masters; of school – school – school – nothing but school; blunt and practical.

But all this was at the front of him, deliberately displayed in the shop-windows.

At the back of him, buried out of sight, there was still the visionary rememberer. Rhoda, who loved him, realized this.

At first she did not dare to speak of the Forest. Then, trying to get at something of the old Hector, she pressed the point; pressed it and pressed it. It was she now who kept on with that eternal, 'Don't you remember?'

The worst of the whole thing was that he did not even pretend to forget. He did worse – he laughed. And in her own pain she now realized how often and how deeply she must have hurt him.

'Oh, that rot! What silly idiots we were! Such rot!'

And yet, at the back of him, at the back of his too-direct gaze, his laughter, there was *something*. Oh yes, there was something. She was certain of that.

Deep, deep, hidden away at the back of him, at the back of that most imperturbable of all reserves, a boy's reserve, he remembered, felt as he had always felt. He shut her out of it, that was all: her – Rhoda.

At the end of a year they ceased to talk of the Forest; all those far-back things dropped away from their intercourse. To outward seeming their love for the countryside, their strange, unyouthful interest in geology, the age-buried world, was a thing of the past.

And it went on, too. Each holiday they seemed to have less in common, less to talk about. They took to glancing at each other curiously, as though each were a stranger whom the other was trying in vain to place.

Hector had a bicycle now: he was often away for hours at a time. He never even spoke of where he had been, what he had been doing. It was always: 'Nowhere in particular; nothing in particular.'

Then, two years later, upon just such a breathless mid-summer day, he burst in upon his sister, his face crimson with excitement.

'I've found it! I never gave up – never for a moment! I pretended – I thought you thought it rot – were drawing me on – but it's there. We were right. It's there – there! Quick! quick! Now the tide's just almost full out … Oh, by Jingo! to think I've found it! Rhoda, hurry up – quick!' He was dancing with impatience.

'I can ride the bike – you on the step,' breathed Rhoda, and snatched up a hat.

They flew. The village shot past them: the flat country swirled like a top. At last they came to a place where there was a tiny rag of torn handkerchief tied to a stick stuck upright in the ground. Here they left the road, laid the bicycle in a dry ditch, and cut away across the marsh, guided by more signals – scraps of cambric, then paper; towards the end, one every ten yards or less, until Rhoda wondered how in the world the boy had curbed himself to such care!

Then – there it was.

They stepped it: just on fifty yards long, indefinitely wide, running out into little bays, here and there tailing off so that it was impossible to discover any definite edge, sinking away out of sight like a dream.

The sun was blazing hot and the top of the mud dry. In places they went down upon their hands and knees, peering; but really one saw most standing a little way off, with one's head bent, eyeing it sideways.

It was in this way that Rhoda found It – Him!

'Look – look! Oh, I say – there's something … A thing – an animal! No – no – a – a –'

'Sabre-toothed tiger!' The boy's wild shriek of triumph showed how he had hugged that old conjecture.

He came running, but till he got his head at exactly the same slant as hers he could see nothing, and was furiously petulant.

'Idiot! Silly fool! – nothing but a bough. You –' A lucky angle, and, 'Oh, I say, by Jove! I've got it now! A man – a man!'

'A monkey – a great ape; there were no men, then, with "It".' There, it seemed, she conceded him his tiger. 'A little nearer – now again, there!'

They crept towards it. It was clear enough at a little distance; but nearer, what with the blazing sun and the queer incandescent lights on the mud, they found difficulty in exactly placing it. At last they had it, found themselves immediately over it; were able, kneeling side by side, to gaze down at the strange, age-old figure, lying huddled together, face forward.

It was not more than a couple of feet down; the semi-transparent mud must have been silting over it for years and years: silted away again through centuries. And all for them – just for them. What a thought!

Hector raced off for his bicycle, and so on to the nearest cottage to borrow a spade.

The mental picture of the 'man' and the sabre-toothed tiger met and clashed in his brain. If he was so certain of the man he must concede the tiger, give in to Rhoda and her later period. Unless – unless … Suddenly he clapped his hands to his ears as though someone were shouting: his eyes closed, shutting out sight and sound. There *was* a tiger, he remembered – of course he remembered! And if he were there, others were there also – not one tiger, not one man, but tigers and men; both, both!

By the time he got back to where he had left his sister, the water was above her knees, the tide racing inwards.

They were not going to be done this time, however.

It was five o'clock in the afternoon, and their father was away from home. Rhoda went back and ordered the household with as much sobriety as possible; collected a supply of food and a couple of blankets – they had camped out before; there was nothing so very amazing in their behaviour; to the old servant's mind they couldn't possibly be more crazed than they had always been, and this is the truly comfortable estimate in which to find oneself – then returned to the shore, the shrine.

Hector was sitting at the edge of the water, staring fixedly, white as a sheet.

Rhoda collected driftwood and built a fire; almost fed him, for he took nothing but what was put into his hand.

'It will still be there, even if we go to sleep,' she said: then, 'Anyhow, we'll watch turn and turn about.'

But it was all of no use. The boy might lie down in his turn, but he still faced the sea with steady, staring eyes.

Soon after three he woke his sister, shaking her in a frenzy of impatience. Oh, these sleepers!

'Sleeping! Sleeping! You great stupid, you! I never! I … Just look at the tide – only look!'

The tide was pretty far out, the whole world a mist of pinkish-grey. Step by step they followed the retreating lap of water.

Hector's very lips were white; he was trembling from head to foot with anxiety, damp with sweat.

He had been certain of the place; but even when they reached it he had to wipe his blurred eyes; was too on edge to get his head at the proper angle, and it was Rhoda who saw it first, crying: 'It's there, old boy! It's all right – all right!' – while he was forced to turn aside, retching from sheer relief.

By six o'clock they had the heavy body out, and were dragging it across the rapidly-drying mud.

It was not as big as Hector: five-foot-one at the most, but almost incredibly heavy, with immense rounded shoulders.

By the time they reached the true shore they were done, and flung themselves down, panting, exhausted. But they could not rest. A few minutes more and they were up again, turning the creature over, rubbing the mud away from the hairy body with bunches of grass; parting the long, matted locks which hung over its lowering face, with the overhung brow, flat nose, almost non-existent chin.

'I declare to goodness it's like you, old chap,' cried Rhoda, and they rolled upon the ground, laughing hysterically.

'A little more chin, I should hope!' protested the boy. 'But the forehead … Oh, Lord!'

'Exactly – exactly like, only … I say, I wonder how he'd look after a shave.'

'Like me! My hat! Trust you!'

They had the thing on its back, and the hairy face was pretty well clear of mud. The eyes were shut, but oddly unsunken: it smelt of marsh slime, of decayed vegetation, but nothing more.

Hector poked forward a finger to see if he could push up one eyelid, and drew back sharply.

'Why – hang it all – the thing's warm!'

'No wonder, with this sun. I'm dripping from head to foot. Hector, we must go home. Matty will tell; there'll be the eyes of a row.'

For all her insistence it was another hour before Rhoda could get her brother away. Again and again he met the returning tide with her hat, bringing it back full of water; washing their find from head to foot, combing its matted hair with a chipped fragment of driftwood. But at last they dragged it to a dry dyke, covered it with dry yellow grass, and were off, Rhoda on the step this time, Hector draped limply over the handle of the bicycle.

He slept like a dead thing for the best part of that day. But soon after three they were away again: no use for Rhoda to raise objections; the unrest of an intense excitement was in her bones as in his, and he knew it.

It had been a cloudless day, the veil of mist fainter than usual, the sky bluer.

As they left the bicycle and cut across the rough foreshore the sun beat down upon them with an almost unbearable fierceness. There was a shimmer like a mirage across the marshes: the sea was the colour of burnt steel.

They dog-trotted half the way, arguing as they ran. Hector, still fixed, pivoting upon his sabre-toothed tiger, and yet insistent that *this* was a man – a real man – contemporary with it: the first absolute proof of human existence anterior to the First Glacial Age.

'An ape – a sort of ape – nearish to a man, but – well, look at its hair.' She'd give him his tiger, but not his man.

'By Gad, you'd grow hair, running wild as he did – a man –'

'Hector, what rot! Why, anyone – anyone could see –' She thought of her father, the smooth curate, the rubicund farmers … A man!

'Well, stick to it – stick to it! But I bet you anything – anything…'

Hector's words were jerked out of him as he padded on: 'We'll get hundreds and hundreds of pounds for him! Travel – see the world – go to Java, where that other chap – what's-his-name – was found. Why, he's older than the Heidelberg Johnny – a thousand thousand times great-grandfather to that Pitcairn thing – older – older – oh, older than any!'

Panting, stumbling, half-blind with exhaustion, the boy was still a good six yards in front of his sister as he reached the dry dyke where they had left their treasure.

Rhoda saw him stand for a moment, staring, then spin round as though he had been shot, throwing up his arms with a hoarse scream.

By the time she had her own arms about him, he could only point, trembling from head to foot.

There was nothing there! Torn grass where they had pulled it to rub down their find; the very shape of the body distinct upon the sandy, sparsely-covered soil; the stick with the pennant of blue ribbon which Rhoda had taken from her hat to mark the spot … Nothing more, nothing whatever.

Up and down the girl ran, circling like a plover, her head bent. It must be somewhere, it must – it must!

She glanced at her brother, who stood as though turned

to stone: this was the sort of thing which sent people mad, killed them – to be so frightfully disappointed, and yet to stand still, to say nothing.

She caught at his arm and faced him, the tears streaming down her cheeks.

'Oh, my dear, my dear –' she began; then broke off, staring beyond him.

'Why … why – Hector – I say –' Her voice broke to a whisper: she had a feeling as though she must be taking part in some mad dream. Quite inconsequently the thought of Balaam came to her. How did Balaam feel when the ass spoke to him? As she did – with eye more amazed than any ears could ever be.

'Hector – look … It – It …'

As her brother still stood speechless, with bent head and ashen face, she dropped to silence: too terrified of It, of her plainly deluded self, of everything on earth, to say more …

One simply could not trust one's own eyes: that's what it came to.

Her legs were trembling; she could feel her knees touching each other, cold and clammy.

It would have been impossible to say a word, even if she had dared to reveal her own insanity; she could only pluck the lapels of her brother's coat, running her dry tongue along her lips.

Something in her unusual silence must have stirred through the boy's own misery, for after a moment or so he looked up, at first dimly, as though scarcely recognizing her. Then – slowly realizing her intent glance fixed on something beyond his own shoulder, he turned – and saw.

Twenty yards or more off, on a mound of coarse grass and sand just above the high-tide mark, 'It' was sitting, its long arms wound round its knees, staring out to sea.

For a moment or so they hung, open-mouthed, wide-eyed.

For the life of her, Rhoda could not have moved a step nearer. The creature's heavy shoulders were rounded, its head thrust forward. Silhouetted against the sea and sky, white in contrast to its darkness, it had the aloofness of incredible age; drawn apart, almost sanctified by its immeasurable remoteness, its detachment from all that meant life to the men and women of the twentieth century: the web of fancied necessities, trivial possessions, absorptions.

'There was no sea – of course, there was no sea anywhere near here then!' The boy's whisper opened an incalculable panorama of world-wide change.

There had been no sea here then; no Bristol Channel, no Irish Sea. Valley and river, that was all!

This alien being who had lived, and more than half-died, in this very spot, was gazing at something altogether strange: a vast, uneasy sheet of water with but one visible bank; no golden-brown lights, no shadows, no reflections: a strange, restless and indifferent god.

'Well – anyhow ... Oh, blazes! here goes! If –' Young Fane broke off with a decision that cut his doubts, and moved forward.

In a moment the creature was alert, its head flung sideways and up, sniffing the air like a dog.

It half-turned, as though to run; then, as the boy stopped short, it paused.

'Rhoda – get the grub – go quietly – don't run ... Bread-and-butter – anything!'

They had flung down the frail with the bottle of milk, cake, bread-and-butter that they had brought with them – enough for tea and supper – heedless in their despair. Rhoda moved a step or two away, picked up a packet, unfolded it and thrust the food into her brother's hand – cake, a propitiation!

The strange figure, upright – and yet not upright as it is counted in these days – remained stationary; there was one quick turn of the head following her, then the poise of it showed eyes immovably fixed upon the male.

Rhoda remembered her skirt, and almost tittered. 'It knows by…' she thought; then broke off, appalled at the immensity of the differences. There had been no skirts then; as there had been no sea, where it now washed, creeping in across the mud. The creature's evident realization of her as the female creature, lesser of the two to be feared, was based upon an instinct deeper and truer than all deductions of dress or long hair.

Hector moved forward very slowly, one smooth step after another. Rhoda had seen him like that with wild birds and rabbits. He wore an old suit of shrunken flannels, faded to a yellowish-grey, which blurred him into the landscape. Far enough off to catch his outline against the molten glare of the sea, she noted that his shoulders were almost as bent as those of that Other … Other what? – man? – ape? The speculation zigzagged to and fro like lightning through her mind. She could scarcely breathe for anxiety.

As the boy drew quite near to the dull, brownish figure it jerked its head uneasily aside – she knew what Hector's eyes were like, a steady, luminous grey under the bent brows – made a swinging movement with its arms, half-turned; then stopped, stared sideways, crouching, sniffing.

The boy's arm was held out at its fullest stretch in front of him. Heaven – the old, old gods – only knew upon what beast-torn carrion the creature had once fed; but it was famished, and some instinct must have told it that here was food, for it snatched and crammed its mouth.

Hector turned, and Rhoda's heart was in her throat, for there was no knowing what it might do at that. But as he moved steadily away, without so much as a glance behind him, it hesitated, threw up its hand, as though to strike or throw; then followed.

⁂

That was the beginning of it. During those first days it would have followed him to the end of the world. Later on, he told himself bitterly that he had been a fool not to have seen further; gone off anywhere – oh, anywhere so long as it was far enough – dragging the brute after him while his leadership still held.

It was with difficulty that they prevented it from dogging them back to the Rectory – just imagine it tailing through the village at their heels! But once it understood that it must stay where it was, it sat down on a grassy hummock, crouching with its arms round its knees, one hand tightly clenched, its small, light eyes, overhung by that portentous brow, following them with a look of desolate loneliness.

Again and again the boy and girl glanced back, but it still sat there staring after them, immovable in the spot which Hector had indicated to it. They had left it all the food they had with them, and one of the blankets which they had been too hot to carry home that morning. As it plainly had not known what to do with the thing, Rhoda, overcome by a sort of motherliness, had thrown it over its shoulders. Thus it sat, shrouded like an Arab, its shaggy head cut like a giant burr against the pale primrose sky.

'A beastly shame leaving it alone like that!' They both felt it; scarcely liked to meet each other's eyes over it. And yet, pity it as they might, engrossed in it as they were, they couldn't stay there with it after dark. No reason, no fear – just couldn't! Why? Oh, well, for all its new-found life, it was as far away as any ghost.

'Poor brute!' said Rhoda.

'Poor chap!' Hector's under-lip was thrust out, his look

aggressive. But there was no argument; and when he treated her – 'Don't be silly; of course it's not a man; any duffer could see that' – with contemptuous silence, Rhoda knew that he was absolutely fixed in his convictions.

He proved it, too, next morning, leading the creature out into the half-dried mud and back again to where his sister sat, following his apparently aimless movements with puzzled eyes.

'Now, look,' he crowed. 'Just you look, Miss Blooming-Cocksure!'

He was right. There was the mark of his own heavy nailed boot, and beside it the track of other feet; oddly-shaped enough, but with the weight distinctly thrown upon the heel and great-toe, as no beast save man has ever yet thrown it – that fine developed great-toe, the emblem of leadership. Hardly a trace of such pressure as the three greater apes show, all on the outer edge of the foot; not even flat and even as the baboon throws his.

It was after this that – without another word said – Rhoda, meek for once, followed her brother's example, and began to speak of the creature as 'He'.

They even gave him a name. They called him Hodge; only in fun, and yet with a feeling that here was one of the first of all countrymen: less learned, and yet in some ways so much more observant, self-sufficing, than his machine-made successors.

He could run at an almost incredible rate, bent as he was; climb any tree; out-throw either of them, doubling the distance. It was there that they got at the meaning of that closed fist; for at least three days he had never let go of his stone – his one weapon.

'He didn't trust us.' Rhoda was hurt, her vanity touched; and when they had seemed to be making such progress, too!

'Not that – a sort of ingrained habit; the poor devil didn't feel dressed without it,' protested Hector. 'Of course he trusts us as much as a perfectly natural creature ever trusts anything or anybody.'

That was enough for the boy, but not for his sister. In absolute innocence, still thinking – despite that 'He' – of their new acquisition as an animal, a strange, uncouth sort of pet, she wanted him to be 'really fond' of her, to trust her completely; as much hers as any dog domesticated through the ages.

And this was the beginning of the trouble.

⁂

The Rector had gone on a visit to their only relative, an old aunt, who was dying in as leisurely a fashion as she had lived, and was unable to leave her. A neighbouring curate took that next Sunday's service.

It had been a Monday when Hector found Hodge, and a very great deal can happen in that time.

From the first it had seemed clear that nothing in the way of communicating with authorities, experts, could be done until their father was there to back them, adding his own testimony. It was no good just writing – Hector did, indeed, begin a letter to Sir Ray Lankester, but tore it up, appalled by his own formless, boyish handwriting. 'He'd think we were just getting at him – a couple of silly kids,' was his reflection.

He knew a lot for his age; was very certain of his own knowledge; felt no personal fear of this wild man of his. But ordinary grown-up people! That was altogether a different matter. And here he touched the primitive mistrust of all real youth for anything too completely finished and sophisticated.

Of course, from the very beginning, there were all sorts of minor troubles with Matty over their continued thefts of food; difficulties in keeping the creature away from the house and village.

But all that was nothing to what followed.

The first dim, unformulated sense of fear began on the night when Hector, awakened by a loud rustling among the leaves of that one tree, discovered Hodge there, climbing along a bough which ended close against Rhoda's window.

Rhoda's, not his – that was the queer part of it!

The boy felt half huffed as he drove him off. But when he came again, some instinct, something far less plain than thought, began to worry him: something which seemed ludicrous, until it gathered and grew to a feeling of nausea so horrible that the cold sweat pricked out upon his breast and forehead.

At the third visit the fear was more defined. But still … That brute 'smitten' with Rhoda! He tried to laugh it off. Anyhow, what did it matter? And yet … Hang it all! there was something sickening about it all. It was impossible to sleep at night, listening, always listening.

He was only thirteen. Of course he had heard other chaps talking, but he had no real idea of the fierce drive of physical desire. And yet it was plain enough that here was something 'beastly' beyond all words.

He told Rhoda to keep her window bolted, and when she protested against such 'fugging', touched on his own fears, tried, awkwardly enough, to explain without explaining.

'I'm funky about Hodge – he's taken to following us. He might get in – bag something.'

'The darling!' cried Rhoda. 'Look here, old chap, I really believe he's fond of me; fonder of me than of you!'

She persisted in putting it to the test next day; left Hodge sitting by her brother, and walked away.

The creature moved his head uneasily from side to side, glanced at Hector, and his glance was full of hatred, malevolence; then, scrambling furtively to his feet, helping himself up with his hands, one fist tight-closed, in the old fashion, he passed round the back of the boy, and followed her.

For a minute or two Hector sat hunched together, staring doggedly out to sea. If Rhoda chose to make an ass of herself – well, let her. After all, what could the brute do? She was bigger than he was, had nothing on her worth stealing; nothing of any use to Hodge, anyhow, he told himself.

Then, of a sudden, that half-formulated dread, that sick panic seized him afresh. He glanced round; both Hodge and his sister were out of sight, and he started to run with all his might, shouting.

There was an answering cry from Rhoda, shriller than usual, with a note of panic in it. This gave him the direction; and, plunging off among a group of shallow sand-dunes, he found himself almost upon them.

Rhoda was drawn up very straight, laughing nervously, her shoulders back, flushed to the eyes, while Hodge stood close in front of her, gabbling – they had tried him with their own words, but the oddly-angled jaw had seemed to cramp the tongue beyond hope of articulate speech – gabbling, gesticulating.

'Oh, Hector!' The girl's cry was full of relief as she swung sideways toward him; while Hodge, glancing round, saw him, raised his hand, and threw.

The stone just grazed the boy's cheek, drawing a spurt of blood; but this was enough for Rhoda, who forgot her own panic in a flame of indignation.

The creature could not have understood a word of what she said: her denunciation, abuse, 'the wigging' she gave him. But her look was enough, and he shrank aside, shamed as a beaten dog.

They did not bid him good-night. They had taught him to

shake hands; but now he was in disgrace all that was over, and they turned aside with the set severity of youth: bent brows and straightened, hard mouths.

Rhoda was the first to relent, halfway home, breaking their silence with a laugh: 'Poor old Hodge! I don't know why I was so scared – I must have got him rattled, or he'd never have thrown that stone. Why, it was always you he liked best, followed,' she added magnanimously.

And yet she was puzzled, all on edge, as she had never been before. The look Hodge had cast at her brother was unmistakable; but why? – why? What had changed him? She never even thought of that passion common to man and beast, interwoven with all desire, hatred – the lees of love – jealousy.

All that evening Hector scarcely spoke. He was not so much scared as gravely anxious in a man's way. If that brute got him with a stone, what would happen to Rhoda? Even supposing that there had been anyone to consult, he could not, for the life of him, have put his fear into words. So much a man, he was yet too much a boy for that. Terrified of ridicule, incredulity, he hugged his secret, as that strange man-beast hugged his – the highest and lowest – the most primitive and the most cultured – forever uncommunicative; those in the midway the babblers.

He was so firm in his insistence upon Rhoda changing her room that night that she gave way, without argument, overawed by his gravity, by an odd, chill sense of fear which hung about her. 'I must have got a cold. I've a sort of feeling of a goose walking over my grave,' was what she said laughingly, half-shamefaced, accustomed as she was to attribute every feeling to some natural cause.

That night, soon after midnight, the brute was back in the tree. Hector heard the rustling, then the spring and swish of a released bough. Before he lay down he had unbolted one of the long bars from the underneath part of his old-fashioned iron bedstead; and now, taking it in his hand, he ran to Rhoda's room.

The white-washed walls and ceiling were so flooded with moonlight that it was almost as light as day.

Hodge was already in the room: the clothes were torn from the bed; the cupboard doors wide open; the whole place littered with feminine attire.

He – It – the impersonal pronoun slid into its place in the boy's mind, and no words of self-reproach or condemnation could have said more – stood at the foot of the empty bed, with something white – it might have been a chemise – in its hand, held up to its face. Hector could not catch its expression, but there was something inexpressibly bestial in the silhouette of its head, bent, sniffing; he could actually hear the whistling breath.

He would have given anything if only it had stayed, fought it out then. But it belonged to a state too far away for that – defensive, at times aggressive, but forever running, hiding, slinking: a thrower among thick boughs behind tree-trunks – and in a moment it was out of the window, bundling over the sill, so clumsy and yet so amazingly quick.

He could hear the swing of a bough as it caught it. There was a loud rustle of leaves, and a stone hurtled in through the window; but that was all.

Hector tidied the room, tossed the scattered garments into the bottom of the wardrobe, and re-made the bed in his awkward boy-fashion, moving mechanically, as if in a dream; his hands busied over his petty tasks, his mind engrossed with something so tremendous that he seemed to be two separate people, of which the one, the greater, revolved slowly and certainly in an unalterable orbit, quite apart from his old everyday life, from that of Hector Fane whom he had always known, thought of, spoken of as 'myself'.

※

He went to his own room, put on his collar and coat – for he had lain down upon his bed without undressing, every nerve on edge – laced up his boots with meticulous care. He was no longer frightened or hurried; he knew exactly what he was going to do, and that alone hung him – moving slowly, surely – as upon a pivot.

The moonlight was so clear that there was no need for a candle, flooding the stairway, the study with its shabby book-shelves.

Easy enough to take the old shot-gun from the nails over the mantelshelf; only last holiday – years and years ago, while he was still a child – he had been allowed to use it for wild-duck shooting – and run his hand along the back of the writing-table drawer in search of those three or four cartridges which he had seen there a couple of days earlier.

The cartridges in his pocket swung against his hip as he mounted his bicycle and rode away – guiding himself with one hand, the gun lying heavily along his left arm; it was like someone nudging, reminding.

The scene was entirely familiar; but what was so strange in himself lent it an air of something new and uncanny. The winding road had a swing, drawing him with it; the mingled mist and moonlight were sentient, watchful, holding their breath.

Once or twice he seemed to catch sight of a low, stooping figure amid the rough grass and rush-tufted hollows to the left of him; but he could not be sure until he reached the very shore, left his bicycle in the old place.

Then a stone grazed his shoulder, and there was a blurred scurry of brown, from hummock to hummock, low as a hare to the ground.

Once in the open he got a clear sight of Hodge. The far-away tide was on the flow, but there was still a good half-mile of mud, like lead in the silvery dawn.

The man-beast bundled down the sandy strip of shore and out on to the mud: ungainly, stumbling; the boy behind it – 'It.' Hector held to that: the pronoun was altogether reassuring now – something to hold to, hard as a bone in his brain.

On the edge of the tide it tried to turn, double; then paused, fascinated, amazed: numb with fear of the strange level pipe pointing, oddly threatening, the first ray of sunlight running like an arrow of gold along the top of it.

There was something utterly naïve and piteous in the misplaced creature's gesture: the way in which it stood – long arms, short, bandy legs – moving its head uneasily from side to side; bewildered, yet fascinated.

'Poor beggar!' muttered Hector. He could not have said why, but he was horribly sorry, ashamed, saddened.

Years later he thought more clearly – 'Poor beggar! After all, what did he want but life – more life – the complete life of any man – or animal, either, come to that!'

As he pressed his finger to the trigger he saw the rough brown figure throw up its arms, leap high in the air, and drop.

Something like a red-hot iron burnt up the back of his own neck; his head throbbed. After all, what did death matter when life was so rotten, so inexplicable? It wasn't that, only – only … Well, it was beastly to feel so tired, so altogether gone to pieces.

With bent head he made his way, ploughing through the mud and sand, back to the shore; sat down rather suddenly, with a feeling as though the ground had risen up to meet him, and winding his arms round his knees, stared out to sea; washed through and through, swept by an immense sense of grief, a desperate regret which had nothing whatever to do with immediate action – the death of Hodge.

That was something which had to be gone through with; it wasn't that – not exactly that … But, oh, the futility, the waste of … well, of everything!

With a sense of appalling weariness he seemed to see the centuries which had passed sweep by him, wave upon wave, era upon era, each so superficially different, and yet so tragically, so stupidly alike: man driven like a dry leaf before the wind of destiny; man the soul-burdened brute.

'Rotten luck!' He shuddered as he dragged himself wearily to his feet. He could not have gone before: not while there was the mud with 'that' on it; not even so long as the shining sands were bare. It would have seemed too hurried, almost indecent. But now that an unbroken, glittering sheet of water lapped the very edge of the shore, the funeral ceremony – with all its pomp of sunrise – was over; and, turning aside, he stumbled wearily through the rough grass to the place where he had left his bicycle.

5 The Fountain (1921)

Not of father or mother was I produced, but of nine
elementary forms: of the fruit of the trees; of the fruit
of the primordial god; of primroses, the blossoms of the
mount; of the flowers of trees and shrubs; of the earth in
its terrene state was I modelled; of the flower of nettles
and the water of the ninth wave.

— TALIESIN

In some way or other we are most of us peculiarly touched by
one special attribute of nature: by the sea, by running water,
by winds, mountains, trees; some more so, some less; others,
again, so little that nothing, apart from their own appetites,
appears to move them.

I judge these people by certain fixed insensibilities. They
are neither depressed nor elated by the weather; they are
unable to hear the bat's sharp note, the singing sound of a
pigeon's wings in the air, or catch the scent of the bean-flower.
They cannot tell the time of day without a watch, and sleep
through that night-hour when the world turns, half rises, and
shakes itself. Unless it be so suddenly warm as to force them
to change their underwear, they are perfectly unaware of the
coming of spring, that time when the blackbird's song thrills
like the passing of the Holy Spirit; when the adder slips its
skin in the warm quarry, while the bark upon the beech is
soft and supple as a lady's glove.

And yet those who feel nothing whatever – though they
seem to be standing for ever in their own light, blocking their
own view – are an easier fit into the scheme of things than
those who are ruled by one single element of nature, far more
completely a part of it than the sailor and his ship are a part

of the sea; living by it and with it: in some strange way – not physically, but spiritually – a part of it. How can I explain? Well, as the old gods were one with their fountains, woods, groves.

Of all these people the most elusive are those who have this – far and away, pre-natal – affinity with running water. Between these and the people of the marshes, leaden-eyed, straight-haired, heavy-footed, slow and deep as the turgid waters which rule them, there is so much difference that it seems impossible to believe that any single function of their lives can be the same.

You, my friend, to whom I write, may wonder at this long preamble; and yet without it how could I tell my story, gain the point I would impress, that point without which the whole thing – tragic enough in all conscience – would be nothing more than a confused medley of mishaps?

People of a single element and people of combined elements, however weighed with one or another, but more particularly if one sink ever so little to the mere animal, can never mix. Their consciences, their training may force them to compliance; but only for a while, however much they themselves may agonize over their own inadaptability. For it is ludicrous to imagine that cold people never feel their own coldness, inarticulate people fret at their own lack of expression; or that the dull and quiet are free from all desire for the lightness and gaiety of some more vivacious neighbour. The thing is that we may alter ourselves for a time, more particularly at the call of love, but forever must we spring back again like a bent bough to our own natural habit.

Sylvia Colquhoun belonged by nature to the people of the springs, with a nature so refined, so crystal clear, yet in a way so detached that there was nothing for her husband's clumsy hands to grasp. She poured herself into them. Oh yes; she gave and gave, for she had been taught that everything, the whole body and soul of a woman, belongs to the man she marries; was as dismayed as he was – more so, for she was so much the more sensitive when she realized her failure – that they were sliding apart, that she could no more keep herself within his grasp than he, with his nature, could help letting her go.

One thing I know, and that is her heart was broken – as surely as the heart of 'The Little Mermaid' – between self-reproach and sorrow. For she believed that, from the very beginning, it was all her fault; realizing how she shrank from her husband's obvious passions, drawn herself back within herself, conscious of a sense of pollution. What she failed to realize was how little Colquhoun realized anything of the sort: if he had possessed discrimination enough for that it might have been possible for him to cool his hot mouth at the fount of a love which was infinitely pure and unchanging, 'forever fresh and still to be enjoyed'; to realize that there is more than one sort of happiness to be found with a woman.

She was fresh from a convent when he married her: friendship and kindred interests, the ordered shaping of thought and time, had surrounded her like a close-woven fence of wattles, sprouting green enough with innocent mirth. When first I knew her I thought I had never heard anything so delicious as her laugh, and there is no doubt about it that she felt stripped, alone in the open of life with this man and his boisterous moods, his noisy greed, his absorption in his appetites.

Of course, everything he said and did must be right, because he was her husband. But, then, what of the delicacies, the reservations which had been instilled into her from her cradle upward? Someone or something was wrong here.

The honeymoon was spent in Paris. I think she was too bewildered at that time to realize anything over-clearly; but she was very tired, drawn to a milk-like whiteness by the time she reached her new home. Her portrait is hanging on the wall opposite to me now, as I write. I painted it myself, and I kept it. Colquhoun had her – her, herself – as much as he was capable of grasping, and I had my picture, and have it still, while he … But that comes later.

She was very fair and delicately made, reminding me of a wood-anemone from the first day I saw her; her hair almost silver, her complexion pale and clear. Her head drooped a little on her slender neck, her shoulders sloped a trifle: her hands were long and slender and very white; she was the most graceful thing I ever saw. The portrait – as I word it, not the picture itself – carries something of an early Victorianism, a certain insipidity. But she could never have been insipid, for her eyes remained to be reckoned with – hazel-golden-brown – or grey with the warm lights of the willow catkin – it was difficult to say precisely which: they were so seldom the same for two minutes together, were like a stream for ever changing and reflecting; though I inclined to hazel in my picture, and I think that was the tint they most often showed when she was thoughtful and at rest.

The window of her own sitting-room fronted the long path which ends in the half-circle of ilex trees with the mountains beyond them; beneath the shadow of the ilex lay the pool in its blackness.

She went to her room almost immediately after her arrival home from her honeymoon, and passing through to the boudoir stood gazing out while her maid opened her trunks and lifted out the trays. Her husband found her there, and coming behind her put both hands over her shoulders, undid the wide blue ribbon of her little grey motor-bonnet, and taking it off, smoothed her silvery fair hair, already silky-smooth either side of the parting, breaking into curls above the ears; then tipped back her face and kissed her on the lips more quietly than was his wont.

'Well, little wife, what do you think of it all?'

She pressed back against him, thankful for his nearness in the vaguely sad mood which had overcome her; for it was a still evening, an evening which showed that curious detachment and calm which comes with a colourless sunset and still air, which there was nothing in Colquhoun's touch to disturb her.

'It is sad; the dark trees and mountains and the dark water; still-water always hurts me – I don't know why, but seems to hurt me here.' She touched her breast as she spoke, with a little laugh at herself.

The man answered her laugh indulgently, for she was still a new and curious toy: 'You women! All alike, all full of whimsies. But the pool is not so still as it looks; there's a damnable underpull, as I know to my cost, for I was nearly drowned there as a boy. The water runs in and out, is fed continuously by seven springs which lie close together farther up the hill.'

'Then if there are springs to feed it with there should be a fountain,' she cried, laughing and clapping her hands, her pensiveness swept clear away by her childish pleasure at the thought. 'How I would love to see it spraying up against those dark trees! All sparkling, rising and falling, full of light and shade – like life,' she added more slowly, as if struck with some premonition, for there had been little enough of shade in her eighteen summers. But the mood was soon past, and she turned, clinging coaxingly to her husband's arm, looking up at him, her eyes alight, her face delicately flushed. 'Oh, Harry, do make me a fountain in the pool, so that I may see the moving water from my window; and let us grow a high hedge of pink and crimson roses either side of the path which leads to it – "The Way of Love" – that's what we will call it – "The Way of Love".'

Alas, she had another name for it not so many months later

– '"Via Dolorosa" – that's what I call it,' she said; and then added, as though afraid that she had betrayed too much, 'I'm sure there were never any roses with such thorns!'

For she got her flowers and her fountain, as I think she could have got anything at the time: a naked boy carved in stone, with head thrown back and a curved horn through which, night and day, he blew a feathery plume of water high into the air. But by the time it was completed Harry Colquhoun was already a trifle tired of his idyll, and all pastoral pleasures apart from sport.

Luckily there were neighbouring squires, and London friends who came to stay, sometimes for weeks at a time. His friends, not hers, for she hardly knew anyone apart from her school companions, who would scarcely have met the case, unless it were one, a dashing, bold-eyed brunette, named Judith, who had been the despair of the nuns, and who wrote more than once declaring that she meant to come and stay with her 'darling sweet Sylvia', for whom she had professed an almost overwhelming devotion; though it was not sufficient, during some two years, to prevent her finding the prospect of other visits more alluring.

It was during those months of early summer, just after her marriage, that I painted that portrait of my lady; and well I remember that Colquhoun was in a fury because she shivered ever so little in her white dress, rounding on me as though I were a servant for allowing her to stand in a draught. But I swallowed it as I would have swallowed anything for her sake, and kept him reminded of the careless invitation, which he gave me at parting, to look them up again some day soon; for I was certain, even then, that life was not going to prove too easy for the young wife.

Perhaps that first summer was not so bad; but then came the sad autumn with haunting winds, and a long dank winter – 'an open season', I believe they call it – during which Colquhoun spent most of his days with the hounds, and his evenings sleeping in a big chair before the fire, very red in the face and heavy in the jowl, save when there were visitors staying in the house: silent men with a passion for cards, noisy men with an equal passion for practical jokes; and loud-voiced, smartly-dressed women who brought their own special friends with them, and regarded their hostess no more than the flowers on the dinner-table.

The rose trees at either side of the long path grew apace, but they did not flower as they ought to have done. To make up for this, however, the fountain was like a perpetual, ever-fresh spray of blossom against the background of dark trees, and directly spring crept round again Sylvia Colquhoun, more and more alone, began to spend hours by its side, trailing her white fingers in the water, all dimpled and alive with showering drops.

Colquhoun laughed at her, jeered rather. 'A pretty sort of wife, like a fish! For all the world like a fish!'

A friend sent him a live carp and he put it in the pool – 'Just the sort of mate for that cold-blooded wife of mine,' he declared.

He insisted more and more on her coldness; it served as an excuse for much, both to himself and others.

'Poor dear Harry' – that was what the women said. 'What can anyone expect of a man tied to an insipid creature like that?'

'She doesn't care.'

'No, she doesn't care; a woman like that has milk and water instead of blood in her veins.'

'And a damned good thing too,' put in Lady Hardy, who looked and spoke like a fish-wife, but had more heart than the rest of them all put together. I heard her myself slap out at them, in response to the oft-repeated excuse for anything which might seem amiss in Colquhoun's morals:

'I'd be devilish sorry for any gal that cared two pins for that wine-laden, dog-eyed creature!'

There was a universal squeak at this. 'Oh, Lady Hardy! How can you! We all love him; the dearest thing in the world, poor Harry!'

'You, you! You love him with your skins; it goes no deeper than that. Stroke you and you purr; give you cream to lap and another woman to sharpen your claws upon and you're happy.'

I suppose that by this time pretty well everyone knew of Colquhoun's infidelities, all, that is, save Sylvia herself.

I went down once for a Saturday to Monday during the next autumn, but got little happiness out of my visit, for the house was full, and the mistress of it white and wistful-eyed, as elusive as a shadow.

'She mopes,' said Colquhoun. 'That damned pool! – she'll tumble in some day and drown herself, and that will be the end of it.'

He did not ask me to repeat my visit to Cattraeth again that time, perhaps because, going down to the smoking-room in search of a pet pipe, late one night when I thought the whole household was well asleep, I found him with 'a damsel dark upon his knee' – plump and dark, and after all no damsel, but another man's wife.

I well remember his incongruous demand, as I stood hesitating, between awkwardness and disgust, as to 'what in the name of God' I wanted there. He was not in the least ashamed or frightened, I grant him that, only angry and impatient to get on with his *amour*.

Close on two years slipped by before I went down to North Wales again. It was the first week in August, and Harry Colquhoun was just back from Monte Carlo, very ill-tempered and restless and – or so I believe – short of money. There was no one else staying in the house, and perhaps he had been bored enough to suggest my being asked, for it was out of season for most sport and he had no patience for fishing. It is certain that he was more bored than any man I have ever seen, and scarcely stirred out, sat indoors, smoked, yawned, drank.

'My Lady of the Fountain', as I had grown to call her, was more elusive than ever; she did not avoid me, but she was no longer friendly and intimate as she had been; though it was evident that she liked having me there, for each time I spoke of leaving she was in a sort of panic, as though afraid of being more alone.

'I shall slip quite away if you go,' she cried one day, actually tugging at my sleeve with something of her old childish impulse, between laughter and tears, with that sort of friendliness which I had grown to miss.

I remember well how the phrase, 'slip quite away', haunted me, with a sense of some sub-conscious meaning: until several nights later, when I lay awake thinking of her, as always – listening to the owl's dismal cry – it came to me that this, after all, was what she had been doing, all those months – slipping away.

And I remember thinking that there was really very little of her left to follow. To follow what? I can scarcely say – but that part of her which seemed to have already stolen away. To put it more plainly, I thought that if anything happened to her body now there would be no great uprooting, so impressed was I by her air as of a creature apart, and – I know the word must give a wrong impression of something heartless, but I cannot help it – inhuman.

It was like Daphne, and had Colquhoun been one whit less gross I might have felt some sympathy for him, 'pursuing a maiden and clasping a tree' – or even less warm, less lifelike in … well, in the sense in which we count life.

And yet though she seemed all spirit, she was not the sort

of woman to whom one could apply the word 'spiritually-minded', with whom one could even connect the idea of a conventional heaven; for it was not the earth – the world of pure nature – for which she was unfitted. In her sadness and gladness, in her every mood, she was essentially of it, at its purest and best; it was the people in it whom she found so difficult. I often wonder what they had really made of her at the convent. There were so many things she could not grasp, things which are part of the faith of our country which must have seemed to her just stupid or cruel.

I remember Colquhoun, with the odd inconsequency of such people, actually complaining that she never went to church. 'Damn it all!' he said, 'but a man likes to see his wife a bit religious; proper sort of thing, you know, particularly in the country.'

But she was not religious, or spiritually-minded; and she was not – as I have said before – in all ways quite human. There was that coldness and elusiveness; there was the fact of her not caring for children, shrinking from them, indeed, which was the one trait in her character that jarred me, until I caught sight of her face one day, as she stood watching a mother playing with a two-year-old on a cottage doorstep, and realized an expression in her eyes as piteously sad as any Peri at the gate of Paradise. I think – and I grew to realize her in a way that was almost uncanny, 'felt' her every mood – it was not so much that she desired a child (I remember her shrinking when someone offered to let her hold a baby in her arms), as that she wished, with a desperate craving of her heart, that she were *able* to feel as other women felt.

For a while Harry Colquhoun had held her to humanity. I verily believe it was his kisses which first woke her to life as we know it; for red-faced and blustering, he was yet the sun of her springtime. And, strange to say, he held her still, though she seemed to have given up her strained endeavour to satisfy him, standing apart with the puzzled pain of a child who cannot realize where it has failed.

Then there came a letter from Judith Farroll, actually fixing a date when she would be free to visit her 'darling Sylvia'.

My lady broached the subject at luncheon – which was Harry Colquhoun's breakfast out of the hunting season – nervously enough, for one never knew what tiny spark might set him off in a blaze.

'More milk and water!' he sneered; but still he took it well enough; there was a blank fortnight before his own friends were due to arrive, a houseful of them, and anything was better than nothing.

'Anything better than nothing!' – as if there could be anything negative about Judith. 'Milk and water!' – flesh and flame rather!

She was tall, small-waisted, deep-bosomed, with luscious dark eyes, the colour of carnations in her cheeks, and a full red underlip, pulled a little out of shape with biting and pouting. She was glancing sideways at Harry as she folded her friend in her arms that first evening, and he was fired in a moment. I saw that.

She permeated the house. She was like a flower with an over-heavy perfume; upon my soul, I believe there was something noxiously sweet in her very atmosphere; between that and her rich voice at the piano, when she sang to Colquhoun, looking up as he lounged across it, one knee on a stool at her side, her floating chiffon scarves, the tap of her high heels on the polished floors, the house was never free to draw breath. Only in the garden by the fountain was coolness and quiet, my lady sitting trailing her white fingers in the water, none the less lonely for the advent of her friend.

Even when the other visitors arrived Judith queened it over them. One night when the mistress of the house was unwell she sat at the head of the table, wearing a satin gown of the rich colour of the outer cup of a wine-tinted magnolia, and a diamond necklace, which she involuntarily fingered as though it were something new and she was not yet accustomed to the weight of it on her firm white neck; while Harry Colquhoun drank steadily and devoured her – there is no other word for it – with his moist, bloodshot eyes.

I stayed on and on. I don't think Colquhoun troubled his head about me, and I would not have cared if he had, for the time had come when I believed that my lady might need me.

But she did not; I might have known that. She never really needed anyone save that coarse brute who owned her; and when the trouble came she took her own quiet way of dealing with it.

Perhaps she could not sleep; she had often complained of sleeplessness, and I believe she was as restless as the wind of dawn, that wind which the sailors learn to look for with dread. Anyhow, slipping silently downstairs one morning, with what restless longing for the open God only knows, she encountered her husband coming out of Judith Farroll's room.

She might have sought the solace which had never failed her at the side of the pool with its fountain, grown faint and fallen in. Anyhow that is what Colquhoun declared must have happened.

'She would not have been such a fool as to – to...' Even his lips, looking all the grosser for their trembling pallor, refused to frame that word. It would put him 'in such a damned awkward position' if anyone suspected anything of the sort. Anyhow it was all part of his pestilential ill-luck that his wife, of all people, should have encountered him that morning. He was always perfectly indifferent to the servants, and would no more have thought of saving Judith's character than his own.

It was her maid who found her, going to the usual place to warn her mistress that it was time to come in and make ready for breakfast; and it was I – thank Heaven that I was at least able to save her from more indifferent hands – who carried her indoors and upstairs to her own room, where I laid her on the bed: very sweet and wise-looking, and no whit disfigured, save that her hair hanging either side of her face in two long plaits was slightly darkened by the water.

I stayed on for the funeral, then I went back to town. I was deadened by grief, and yet in some way relieved. For no one could touch her now; something of her had merged with the element to which she rightly belonged, and as for the rest, the kindly earth would see to that. The main thing was that she was free.

As to Colquhoun, I was conscious of no particular resentment against him; it seemed scarcely his fault that he was sheer animal, warped out of all image of divinity by his hard-drinking progenitors; as little responsible as the swine for the pearls, infinitely preferring husks.

After a while I even grew to feel sorry for him. He told me, at parting that time, to use the place when I needed a breath of country air, wringing my hand, with tears in his eyes; for he seemed to have grown to count on me in his blundering way during that dreadful week of the inquest and funeral.

I went down for a few days that autumn, just before the beginning of the hunting season, while Colquhoun was still abroad, gambling wildly, from what I had heard, with a train of dissolute men and women for ever at his heels.

I do not know why I went; but the kind of impulse which one feels must be obeyed came to me, and I telegraphed to the housekeeper, asking her to expect me the very next day.

She was glad enough to see anyone, poor thing. The house was half empty; she would not keep the servants. That was what she told me at dinner the first night, supplementing the services of a raw young footman. She made the remark with an air of close-lipped secrecy; but as I forbore to question her she came out with the whole story when she looked in at the smoking-room the last thing that night, on the pretence of asking if I needed anything more, but really, I am sure, to unburden her soul.

There was something queer about the house. The fountain had ceased to play! I interrupted her there. Of course I remembered it had stopped working that – that day; but surely it had been put right since then.

The housekeeper drew down her underlip and smoothed out the front of her black silk gown with an 'Um, um,' which said as plainly as any more definite words, 'Things are not so simple as they may seem to you, in your ignorance, if you'll excuse me, sir.'

Her broad, colourless face was coruscated with numberless lines which seemed to come from nowhere and go nowhere, as though some mad surveyor had scratched out the track of innumerable roads across some wide, mud-caked flat; lines which marked the passage of no particular emotion or passion, though at the moment the whole was stamped with a look of almost defiant fear. And yet there was that sort of pride, as of a person who has something dreadful to divulge.

'Well, sir, I'm sure I hope you won't be disturbed or made uncomfortable in any way,' she remarked with an air of one who cherished an almost pleasurable knowledge that such would be the case. From the mere words one might have imagined that she had dropped the subject of the fountain; but I was convinced to the contrary and drew her on by the simple expedient of saying nothing, looking at her with that air of grave inquiry which forces people of her stamp to words.

'There's no repairing the danged thing!' she burst out suddenly, in vehement contradiction to my former words; 'how is it possible to do anything with it? At the outside the springs *seem* to have run dry! There's no water coming from the hillside – none to be seen, out there. Bone dry! All of them, every single one, the whole seven! up above the ground, as deep as they can dig. But there's deeper places than that – the water's somewhere for certain – certain sure. An' if you don't believe me –' Suddenly she drew herself together. 'I'm sure I beg your pardon, sir, to seem so excited – upset. But it's lonely when the house is empty, an' not be able to talk to the maids an' all.'

'You'd better sit down, Mrs Brice.'

She sat down at once, almost as if her knees were shaking under her; well into the chair, too, not on the edge as she would ordinarily have done.

'It's silly of me – but it gets on my nerves. An' those girls, as won't go upstairs in the dark, running with their ears back like hares, so to speak, and their eyes half out of their heads. And the water – well, where *did* it go?' She leant a little forward, her hand pressed against the edge of the table at which I had been writing. 'That's what they – what we all want to know and are yet scared o' knowing, for certain that is. Inside us' – she went on with a sudden gesture, strangely dramatic in one so servile – 'inside us we *know* – we all know; those of us that don't run ourselves out in hysterics, and shriekings and gigglings: we know things we daren't say – making them more real by exact words, as it were.'

'About the fountain, you mean? Oh, well, I suppose it's just that the springs have run dry; they do sometimes, you know.'

'If I thought that was all – could think that – should I be sitting here now? Listen!' She held up her finger, the further to attract my attention. 'The maids are in bed, there's no one to draw water, no one in the house save us two; where's the water coming from now, where is it? Tell me that, sir?' She was almost triumphant, forgetting her fear.

For I was conscious of it, and she knew it, had been ever since the quiet of the evening fell upon the house – that soft, continuous sound of running water.

'Some defective pipe, with the air in it.'

'Not it!' All the woman's obsequiousness was lost in the sense of having got me there. 'I've had man after man in to see about it, an' there's nothing to be done, *nothing*! Of course there's nothing. I've never told the maids, I've told no one.' She spoke proudly there, and indeed there was something like heroism in what, by her next words, she proved to have kept to herself. 'But when they turned it off at the main it was the same – running, running, just the same; forever running, till it near drives me mad with its trickle. Though only at evening, mind you. Night after night it goes up and down the stairs, filling the house with damp – reeking it is, reeking.'

'Nonsense, nonsense!'

The housekeeper pushed back her chair and rose. There was a fire in the room in which I was sitting, and an immense pile of logs burnt in the hall. When I arrived about tea-time the atmosphere had felt stifling after the frosty air outside; but now, as she led me to the foot of the stairs, I was struck by a dank moisture, which chilled me to the bone, set me shivering with a sense of cold water down my back.

'We were obliged to take the carpet off the stairs; I dare say you noticed that, sir,' she remarked, in a monotonous, droning voice, as though determined to put everything in as matter-of-fact a light as possible. 'I would have put it down when I heard that you were coming, but it wasn't fit. Besides – I'll trouble you to look what would it have been like in one night? – There, now! See there!' She stooped, lowering the candle to the level of the third step, and drew with her finger upon the dark oak, all greyed with moisture.

Straightening herself, she ran her fingers along the top of

the wide, flat banisters, then made me touch my own hand to the underside, where the drops hung.

'The house is damp.'

'Yes, sir, you're right there. It *is* damp.' She stood for a moment with the candle in one hand, the other over her mouth as though she felt her lips tremble. 'But it was never damp before, when the water in the springs ran the way God made it to run. Why wasn't it never damp before? – if you'll excuse my asking you that question, sir. I've been here close on thirty years, an' a drier house I never came across. But now! It's wringing, fair wringing! If it was all over the house there'd be no grappling with it. But it's only across the hall and up the stairs, and in two rooms – as yet – as yet. But the damp and the mould of it! It's beyond all belief! I keep the rooms aired as best I can, kindle the fires myself, have them going pretty well night and day. I'm fond of the place, fond of Mr Harry ... Well, I held him on my knee when he was a baby – though he has his faults, as we all have.' She dropped to silence for a moment, glaring at me. 'There never used to be anything wrong with the house, an' I won't give it up unless I'm driven; it's my duty to stand by it. But – but – well, it curdles my blood. Nothing to be seen, as far as I'm concerned, only the sound of running water and the dampness. Though the maids do say –'

'What do they say?'

'Some say that it's – it's – against the light there's nothing, but against anything dark, as it were, a picture on the stairway – well, they say as how it's the shadow of the –' she hesitated, drawing her shoulders together and turning her head furtively, as though the mere words were enough to bring the thing to her elbow – 'the ghost of – of –'

'The ghost of what?' I was in terror as to what her next words might be, and gave vent to a boisterous laugh of pure relief when she replied that it was 'the ghost of the fountain' which the maids swore to seeing.

'That's good! That's a joke! I never heard of anything like that! The ghost of a fountain! As though it had actually lived, possessed a soul. Really, Mrs Brice, really!'

Still laughing, I took the candle from her hand and went upstairs.

But as I lay awake that night I remembered how she had tried to tell me something else, which I had half heard as I moved away: confused words to the effect that, while to some it seemed like a shadowy plume of water, to others it bore the aspect of a woman, ethereal as mist. 'Both!' cried one hussy, brazen with fear, asserting what must have seemed, to her own limited intelligence, an impossibility. 'Both at once! Not altogether a woman, nor altogether water.'

This elaboration of what I endeavoured, against my own convictions, to regard as a senseless joke, came out later, for I lingered on for several weeks, restless and miserable, yet unable to tear myself away.

There was a blank air of repression about the place. The weather was warm for the time of year and very dry, so that it seemed strange to look up into the hard, brilliant blue sky and see it crossed by nothing more than bare boughs. The few early spring flowers were warped and stunted, the parched ground cracked; at the bottom of the fountain basin was a layer of crusted grey mud; even the Cupid with his horn appeared shrunken and grey with drought.

I haunted the empty pool at all hours of the day and night, gazing into it as one might gaze into the face of a deaf-mute who holds some secret upon which one's whole life depends, with a will so intense that it seemed as though it were bound to force speech.

And yet I had no idea what I expected to see or hear there; I only knew that I could not keep away; that the moment

I awoke some formless necessity seemed to drag me out of bed, to sit on the crumbling stonework at the edge of that featureless expanse of stinking soil, my whole heart and mind drawn to a fine point by my desire to get at the secret of something I could not fathom; to understand, to help, to comfort: striving against nothing and for nothing, with a soul as thirsty and arid as the parched earth itself.

Sometimes when I was alone at night the soft sound of running water through the house grew to something so like a desolate weeping that I would actually cry aloud, asking what was amiss, what could be done; and yet out there by the side of that empty basin it was even worse.

At last I could endure my impotency no longer and went away, off to Norway for the summer months and then back to London.

It was mid-December when I received a curiously urgent telegram from Colquhoun asking me to stay with him, and to come as soon as possible – 'for God's sake.'

The autumn had been one of furious winds and heavy rain. As I drove from the station I saw that some of the finest elms in Cattraeth Park had been torn up by the roots; one monster, indeed, lay right across the road, so that Colquhoun was obliged to turn the restive, thin-skinned chestnut which he was driving on to the grass to avoid it. He had formerly been very gentle with animals, was noted for his light hands; but I could not help noticing how he mismanaged the nervous beast, and wondering if I should ever reach the house alive between the two of them; whether we should both be overturned, and pitched out, or killed by a falling tree. For even then there was half a gale blowing, the sky was whipped into tangled hanks of grey and white, while the dead leaves were driven to heaps in every hollow, the short grass flattened to a curious whiteness.

Colquhoun had almost entreated me to come, but he did

not appear over-glad to see me. Indeed, excepting to curse the trembling mare, he never opened his mouth during the whole of the six-mile drive.

We had tea in the smoking-room. At least, I had tea; Colquhoun himself took whisky. I noticed how his hand shook as he poured it out, how he was changed, bloated and yet haggard, standing by the fire with his glass on the mantelpiece, his head drooping between his shrunken shoulders, save when he jerked it backwards, staring round defiantly as though asking what right anyone had to be up to – God only knows what, right at his elbow there; until at last, breaking off in the midst of an attempt at conversation, he turned and left the room, while a moment later I heard him cross the hall, open the door that led into the garden, and slam it behind him.

After a while the housekeeper came to ask if I would not like to see my room, for there seemed to be no proper servants about the place, an uncouth boy with frightfully creaking boots and not over-clean hands having brought in the tea.

As I followed her through the hall and up the stairs, I was struck by the same overwhelming odour of damp as on my last visit. But Mrs Brice volunteered no remark, contented herself with merely answering mine; while I noticed something taut and rigid about the woman – who had grown thinner, and even more leaden-coloured and lined – as though she were determined not to say a word.

There was a good fire burning in my room and I sat before it, smoking; then, while I was upstairs, dressed for dinner in leisurely comfort.

As I crossed the hall, rather after seven, the outer door opened and a boisterous, wet wind eddied in, setting every other door in the place slamming; while it must have whirled right up the stairs, for there was a sound like the report of guns along the two corridors above me, and the whole house echoed in its emptiness.

A little Aberdeen bitch, which had left the smoking-room at Colquhoun's heels, ran past me yelping, and down the long passage towards the kitchen quarters, where she threw herself against the baize door and disappeared.

As I turned I saw that my host had entered the hall, and wondered if he had kicked the poor beast, or what had happened to upset it so.

But the next moment I was undeceived on this point, for he began whistling and calling to her, almost tenderly.

'She's gone through the baize door to the kitchen,' said I.

'Ah, well, she's chosen the best part of the house, it's warm and dry there. Poor bitch, she can't stand it, and no wonder.'

'Can't stand what?'

'What – what! why, what's with me, to be sure,' he answered morosely, and brushed past, too much absorbed in his own misery to realize his rudeness or trouble himself as to whether or no I understood his words.

He had been out for at least two hours, and all that time I had heard the rain beating against the windows.

'You must be wringing wet; you'll catch your death,' I said, for I saw he had no overcoat, that his clothes clung round him, while the water poured from him in pools.

At this he laughed wildly, pausing half-way up the stairs and looking down at me, with a sort of fierce raillery in his glance.

'Catch my death! Not I, not that way, anyhow! I'm used to it, or ought to be,' he said, and then I thought I heard him add, as he turned and stumped upwards – as heavily as though his limbs were leaden-weighted – 'Catch my death! No such luck; I only wish I could!'

That evening, dinner over, we sat in the smoking-room,

silent, for my brain had already exhausted itself in the search for some topic of conversation which would not drop dead the moment it was launched, killed by a dark, uncomprehending stare from my host, or, worse still, an utterly misplaced comment.

We were both smoking, Colquhoun sitting with his chair almost into the fire, bending forward with his elbows on his knees – save when he jerked round with that defiant stare – shivering as though he were in an ague; while Wasp, the Aberdeen, sitting pressed against her master's knee, shivered as he shivered, with her eyes fixed on his face as though awaiting some word of command.

The ripple of running water was very distinct through the house, and there was a desperate sadness in the sound which can be so pleasant and cheerful.

I think I must have said something to start Colquhoun off; I don't know. If I did it was wiped out of my mind by the torrent of words into which he suddenly launched forth.

'I can't stand it any longer, Herries; that's why I sent for you. No one else will come, no one else will stay in the house, and no wonder! That infernal din of running water. I tell you it is driving me mad. Water on the brain, I suppose that's what it is, eh, eh? A funny thing for me to have!' He gave an ugly laugh, which terminated suddenly, as though it were broken off. 'That damned tricklin' an' gurglin'! Hear it now? … Or perhaps you can't hear it, eh? It's not there; I was only humbugging.' A furtive look came into his face, turned over his shoulder towards me, as he rose, took a tobacco pouch from the mantelshelf and filled his pipe afresh. 'Only a joke – a man must have his joke, you know. It's dull enough here, in all conscience; somehow I'm clean off hunting this season.'

'Well, there is the sound, clear enough,' I said, and at that he gave a sort of gasp, as though of relief.

'That's right, now! You hear it too. Then we know where we are. Sometimes I think I've "got 'em". Only other people *do* hear it, though they pretend not to … Hear it, feel it, smell it, *rot with it*! Why, it's everywhere – at least everywhere I go. I changed my room, went and slept in the other wing, but it was there too, damn it all, driving old Brice nearly mad. "I can deal with it when it keeps to its own place, Master Harry," she said, with her mouth like a rat-trap, "but if it once starts stavanging all over the house we're done for." Its own place! That shows how people can get used to things. Its own place! – as though its own place was across my front hall, up my stairs and into my bedroom. Good God! I sometimes wonder if I shall sleep in a dry bed again, or get free of the sound of that damned trickle; and … hang it all, Herries, it isn't as though it were like the sound of ordinary water; it weeps, that's what it does – weeps, there's no other word for it.'

'What do you make of it?'

'I don't know.' He leant back with his two elbows pushed out behind him on to the mantelshelf, glowering at me so desperately that I was as sorry for him as I had once been for her. 'People can't be *things*; there's animate and inanimate nature. Oh, hang it all, running water is animate enough, but … Well, I learnt it all at school, but I can't put it into words; you know what I mean – water's not like – well, human beings.'

'You mean it's not life.'

'No, it's not life,' he answered very slowly; then in a burst: 'But what is life? Tell me that. It used to seem easy enough – animal, vegetable, mineral, that's what they taught us – but there's nothing clear or separate these days. Look here, I don't believe *She* was ever quite true to life, as we count it – you know, warm blood an' passion, an' making goats of ourselves, an' all that. There's something one could never quite get hold of – it used to drive me mad at first.'

'Yes, I know.' There was no need for me to ask whom he meant, though he had not mentioned his wife's name since I came to the house.

'Though in her own way she was chock full of life,' he went on sadly; 'a *sort* of life: gay as a bird, until I started playing the fool, breaking her up. For that's what I did, you know that; you always knew it. You womanish sort o' artist chaps know a damned sight too much of both sides; but you were right there. And yet – look here, Herries, I believe, 'pon my soul, I believe she loved me, in her own way. She wouldn't give me all this devilish uneasiness if she could help it; I take my oath on that! She's uncommon sorry. Sorry! Well, listen, doesn't it sound for all the world as though she were crying over it? Wandering, don't you know, sort of wandering up and down like a lost child: driven – well, damn it all, driven as I'm driven.'

'She … What do you mean?' I asked, curious to hear what he really did make of it all.

'She – why, she —' He paused, his face flushed to a heavy crimson, and he stared at me hardly, as though he were putting me to the test, wondering how much he might dare to tell me, without the risk of a burst of asinine laughter. I think he was reassured by what he saw on my face, but anyhow the thing was beyond his power of expression and he could only murmur something about its being 'all the same thing'.

'You mean she' – for the life of me I couldn't use the words 'your wife' – 'or the soul of her, and the running water are one?' He nodded, and I went on: 'That she was so fond of the fountain, so one with it?' I paused. I too was helpless; it would have needed one of the ancient Greeks, with whom such strange interminglings were an integral part of nature, to put the thing into words. But he realized what I meant and nodded again, with a quick glance of relief at my ready comprehension.

Presently we sat down and lit another pipe, while we tried to talk it out in our English tongue-tied fashion.

One conclusion to which he was drawn and from which he was by no means to be separated, surprised me. Sylvia was not responsible, though she was the instrument. She was being revenged for the slights which had been put upon her. But she was not responsible: was rather the tool of some power infinitely old, pagan and fearful, which demanded a certain sacrifice in payment of all that she had endured; some power which had said, 'She is mine, of my kingdom, and you must pay the price, even if it is through her, the sufferer.'

It was strange how Colquhoun had reached such a conclusion, following out, perhaps for the first time in his life, a definite train of thought. Maybe he had, also for the first time, known what it was to endure sleepless nights, those forcing hours of fancy.

'That she should suffer too? That's nothing! The old God of the Bible was the same: it did not matter who was hurt as long as it was not His pride. And now "They're" just the same – "They" or "He" – I don't know what; maybe you know, you've studied those sort of things – but those old Druidical beliefs, I have heard of them, as who hasn't, living down here? – and all my people before me. Well, it seems to me that it's something like that – *something left over.* There's the blood sacrifice, now. The old chaps 'ud do nothing without it – build a house, launch a ship, raise an altar. And if any damned silly thing went wrong it was the same old cry, "A blood offering". Well, that's what They want of me – an' that's what she knows They want.'

'Sylvia! Sylvia, the gentlest creature on God's earth.'

He looked at me with a sudden unexpected shrewdness. 'And yet not quite of God's earth – you know that. I remember when first we married I felt – well, you wouldn't believe it, the sort I am – but I felt that I'd jolly well try to be different, she was so sweet and white, so apart from anything I had ever come across. And I remembered how my old mother used to say her prayers, thought no end of 'em, taught them to me when I was a kid. I suggested to her that we should – should' – he coloured shamefacedly – 'you know what a man feels like when he first marries a girl of that sort; it doesn't last, I grant it doesn't last: but somehow, as if he was in church … Well, I half suggested that we should pray together, that she should help to make me somehow decenter. It wasn't that I was drunk or anything,' he added rather pitifully. 'I suppose even the worst of us get queer notions of that sort into our heads at times. I've known men – well, it would surprise you. She was ready enough, eager as a child, she would have done anything in the world for me; you know that, Herries – anything. Oh, but it wasn't there, simply wasn't there. I can't explain. Sweet through and through she was, but certain things which used to count with my womenkind – it was no good, she couldn't grasp them. She had been through everything, they had drilled her in the convent, but you could tell that it didn't touch her, the real her. It's like inoculating a man – you can't make it take. Beauty she understood, and the trees and the flowers, and – well, you know the water, Herries, running water. I once heard an awfully clever chap say that you created your own God, or became part of Him. I couldn't make head or tail of it at the time, but somehow I remembered and it came back to me. It seemed to be like that with Sylvia; she – she' – he hesitated, then out of a sheer lack of words he blundered into the most convincing sentence imaginable: 'She worshipped, and she was.'

He drank a good deal of whisky after that and began to wander, embarking on a long tale of some dream which he could never get away from, a dream of a white woman and seven white hounds with crimson ears, which I counted as balderdash, until after I had helped him up the reeking stairs and into his bed; when, sitting smoking by the fire in my own room, the sudden memory came to me of how the sacred hounds of the Druidical gods were white with scarlet ears, and how the springs which had fed the fountain were seven in number.

Next morning I tackled Colquhoun in real earnest, begging him to go away, abroad, big-game hunting in South Africa or heiress-hunting in America – anywhere. But he would not even hear of it; he had not been away for more than a night or two since early that spring when he was at Monte Carlo, and somehow he seemed to be bitten with the idea that he *could* not go. 'It was worse when I was away last time, an' far worse when I came back.' That was what he said. 'No, by God, I'll stick it out somehow. Who knows, perhaps *They'll* get what they want, then there'll be peace for the old place and the whole bally lot of us. Six foot by two of dry sod – it wouldn't be so bad, anyhow.'

I told him not to be an ass; I was frankly alarmed at his manner, and I talked it over with Mrs Brice next day while I watched Colquhoun from the window of her room, sitting on the stone margin of the pool, poking holes in the dry mud with his stick. It was then that she told me something of what had happened, that last summer after he came back from abroad. Things had been queer before – well, I knew; when was it I had been there? – March, was it not?

Colquhoun came home at the end of June and had a party of friends to stay in the house. It had been terribly hot in London and they were glad to get away; besides, they weren't the sort of people who would ever stay anywhere for a regular season. The housekeeper stiffened visibly as she spoke, and I gathered from that what sort they were. There had been many a wild crew there before; still, people with a more or less assured position. Gradually it all came out; the 'ladies' – the word was uttered with a sniff which discounted it – drank whisky and water and smoked in their bedrooms – and not alone either. They ruined the best carpets by powdering from head to foot, to judge by the mess they made. Mrs Brice opined that it was to save themselves the trouble of bathing, but I know better; the sort she described are impeccable in that direction, anyhow. They larked up and down the passages in their nightdresses, transparent crêpe-de-chine – at least, at the very beginning. Later on they flew through them, wrapping their filmy draperies as close as though they were afraid of some clutching hand, for they were more scared than the maids; showed it too, as real ladies would never have done; while – cause for the crowning condemnation – they called the housekeeper 'Bricey' – she who knew her place and kept it – one of them actually throwing an arm round her waist one evening and laying her head on her shoulder, declaring that she was 'a dear old dug-up', and made her 'sick with laughing' – 'In front of the gentlemen and all' – she, Brice, having been sent for with a needle and thread to mend a torn flounce.

Colquhoun, as it seemed, favoured no one in particular, though the women hung round him, fought over him. 'You could tell how he saw clean through them,' remarked the housekeeper with pride, as though this freed her master from all blame.

At first the women quarrelled, abused each other like fishwives. Mrs Brice gave a graphic account of how she saw a little one fly at a big one and actually stamp on her insteps with sharp Louis Quinze heels.

Then suddenly they drew together. 'There's something damned funny about the bloomin' house!' That was what they said.

No single one of the women would go up to bed alone: they would gather together in the hall, with the men laughing at them uproariously, and then fly upstairs. And there was something to be frightened at, too – their satin slippers were all blotched with damp in the morning – the housemaid used to put them to dry on the window-sills; the tails of their delicate gowns 'such a sight as never was!' They shuddered as they touched their fingers to the banisters.

Then one evening they all came down again, pouring into the hall, and across to the dining-room, where such of the men as were not playing cards still sat over their wine, clinging together, shrieking like nothing so much as a flock of brightly-plumaged parrots.

They had gone up the stairs together, kept together, but all the same they had felt 'as chirpy as anything' till they reached the top, when on a sudden they realized that there was Something – or Somebody – before them.

It touched Rosie Vallenge. Rosie was sitting on a man's knee with her arms round his neck, sobbing and gasping. 'Good Lord!' he cried suddenly, and made a movement as though to fling her aside. 'Look at the front of your frock – all wet, girl!'

Then it *had* touched her ... It was like a woman against the dark panelling; they were all agreed as to that: and yet transparent, silvery as water. Like water – well, only look at Rosie's dress, a delicate mauve satin all splashed and stained.

Mrs Brice had run out into the hall, hearing the clamour even behind her baize door; the other men had come in from the smoking-room and were laughing boisterously enough at the women, yet with an edge on their laugh, for they had only just been talking over it all – 'the confounded queerness of the place.'

Harry Colquhoun had risen from the table and stood leaning against the mantelpiece in his favourite attitude, with his shoulders raised, his elbows stuck out behind him, resting upon it.

His head was bent, his face grey; at least, that is what Mrs Brice said.

Suddenly he looked up and shouted at her for the keys of

his wife's rooms, which had not been used since her death, mentioning her name there in front of them all, which he would never have done had he been in his right mind.

When Mrs Brice pretended that she had not got them – she had never cared for her late mistress, but she did not like the idea of her rooms being invaded by 'that muck' – Colquhoun yelled at her with a curse: 'Well, get 'em, woman!' and she was obliged to obey.

When she came back with the keys he was upstairs, outside Mrs Colquhoun's door, and his face had turned from white to a heavy crimson. The women were at the other side of the landing, which ran round the top of the hall like a balcony – clinging together, staring across at the group of men who were gathered about him – more than one propping himself against the wall, scarcely able to stand upright – laughing, giving advice, making suggestions.

Colquhoun was the only one who seemed quite sober, sure of himself; though so queer and 'stony like' that it might be he had passed the convivial stage.

He took the key from the housekeeper with a steady hand and opened the door into his wife's bedroom, passed through it into a little dividing dressing-room, and so on into the boudoir.

It had been a breathlessly hot day, there had been no rain for close on a month, and yet the damp of it, the awful dank chilliness struck to the bone. Some of the men, so Mrs Brice said, actually turned up their collars as though not thinking what they were doing.

The room had been done in pale blue and white, very fresh and delicate. But now the blue hangings at the windows were stained with damp; great blotches stood out against the walls; the muslin draperies of the dressing-table clung round it like the clothes round a drowned man. In the boudoir someone pulled a book from the shelves and found the sides of it grey with mould.

'For the Lord's sake why don't you open the window and let in a little fresh air!' cried one man; then, pulling aside the curtain, found that the windows were all pushed up as far as they would go, while the breath of the outer air was hot and dry as an oven.

Some of the women had crept in; one put her hand on the bed and shuddered: there was a damp patch on the pillow, the dark blue carpet was all paddled over with it.

Suddenly she gave a shriek, crying out, 'A toad! Toad – ugh, the nasty thing!' and gathering together, they fled.

But it was not a toad, only a dead leaf lying on the carpet which Mrs Brice herself had brushed over, that very morning, locking the door after her when she had finished: a dark, water-rotted leaf, almost a skeleton, such as one might find at the bottom of a well.

The house-party broke up after that. One or two of the men lingered on, but not for long; they declared that the place affected their livers.

Now and then a chance visitor turned up, but never stayed for long. The most persistent was what Mrs Brice called 'a poor frayed piece' who seemed to have nowhere else to go. One of the men had left her behind, as though forgotten, and Colquhoun took no notice of her; perhaps that was why the housekeeper, in whose comfortable room she took occasional refuge, declared her to have been 'more sinned against than sinning'. But even she left at last, saying that she would rather be in the morgue.

Several times Colquhoun went away, but he always came back sooner than he was expected, 'dropping in upon me all of a sudden', as Mrs Brice put it, 'with a look in his eyes – God forgive me for comparing any Christian, above all my own master, to a heathen beast with no soul – but for all the world the same as that there dog of his.'

I knew that look in Wasp's eyes, puzzled, anxious, in a way licentious; and I remembered now that Lady Hardy had spoken of Colquhoun – though whether she quoted consciously I cannot tell – as 'dog-eyed, wine-laden'.

Poor devil! I was sorry enough for him now in all conscience, his whole life turned upside down by some power which was past his understanding. Indeed, he was like a dog in more ways than one, for he had all a dog's hatred of what was beyond his comprehension, with none of that prying, tiptoeing delight and curiosity regarding the supernatural which possesses the feline race and all that are kindred with it.

After a great deal of persuasion I got him to go abroad with me, and we started off to the Austrian Tyrol; but we had not been there a week when I awoke one morning to find that he was gone, leaving an explanatory note – in the calligraphy and spelling of a boy of twelve – to say that he felt he had to go, or rather, 'must be there'.

I followed him as quickly as possible, very much frightened, for he still held to that belief as to what was expected of him. It is strange how the pure Welsh strain of his mother's race – through whom he had inherited Cattraeth – came out in this, as it already had done in his mobile mouth, the straight, densely-black hair. Some old nurse might have told him stories of atonement by blood; but those white hounds with the red ears, surely they hunted him down through the dreams of untold ancestors.

It was Mrs Brice who opened the door to me; and I do not believe that I was ever so welcome a sight to any woman's eyes, for her flat, rubber-like face awoke to a sort of humanity as she realized who it was.

'He's come,' she said.

'What does he say?'

'He says nothing – to me, at any rate,' she answered. Then, to my surprise, she led me through the hall and down the passage to the servants' quarters, without so much as a word of apology or explanation.

Upon the window-seat of her own sanctum, the only one of the lower rooms from which there was a clear view of the fountain pool, sat Wasp staring out, shivering. She had gone to skin and bone, her coat was dry and colourless. When I spoke to her she glanced round hastily and then back again out of the window, making no movement to come to me.

'There she sits,' remarked the housekeeper. 'It seems that she won't go out with Master Harry.' The old name slipped out in her perturbation; she spoke with that sort of flat blankness which comes to us when we feel there is nothing more to be done. 'She seems to know where he is going, poor bitch!'

'Where?' I asked; and she answered dully enough that I could see for myself; as I could by leaning over the dog – who growled as though in fear that I should oust her from her vigil – for there was Colquhoun on the edge of the pool, digging holes in the mud. The whole aspect of him, the attitude, had something eternal about it to my mind; I felt I must have seen him thus thousands of times, could remember no other position, with no more reasonable occupation.

'He slept on the floor last night,' said Mrs Brice; then added bitterly, 'An' no wonder – no wonder, I say. For his bed was wringing, though I've moved him to the far wing – and now everything's spoilt there, for it's everywhere, everywhere where he goes. Well, it's past me!' She drew her hand over her mouth with an odd grimace as though her muscles had grown stiff with keeping her teeth clenched over the thing. 'I say to myself, "'God only knows'", but does He – does He? An' counting Him out there's no one.'

I went into the garden and managed to coax Colquhoun indoors. It was a warm spring day, but we had an enormous fire and sat over it, both before dinner and then again later on, Colquhoun leaning forward with his forearms along his knees, his hands hanging, while little Wasp sat and stared up at him.

I noticed that he had lost that habit of sudden turning and staring; but it was not because he was more at ease, rather that everything had come to such a pass it was beyond troubling about. Only once did I see him roused.

Something came into the room. I do not know what it was; I could see nothing, but I could feel it. Colquhoun did not look round. He knew it was there, I saw that by the twitch of his mouth; but his despair seemed to have bred in him a sort of sullen indifference which said, 'Oh, let it come!' He was like Sir Roland at his Dark Tower.

The something, whatever it might have been, passed behind me where I sat in a low chair to the right of the fire, I knew that by the breath of moist air, so different from the mustiness which hung about the house – sweet as spring flowers – and moved on until it stood in front of Colquhoun.

Oh, it was so distinct, the feeling of it – a slender column of water: so distinct that I actually knew when it stooped. And it was then that Wasp leapt up with a howl of terror and ran to the furthest corner of the room, where she sat with her muzzle pressed against the wall, shivering.

I could hear my host rap out a fierce oath at that, but I could hear something else, as he got up to follow his dog – a soft cry, bitter and heart-broken, such a cry as might come from one who, stopping to caress, is cruelly repulsed, driven back for some reason it cannot comprehend.

'Look here, Herries,' Colquhoun called to me, his white face flushed. Then: 'Damn it all! They might as well leave my bitch alone!' he burst out, and lifting the trembling creature in his arms, pointed out a dark patch upon the dry, starting hair, as though a wet hand had been laid there.

I can never forget the atmosphere of the room at that moment. It seemed as though it *must* become articulate, so over-charged was it with misery and fear and pain, and the desperate striving to understand and explain of at least one of the Four of us – counting Wasp as one.

Then that other one slid away, with a sort of sob, as I thought; passed across the hall and up the stairs, the sound of its weeping mingling with the sound of the running water.

'It's everywhere,' said Colquhoun. 'Look here, Herries, it lies on the pillow beside me at night, 'pon my oath it does! It's already in the chair that I go to sit in; it mists over the glass so that I can scarcely see to shave. An' the damnable part of it is that it's being driven just as I'm driven. Cruel! Oh, rank cruelty, I call it. It's got to be done with, given a chance to rest. It's no good haggling over the price – I know that, have known it all along. I cursed when my dog was touched! somehow a fellow can stand things for himself that he can't stand for his dog – poor Wasp, poor little bitch! But the reason for it was that she, an' I, were both scared – dead scared. An' you too, though you loved her ... Oh yes, I know that, always knew it: it amused me – once. But scared! Of her, of her! That's the desperate part of it, Herries ... Confoundedly lonely ... Oh yes, I know, the same way as I'm lonely; an' driven the way I'm driven: an' comin' in here to us to the light and the warmth, and us scared of her! Poor little thing, poor kid, so soft and sweet and white.

'She had on a little grey motor-bonnet the *first* day we came home here, with blue ribbons under her dinky round chin; an' now I'm dead scared of her – or what's at the back of her drivin' her on. Some horrible thing – tremendous somehow

– I don't know how to put it – but it seems something like what you call the forces of nature, not our God or Christ, but that old bloody thing –'

'The pagan belief …'

'That's it, the pagan belief! It strikes me that it made something. Can a lot of people believing in a thing *make*, create it? – O God, I don't know, I can't get it into words. But if they did make it – that way – they mightn't be able to drop it when they wanted to – by simply ceasing to believe. Damn it all – but it seems like this: that a chap might make a god of clay and break it in a paddy, and there'd still be something left – something he used to count on.'

He sat down in his chair cuddling the little dog up against his face, looking at me with eyes which seemed somewhat cleared of their desperation, as though by some definite decision. Mrs Brice brought in the tray with decanter and glasses, but he did not touch anything, and saw me to my room himself that night, playing the host, careful that I had everything I needed.

I think I knew what was going to happen: certainly I was not surprised when the housekeeper came to my room soon after dawn next day to say that she had been awakened by the sound of a shot, and running to her master's room, found him dead, lying upon the floor. I had done all that I felt I had any right to do, and I could not grieve.

I think Mrs Brice felt that too.

'Anyhow, his troubles are over now,' she said, and I hope and believe that she was right.

I still go to the house. It is there, indeed, that I have written the greater part of these memories – and speculations.

At the moment I have just returned from a visit to the housekeeper's room, where she spends most of her time – for she is growing old now – in a great winged chair by the window.

On this particular morning it was wide open, for it is midsummer, and old Wasp, very feeble and almost blind, was lying asleep on the cushioned seat. The roses have grown tall, and flourished exceedingly, so that it was only above their long flower-laden sprays that I caught a glimpse of the fountain's sparkling plume, which we found sprung to life again on the morning of poor Harry Colquhoun's death.

A four of schoolboys, two of them Colquhoun's nephews – for the place went to his sister at his death – were playing tennis on the lawn, with a vast amount of noise and very little science. Out from the door of the housekeeper's room I could look straight along the passage, as down the dark barrel of a gun – for the baize door is permanently fastened back in these days – right into the hall.

A light silk curtain billowed out in the draught from some unseen window, and a woman in a white gown pranced across the upright panel of light, a four-year-old hanging on to her sash ribbons with shouts of 'Gee-up, there'; while from a distant piano came a whole-souled clash of notes, and a girl's clear voice singing 'The Low-backed Car.'

'I suppose there's no damp here now,' I ventured, half-turned to leave the room. For conversation is difficult with Mrs Brice these days. I have seen her soul stripped bare, unashamed and very much afraid, and she can never forget that against me.

Sitting there immovable in her great chair, with its curving back giving her something of the air of a tortoise turned up sideways encircled by its shell – she treated me to a cold stare out of her dull grey eyes.

'Damp!' she said. 'There's no damp here, never has been. It's the driest house I was ever in; that's what I always have said, always will say, no matter what folks, that have got the habit of novel-writing, demean themselves by making out.'

6 'Luz' (1922)

The blind man passed my flat between seven and eight each night. I never remember having heard him during the summer months, but directly the days began to darken – perhaps because I was more indoors – I noticed the tap-tap of his stick beneath my window. Even if it had been light enough to see I could not have caught sight of him, for the pavement was obscured by a jutting bay-window immediately below mine, and inevitably he walked upon the near side of the street.

I have always felt acute sympathy for all who are maimed and defrauded; above all for the blind, shut away from light and colour, which mean more to me than speech or music. But I feared and hated that blind man: from the beginning I hated him, though I saw nothing of him, heard nothing – not even so much as cough or sigh – apart from that tapping stick.

I was curious about him, and yet I never tried to meet him. The truth is, I was more frightened than curious, would hurry down my short street at the hour when he might be returning that way, thankful to reach my own door, or the roaring traffic, the lights of the wider thoroughfare.

'Returning,' I say: but when did he set out? and what did he return from? I had a fancy that he reached the scene of his day's labours – pleasure, solicitation, whatever it might be – by some altogether uncanny means; that his every action, his whole life, indeed, was nefarious.

During a long illness I thought of him continually. 'When I get better,' I said to myself, 'I will ask the policeman at the corner about him under some pretence of charity; find out what he is like, where he comes from.'

And yet, when I was about again I spoke of him to no one.

If there were visitors with me at the time of his passing, I was all on edge, in case they might lift their heads to listen to the sound of the tapping stick, and put something that I feared – I had no idea what – into words!

Then, one evening during the last week of February, coming away from a tea-party in the higher part of London, I dipped to Chelsea and found myself completely enveloped by a thick yellow fog.

I ought to have turned back at once; but I pushed on, anxious to reach home, confident that I knew the way far too well to miss it.

The secluded streets and squares, through which I had attempted a short cut, were very quiet. The roadways seemed to be empty. Now and then people passed me; but when I entreated their help I was met with nothing but vague complaints of their own troubles; bewildered questions. At times they did not even answer; if they shook their heads I could not see them do so.

Once, some strange fluttering form caught at my arm and in a shrill voice entreated guidance to Parsons Green – of all places! – cursing me shrilly when I declared my inability to help; fluttering off again with shoes that flapped at the heels like broken wings.

Sharp, jutting angles of wall and railing shot out before me. There was no accounting for them; avoiding one, I turned a corner and there was another like a sharp elbow; a wall flat against my face, or a *chevaux de frise* of spiked paling; and everywhere a smell of sulphurous damp. The fur beneath my chin was wet; my gloves clammy, clinging to my fingers.

Quite suddenly hope gave way within me. I convicted myself of having walked round and round the same square, and tears, of self-pity, exasperation, fatigue, mingled with the foggy moisture on my veil.

Then a man standing motionless at a corner – so close that I must have almost touched him as I leant against the rail fumbling for my pocket-handkerchief – spoke to me:

'You have lost your way?'

'What is that – who – ?' I put out one hand, involuntarily groping. There was a movement; a shadow darker than the fog; a strange, musty smell of something dry and desiccated – yes, dry, in all that damp – inexpressibly frowsty; and a dry, cold hand was laid upon mine.

'I will lead you. Where are you going?'

'Hunter's Grove –' I began, then drew back, my fear of the fog overcome by something more poignant, though perfectly vague. 'Thank you, but I can manage. I – I am all right – I am only resting.'

There was a laugh at this – a hoarse chuckle – then: 'Oh, very well.'

The air around me cleared: I was alone once more.

With an effort of determination I started off again: straight on for a dozen yards or so, then round the first corner; stupefied by the feeling which comes to one upon waking suddenly in a strange room, uncertain which way one faces, which side the wall lies.

To my bewilderment, the ground grew rough beneath my feet. I tapped my way with my umbrella; there were ruts and loose stones. It became worse and worse; I fell against something which caught me just above my knees; followed it with one hand and found a broken piece of wall zigzagging up and down – in some places above my reach. I stumbled again and fell forward, bruising my knees upon a pile of loose masonry.

Evidently enough, that turning from the main street, the baffling square, debouched upon nothing more than a piece of waste ground, bestrewn with remnants of half-destroyed buildings: an old deserted nest of slums.

If I went on, ten to one I would fall into some unguarded cellar or clay pit; lie there with a broken leg; perish of cold and hunger.

Why, here – right in the midst of London – I might have been miles and miles away from humanity.

Best to retrace my steps. But how? I turned, then hesitated, trembling. There was not so much as a kerb to guide me.

I cried aloud: shouted for help, overcome by that sense of wild panic which attacks a child, realizing itself alone in the darkness. I heard the tapping of a stick, then someone sniggered, close to my elbow.

Of course, oh, of course *anyone* must feel their way with a stick, in darkness such as this. All the same, the sound struck some shrinking dread in the depths of my being. It was as though that tap-tap were upon my heart as well as the ground, emphasizing some fear.

Tap-tap-tap.

With an extraordinary effort I kept the thought of whom it *might* be at the back of my mind.

'Come, come now; be sensible.' It was the same oddly smooth voice which had accosted me half an hour earlier: empty and flattened, like that of a man talking in his sleep.

I hesitated a moment, then brought my common sense to my aid, arguing with myself: 'Anyhow, I have got to get home; I can't stay here all night.'

'If you think you can find your way – but how?' I began.

It was in my mind to say, 'If I can't see, how can you?' but I changed it to, 'If you will take me to my own door I'll give you five shillings.'

'All right – all right.' A hand was laid upon my arm; that strange mouse-like odour was about me once more. There was that laugh, malevolent and mocking.

'Now – now – use your eyes; look where you're going.'

I shook off the hand, half hysterically. 'I'll follow – don't touch me.' There must have been some servile fear of him in my heart, which made me add, 'I might stumble if you held me – I am not used – accustomed…' My awkward words tailed off as he moved away, without a protest, keeping close in front of me.

I could see him and yet not see him: nothing more than a darker blur, magnified by the yellow fog.

After a time I found my feet once again upon the pavement, and that cheered me. My spirits leapt up with the thought that I must be near home.

Now and then people passed by, all alike mere slips of denser darkness: now and then a flashlight blazed full in my face, then vanished, leaving me blinder than before.

Still we went on and on. I could not be sure how far I had strayed out of my way, and yet I could not have believed that we would take so long.

Oppressed by the darkness, by fatigue, by the strain of fear, I began to feel as though I were in a dream. On and on and on we went.

Now and then the thought came to me: 'Why, it's years since I first made sure that we had come more than far enough.'

Now and then I called to my guide, but he took no notice, though my voice sounded shrill and almost indecently loud in my own ears. A certain sense of awe is the outcome of everything over which we have no influence, with which we find ourselves unable to grapple: and hearing my own voice shrieking in that darkness, silence, I felt as suddenly ashamed as though I had set up a clamour in church.

Once I stopped dead: 'I won't go on – I won't. I am certain that you are taking me wrong.'

He was so sure of me that he moved on. And rightly enough, for as he melted away I stumbled after him, caught at his sleeve.

'Wait a minute – wait! You promised to guide me. Only – well, we must ask the way. I'm sure you're doing your best, but – but…' I was servile in my fear, my conciliation.

Keeping close to the frowsty form, feeling my way along palings, the sides of walls, I would suddenly encounter other fingers, cold or damply gloved: other people groping their way as I did. There would be a moment's pause; then one or the other would reluctantly move out from the place of vantage. I think we all hated each other in that fog – without sight or reason.

I never failed to shoot out a question: 'Am I right for Hunter's Grove?' – 'Can you tell me the way to Hunter's Grove?' And every time I was answered, if at all, in the negative: briefly and pettishly, as though each wayfarer were engrossed in his own troubles alone.

'Down Church Street, across King's Road, down Oakley Street – then to the left,' my guide had said mockingly enough; and yet… Well, after all, he seemed the only person who even knew of Hunter's Grove; the only one willing to help or even consider me.

We did cross King's Road: I was certain of that; and it relieved my mind. There was none of the usual roar of traffic; but there were faint blurs of light, the sound of something like a motor-lorry moving at a foot's pace, the stench of petrol.

Then I smelt the river. Smell, indeed, seemed the only sense left to me: speech and hearing were alike deadened, sight useless; but I caught up scents like a dog.

If they blindfolded me, placed that sour, musty form among a hundred others, I should recognize it, even now.

It was quite suddenly that I became conscious of a sort of hollowness beneath my feet; a freshening air, the moan and shriek of fog-signals.

I stopped dead. 'We are on the bridge,' I cried. 'We have come wrong – too far…'

He turned at that, came close to me. 'Dear, dear – I'm afraid – and I was so certain … Sir, can you tell us how far we are out of our way for Hunter's Grove?' He plucked at the sleeve of a passing shadow.

'I don't know – how should I know? I don't know my own way,' wailed the stranger. "Let me go – everyone for himself.'

'I would not have had this happen for worlds. I was so sure – oh, so sure!' lamented my guide. 'We must turn and go back.'

The kerb was very high, and I stumbled over it. Somehow or other, we must have got into one of the recesses of the bridge, for I felt the coping upon three sides; the damp reek of the river came up to meet me.

I was actually glad of a hand upon my arm. There was no reason why I should fall over a wall which reached almost to my waist; but, all the same, I was frightened.

The fact that my companion acknowledged himself at fault – this and that other fear drew me to him. When he said, 'We must turn back,' I turned, without realizing which way I already faced.

Yet it must have been there that I turned – not for the first but for the second time; the first time was in the recess; and that was why, with his diabolical cleverness, he had led me there, working upon me so that I moved in a restricted circle.

'All right now – all right now,' he chuckled, and moved on in front of me. 'In another moment we shall be off the bridge again. Now – now – to the left, and then to the right; twice to the right, and then to the left again.'

We were clear of the bridge. Battersea Bridge was but a little distance from my flat: I tried to follow the route in my mind's eye, to remember how one turned. But I was without any special bump of locality; was too wearied for clear thought.

We turned and turned. My brain, bedizzied with fatigue, refused to register the number of turns, to exert itself further.

The atmosphere became more airless and dank, as though

there were high, sordid buildings close at either side – but there are many such in the vicinity of Hunter's Grove – impregnated with the sour smell of stale cabbage-water and garbage. The pavement was greasy and uneven beneath my feet.

My guide came to a pause.

'I have missed my way again – tch! tch!' He stood tapping the ground with his stick.

Wrapped in the yellow mist, I could just make out his figure, a sooty blur; there was a dim movement of his head, as though he were listening or – or sniffing: indeed, I seemed to hear the quickened breath in his nostrils.

Though we could see nothing there was the sound of a low humanity all about us. In some cases people seemed to be divided from us by walls; in others the sound came from upper storeys: raucous voices, gruntings, snorings, oaths, cries – all in some way muffled by distance, by the fog; but all alike hoarse and almost unimaginably bestial.

To one side of us was the dim square of an open doorway, made visible through a speck of gas which burned within it.

'I think I know where I am. I will go in and inquire.'

He did not ask me to follow him. I see now how clever he was in that as in all else – he did not *ask* me to follow!

There was a stairway facing the door. He did not pause to make any inquiries upon the ground floor; I realized that as I heard his stick go tap-tap up it.

'Wait, wait!' I cried. 'Don't leave me – I –'

A heavy form, reeking of beer, rolled against me, steadied itself by a hand upon my shoulder, and hiccoughed out a stream of curses.

I wrenched myself free and fled to the shelter of the open door, stumbled on the stairs, and mounted the first three steps, with the idea that there was a point of vantage where I might be safer than in the open streets.

I called up to my guide, 'Is there anyone there? Can you find anyone to help?'

'What the b — hell –?' There was a roar like a wild beast.

A door was dashed open to the right of the stairs and a huge figure – just visible in that single light, which fought with the incoming fog – shot forward to the foot of the stairs; immense shoulders, clothed in a ragged shirt, a shaggy head, swollen eyes beneath a shock of hair showed themselves, leaving the rest lost in darkness, like a body half in and half out of a pool of black water.

For all that, it was enough. I turned and ran stumbling up the stairway. There were more oaths, something about 'squawking', twisting a 'gory bullet' – but that was all: no pursuit further than a bare half-dozen steps.

At the first landing I was in total darkness: below I could just see the head of the brute moving from side to side like a threatening bull: the flickering, far-away spurt of gas: nothing more.

I called to my guide in a shrill whisper: 'Are you there? What is it? – what –' I moved a step and caught my foot in a hole in the flooring.

'Mind – mind …' It was the smooth, slurred voice to which I had grown accustomed; almost – as it seemed in my panic – the voice of a friend. 'Be careful – there's …'

I made another step forward, and my foot broke through a rotten plank.

There was a shrill squeak and something heavier than a mouse brushed across my instep: little wonder that I shrieked aloud, wild with fear.

'A rat – only a rat. Mind, or you'll fall.'

A hand drew me aside – just aside, as I thought – while a raucous voice shouted: 'Come in, come in! Oh, damn it all, come in!'

A door banged; there was the snap of a latch, the rattle of a withdrawn key.

Even then I did not realize how I had been trapped, until I flung out both hands, struck the back of one against the hollow-sounding wood.

'And now we shall do nicely – oh yes, nicely,' chuckled the smooth voice.

Whoever it was who had shouted 'Come in!' had dropped to grumbling, cursing hoarsely, in one corner of the room, or so it seemed to me. I don't know why, but at that moment I got the clear impression of a madman, crouching, muttering.

'I must get out! Open the door … I … How dare you! … How …' My own voice broke shrilly. I felt along the surface of the door, found the handle and rattled it furiously.

It is impossible to chronicle my terror. And yet why – why was I so frightened? I was a young, strong woman: there might be the possible loss of my purse and watch before me, but what else?

Maybe my fear was all the wilder in that it was concerned with nothing definite. I did not even think of death. In truth, I did not fear *anything* – 'to fear', that is the verb, carrying a different, and, for me at least, a less dreadful meaning. It was Fear itself which had me in its grip, stark, unreasoning – 'shrill, hair-bristling Fear'.

Foolish enough, eh? But remember the darkness, the absolute and unbroken darkness: those two of whom I knew nothing beyond their voices: the awful stench of the place; the close air like a foul blanket against my face.

Ah, but above all, the darkness. Not a mere absence of light, but something tangible, alive, threatening.

Once again I shrieked, so wildly that I felt the cords of my throat crack.

God – the devil, rather – only knows to what desperate

sounds that house, that district, was accustomed that no one came in answer to my clamour; that my captor made no attempt to stop it.

'Now, now!' The oily voice slid in between that long-drawn cry and the sobs which followed it.

'Supposing you sit down' – a chair was pushed against my legs, and out of sheer weakness I collapsed into it – 'and let us have a little quiet talk together. For wine I love, women I worship.'

What was it made me feel – was it some stir of the frowsty atmosphere? – that he bowed towards me at this? 'But talk – ah, there you have it – talk is the breath of my nostrils.

'As for a subject – What about Eternity, now? – just to begin with: a small matter. How does Eternity strike you? The problematical after-life of the Soul as Plato conceived it, or the far more satisfying, infinite prolongation of the life of the body, the secret of which so many philosophers, physicians, have sought for, and found … Oh yes, without doubt found.

'There are cases chronicled, quite a number, for those who know where to search for such records; and many more, you may take my word for it, many more still unchronicled. If I had a mind to write a book on the subject – to register all I have heard, guessed – once read – of eternal mortal life, unending youth …'

Of course he was mad, and I should have humoured him: two of them – both mad – close to me – how close I could not tell, there in the darkness. Do you realize all this? The only wonder seems that I did not make a third among them. It was evident that this fellow's fellow knew how to take him, for he broke in, laughing loudly; then began to whistle, 'Tiddley-winks the Barber' – of all things!

The whole situation had its ludicrous side, I allow that, *now*. But is not all fear more of less ludicrous, grotesque; bearing no true relation to the thing feared; devoid of personal dignity?

'A light – for God's sake let us have a light – a candle – a match – anything!' I cried.

'Dear, dear, how dependent you people are.' I could place that voice, and I began to move round the room away from it, feeling along the wall with my right hand, the left stretched out in front of me: horribly afraid lest I should find myself up against that Other, whose whistling it was so impossible to locate.

'Two orbs – orbs! As well say oysters! So much slimy matter, tied in a network of nerves: vulnerable to every sort of hurt! – and silly fools banking their entire existence on this sight – light. Calling for "light – light" ... Oh, damn your eyes! And "for God's sake!" you say.... Now, I tell you this: God 'ud take it coolly enough if you never saw again. Here am I in the dark for all eternity, an' you squawking – "Light – light! – a match! – candle!"'

Of course I had known it all the time! It was the blind man! That certainty leapt into the open: no shooting it back.

Picture to yourself a traveller making his way through the jungle at night; telling himself that such and such a rustle was only a large bird, the wind among the leaves: those bright lights two fire-flies: and knowing all the while what it was – 'burning' – 'burning bright' ... It came into my head then. 'Tiger, tiger, burning bright ...'

If I could only reach a window I might throw it up, shriek so that someone must hear.

I stumbled against something which might have been a stool; there was the rattle of a chain, a harsh string of curses.

A hand shot out and drew me aside. 'Come, be careful now. Even we – *nous autres*, in our own dark world – we have our rights – the urbane attention of any guest to any host. But you of the younger generation have done away with that. You of the younger generation' – the smooth voice broke in a snarl – 'you of the younger generation, damn you! – devouring, trampling – "Blind mouths" – who is it speaks of "blind mouths?" Come now!'

I caught myself together at that, thinking to humour him. 'Milton'.

'Then you do know something, have read. Strange how one mistrusts the brains of any woman who wears a rustling silk petticoat. And yet … Ah, well, my choice, my means of selection, was limited. Come now – let's have a look at you.'

I was past protesting as he drew me towards him: those hot, dry hands as strong as steel hooks, as inhuman. For a moment or so I struggled weakly; then stood still, shaken with rigors which ran through and through me at his hateful touch.

What use had a man like that for anything so humane as sight? – eyes to see, love, admire, shed tears of pity?

He drew the pins from my hat and removed it; felt me over, commenting aloud: 'Hair crisp and springy – not fair, though; there is the feel of gloss, that is good. With fair-headed people one is liable to suspect *status lymphaticus* and … Ah, well, who knows? – who knows? – possibly communicable even through the bony tissue.'

He felt round my eyes, the curve of my brow. I retched with nausea as, following the line of my nose, he fingered my lips, ran his hand down my shoulder and bust; summing me up the while, like a cattle-buyer at a fair summing up the merits and demerits of a possible purchase.

He had drawn off my fur coat. You ask me why I allowed it? why – or how – it was I did not struggle in earnest? The truth is I was as helpless as a wild doe with a boa-constrictor sliming it over. There was no question of relative size or weight: twice his size, I believe I should have still been helpless. I am thin and slimly made, and was wearing a thin crêpe blouse. As he ran his dry, gritty fingers down my spine, with its unusually prominent vertebrae – never, never even by the people I love can I bear to be touched there – I felt as though the very soul were being drawn from out of my body.

I did not, could not shriek, even then, but I heard myself give a shrill squeak, like a mouse; upon which the third occupant of the room – or were there more? – 'There might be more,' that thought came to me, 'all silent and all damned' – shouted out hoarsely and solemnly, with a long interval between each word:

'Battle – murder – and sudden death!' Then, with a shriek: 'Damn your eyes, I say! Damn your eyes!'

'Strophe and antistrophe,' tittered the smooth voice at my ear.

I repeated the words to myself dully enough: 'Strophe and antistrophe.' Of course I had heard them, but how? – where?

My brain, like my body, was sick; so deadened that all fear had left me with that small, contemptible cry.

'You do not like to have your spine touched – there – there ...' Once again I felt his fingers upon me, but my long-drawn shudder was purely physical. 'How men have wrangled over the soul, the spirit, the vital spark, the centre of life, reason, of all emotion – love – hate. And yet the Egyptians mastered the secret, the Ethiopians. In the days of Hadrian it had its name: that one small bone which to another – not to its owner, never to its original owner, mind you! – carries the secret of eternal life in life; the only immortality worth a pinch of salt.

'Come now, you shan't say that, mentally at least, I have left you in the dark regarding our venture. *Ours,* mind you – an undertaking of the most supreme issues, the highest possible interest to mankind.

'There are so many people who do not count, who do not matter, who would not be missed – if you will excuse my saying so. Others who need nothing more than time – time – to develop their ideas, something more than the mere apprenticeship of fourscore and ten years. It comes to this: two futile, semi-lives, or one complete super-life. Some small sacrifice for the lesser, I grant you; but then, what has existence ever held for such people? And after all, they are the ones who, lacking courage to make the best of this world, drug themselves with hopes of heaven. Put it to them plainly: you are but helping them on their way, and they must see it. With you, now, it's a pity – ah, yes, I grant you that – a pity you cannot be here to witness the effect of the operation to which you will so largely contribute. But, believe me, I shall not forget you – you will live again, in fame, in actuality – bone of my bone – "Luz"!'

The words were laughable enough; uttered with the deliberate pomposity of the lunatic who floats upon the stream of his own monstrous illusions, egotism. And yet – even now I do not understand why – it was in connection with myself, not with my gaoler or his companion, that I began to have fears of madness.

'I shall go mad. I'm going mad …' That was my thought.

Light! Light! There was the only possible remedy, hope. At that moment it seemed as though in light alone, any light – the light of day, electric light, the merest farthing dip, the spurt of a match – might be found the one panacea for all ills of body and mind; the preservation of that sanity which was being distilled out of me by cold sweats, shaken from me by such tremblings that my very teeth chattered; the balm against that horror, gathering to some dreadful head in the darkness.

'You must let me have a light. I can't – I can't endure this!'

'Tut, tut! so impatient! But it will come; in a better, brighter world, according to your divines, who offer you a letter of credit to some sort of glorified gin-palace, with no close hours …

'"Oh, for the golden gates of heaven!" etc, etc, "The Sun of Righteousness, that setteth nevermore" ... There you have it, eh? Yes, there you have it. As I said, I cannot but regret that you will not be here visibly – shall we say, completely? – to join in my triumph, the triumph of an ancient belief resuscitated by me – by *me*!'

His voice swelled with vanity. I knew that he smote his breast, for by this time I had grown sensitive to the faintest sound, to every stir of the foul air: that mouse-like stench already carried its own personality.

'Still, I daresay you will be better suited – "Leaving to better oneself" – it is an expression confined, I believe, to the servant-class. But the clergy might well adopt it – a pretty heading for a tombstone, eh? Good! Very good!'

He chuckled, tapping my knee with a forefinger like a thin bar of iron.

'Battle! – murder! – and sudden – death!'

The third occupant of the room broke the silence with a piercing shrillness. Odd how he affected me: I think I was more frightened of him than of the other who threatened me – for I knew he threatened, menaced – perhaps because I had not seen so much as a shadow of him; because he held all the dreaded quality of the completely unknown.

'If only – you – would – would – light the gas – a candle – anything – I promise –' I began, slowly, laboriously, trying to think and speak with reason.

'Oh, damn your eyes!' Again it was that other. The tone was fretful, the outburst followed by a low, muttered soliloquy:

'There – you hear that? It is two to one. My companion is against you: both alike, we are creatures of darkness. To master conditions, that is the secret of life. If you had lived long enough ...'

The speaker was moving round me, feeling me over. He had taken off a long scarf which I had worn under my coat, and I fancied I heard him running the silk through his slightly roughened fingers.

'What are you doing? What –' I cried, and, waking from my inertia, made one desperate effort to escape. But I was too late – I had once complained of that scarf being over-long – it went three times round my body now, widened out like a bandage, pressing my arms close to my sides; and even then there was the fringe left for knotting.

'We were talking of Eternity –' The smooth voice was a trifle broken; the creature panted. It seemed as though all his strength must lie in those steel-like muscles, those iron bones, for there had been nothing which could be called a tussle – I was past that. 'Life eternal! Now, I wonder if you ever heard of the belief I mentioned – the fact proved – proved, I tell you! – that there in one of the smaller vertebrae of the human spine which the Romans distinguished by the name of *Luz* – there – just there –'

Somehow or other, more by the pressure of will than by any actual force, I was being propelled across the floor.

'– just there – above, rather than between, the shoulder-blades – nearer to the seat of the intellect than that of the animal passions, though partaking of both – which has the power of conferring immortality upon another who removes it from the still living body! Think of it – only think of it – the infinite sense of time in which to work out one's ideas – crowding, all crowding in upon one, as they do now, with no time for completion – making man one with the gods.'

His voice rose shrilly. '"A life for a life" – this was what was meant. I've proved it – proved it, I tell you!'

He was panting with excitement. I could actually feel it in the air, vibrant, distinct; could have sworn that I heard his heart beat – quick, like a small animal's.

'Your life for mine! But only think what I know, what it'll mean to the world – my life – unhurried, calm, eternal! Here – just here – one little bone!'

Again he touched my spine, and I shuddered from head to foot. My knees were like water under me as I was lowered on to some sort of couch or bed.

I suppose he made certain that I was past all further effort, or else he had half-forgotten me as an individual, as anything apart from a means by which to carry out his own chimerical desires, for he started to move about the room, humming to himself.

I heard him pouring out water – can you imagine how it affected me in that blackness? It was, indeed, as though I were blind, and this stranger seeing, pursuing the ordinary avocations of life.

'Ba-a-a-tle – mur-mur-mur-der,' his companion muttered senilely; then – suddenly, decisively – broke out with: 'Sudden death! Sudden death, I say! Damn your eyes!'

There was an odd little click; a moment's pause, and then it came again.

For what seemed like an eternity my mind fumbled over memories of just such a sound.

Once again, and I had it!

For three years during the war I had been nursing. During the last twelve months my work lay in the operating-theatre, and here the greater part of my time was given to the sterilizing of the instruments, keeping them scrupulously clean.

Well, there you had it – the click-click of the pieces of steel against each other as they were washed, and laid down, side by side.

Panic overcame me, my sense of deadly weakness. I flung my feet to the floor, and made a dash – all on one side, with my arms pinned close – for the place where I imagined the door to be: struck the corner of a table, struck the wall and hurtled round it, frantically beating myself against it, like a bird with clipped wings dashing itself against the bars of its cage; screaming at the top of my voice.

I caught my foot against something which fell with a clatter followed by a hail of shrill curses – 'Damn your eyes – you … you … damn your eyes, I say! Battle – murder – murder … Death!' – stumbled on a few steps, and crashed to the floor, conscious of a sudden sharp agony of pain in my left arm.

That mouse-like frowsty odour was close to me again; there was the sound of that quick, panting breath; then a scent stronger, sicklier than all else.

'Mur-u-u-rder!' repeated a far, far-away voice.

A vision of the operating theatre at B –, the patient strapped upon the table, floated clear and clean-cut before me.

I was overcome by a sharp dread of passing the wrong instrument. 'If …' I began – and that was all.

It was an hour or more later when they found me … *us*. … That was, somehow or other, the most awful part of the whole thing; haunting my dreams, even now.

The fog had lifted a little, and my informant – a stolid constable – and his mate had been going down the alley together when they heard that strange, discordant shriek of 'Murder!' – more words that they could not catch, and again, 'Murder! Murder!'

Even then it had been difficult to find the right room.

'No good asking.' That was what he said. I had sent for him directly I was well enough to see anybody, feeling that I must know everything, *everything*. There was one memory …

'People in places like that there, great old rookeries o' places, will never tell on each other, never let on ter knowing anything that's going on. Everlastingly on the move from one room to another, taking their bits o' sticks with 'em; changing with each other – why, half o' them never sleep in the same room for two nights together – changing with each other, a regular put-up job, so that the police can never drop across the same people in the same place. Nobody knows nothing, nobody's seen nothing, nobody's heard nothing.

'Not as how that was the case with this old chap. Far from it: lived there for years, he had, or so we reckon. An', my word! but the place looked like it, choked up with dirt and rubbish!

'A doctor, too – oh yes, a fully-qualified doctor, turned out o' 'is Union, or whatever they call 'em – for some reason or other. Queer goings-on: that's what they say. Clever enough, too; in the surgical line, they tell me; out o' the ordinary clever. But all that happened years before he went blind. There was an old friend o' his, a doctor up West Kensington way, stood by him as best he could; an' when he got pretty well to the end of everything, he gave him a good suit of clothes and a trifle o' money for answering the door and showing in patients; for, blind as he was, there seemed nothing he couldn't do. But lately there'd been a lot of odds and ends of instruments disappearing out of the surgery, and he was forced to get rid o' him. He made sure as he'd just sold 'em for drink, until … But, well, there you were, miss.'

Yes, there I was.

There was a long, shallow cut – the mere outline of an incision – between my shoulder-blades.

And yet 'more above than between' – just as he had said. Fortunate that the instrument had been clean, clean as I myself could have kept it.

'Them bits o' steel, knives an' such-like, the only things as wasn't thick in filth. I've seen some queer places in my time, but never none ter equal that there.

'Books, too, any amount o' 'em; though it must have been years since he could see ter read 'em. One book as they said must 'a set him on ter do what he was after doing – all about taking a bit o' the bone out o' a person's back, and the one as did it living for ever; a sort of contrariwise ter the Adam and Eve business, seems to me – saving your presence, miss. Ah, well, it was Providence as he was took when he was.'

'What do you mean? Is he –?'

'Didn't you know? I'm sure I'm sorry, miss, but I took it for granted – seein' as how he had fallen right across you –'

So that was it – that memory, the meaning of my nightmare sense of something intolerably heavy – horrible beyond all words – lying across me, pressing me down.

There was another memory – something else … but …

'Heart-failure from over-excitement, or so they said at the inquest.' The policeman was still speaking, as I pieced it all together. 'But Providence, as I said afore … the knife – a queer-shaped sorter thing – still in his hand, an' all.

'Seems as how he'd been trying ter get people ter go home with him before, pretending ter guide 'em. But o' course no 'un 'ud trust themselves ter be guided by a blind man unless it were in a fog like that there; an' then the blind see better than the seein', so ter speak. Well, anyhow, it's over an' done with now. An, if you'll take my advice, miss, you'll not think no more of it than you can help – such-like things ain't wholesome ter get broodin' on.'

He picked up his helmet from the floor and rose to go, eyeing me kindly. 'To my mind you got off easy with that bit o' a scratch an' a broken arm.'

'Oh, that's all right.' … There was still that other memory, something else I wanted to ask him; but I was frightened. My heart beat faster. It was as though, speaking of the thing, putting it into words, would bring the whole horror back again, there in my own brightly-lighted drawing-room.

'But – the other…'

The constable paused, his helmet in his hand: 'Beg pardon, miss? The –?'

'The other…' The stench of the place was in my nostrils, the chill sweat of fear lapped me round. I moistened my lips with my tongue. 'The – the other man?'

He looked puzzled. 'There weren't no other man, leastways there wasn't when we got there. Just you and – and – 'im: and a mangy old parrot, with his stand overturned on the floor, shrieking … well, miss, I've told you how it was we came to find you at all – shrieking for all he was worth – poor brute! He'd had both his eyes put out with a red-hot needle, or something o' that sort, to make him talk better, I suppose – shrieking fit ter deafen yer:

'"Battle – murder – an' sudden death!"'

7 The Landlady (1923)

The word 'ghost' brings to the mind's eye – shrinking even in thought – an apparition of the dead, the dank smell of death. At least that is how I used to take it; though I am sure I do not know why, for after all I believed, as we are all taught to believe, that the spirit – that impalpable essence of a ghost – is stronger than the body; and that being so there is no reason why it should not shake itself free at any time, and fluttering its wings be off on its own business, or pleasure, untrammeled by time or space. Why should there not be ghosts of the living as well as of the dead? Why – come to that – should not the word stand, simply and solely, for the true ego of any one of us?

Still, as I have said, there was that dread of the very word 'ghost' until we took Number Eight, The Paragon, Denis and I.

The Paragon was built in an oval, with a garden and plane trees in the centre of it; an oval of tall, narrow houses; all the rooms apart from the attics and basement panelled in white painted wood.

Some of the houses were detached or semi-detached. But Number Eight was not even this; though in some strange, spiritual way there was never any house more completely detached and aloof, so that I do not believe that it so much as acknowledged the others, unless by the support they gave it; any more than a proud woman of the exclusive Victorian day acknowledged the individuality of the servants who ministered to her wants.

Apart from a small writing-room, which fronted the staircase, the whole of the first floor was occupied by the drawing-room, running the entire depth of the house, with two tall, narrow windows at the front, overlooking the oval; an arch in the middle and a large rounded bay-window at the back.

From this window, above the hawthorns and laburnums, the one giant chestnut in the long narrow back garden, above the steep slope of the red-tiled roofs and chimneys of the lower part of the town, one caught a glimpse of the river, with its forest of masts and funnels, its haze of silvery smoke or mist; and far, far away, the blue hills of Highgate.

We took the house, furnished, through land agents and lawyers, without any real idea to whom it belonged. The drawing-room was done in silk rep of a palish green – neither emerald nor willow, but something between both – and a shiny chintz, white, powdered with tiny black specks and bunches of rose-buds. The writing-table was very small with a sloping top; the other tables, all of rosewood, and unnecessarily large, were like pools of reflected light dotted with islands of morocco-bound books. There were a good many mirrors and a good deal of valuable china, vases and Dresden figures and bowls filled with pot-pourri, the scent of which permeated the whole room and the landing outside.

It sounds like a silly sort of a room, but it had charm as everything which belongs to a past generation does have, at least for me; and during that exceptionally hot summer it was grateful as a woodland bathing pool, overhung with willows.

Denis and I laughed at it and laughed at ourselves for liking it, but like it we did; not only the drawing-room but the whole house; the elegant twirl of the staircase; our immense mahogany bed, the huge wardrobe, the washing-ware – big basin and jug and tiny basin and jug side by side, like mother and child; the scent in the upper rooms, not of pot-pourri but sandal-wood: sandal-wood everywhere, in the drawers and wardrobes – wardrobes like houses.

Still, it was the drawing-room which held me most. Young and newly married, one of a large, cheerful family, I had begun by being almost unendurably restless during the long hours when Denis was away attending to his duties at Woolwich; noisy too, banging doors and swishing about, singing, whistling, too busy to settle down to anything.

But the drawing-room at Number Eight quietened me; so that before a couple of months had passed, the rather boisterous spring merged into a tranquil summer, I moved more sedately. How Denis laughed when I replaced my high-heeled shoes, with their irritating tap over the polished floors, with a pair of child's flat dancing slippers; while for the first time in my life I sat down to sewing – hand sewing, none of that feverish rattle and whirr of a machine, with the good, the tender excuse that the tiniest of all garments call for the softest of seams.

Hour after hour I sat still in that pensive room with the wash of pale, green-tinted air passing through its entire length from window to window – I who had been for ever on the jig, never for one moment alone – choosing by preference what must have been known as the back drawing-room; laying down my work for long intervals at a time, and gazing out of the window over that expanse of which I have already spoken.

At first my mind was curiously blank; then – for the first time in my life, as with the sewing – I began to think; to reflect, to speculate, with no chance of running myself out in words, upon life: suffering; the unreason, the waste: generation after generation like seasons, waxing and waning: the hopes of spring: the fulfilment of summer; the ripening and decay of autumn; and then old age and death, like a shut mouth, grim and undeviatingly silent. Along with all this I pictured my mother's thoughts and feelings before my own birth: my own unborn child grown to maturity and I, myself, with all earthly desires dropping from me like leaves from a tree: Denis and I old, old people, having spent years in the difficult support of life which must inevitably end, for all our pains; a life which could, by no manner of means, prove uninterruptedly happy. Though, after all, what was happiness? For the first time in my life, twenty-two long years, I differentiated between happiness and pleasure, amusements.

The days, wonderful late spring and early summer days, flowed by me like the air. I grew curiously intimate with the portraits on the white wall, water colours and pastels of young women in short-waisted dresses and side curls; young naval officers with immensely high collars; an admiral smiling and scowling: a group of children with a liver-and-white spaniel: a portly divine in a black gown with white bands. I knew them all, I even talked to them – to them, and to *that other*.

Denis caught me at it one day. I felt like a lunatic and said so: 'Everyone's a bit queer at these sort of times,' that was the excuse I made, though he had showed no special surprise; I remembered that later, puzzled over it; for after all, we were not the sort of people who, normally, talked to ourselves.

'You're far too much alone.' Even that was tentative, at half question. 'Why don't you have Stella here?' – Stella was my sister – 'or if you can't stand relations, one of your own friends to stay with you for a bit? Molly Seton, or that Morris girl you used to be such desperate pals with?'

Stella! – Molly Seton, the Morris girl! In that house with – well, with *that*!

'I don't feel as though I were alone,' I answered slowly, thinking not so much of my words as of the queer meaning they had for me.

'You don't seem very sure about it.' Denis eyed me curiously; if I had not been so wrapped up in myself, I might have known that he too was wondering, trying to find out, test something he himself guessed at, the something which I might have in my own mind.

'Dear thing, all I know is that I've never been so happy in all my life.'

'Oh, well, so long as you *are* happy – though it doesn't do to mope; nothing so bad as moping, my mater says; and she ought to know, with eight of us all told.' He was very abrupt and matter-of-fact; a little disappointed too, or so it seemed.

But what could I have said? Even if I had realized what it was he wanted to get at: for it was only just then that things really began to shape themselves, become definite; that I, myself, was able to separate realities from pleasant, half-dreaming fancies.

It fixed itself like this, with odd simplicity and clearness. There was a tall vase of clouded glass standing upon one of the many tables in the drawing-room, and when I arranged it with some tall sprays of delphinium I had known the risk I was taking; for it was ridiculously badly balanced, as all Victorian vases are, fashioned for short-stemmed, dumpy bouquets.

The parlour-maid came into the room with a letter; there was a whisk of air between the two windows and the door, and in a moment the vase was over, with a thin stream of water – luckily the thing held next to nothing – running over the table and in among the books.

I called to Ada, but she had noticed nothing, was already half out of the room – one of those tiresome bustling servants – going about their work in a sort of whirlwind, very starched and clean-looking, and nothing more to them.

I jumped to my feet, but someone else was before me. I heard an exclamation which was like a breath of dismay: I saw – yes, I *saw* it, as plainly as I can see my own hand, now, stretched out in front of me – a small white hand, a wisp of a handkerchief, stemming the stream. There was some effort to raise the vase – I *felt* rather than saw this; but the sigh at the sense of failure was plain enough, following upon that first exclamation of dismay:

'Oh dear, oh dear!'

It was all like that, the keeping in order I mean, the anxiety over the precious trifles in that tenderly cared-for house, a casket of reliquaries. Sometimes, indeed, it seemed almost beyond bounds. 'Fussing?' No, no – Heaven only knows what I would have called it if I had been subjected to it from any of my own people; but here and now, and coming in the fashion it did, I rather liked it. It gave me a sense of being looked after; for that somebody, whom we seemed to have taken over along with the house, was concerned about me too: sometimes of set purpose, or so it seemed; sometimes because it fitted in that way. For ten to one if the sun threatened the rep curtains or chair-covers, it was tiresomely in my eyes also, though I was too indolent to get up and draw the blinds; lazily watching for, *expecting*, the hand on the cord, the faint flash of turquoise and diamonds – and for a long time that was all I saw.

Running down the polished stairs too – did someone really exhort me to be careful, was it in the air, so to speak, or did I just imagine it? Anyhow, there was nothing of irritation in my quick – 'All right, all right!' While there was real pleasure in the thought that someone else was watchful over the new life already so dear to me.

All the same, there was one thing that did really irritate me, and such a little thing, too. A tall candlestick of turned mahogany stood at Denis' side of the bed. Now Denis never reads in bed and I do, so what more natural than that I should transfer it to my side? – or more exasperating than that it should, each night, be moved back to its old place?

I tried it again, and again and again and again, until my irritation melted into amusement, and the thing became a quite good-natured duel between myself and that other. One night I actually heard it being moved, the soft 'tut, tut' to which I had become accustomed, followed by a distinct banging down – something like temper there! – of the candlestick upon the little table at the further side.

Jumping up, I walked round the foot of the bed in the moonlight, recaptured it and put it back in the place I myself had chosen for it.

'If you go on like that we shall have to leave the house,' I said firmly, and there was a gasp of dismay, followed by a soft chuckle – proving a distinct sense of humour, for *It* – oh, but why should I pretend like that? – *She*, bless her heart, knew that I was joking; was as sure as I myself that I could not bear the thought of my child being born elsewhere.

To my surprise, Denis – who I had thought was asleep – broke in with:

'Easy, old girl. Though, by Jove, it really is getting a bit beyond a joke!'

'What?' I almost screamed at him in my surprise.

'Well, the way she goes on. One can't call the place one's own. As for dropping cigarette ashes on the carpet! You should just have seen her face – never again, as I value my life!'

'Seen!' I was amazed, and dreadfully jealous: Denis to steal such a march upon me! 'Seen! Oh no, it's impossible!'

'What! Do you mean to say you haven't seen her?'

'Well, no, not exactly,' I admitted grudgingly, 'her hand, the whisk of a flounce of handkerchief.'

'Well, I've seen her,' his voice was almost unctuous with pride. 'Look here, light that candle, I suppose it's still at your side.'

'I've got my hand on it – firmly.' I struck a light and we both sat up in bed, for this was the sort of thing that was not to be taken lying down. But for Denis – Denis who, for all that he was such a darling, I had taken as being, in the nicest sort of man-way, a trifle insensitive – to have seen her, actually seen her, was almost beyond bearing.

'But not really – a sort of shadow – not like a real person,' I protested stupidly.

'My dear, she wears a cameo brooch and frocks which touch the ground all the way round – buttoned up to her throat; rows of buttons; and sometimes a fold of lace round her neck, and a what do you call it? – a sort of chest protector of lace stuff.'

'A plastron?'

'I don't know what the devil the thing is, but I've seen old ladies wearing them in real life. Not that she's not real enough! Grey hair puffed out over her ears and a little pink-and-white face, all crumpled up like the petal of a poppy-bud; her mouth drawn together – a tight bud that, but awfully sweet. A good deal bothered with us, the liberties we take with the house, and yet amused, at times; liking us on the whole – sort of tender and wistful. That night when you refused to come up to bed because you were in some sort of a paddy with me – remember that, eh, silly kid! – and I picked you up and carried you upstairs, she drew aside on the landing with a rustle of silk – queer sort of silks she wears, colours running into each other all the time, so you can't tell t'other from which –'

'Shot silk?'

'– Maybe, I'm hanged if I know – anyhow, she drew back to let us pass, flattened out against the wall, and laughed – a charming laugh, so soft and really amused; sort of way as though she liked us to be there and young and in love – eh, old thing? – though we do make hay of her house.'

'Her house – Den, does that mean that you think …?'

We were slipping into that careless married fashion of not finishing our sentences, taking the understanding for granted.

'Well, that's what I do think, that it belongs to her.'

'Belonged, you mean, centuries, oh centuries ago!' I don't know why, but the thought of anyone not seen being near, really near – in point of time, more than anything else – gave me the creeps. 'Ghosts don't come – well, all at once.'

'Don't you believe it, my dear.'

'Well, I shall know when I've seen her. The cheek of it! to let you see her and not me, when I think of the liberties she takes; straightening the things on my dressing-table and all – and *they* do belong to me. Why, she won't even let me leave my rings about loose, hangs them all up on the little china tree thing.'

'She must have taken tremendous care of everything. Look at those polished tables; by Jove, there's not a stain on any single one of them – the Lord only knows what would have happened if I put down a lighted cigarette, or anything like that.'

'The wonder is that the people who came after didn't mess up the things.'

'You bet your life there weren't any, we're the first and only tenants – that's why she feels it so.'

'Oh, Den, but that's impossible.' I was obstinate upon that point.

'How do you mean?'

'Well, ghosts don't come like that – at once.'

'She's not a ghost, I tell you, at least not in the ordinary way. I ought to know, I've seen her.'

That piqued me: 'If she's a ghost, she's dead – dead as a doornail, all ghosts are, so don't be silly,' I said, and turning round on my side I loosed my hold on the candlestick and blew out the candle.

It was in the same place when I awoke next morning, and for some reason or other this made me feel ashamed, in disgrace, left to my own miserable, haphazard ways.

The whole of that day I heard and felt nothing of her, not so much as a breath. 'I've hurt her,' I thought, 'perhaps she'll go away and I will never see her after all.'

I made my confession the first thing when Denis appeared home that night, contrite and abashed; feeling very small, curled up on his knee in the half light before dinner.

'I knew she was really alive, knew it the whole time; only I was jealous – just frightfully jealous, Den – I didn't know it was in me.'

'Jealous! Of a ghost?'

'Idiot! Of you seeing her and not me. But what do you think – really think?'

'Well, they say that there are – it sounds utter bunkum, but still there you have it – and I won't believe for a single moment that she's really dead – emanations or manifestations, or something of that sort. Supposing anyone was everlastingly longing to be back in some place they loved most frightfully – longing and longing, thinking of nothing else; you know when you long for anything like that the way you feel as though something were emptied out of you – it does seem that they might sort of slough themselves clear of the restrictions of space; yearn their spirits out of their bodies – actual bodies – dragging the appearance of it with them. If she, the little lady, had never lived anywhere else, loved this house in the way we love each other, she might – it seems feasible enough – almost *must* come back to it.'

'*She* – you speak as though you know who she was.'

'Why, the owner, of course.' He looked surprised, and no wonder; though it seemed strange to realize that Denis, whom I had thought of as much less subtle than myself, should have jumped at once to what I now realized as the only possible conclusion.

'Our landlady – oh, Den, but it makes us feel awful outsiders, frightfully in the way! Are you sure, though – was it a woman we got the house from?'

'I can't be certain. Don't you remember we just took it through the agent? – but of course it must be. Anyhow, we'll go and see him and find out to-morrow.'

All that evening I went softly, shy and ill at ease, a little resentful; once in bed, however, that queer feeling of half-amused tenderness came back to me. I had planted the disputed candlestick down, almost aggressively, on my own side of the bed, but I now leant across Denis and put it back in its old place. After all, she had been used to have it there, sleeping all alone in that great bed: and where was the sense of letting her worry her soul further out of her poor little body, frail enough already in all conscience as Denis saw it?

We went and saw the house-agent next day, finding him as florid and bland as most of his breed are: a forced geniality masking the most complete indifference to damp and drains, along with life and death in general; that same species of geniality as is achieved by the really competent trained nurse.

It seemed that he could not tell us anything more than we already knew of the owner of the house: a lady – that was all he was sure of, and everything arranged through the lawyers.

We left things as they were for close upon a month after this, and then I began to get really fussed, and so did Denis. By this time we both saw her equally clearly, and it could but strike us that she was somehow or other failing, the heart going out of her. She no longer kept us in such order: that familiar 'tut, tut' gave place to a sigh. I believed that she lay upon the sofa, one of those inconveniently curved and ridiculously small contraptions of Victorian days, for at times I found the cushion dented: my cushions, too, the originals being worked in Berlin wool and beads – there was one of Rebecca at the well, all beads, and only imagine the impress of that against one's cheek! Anyhow, it comforts me now to feel that she did like my cushions, immense and downy; though the very fact of their not being shaken up after use was enough to show you how she was changing! Why, in the beginning – no, even towards the middle part of our acquaintance, she never missed tucking in the loose chintz covers after Denis or his friends had been lounging on the chairs or sofa: more *pretending* to be horrified than anything else, I think, because there is no doubt about it she liked them, laughed at their jokes if they weren't too – oh, well, you know, too modern; the sort of things we do joke about in mixed company nowadays.

Oh yes, there was no doubt about it that she was failing, wearied and played out to indifference: failing and fading, her dear little face growing pinched and pale, her frock rubbed and worn; her plastron – why on earth couldn't they have called them plasters and have done with it? – flattened out and depressed looking.

Then one day she came and stood by the drawing-room fire – for by this time the days were getting chilly, the summer nearly at an end – with one hand on the mantelshelf staring down into the blaze, with just such an air of dwindled faintness as those pale water-colours; so wistful that my heart bled for her.

'Oh, do, do, *do* tell me what it is,' I cried; but she only shook her head, straightened a couple of little Dresden figures on the shelf and moved away with a sigh.

It was not until she was gone that I realized what was wrong with her hands – the rings, turquoise and diamond, all gone, nothing but a fine gold keeper left; while the low-heeled, slim slipper on the foot turned sideways upon the twirly steel fender was rubbed and worn at the side, almost in holes.

'Something's got to be done,' I said to Denis when he came home that evening. 'She's got so frightfully thin, and what do you think – her rings are gone; just slipping off, I suppose, poor dear!'

'There may be another reason.'

'What do you mean?'

'Well, hard up, and all that, you know.'

'Denis!'

For a moment or so we gazed at each other in dismay.

'I believe you're right,' I said at last. 'Always the same dress, and getting very shabby. Oh – but *very* shabby; her shoes too. Fretting her soul out of her body, if she's really alive …' I paused; even then I could not really grasp it. 'And poor as poor. Well, if she is alive – and she won't be for long if she goes on like this – she'll have to come back here. We'll go and see that lawyer man to-morrow, eh, Denny?'

'You can't move house at this juncture, young woman, let me tell you that.'

'Well, I don't see why we should move; the place is big enough in all conscience.'

'Peggy!' I can never forget his look of amazement. 'You! You who wouldn't have anyone, not even one of your own people, here!'

'Well, she *is* my own people! After all, one has spiritual countries of one's own, places which are native to one from the first moment one sees them. And why not spiritual relations, who are far more real relations than the brothers and sisters and children of the man your mother happened to marry; or the woman your father married, either? They only pleased themselves, never really thought of us, or the sort of people that we might like to belong to us. But I've lived in the same house with *her* for six months, and know her and her dear little soft pernickety ways; and I'm sure she'll be a good influence for Thing-um-y-jig – particularly if it's going to be a girl,' I added ungrammatically: 'Thing-um-y-jig' being the temporary name with which we had endowed the impending offspring; anything to make out, even to each other, that we did not care, that there was no sort of sentiment about either of us.

'Well, the Lord knows I'll be only too glad for you to have someone with you, and it will be some sort of a help to her, too, if it's really come to that – pawning her rings and that sort of thing, you know.'

'Oh, Denis, it's too piteous, and here we are making ourselves at home in her house all the time.'

'But look here, old thing, after all there is the rent!' It was the first time we had either of us so much as thought of it. 'She can't actually starve on five guineas a week, you know.'

'Perhaps there are debts. That perfectly horrid-looking man in the portrait over the mantelpiece in the dining-room, with the leer and the underlip, and the *too* fine eyes, for instance – Her father? What do you think?'

'Brother more likely; she's old enough. Blown everything, the devil, and left her to clear up the mess. Anyhow, we'll hunt out the lawyers to-morrow; and it's time for bed now. Come along, old thing.'

We turned out the lamps and left the room; at the door I turned and tweaked Denis' sleeve. The dying fire had flared up in a spurt of flame, and there she was; her arm resting along the mantelshelf, her head drooping upon it – too dispirited even to draw back her skirt from the heat of the fire, and that alone would have shown you if you had known as much of her as I did.

She looked up and gazed around her. For the moment Denis and I were wiped completely out of the picture; I realized that, while the gaze of those pale, wonderfully candid blue eyes was so yearning, so intense and tender that there was no mistaking what it was – a sort of good-bye, a drawing to herself once more, and maybe for the last time, everything that she loved best.

We went up to London next day – for it is only the post-office people who count us as already in it. At first I thought that the lawyer – who looked, as they say of wine, as though he had been 'laid down' for a very long time, his shoulders showing a pure bottle-like slope, his face cobwebby with fine wrinkles – established, or rather binned into, a set of frowsty chambers in Bedford Row, would tell us nothing; but Denis, who can charm a bird off a bough when he likes, gained his point with some very mellifluous lying, something about feeling that we really weren't paying so much for the house as it was worth, and we got her name, Miss Julia Champneys – Julia! Could it have been anything else? Julia, the soft syllables of it! – and the address of a boarding-house in Bloomsbury – such a boarding-house, too!

The maid who answered the door, with an apology for a cap at the back of her head, a general air of having been dragged backward through a gorse-bush, and that insolence which always goes with a certain type of imbecility, said she did not know if Miss Champneys would see us.

'She's here in her room, sick; I ain't sure as she'll see anyone,' that's what she said, scratching the instep of one foot with the heel of the other; though after some time, helped by the passing of a coin, we prevailed upon her to show us up into the drawing-room and go and find out.

Drawing-room! – drawing-room! *This* after the exquisite order and restfulness of Number Eight! What could the bedrooms be like in a house with public reception-rooms such as this? – A mausoleum, with crumbs in the crack of every chair, the dust of ages over the tables, and more woollen-ball-fringed antimacassars than I had ever seen in all my life before; small wonder that our landlady's soul had, at times, longed itself clean out of her body.

After a while the unspeakable maid came to tell us that she would be there 'in a brace of shakes', and then after another considerable pause – I had an idea that she had to travel downwards from the very top storey, some horrible, chilly, sloping-roofed place, for she was blue with cold and trembling with exhaustion – Miss Champneys herself appeared; desperately anxious, her wide blue eyes scared, her mouth tight with small perpendicular lines, braced up against disaster; for it was clear enough that our presence had put the fear of God into her – Denis' expression, not mine – that she made sure we'd come with some complaint about the house, some idea of wriggling out of our agreement, for her very first words were:

'If there's anything I can do to meet you in any way, if there's anything not quite right –' She broke off, staring; timid and bewildered as she well might be. Denis and I had been holding hands like two children when she came into the room, I myself frankly clinging; for – Oh, well, after all, it is not the sort of thing that happens every day, meeting the reality of an appearance, I mean, and she was so *like*, so precisely and amazingly like – stupid of us to be more scared by that than by anything else; but there it was, though after all it was not only our gaucherie which took her aback. There was more to it than this – amazement on her side, too; a slow dawning, unwilling realization, a painful acknowledgment of something which, at first sight, seemed impossible, upsetting every sort of calculation.

'Oh! – but I didn't realize – I couldn't have believed that – the maid said Mr and Mrs Maudesley, and of course I knew that was the name of the tenants, but – but not you – oh, not you!' She wrung her hands together in despair, those thin little hands, as though confronted with some idea which she could not get round: 'I made a mistake, confused you with – Oh, I don't know – I don't *know* – it's beyond me, that's what it is – beyond me. Why, all this time –' She shook her head trembling from head to foot, her face white and piteous, the tears running down her cheeks. 'You – you who I thought –' Her gaze was all for Denis. – 'Oh, of course, of course, at Number Eight – but I didn't realize – that's it, I didn't realize –'

I was on my knees at one side of her, Denis in a low chair at the other; we both held a thin white hand, patting it – I had the one with the thin gold keeper. The whole affair was so completely incredible that it was impossible for anything to seem more out of the way – outrageous, than it was. I even took out my own handkerchief and dried her eyes, pressed one hand to my cheek and kissed it; murmuring over her:

'Don't worry, dear, it's all right – indeed it's all right!'

'I thought – I thought –' She turned from one to the other, her confusion far greater than ours; for, after all, she was true to – what do they call it? – oh, sample – too wonderfully, wonderfully true; every fold of her dress, the rubbed sides of her satin slippers, showing how she sat with her tiny feet crossed – the dear ghost of Number Eight. But she herself was only too evidently disappointed, taken aback, and that hurt me; for we really are – oh well, quite nice.

'What did you think – what could you think? Of course we knew you, you are part of the house – the house we love. But Denis and I? Why – oh, but you don't like us!' I was shocked to the soul.

'I do – I do! I always liked you, loved you. Only I didn't know – oh, I didn't know,' she cried desperately, glancing from one to the other. 'I went back to the house – you know I went back to the house?'

We nodded.

'I couldn't keep away. It seemed dreadful, poking and prying like that, with the place let and all, but believe me, I couldn't keep away. Then when I saw you there – I am getting old and stupid, things confuse me – I forgot about the tenants; it was shocking of me, but I forgot – I quite forgot – I thought you were –'

'Yes – yes?' we bent nearer; I had one arm round her, fragile as a fledgling bird. 'Only just met her,' you say? Why, hadn't I lived with her for weeks and weeks and weeks, at a time when I was thinking and feeling more than I had ever done in all my life before? And anyhow, what does the length of time since you have first actually met a person matter, one way or another?

'Yes, yes,' I prompted her, 'you thought …?'

'I don't know – I don't really know what I thought.' She shook her head helplessly. 'But – my dear – I wasn't always old – people were kind enough to say I was a pretty girl once – and it seemed to me that you were myself, as I used to be, and that you, sir' – she turned and faced Denis bravely, her crumpled cheeks pink, her eyes like sapphires, 'you – you, who are young enough to have been my son – were the gentleman whom I was once going to marry, and who was killed just before our wedding day. It sounds very silly, as everything of that sort does sound silly from old people, though I'm sure I don't know why – and maybe you'll think I am queer in my head – perhaps I am – sometimes I am afraid of that, but there it is – I quite forgot – it was dreadful of me, but I quite forgot about the tenants. You did not seem like real people, you know, just tenants; and it seemed that, perhaps, having given up the house and gone away, which was a very great wrench to me – for I had never lived anywhere else – that – I don't know I'm sure, I don't know – but it seemed that I was to be given a sort of dream life as a compensation; one feels so dreadfully young inside, that's the worst of it all – so young and full of hope. Don't you see – oh, don't you see?' She spoke almost fiercely, beating her two small, ringless hands up and down upon her knee. 'I didn't know what was true – I didn't *want* to know.'

'But lately, dear Miss Champneys,' I said, 'lately you've not been so happy?'

She shook her head, gazing in front of her with so faraway an air that I believe, could I but have opened the door of the drawing-room at Number Eight, at that very moment, I would have found her there. 'It has seemed to be slipping away – everything, everything, but the house. And even that seems difficult to reach – a long way off. I'm not very strong, I sometimes think – my heart, you know, so stupid – that the time will come when I may never see it again. Last night, for instance ...'

She hesitated for so long that Denis prompted her: 'Last night?' with a glance across at me.

'Last night I thought I was saying good-bye to it for ever, and then nothing mattered: nothing! Not even he – the gentleman I spoke of, and who I was stupid enough to take for you, Mr Maudesley – nothing and nobody, only – only the house and the things in it. It is part of me, you see,' she went on eagerly. 'It really is a peculiarly lovely house, and it's part of me, in the same sort of way' – she flushed, turning her head a little aside, her eyes strained and wistful and very bright – 'as I have always felt that married people must be part of each other. It seems as if I can never, never leave it, however much I want to, however much I know I ought to, so long as there is any life left in me.'

'But you mustn't leave it, you mustn't live away from it; that's really what we came about. You belong to each other,' said Denis; then, hesitating a moment, ventured on a joke which sent my heart up into my mouth; but she took it well: 'Why, it really isn't moral for two people like you and that house to live apart.'

'But there are reasons' – she drew herself a little more upright, smiling, yet a trifle chilled, on her guard, as that generation is when it is driven to speak of pecuniary affairs – 'private expenses and obligations which make it impossible. That is unless you don't care for it, you are tired of it,' a piteous blend of hope and anxiety chased themselves across the small, delicately-featured face.

'It isn't that, but we want you to come and stay with us. There isn't any heart in the house without you.'

She flushed scarlet: 'It's sweet and dear of you; but I couldn't – I really couldn't! Why, I hardly –'

'If you're going to say you hardly know us, I can't stand it!' I broke in, rising to my feet and standing before her, with an odd sense of being half child and half judge, looking my very worst, I know, awkward and frightfully determined. 'Look here, I'm supposed to be going to have a baby, and I know something will go wrong if you're not there at Number Eight. Anyhow, I won't have it at all in that case – so there!' I added, perfectly ridiculously.

'She's too much alone, it would be awfully kind of you,' put in Denis.

'Oh, if it's that – if I can really be of any use –' The little old lady rose from her chair, clinging to both our hands, trembling from head to foot. 'Oh, my dears, if you only knew what it will mean – like going to heaven – like other people's heaven!'

She said it again when we parted from her on the landing, for she would not let us take her upstairs back to her own room: 'It will be like going to heaven.'

I went downstairs with Denis, and then ran up again halfway – I dared not venture on more – and listening, heard her move very slowly up that intolerable flight of stairs; with a long pause between every two or three steps, a still longer one at each landing.

The tousled maid came brushing past me with a bucket, and I pressed a ten-shilling note into her hand:

'Don't let her come down again to-day; and see to her, help her pack – my husband's coming to fetch her away to-morrow.'

I believe that she did her best; anyhow, she took her tea up to her own room – and one knows what that means in such places, the utmost concession – it came out later, because:

'She was all right when I took her tea up to her,' that's what she said, crying – actually crying. 'A bit excited and trembly like, that's all!'

I could not settle to anything that evening, neither could Denis; though we were oddly scared of putting our fears into words even to each other.

She had never come into the dining-room – I fancy that she must have shirked that portrait – but anyhow, he left the door open for her, jumped on the parlour-maid when she shut it, naturally enough, for it was a chilly evening, colder in the house than out of doors, or so it seemed.

Upstairs in the drawing-room, we each took a book; but I doubt if we either of us read a word. It was late when we got up to go to bed, and Denis was, oddly enough, making up the fire afresh, when he blurted it out – what I knew to be in both our minds:

'I wish to goodness we'd brought her back with us!' – for there was no sign or sound of her; while it seemed as though every room in the house had drawn itself close together, holding its breath, waiting for something which might be the end of a race.

By some odd chance the housemaid must have put the twisted candlestick at my side of the bed when she did the room; though I did not discover it until about two o'clock in the morning, when I could lie still no longer and stretched out my hand for the matches.

I thought I might have found her in the drawing-room. No, that's wrong, I did not think, I hoped despairingly, for I *knew* – all the time I knew; I had heaped up the fire again, was crouched before it, determinedly waiting, when Denis came down and carried me up to bed in his arms, with no single word of rebuke, or – bless him for his understanding – false optimism.

For of course he knew, and I knew, and the house knew, that there was nothing really to wait for, that the life and soul – yes, yes, despite our own youth, and many friends, and the little Julia who came later – the real life and soul of the house had gone out of it.

Why did she say that, 'Like going to heaven'? Oh, well, I'm sure she would not like heaven, the real heaven; I was bitterly, resentfully sure of that. To take her there, just then, when we were going to make her so happy. She would only peak and pine, I knew she would, was certain of it; so certain that for months and months I thought that God would set her free, that she would come back to us – and Number Eight.

8 Four Wallpapers (1924)

The house looks down upon one from a semi-circular terrace of half a dozen broad steps, running round three sides of a small paved courtyard. The terrace lies across the front only; to enter either of the side wings you must mount the wooden steps to the verandah at the end of each, or else walk through the rooms themselves At the open side of the courtyard is a low wall set with blue flower-pots, overflowing with flowers; and a carved wooden gate painted bright green, let into an arch which is smothered with creepers – deep blue morning glory, and an orange flower like a large honeysuckle, purple bougainvillea and the cool blue-grey of plumbago. Beyond all this is another courtyard, sanded over; with one weeping willow, a high cream-tinted wall and wrought iron gate, flanked with great bushes of crimson poinsettias.

The house is white, with brightly-painted apple-green doors and outside shutters; over the front door is a marble plaque, deeply carved with the arms of an old and very distinguished Irish family, and set in a wide black frame. The sill of the window above this is carved with drooping bunches of fruit; the window itself surmounted by a green wooden panel with 'Quien mal no hace, en mal no piensa' – 'He who does no evil will think none' – written upon it in white letters.

It is called in Spanish 'Quinta de Esperanza' – The House of Fair Hope.

At one side of the house is an orange grove; at the other a red-tiled pergola roofed with vines; flower-beds, fountains and a wide green lawn; while backing it all are the mountains, forever changing from deepest indigo to shot green and blue and rose madder; toppd by the Peak, aloof with its snows and its clouds.

In the front, running straight away from the iron gate, is a wide avenue of cypress trees ending in a deep cliff, the almost unchanging blue of the sea beneath it.

It is impossible to give any idea of the beauty of the place in fine weather; the velvety blackness of the cypresses, the orange and crimson and purple and rose and white of the flowers, the deep blue of the sea and sky, the glow and more – the deep tenderness, the radiance – of it all, like a young and loved woman smiling over some secret joy – the soul of the place.

It was like this when the Erskines first saw it; one solitary hoopoe in sole possession of the freshly watered lawn, or so Eva Erskine said.

They had taken it upon the recommendation of Joan Malcolm, who had been in the island the year before.

'If only *I* had the money!' that was the burden of her plaint; for she could but confess that it would cost a very great deal to make the house itself really habitable.

'All the same, my word, wouldn't it pay for it!' I can hear her say it, and she meant it too, in a way inexplicable to herself, for she is the most unimaginative person in the world. I myself had not seen it then; afterwards – oh, well, I suppose one does not go on one's knees to a house and a garden, it is simply not done – but that's what I felt like.

The Erskines took fire at Joan's description: they had money enough for anything, for they were a short-lived family and one fortune after another kept rolling in to young Tom; though he, himself, would have been content with a great deal less and the lung which went back on him during the last year of the war. But there you are, he might have had neither and no chance whatever of wintering out of England.

All the same, this is not Tom Erskine's story. It is not a story at all in the proper sense of the word; nothing more than the recital of one of those impressions which suggest a realm, a series of hitherto unsuspected possibilities. In people? No, no, of course not, one has always known that, there's no getting to the end of people – in inanimate things, I mean; their power to seize, retain, release at will.

There is one large room and a hall with the staircase leading out of it in the centre of the house; two rooms in either side wing, and two at the top – in the centre alone, for the wings are but one storey high with sloping roofs of goffered red tiles, stained with time.

The two top rooms, with those in the left wing, had been used as bedrooms: the other three were reception rooms; the centre room being by far the largest, with windows at either side and one at the end.

The window in the front of this room was wide and recessed, lined with window seats; the one at the back flat with the wall, opening on to a narrow balcony and green-painted outside staircase which led to the roof; while the end window had a small hanging balcony to itself.

The Erskines – who had taken the house without seeing it, on a ridiculously short lease – had sent over a steady stream of money to a friend of Joan's, an old resident, who had undertaken to have it put in order for them; taking it for granted that, as money can do everything, everything would be done.

Arriving in the island the day before, they had even gone so far as to debate – with no conception of the ways of Spanish workmen, their eternal 'Mañana, mañana' – 'To-morrow, to-morrow' – as to whether it was worth while to go to a hotel at all.

Next morning, even, riding over from the hotel directly after breakfast, they took the house very much for granted; for of course the garden caught them up, as it does – enwrapping, enchanting; and when they tore themselves away from that there was cliff and the sea.

It was coming back between the dark cypress trees, with the sharp blue enamel of the sea behind them, that the first sense of something not altogether right came with the sight of Rees, Eva's English maid, beckoning from the steps in a manifest 'state', as she herself called it; infecting Tom, who was seedy and weak enough for any sort of despair at the first fatigue or set back.

For in the house itself, nothing was done, really done – done to be finished with.

'It won't not be ready for a month; an' not up to much then, so far as I can see.' That is what Rees said, turning in at the door before them, moving from room to room with a triumphant air of 'I told you so!' rejoicing over calamity as her breed do. 'Why, there's nothing done! – Nothing as I calls anything, if you'll excuse me for saying so, marm.'

Eva snapped the woman back into her place, with a sharp glance at her husband. All the same, she was sick with disappointment; for how she had counted on it all, how frightfully she had counted on it! And now, or so it seemed, her maid was right – odiously right, as she had no business to be – and it was hopeless, quite hopeless.

She pulled herself together with what sailors call a 'round turn' – for she was like that – counted out the first impression of general messiness, painters' rubbish, ladders, buckets, and caught the charm of the interior; held to it with the realization that there was really much more done, the house far more habitable, than they had at first supposed.

For one thing the outside of the house was already painted, the woodwork repaired, the bedrooms colour-washed; and though the electric lighting showed no more than tags of loose wire in the sitting-rooms, while the packing-cases, containing all that superfluity of household stuff which Britishers regard as necessary to their comfort, stood about still unpacked, and the scant Spanish furniture was thick with dust, it was still all there; with the makings of something quite out of the ordinary.

'It's really all right, Tom; it will be delightful when it's done. – Light? Oh, well, we've brought lamps, we never really cared for electric light. And only look at that view from the window! It makes up for everything.' Mrs Erskine slipped her hand into Tom's arm, speaking with valiant cheerfulness: 'Let's sit down on the window seat for a jiffy and take stock of things. Rees, if you sniff again I'll take you to the end of the garden and throw you over the cliff. The bedrooms only want scrubbing out, then they're done; and once we get everything cleaned and that old stuff – awfully fine in its way, look here, Tom, I do believe it's real Chippendale – nicely polished, we won't know the place.'

She paused, scanned the faces of the other two with her bright, bird-like glance; and then, deciding that the only thing for it was to get them moving, she packed off Rees down to the town in charge of the gardener's boy to buy lamp-oil and cleaning materials; prevailed upon the gardener's wife to hunt up some soap and a scrubbing-brush, and start scrubbing out the bedrooms; and got the two men who had come over with their mules to help her husband and herself with the packing-cases in what she intended for the drawing-room.

'If we make a couple of bedrooms habitable and get the kitchen clean, we can spend the day in that divine garden and keep an eye on the workmen. Rees? Oh, we'll leave her at the hotel until we get settled. I'll cook for you, my dear, but I'm hanged if I'll cook for Rees!' She was determinably gay about it all; one of those small, courageous, Jenny-wren sort of women, with brown eyes and smooth, shining, brown head; fresh faced, and very English in her short, well-tailored skit and white silk shirt – you know the sort? Not altogether rare, but no less precious for all that.

'We'll be awfully happy here,' she just touched her husband's hand as he piled her arms full of linen, determined and tender; for he must take it in the right way, or it would be all of no use whatever. 'You'll be as right as rain in no time whatever, and you'll owe everything to this queer old house, I feel it in my bones.'

'I can't stand those wallpapers,' said Erskine. He knew it sounded childish, but he could not help himself. 'I simply refuse to live with them.'

'You won't have to live with them, you old ass!' retorted his wife cheerfully. 'They'll all be off in a couple of days, anyhow, and meanwhile who could want to stay indoors, with a garden like that! Only to think that we can come straight out of our rooms the first thing in the morning, go up that twiddley little outside staircase to the roof and have our coffee there in the blazing sunshine; with all this in front of us,' she added, with a large wave of her hand towards the sea, the mountains and garden.

But Tom only shivered with a little sniff of discontent, and she glanced at him anxiously. He was in general almost too bright and plucky, and this was awful. What a fool she was not to have come over by herself, to let him overdo himself on the very first day in this fashion!

'Look here, my dear, the best thing you can do is to go back to the hotel for lunch, and rest all the afternoon. I'll stay here and get things a bit in order now the boxes are undone. You won't know the place when you see it to-morrow, take my word for it.'

'What about your lunch?' Erskine's protest was weak, for he was done to the world, with no more than one idea in his head: to get back to the hotel, lie down in a cool shaded room, and never move again.

'Oh, I've got biscuits and there are oranges, I'll be all right.

I daresay the female here can get me some coffee, they can all make coffee.'

'What about Rees?'

'Oh, Rees will have to go too. If she once gets "that sinking feeling" she's worth nothing.'

'I feel a beast leaving you.'

'Tommy-rot! You know there's nothing I really like better than charing – that's the state of life I ought to have been born in.'

She watched him go off on his mule, waving to him from the gate; conscious, with that awful tightening of her heart-strings, of the way in which he stooped, his increasing thinness. Then she turned back to the house and strolled through the lower rooms, pondering over those wallpapers to which her husband had taken so sudden and strange a dislike.

Why, she liked them, actually liked them! Funny old things as they were, there was something which touched her, appealed to her; some feeling of the life which they had once surrounded, the tastes they had gratified. 'There were people who liked us once,' they seemed to say.

And, after all, when one came to look at them, there was no pattern – no set pattern. They were really more like pictures than wallpapers: all worked out the same in shades of grey and black and white and divided into panels; a different scheme for each room.

In one there were streets and houses and quays, crowded with figures in oriental dress and heaped with merchandise; with ships lying close against the side, or sailing away with billowing sails into the distance.

In another were the interiors of houses, wide pillared halls, and window bays and curved alcoves, with people seated in them: in another gardens and terraces, with children playing on the steps; pergolas, fountains and pleached arbours, where lovers sat holding each other's hands, gazing at each other with the undiminished ardour of immortality.

It would have seemed wicked to strip them off, were it not that they were stained and splotched with time; and in a place like this where people came because they were ill – ugh – Tom was right, and they were far better away.

Eva Erskine gave a little shiver as she turned aside, then shook herself in an odd way she had. It would be fatal if she once began to let things get upon her nerves. Rees was invaluable when Tom was really at his worst, but on the ordinary level of a never altogether normal life the whole burden lay upon her own shoulders.

What was it Rees had once said; the complaint which had grown a classic among them all? She forced her wavering and disturbed mind back to it – the exact, ridiculous words:

'I drops down on a chair, and comes all over like.' Mrs Erskine laughed over it for the hundredth time, quite naturally, for any sort of a joke was, and still is, like a tonic to her.

She was still laughing when Rees herself came back, complaining of a headache; and, having packed her off back to the hotel, to look after the master, she set to work with the added help of a couple of Spaniards whom she had found squatting in the furthest sitting-room, with nothing better to do than watch the workmen languidly starting to strip the paper off the walls of what she intended for Tom's own special sanctum, secure from visitors.

They did wonders between them, flicked on by Eva's laughter and scolding, her ridiculous Spanish. By four o'clock the kitchen was speckless and the upper rooms so really presentable that she hunted out her work-box and sat down on the front steps to sew the rings on to their bedroom curtains.

'In case anyone sees us dressing from the North Pole,' she

thought; with a whimsical delight in the picture of that immense waste of water stretching away from the edge of what she already called 'our cliffs'.

The gardener's wife brought her some coffee, then disappeared; and the men drifted away, feeling that they had done enough for one day; while the boy in charge of her mule alone remained, squatting outside the gates at the end of the long drive which ran along the edge of the garden, and so to the high road, perfectly contented to wait for so long as she would pay him for waiting.

Evening came with a glow of pink, like a half transparent veil, spread over the garden and sea, stretching into grey shadows on the mountain. The silence was so intense that she could hear the waves on the shingle far away at the foot of the cliffs. By degrees the pale grey trunks of the trees seemed to detach themselves from the flat masses of foliage. The cypresses ceased to count, they were too well covered, formless; but the one dragon tree just outside the gate of the courtyard troubled her by its look of age and hard indifference – a tree like a rhinoceros. She had been told that each upright stem with its stiff bouquet of spiked leaves meant a year, and counted to three hundred, then gave it up as the light failed her.

Three hundred! Why, that was nothing, a mere stripling. They had been talking of these trees at dinner the night before, and someone had said there was one further up the mountain which was over two thousand years of age.

Two thousand years, and here was she fretting the soul out of her body over the life of one man – two thousand years! And to think of all who had gone out in that time!

Close against the dragon tree was a datura, with its great, white, trumpet-shaped flowers drenching the air in perfume.

Quite suddenly the colour was wiped out from everything. The birds ceased to sing, while the shrill note of one ciggara pierced her ears; as persistent and unbroken as though it might go on and on and on for ever, defying time like the dragon tree.

She ought to start back to the hotel; Tom would be getting anxious and there was nothing for her to do here. She knew that; but all the same, as she rose from the steps, a trifle chilled and cramped, she moved into the hall and so on to the main sitting-room, instead of towards the gate.

'Anyhow, I must shut up, put my work indoors.' It seemed as though she were excusing herself to herself.

She found matches, lit one of the candles which she had put ready in its candlestick – with the idea of hastening their homecoming by having it all ready to light them to bed – and walked round with it in her hand. A flap of wallpaper was loose at the edge of one window-frame, and pulling it idly aside she found another underneath it; something dark and heavy, with a conventional pattern of green and gold, so far as she could see. Scraping at this with her fingernail, wondering how many papers there were plastered over the top of each other, how long it would take to strip, she reached the next, a geometrical design in violent primary colours; then what must have once been a white paper, and after this – thank goodness! – the plain plastered wall.

She put her candle on a table and, moving to a seat in the large front window, sat down to wait. To wait for what? It was impossible to say, but there it was: the feeling of waiting, as though for a curtain to go up – the oddest feeling, she said; so distinct that there was no idea of combating, let alone ignoring, it.

A host of perfumes – so heavy as to seem almost unpleasantly material – were crowding up from the garden on the still warm air: trumpet flowers, heliotrope, stephanotis, white jasmine.

'I never remember disliking the smell of flowers before; but there was altogether too much of it, and the wrong sort,' that is what she told me.

The window at the end of the room was shut, the table almost against it, well out of the draught from the other two windows and the door; though there was really not so much as a breath of air.

Quite suddenly Eva's eye was caught by the flame of the candle, blown violently all one way; just as though someone had whisked past it. And yet nothing seemed to move. There was indeed no living thing visible in the room; apart from one large white moth, clinging motionless with folded wings to the frame of the window where she sat.

For all that there was something – no, more than that, *someone*; more still – it seemed as though her mind took it in by degrees. Why! the room was full of people passing and re-passing the candle; wafting past it with elaborately puffed draperies, floating sashes.

She told me how odd it was to see it – the flame, I mean – blown this way and that, yet still burning on; the one tangible source of light, though the whole room grew full of it: the sense of that candle as something sturdy and material, holding its own.

The diffused light came first; then the sound of footsteps: the impression of figures, furniture – a green topped card-table with three men and a woman seated at it.

The woman, who seemed somewhere near a well-preserved forty, with a hard, bitterly smiling mouth, and quick, malicious eyes, wore a wine-coloured dress cut square in the front and thickly draped round the hips, a sort of polonaise, that's what Eva called it – with a ruche-edged train wandering round the leg of her chair, and innumerable bracelets and lockets.

The men's evening dress was almost modern, but not quite; less shapely and well cut than it is now. The two elder men, and they were all three young, wore long side-whiskers; the third was clean-shaved with a wide, long-lipped, discontented mouth.

It all sounds very dowdy, but they were not that, Eva was firm upon this point. They were not dowdy because they were the smart people of their time, while she herself seemed to be in it, part of it.

'If I had caught my own reflection in a glass, I should have expected to be dressed in the same sort of way,' she said.

Other people passed and repassed, bent over the card-players. One caught the impression of them in an oddly unequal way, or so Eva declared. Sometimes one made sure of the grey wallpaper shining through them; again it seemed to be cutting them off – or was it *drawing them back*?

It did not seem that one figure was, in itself, more distinct than another; rather that each was more distinct in one position, or light. At one moment she made sure of them all as real solid human beings: the next they were very evidently nothing of the kind. Eva seemed puzzled how to explain it to me: said that it was *the wallpaper* that did it: absorbed them or threw them out, as it were. Her brow was knitted as she told me of it, trying to get it clear to me, to herself.

The card-players laid down their cards; it seemed that they had come to the end of their game. A tall girl in a low-cut black dress, quite off her shoulders, with a rose-coloured carnation in her hair, unmistakably Spanish – but they were all that, apart from the clean-shaven man, who had brilliantly blue eyes allied to very smooth black hair, a fair, clear skin – came up laughing, and made a pretence of snatching at the money which lay in little heaps at either corner of the table.

The players caught up their winnings, the men laughing indulgently. – 'No, the woman didn't laugh – the sort of woman who hates youth, you know,' said Eva – upon which the girl pounced on the cards with one hand; and raised the branching silver candlestick in the other, spoke quickly and vivaciously, glancing from one to another, tossing her head.

The strangest thing about the whole affair was, as Eva said, the fact that she could hear certain sounds, footsteps, music, the rustle of draperies, while the voices were entirely lost. And yet she seemed to know perfectly well what was said.

I suggested lip-reading, but she was positive that there was nothing of that sort about it. 'I just *knew*,' she declared, adding ridiculously: 'I believe if my eyes had been shut I should have seen them, in the same way that I *knew* what they said, heard without hearing: with all my nerves.'

The table was folded to one third its size and pushed back against the wall; and three or four other young girls gathered round the first, holding aloft the tall branching candlestick.

She called for music, and after a moment there were the clear notes of a fiddle, so strange among these soundless speakers. It seemed, indeed, as though they were alive – intensely alive whenever one got a really clear view of them, and yet not *all* alive; live people with dead voices, that's what Eva said.

Men came up to the little group of girls, and one by one they were detached until the first, the girl in the black frock, stood alone.

She turned and put her tall candlestick down on the narrowed card-table, moving as though she were in a dream; watching the clean-shaven man who was standing alone, leaning against the wall with bent eyes and folded arms.

He was solid enough there, wallpaper or no wallpaper; nothing affected him. He was feeling too intensely – *felt* himself into solidity, was what Eva said.

The flames of the branching candlestick were blown from this side to that – there was nothing more puzzling about the whole affair than the difference between her candle and these, the sort of light they gave – and the girl in black blew them out; one by one, glancing sideways at the young man.

The dancers passed and repassed. They were quite different.

'How different?'

'Oh, well…' Eva hesitated, then tried to explain it by saying that the others, the girl and the young man, and, a moment later, the lady in the wine-coloured dress who had gone out of the window at the back – the window which led on to the balcony with the little staircase – were growing every moment more real, wiping out the others, the ones who did not really count, were moved by less intense emotion; while the dancers, young men, and girls with their pale tinted dresses – innumerable layers of tarleton and tulle, like brilliant, many-petalled flowers – counted for no more than so many transparent, sunlit clouds, floating over a solid mountain side.

'In the places where the paper was torn they vanished; or else became broken and dim – like the reflections you see in a pool, so bent by ripples that you can't make sure of them. Apart from that they got mixed.'

'How mixed?' she repeated my question. 'Well, it's difficult to explain. But it seemed as though, in a queer, horrid sort of way the people in the other papers beneath the grey one were trying to get free too, fight their way through them. Oh, yes, it was all the papers, I was certain of that.'

The woman in the wine-coloured dress came back into the room; touched the young man's arm, and spoke to him. She said: 'They seem very happy up there and, of course, so long as you don't mind' – Eva was certain of this – what she said, I mean, declared that she was like a live wire with malice; while the expression of the man to whom she spoke quickened from dejection to anger; and there were tears in the eyes of the girl in the black dress, who turned aside with a little toss of her head and drifted out of the picture.

'I suppose she did not really belong – count. It's awful to think how little love really matters, the love of one person, I mean; for I'm sure she loved him.' That's what Eva said. 'And she was frightfully unhappy. Of course she was unhappy, I realized this from the first moment I saw her; she was too gay, that's what it came to. Anyhow, she dropped out. I suppose the picture was set for something; and she just wasn't in it for all her love. It was queer how I felt her sharper pain through the general sense of uneasiness; for they weren't really happy, any of them. It seemed as if there was something going on that they were trying to ignore, pretend they knew nothing of; all excepting the lady in the wine-coloured dress – she wore long, dangling, gold earrings, I remember, realizing them so plainly that I actually wished for them – she alone had only one desire in life, to press it home – whatever it was, so long as it hurt.'

The young man stared at her a moment, his head raised, his mouth scornful. Then he flung round to the window, drawing back at the sound of steps on the wooden stairway.

'Oh, yes, I could hear *them*,' said Eva, 'a man's and a woman's: though the woman had no heels to her satin slippers.'

It seemed as though the whole picture was now concentrated upon the new comers: the woman in white satin entering the open window, the man at her heels and the first man.

She was fair, with that rather opaque fairness of those Spaniards who have in their veins the blood of the original islanders, and very beautiful; her hair, of that colour the French term *ceindre*, piled high upon her head, apart from one long curl which fell over her bare shoulder.

She gave the man with the blue eyes a single glance, too slighting for contempt – it was as though she saw him and yet did not see him, in the way one does with servants – and inclined herself to her companion, who put one arm round her waist; while, stooping a little, turning sideways with inimitable grace, she gathered up her train in readiness for the dance.

Eva was certain that something dreadful was about to

happen; that the husband – oh, yes, that's what it was, the eternal triangle – would strike her – 'I never saw such insolence, the sort of woman who ought to be turned up and spanked,' said Eva – or else fall upon her partner and kill him.

I asked 'How?' – and she said that she had not thought of that, but there was always a way, and he was much the heavier built, stronger man of the two; and anyhow, there seemed no other reason for such a scene without it.

I questioned her as to what she meant, and she answered: 'For the perpetuation of it all'; and that was what was in her mind even then; which shows that her thoughts were still clear and cool.

'People are ghosts because of things like that – murder, sudden death – at least, that's how I have always taken it,' she said. 'And goodness knows, there was hate enough in all conscience between them, the two of them, anyhow; that worst sort of hate, as between people who have been lovers, husband and wife. The second man was a very fine type of Spaniard, handsome and virile with – oh, well, you know the look they have in their eyes where a woman is concerned. He didn't care, he was master. But the other –! How he could stand it, that's what beat me! I felt all screwed up with the sort of intensity which is like a tight hand on one's heart. You know the feeling, when one's waiting for a gun to go off, if one's at all the jumpy sort.

'He ought to have done something – he ought – he ought! There was enough following after – No, what am I saying? – really going before, for this is the sort of story that's bound to begin at the end – to excuse, even warrant him. It was all too horribly plain, the awful feelings, the suspicion – no, more, *certainty* – of evil; the lust, cruelty, scorn, the will to kill – all soaked into that room. But action seemed to have petered out. I suppose that's why the sense of misery hung about in that fashion, permeating the whole atmosphere. Anyhow, he did nothing, just turned aside with a moan; and that was the first, the only human sound I heard throughout the entire scene. It went out at that.'

Eva herself seems to have been quite cool about it; almost as though it were the end of a play – women are wonderful like that, one never knows what they'll take with an irritating coolness – for she bolted the window, blew out the light, and moving through the hall locked the front door behind her; found her mule boy, by this time asleep, and rode back to the hotel.

I asked her if she had been frightened, and she said 'No' – only quite furious with that poor thing of a man who had lacked the strength to assert himself, uphold his own honour: 'Though if I had known all that he must have known about the place, I might have felt different,' she acknowledged this.

Anyhow, it is certain that she was not frightened, for she said nothing whatever to Tom, and they established themselves in the house the very next day.

'We didn't use the sitting-room but lived in the garden, or on the roof,' that's what she said. 'I didn't mean to have Tom upset; but the bedrooms were quite all right. It was queer what a difference the colour wash – or was it the stripping of the walls? – made to the rooms: all the difference. It was queer, too, the dislike Tom had at once felt for the big room with the grey paper; though it was the paper, not the room. To prove it – well, I defy anyone to say that there's anything wrong with, uncanny about, the room now.'

She did not need the tribute of my agreement or approbation, but for all that I gave it. It was perfectly impossible to imagine any room more completely charming and restful.

'That's it, you see. They'd soaked it all in, layering the impress of one misery close down above the other with their – I can't help it – *infernal papers*; given it no chance to get free. In this first scene – which was really the last, the scene of the topmost paper, you know – they were all just as miserably infected though they were hardly related to anyone who came before. Oh, you can catch things apart from physical diseases, there's no doubt about that. Supposing I'd plastered another paper on the top of all those others, what on earth would have happened to Tom and me?'

I said I really didn't know, and she answered that she did, no mistake about it either. It had started even then, during those few days they took to strip the walls.

She had gone back to the house early next morning, and worked hard all day. 'It was really beginning to look quite homelike and charming,' she said, 'impossible to believe that I had been in the depths over it only twenty-four hours earlier. "How about what happened the evening before?" Oh, that didn't upset me, I don't know why, but it didn't. It was all rather like a bad voyage, you know, a thing one has to get to the end of somehow or other – but with an end, a real end, in sight. I never seemed to have thought that it might go on for ever, beat us; that the house was really irrevocably tainted.'

The workmen had got the walls of the other two sitting-rooms pretty well clean that day and the grey paper stripped from the big room. Here and there the next one, the green, had gone with it; but only in a very few places, and they were plainly puzzled over this, accustomed to have them all come off in a bulk; get down to the plain wall at once.

Tom drove over with Rees and the baggage just in time for tea, which they had in the garden; then, as the evening began to get chilly, he went upstairs, and ate his dinner in bed: a good deal depressed and taking very little notice of anything.

Soon after nine Eva lit a candle and went down to the big room. She said she had a feeling as though she need only just take her seat and wait for the curtain to go up; was as sure as that of the first act, alone, having been played out with the grey paper, I mean.

When she opened the door, however, she saw, to her surprise, that there was an old man sitting in a chair sideways to the window which leads out on to the back balcony, and apologised for having kept him waiting, taking it for granted that he was a neighbour.

'Someone ought to have told me you were here,' she said, 'but we're still in such a state of confusion – only really moving in to-day, you know, and no proper servants or anything. I do hope you haven't been here for long.' She was very profuse, she said, and ran on and on because – oh, well, there *was* something queer about it.

For her visitor did not turn his head or look at her; continued gazing steadily, and with infinite melancholy, out of the window, towards the deep blue sky, the shadowy depth of the trees.

She spoke again, but still he took no notice; and as she placed her candle on the table, sat down on the window seat, she thought to herself: 'He must be as deaf as a post.' Then: 'What in the world will he make of *Them*, when *They* come?'

You see she was quite certain that she was not to spend the evening alone. All the same, it was not until she had been sitting for some time with this silent figure, dropping out an occasional unanswered sentence from sheer nervousness, that she realized that here was all that there was to be of *Them*, for that one evening at least.

The dark paper absorbed the light, so that it was difficult to see anything very plainly. All the same, as she grew more used to it she realized the stranger was a very, very old man. – Oh, quite ninety, frail and yellowed by time, in an old-fashioned, high-collar coat; his hands like ivory spillikins laid out upon either arm of the straight-backed chair.

'I have never felt more hopelessly miserable in my life,' she declared. 'There were dreadful things to come – dreadful things already passed, well, from his point of view, for you must – you just *must* – keep on remembering that it was all working backwards in so far as I was concerned; but nothing could touch the sense of despair diffused by that lonely figure. For looking and feeling lonely, and just *being* alone, are quite amazingly different, aren't they?

'I got up at last, for I simply could not bear it; and leaving the house walked down to the cliff and sat on a stone bench just outside the garden wall for a good half-hour. When I got back I meant to go straight up to bed, but I couldn't – just couldn't – leave him like that. As I opened the drawing-room door, however, I saw that he was gone, and I must say I was relieved; for that was in some ways the worst of all the evenings. I wonder if you can catch it, realize it: the desperate and diffused despair of a fellow-creature, who ought to have been really dead, which hung about that room throughout the entire evening? The worst of them all, I think, for – oh, yes, of course there was more to come: the geometrical pattern and the white paper, I realized this, from the very beginning.'

I asked her how she had stood it, and she seemed honestly puzzled by the question: 'I? Oh, but don't you see *I* was getting to the end of it all the time? It was *Them* I was concerned about, thinking of. Of course I could have kept away until the men had finished their work, and yet – Well, I did feel that it was somehow or other up to me to pay them the last respects possible, rather like attending a funeral, you know.'

I enquired here, rather stupidly – trying to make a sort of joke of it, lighten the atmosphere – if she imagined that the people of the grey wallpaper had held the field all those years, forty or more, since it was first hung, while the others remained quiescent, packed away beneath it.

The moment the words were out of my mouth, however, I was ashamed; for a curiously baulked, scared look came into Eva Erskine's face; completely changing her, showing that the whole thing had bitten more deeply than I imagined.

'I don't know what to think – I just don't know. I've thought and thought, but it's all beyond me!' she exclaimed rather wildly; and was silent for so long that I was half afraid I was going to lose the rest of it.

As it was, she jerked back almost violently to her old self; a little too matter-of-fact, though.

'The next paper was awful, you know – you can't imagine how awful: blue and scarlet and gold on a pale French grey ground; octagonals, triangles, circles and all sorts of meaningless interlacings, running off into sharp unrelated angles. After all, it was not a pattern at all, nothing more than a kaleidoscope gone mad. He must have put it up as a relief, the furthest possible thing from the pure white paper that had come before.'

I think I looked puzzled at this, for she repeated again: 'You simply must remember that it was all backwards, as I saw it!' and went on before I had time to grasp anything.

She was in the drawing-room rather earlier that night, for she was anxious to see the thing from the beginning, and – 'Oh, well, it did not seem very polite to be late,' she said, with her odd simplicity.

'Come now, after all, you didn't invite them?'

'No, but all the same it was their house. People can't help dying, you know. – Or, worse still, not dying, like that poor old man of the night before. I had been reproaching myself about that all day – my rudeness, my lack of patience.

'However, he was there again that evening: not when I went into the room, but later on. I'm sure it was him, though he looked pretty well fifty years younger, not more than forty. Only think of it, fifty years of loneliness and regret – nothing for a dragon tree, but for a man! – Oh, too awful! I saw him once more next night, the fourth night, in his first youth. You want to know about the people of the grey paper – the last of all? Oh, yes, I've found out about them too. This old man was the last of his line, and left the house to distant cousins of his wife's, as a sort of make up, I suppose. For what? Oh, we get down to that later: anyhow, there was no one of his own left to him after his daughter, his only child, put an end to herself, threw herself over the cliff.

'Oh, yes, that was true enough, I verified that, though of course I saw nothing of it, only what led up to it!

'The daughter and her lover were upon the roof that evening, the evening of the geometrically patterned paper, years and years before the scene of the green paper, remember. I heard them come down the little outside stairway, but they must have remained on the balcony for a moment or two, or else in front of the window which gave nothing back.

'Then the girl moved sideways into the room, with her lover just behind her, his hand on her waist, and stopped by that old papier maché settee.'

Eva Erskine indicated it with a gesture; for it is there now, back in its old place, a little sideways to the right of the window, rescued from one of the tool-houses, repaired and re-varnished, by Eva herself: black painted wood, decorated with bunches of flowers in bright colours and inlays of mother-of-pearl, the whole powdered with gold, the back and seat of finely-woven canework.

'They were both standing, though he had one knee on the settee,' she went on. 'I seem to see them the more plainly because they were the only people there, concentrated, as it were, clear against that awful paper. He was urging her to run away with him, but she would not.' Eva was quite clear about this.

'It seemed that her father had some very special dislike to him, reason against him, as suitor or husband. All the same, the girl seemed absolutely convinced that she could win him round. She was just the sort who *would* be so pathetically sure of anything she really wished to believe: the sort to whom life comes most hardly; while I don't for a moment think that she, that either of them, knew of any very definite reason against their marriage. It remained for him to tell them that – the father, you know. It was the year eighteen-thirty, the date of that dreadful paper, and there were old people alive when we first came here, whose parents had told them something of what had happened. For the rest of the story – oh, well, when I worked back over it, again and again, it was wonderful how clear it all grew!

'They were desperately in love, and little wonder either, for a handsomer couple it would have been difficult to imagine: the girl had an oval face, very pale, with deep red lips and dark eyes full of spirit. Her finely marked black eyebrows, her chin and nostrils, the way in which she held her head on her long slender neck, all showed character; temper too, but nothing mean or petty.

'She was wearing a full, straight white gown, drawn up by a girdle under the breast, and with a narrow white tucker run with velvet holding it in place; while her hair was dressed high, in smooth loops, with short falling curls over either cheek.

'She had assured her lover that everything would come right; though, anyhow, she would not run away with him, she was too proud for that, as she was too proud to live when she realized it all – the dreadful inevitability of some sort of misfortunes, I mean. They were in each other's arms, saying good-bye, when she seemed to hear someone coming along the garden path, beneath the pergola, and ran to the little end balcony to see who it was, whisking past the candle, driving the flame all sideways with the wind of her going.

'I think her lover might have beaten his retreat down the verandah at the back, had she allowed him, when she came back and told him who it was. Anyhow, he was less confident than herself; perhaps he knew something, not all, of course, but *something*.

'She would not let him go, however; put her arm through his and stood boldly by his side, facing the door; a little pale, but for all that erect and gallant – you don't often hear that word used of a woman, yet there it was, gallant.

'And he? Oh, yes, on the whole he was glad enough to face it out, too,' that's what Eva said; 'for after all, he was a fine fellow – they were both dears.'

For a minute or two she could not see who came into the room – for the paper was unevenly stripped, leaving blanks in the scene – but it was evident that they were defending themselves, explaining, pleading.

'The girl moved forward a step or so in front of her companions. At first she was really half smiling, as sure of herself as all that – and it was this that made it the more heart-breaking, the change in her face, you know; that look of youth up against the dreadful, the disgraceful, things of life for the very first time, anyhow in connection with itself – things that there's no getting over or round. I tell you it was dreadful to see it: the more than half-amused pretence of awe; the hardening, the defiance, and then that impression of blank amazement and despair – the ageing and stiffening of that young, confident face.

'The father moved forward into the picture as he told them – Told them what? Oh, of course, you could not know: that her lover was a near relation, some people here said the son – and I think it must have been that, for it seems to explain everything, the feeling of there being nothing left to fight for, no sort of chance – of the man who had betrayed her mother; the real cause of her death, the manner of which must have cast such an awful shadow of regret over her father's whole life. For, by then, I saw him too; his still young face lined and grey with the misery, not of a day, but of years: so accumulated, so bitten in by the time he reached that period of the green wall – for you must still remember that we are moving backwards – that the thing which had happened when the white paper was on the wall was the thing which was killing them now.

'The girl dropped her lover's hand, which she had still held in her own when she moved forward. She did not approach her father – and I can't tell you the effect of finished misery which they gave me, standing there like that; all three hopelessly detached.

'The father spoke again, and what he said only made it worse. It was beyond all anger, anyhow. For don't you see there may have been some actual relationship? He knew that his wife had been unfaithful, and he *could* not be sure that she was, in truth, his own daughter; never had been, though he loved her. And only think of having to put this to any girl! What? Oh, don't you see, are you too stupid to realize that they might have been half-brother and sister – for that's what it came to? Now you've got it, eh? Need he have told her? Well, yes, I think so – I was sure of it then, for it was plain that she was not the sort of young woman to be put off by any merely sentimental reasons, the differences of an older generation. But this hit home. Well, I know how I felt, the merest looker-on, as though it were all beyond belief, an exaggeration of coincidence: "It can't be true, it can't!" sort of thing. Even now, in thinking it over, the memory of her face hurts me so that I feel I must find some solution, some way out of it all – the face, mind you, of a woman, even then, many years dead.'

Anyhow, it was one of those things which left nothing more to talk about; no amount of talking could have done anything, and picking up his hat, which lay on the cane-backed settee, the young man bowed and turned away. He was wearing spurs; Eva said that she could hear them click as he moved down the stone steps.

For a moment or two the father and daughter stood gazing at each other; then he put out one hand towards her, but she did not seem to see it and with a deep sigh he turned aside and dropped into a chair at the opposite side of the window: sat with one elbow resting on the arm, his head bowed forward upon his hand – the same chair in which Eva had already seen him, the old, old man of the green wallpaper. 'I must put it like that; I can't say "the evening before", for the evening before was years and years afterwards.'

It was impossible to see the girl's face because she was standing more than half sideways, staring out of the window. After a minute or two – ages, it seemed – she stepped forward into the balcony and vanished; came back again and moved towards the door. She did not even glance at her father, and there was something in her expression, though it showed little more than the profile, which frightened Eva so that she called out, 'Oh, stop, stop!' and ran after her into the hall.

Of course there was nothing there, or in the long cypress walk; though she gathered up her skirt and ran, as she had never run in her life before, while there was moonlight enough to have seen anyone in a white dress cutting the shadows of those sentinel-like trees.

There was no one on the edge of the cliff either; though as she stood there, panting from her run, she was conscious of something apart from her own fear and depression, an atmosphere of loss and despair beyond all words.

'If one could be Irish enough to speak of a vacuum filled with horror, that's what it was,' she said, and ridiculous as the words sound, I know what she meant.

✕

On the fourth day she did not go near the large room until evening. It was hot and oppressive, as the weather so often is in the islands, the mountain wrapped round, almost swathed in dark clouds; the sort of day when, in England, one would have felt sure of a thunderstorm.

There, however, nothing happened, though the clouds spread out like a mantle; pressing closer every hour, until the weight of air, the stifling heat, became almost unendurable; something menacing and definite, something to struggle against like chloroform.

Tom Erskine, overcome by a sense of deadly fatigue, had lain in a long chair on the roof throughout the entire day, while his wife had been continually up and down stairs seeing to his comfort and trying to keep him amused.

He had been very silent, and this silence weighed on her like the weather, adding to her sense of numbed depression and bewilderment; as though she had been, or so she put it, knocked silly, hit on the head.

Though Tom had hardly spoken, and this in itself was so unlike him, or, more properly – she was forced to this – unlike what he had been before they came to the house; his eyes had followed her with a sort of queer suspicion and resentment; half savage and yet infinitely pathetic.

'If things are going on like this, if he's going to get like that towards me, I can't stand it,' she thought passionately, and then once more caught herself up. If Tom was different, she was different too. 'I can't stand it!' What on earth was coming over her to say a thing like that? Can't stand it! – there was nothing people couldn't stand if they made up their mind to it. 'I'm going dotty,' she said to herself; and then: 'He must be getting better; all convalescents are more or less difficult.'

Towards evening he had hit out at her in an astounding way, from the blue, as it were: or, rather, from the blackness of his brooding silence. 'You might have the decency to try and not look so damnably bored – that holy martyr's business! Of course I am an infernal nuisance. I know that well enough. But after all, it will pretty soon be over and you'll be able to shake a loose leg' – 'to shake a loose leg! – this from Tom with his delightful courtesy, and to her! – 'marry your precious Bobby Harland – "funeral baked meats" and "wedding feast" sort of thing: fresh husband, fresh trousseau, fresh everything. Though you might remember it's not been all beer and skittles for me. Hang it all, one's dead a long time, and death's a pretty mouldy sort of thing, anyhow!'

That cut her, though if she had not been so completely over strained she would have laughed. To marry Bobby Harland! – Bobby, to whom she had been so nice because she was determined that no one should ever say that she did not like her husband's old friends, tried to keep them apart; more especially nice because this one really did bore her, poor, well-meaning, uproarious Bobby!

Erskine did not speak again until he pushed aside the little table which had held his dinner, dragged himself upright with a bitter refusal of his wife's arm, and went off to bed; remarking that it wasn't very festive for either of them, but it would soon be over – for her, anyhow.

After that she had gone down the cypress drive and sat on a stone bench at the top of the cliff for close upon an hour. 'I won't go into that beastly room to-night,' she had thought, repeating the words to herself again and again as she weakened; then, after all, she jumped up and hurried off, almost running.

She was trembling as she mounted the steps, lit the candle put ready on the table in the hall, and stood hesitating after all her haste: that almost panic-stricken fear of not being in time for an assignation to which she was forced, the neglect of which would spell some inexplicable, yet no less fatal, loss. For there it was: without the least being able to understand it realized that this evening would bring something very terrible, something which, for all that, must be seen out to the end – any sort of end – clearing the air like that long delayed thunderstorm; something without which everything else was, and would for ever remain, meaningless.

She wiped the perspiration from her forehead, for the heat was almost unbearable if one moved at all quickly, far worse than it had been throughout the entire day, and picking up the candle moved towards the drawing-room door; then hesitated again, with her hand on the handle.

Her heart felt small and quick-beating, like that of a mouse; she was conscious, with self-contempt, of the fact that her knees touched each other, damp and chilly.

'I must be going to pieces,' she thought, and pulled herself together with an exasperated shake; for this was getting beyond everything, would end in doddering idiocy – to lack courage either to go into the room or keep away from it.

With a sharp click she turned the handle and entered.

The workmen had been astonishingly industrious, for them – or was it merely that the last two papers had been less adhesive? – for the whole room was stripped, apart from a large patch to one side of the window at the back of it, running up two-thirds of the height of the wall and spreading some twelve feet wide; showing an entirely white paper, raised in a design of a seemingly different texture like a brocade, with a pattern of baskets of flowers and long streamers of broad riband.

She walked round the room, touching the bare walls with her fingers, conscious of a sense of relief and coolness. It was as though the place was emptier than it had ever before been; a crowd of people gone out of it, leaving more room to breathe, a greater plentitude of air, in spite of the heavy atmosphere outside.

When she reached that part of the wall where the paper still remained she drew back; placed the candle on the table and sat down facing it, trembling from head to foot, with a distinct feeling as though someone had put out a burning hand and laid it upon her face, pressing her back. And it was not only this: something else came out from that white paper with its innocent pattern – and here, even more distinctly than ever, she was sure of it being the paper, thanked God to see it so near its end – something hot and indescribably dreadful: an atmosphere not altogether foul but weighted with the accumulated heat of gross passions, desires and hatred: distinct as the hot air from an open oven door.

As the papers were in the process of being unevenly stripped from the wall, the absorbed emotions – out of which the whole thing seemed to have resolved itself – had shifted, here and there, with a gradually narrowing stage, an increased concentration; as though it were all leading up to something definitely fixed.

She had felt that before, but there had been nothing like this. Now, before a single actor appeared upon the scene, it seemed to Eva Erskine as though, in place of mere seeing and feeling, her whole being were being spun out towards the wall in front of her, with the waving candlelight playing across it, as though she herself were being torn out of herself with a sense of the sharpest agony: all there was to her – body, soul, mind, sight, hearing – drawn to a sort of cone, with the apex focused, depending for life itself upon that one patch of wall. Her body, indeed, seeming to count for something less permanent than a wet glove on a cold and trembling hand.

Once again someone moved forward from the little balcony and the flame of the candle swayed outward as it caught the waft of a light sleeve, sash or pannier.

Another moment and a woman's form appeared against the

narrow strip of paper: so distinct, so almost *more* real than life, as Eva said, that it seemed like some sort of essence, concentrated by the narrow circle of visibility: poising there with an air of hard bright triumph, as though to say, 'Here I am!' The oldest of all four impressions and yet the youngest, in the hardness, the cocksureness of it all; the brutally selfish and triumphant youth: a tall, slender woman, with her auburn hair piled high in light curls, crossed by a blue riband, a low bodice, a long skirt, and looped panniers of peach colour and white. Later than a Romney, but rather like that.

Transparent? What, hadn't I caught that yet; in a sort of way it was all transparent! Eva had spoken of it as solidifying; but wasn't a glass at once solid and transparent? And yet this was far more than that – one could not actually see *through* it; besides, there was the colour. All the same, one must not underrate the transparency; for it was far more transparent than all that had gone before. Eva tried to make it clear, and I think I caught it, visualised it. The whole thing was, in fact, so much the *more* real because of the transparency: impressing her with a feeling that here, indeed, was the very essence of individuality. Too much of it, in fact; for it seemed as though something personal and sacred was being almost indecently thrust upon her.

You know the sort of thing, the idea of catching people out of their skins, souls and all – what they have of them – feeling oneself mean and abashed.

Anyhow, it was all there plain enough, the appearance of life, I mean – raised head, sparkling eyes, the quick rise and fall of the breast beneath the light, floating gauze scarf: the whole woman more alive than life; dreadfully alive against the white paper.

She was all on edge with impatience. Oh, yes, she had darted forward because she heard someone coming, a lover too. Eva was certain of this, no woman ever looked like that for any other reason; and yet she had set her own limit, was held back by pride, would not allow herself to be actually caught moving one step towards him.

'The sort of woman to keep a lover.'

'Yes, yes, and had kept him too, if the child, who came later, the girl of the geometrical paper, was, indeed, theirs.'

Her lips were parted: a very short upper, and full under lip, smooth carnation red. She panted a little, seemed to glow. Yes, that was it; and they had glowed before, changed colour, these people of the wallpapers.

It was no use my saying that a changing colour presupposes, rather assures one of, a beating heart, a normal circulation; for there it was, it had happened before, or so Eva Erskine assured me.

Her feet moved; she did not tap on the ground as people are popularly supposed to do in moments of excitement, but rose upon her toes and dropped, rose and dropped again, like a dancer tantalised by the sound of music.

It was at this moment that Eva caught the sound of a man's footsteps upon the flags outside, crossing the inner court, hurrying up the steps.

The woman raised her shoulders a little, stretched out her hands and caught them back upon her breast with a smile: it came to Eva then, the same noticeably short upper lip, poise of the head, not the same person, but the likeness between mother and child – the girl of the geometrical paper; though here was something crueller, harder, more 'having', a sense of power, an intense pride, a toss of the head, which seemed to say: 'What need to draw him to me?' though Eva caught the quick breath, almost shudder, of intense excitement, an excitement as palpable as a shimmer of heat on a hot day, charged with electricity.

She could hear the newcomer cross the hall, enter the drawing-room; caught the change in the sound of the footsteps from marble to polished boards as he moved forward a step or two, then paused and stood there, 'devouring her with his eyes, smiling', that's what Eva said. It was all so clear, even without the light in her face, that no one could help feeling it. 'The very expression of her face painted his clear for me: no woman could look like that for a lover who was not at least physically splendid. Anyhow, it was all there – in the air, as it were: this immense confidence and pride in one another; the complete and passionate selfishness of two people who care for no one on earth apart from themselves; brutal in their denial of every other claim.

'I think he must have tantalised her, teased her pride, just standing there, smiling at her, drawing her with his eyes; for after a moment or two she gave a queer, muffled little cry, like an animal, and raised both arms, ready for her lover's neck – ready for anything he should ask: no reservation about it, either!' Eva was certain of this; as, all along, she had realized that there was something wrong, illicit in the whole thing; something bestial in the woman, for all her delicacy.

The two were almost touching each other: there was a man's hand in the picture, so to speak – that circumscribed patch of white paper – a dark cuff and lace ruffles as he reached forward towards her, when another footstep sounded upon the small outer staircase leading to the roof and a third person ran down it, two steps at a time; moving lightly as though, whoever it was, wished not to be heard, and was yet in too great haste to take any real pains about it.

'I knew there was someone listening, all the time I knew,' that was what Eva said; and remember that Eva Erskine is one of the last people one could think of as being led away by her imagination. 'There was that there too, hanging in the air on that side of the room – the sense of an almost unbearable weight of suspicion, suspense, of – oh, well, of everything that is horrible.'

The hand was drawn back: there was nothing left in the picture excepting the woman. Remember that, she alone with those other two reacting upon her, as plainly as though they were all in it; the second man at the further side of his wife. Oh, yes, Eva knew that too, though she did not know how she knew it. – Anyhow, there was a clear sight of the woman, with all the colour drained out of her; more upright than ever, her head turned a little backwards over one shoulder, quivering from head to foot; and the *sensation* of the other two: nothing further needed in the way of plainness.

From what Eva said I see them like this, in a waved diagonal line; the two men a little more backward, very little, but enough to make sure that anything which happened between them would naturally happen behind her – anything moving in a straight line from one to another, I mean.

Quite suddenly she must have realized what was about to happen, with frightful quickness too; one could see it sweep over her – the sense of death – for her scornful mouth dropped wide open, foolish with horror, and throwing up both hands she stepped, swung rather, backwards and sideways, with an extraordinary effect, for during that one moment the wallpaper was clear, all three of them out of it, until at the sound of a shot, a piercingly sharp cry, she fell backwards, and the whole screen – what there was of it – was full again, crowded.

First the two men leaning over her: the one had let fall his pistol – Eva heard it clatter – as he came into the picture, dropped upon his knees. But it was the lover who took her in his arms, raising her, with one hand to her heart. Eva saw the blood soaking from the laces over his hand, while the husband bent forward, without touching her, the tears streaming down his face.

There was a clamour of voices and hurrying footsteps: more people ran into the room, brushing past Eva, passing and repassing the small area of the picture: the principal figures, all that mattered, standing out through them.

Then came the sound of a child crying – frantically and unrestrainedly as a child will, the crying breaking into shrieks, and catching itself up – on the stairs, then in the room itself, with the words, 'Mamma – mamma – mamma!' and a small, fair-haired girl broke into the picture, dropped to the floor at the woman's side, wide-eyed with fear: crouched there tugging at the lace of her sleeve, putting one hand to the side of her face, trying to turn it toward her: and unceasingly, in its child's way, all upon one note, repeating that same cry:

'Mamma – mamma – mamma!'

And remember that here alone, in all the records, was any human sounds, beyond a sigh: the sharp cry of the woman, the actual words of the child. 'In English?' you ask. Oh, yes, it seemed as though the type was persistently more English than Spanish, as it went on. But no, I'm only confusing you again, it is so difficult to remember that the end was really the beginning of the story, starting with the white wallpaper; more English in the beginning, I should say; the lover alone, in this, the first act, pure Spanish.

With the coming of the child, the whole scene wavered and grew confused; at first too crowded, then altogether fainter and fainter; while that heart-breaking cry still continued, stifled, as it were, and yet the more poignant for that – 'Mamma – mamma – mamma!' – until Eva flung to her feet with a sharp exclamation of:

'Oh, but I can't stand this!'

She had no idea what she was going to do, she told me that later.

'I was quite incapable of putting two and two together, that's all I know,' she said, 'though I do remember wondering – not what I was doing, or why I was doing it, but if it was *I* at all – when I found myself in the little scullery filling a bucket with water. The sound of the water running from the tap into the bucket struck me as peculiarly unreal – just because it *was* real, do you know what I mean? I seemed to have got used to other things: I don't know what to call them – appearances of things. Anyhow, I acted perfectly rationally, as one does when one doesn't really know what one's doing; with a queer sort of care, deliberation. I remember how concerned I was not to spill any water on my way through the kitchen and the hall into the large room; trying the bristles of the scrubbing-brush with my thumb, collecting the soap and all that, you know, with the calmest deliberation.

'I often wonder what I would have done if *They* had been there when I got back. I believe I should have sort of pushed my way through them – if one can push through a thing of that sort – and gone straight up to that patch of wallpaper. I was so "set", as the old nurses say, so absolutely certain of where the mischief lay. But, thank goodness, they were all gone, not a sign, not a sound of them: the whole wretched atmosphere gone too: a sort of added chilliness – rather graveyardish – that was all, and what remained of my candle; burning with perfect steadiness, though even that did not satisfy me.

'I had to go back to the kitchen for a knife. I had been furiously impatient with the Spanish workmen for being so slow over stripping those walls; but I could not have believed any paper could stick like that, so diabolically tight! It was a good hour before I got even that much clear, with the floor flooded and myself drenched with water. But at last it was done – *over and done with!* That's what I felt in, oh, the intensest sort of way.

'I went outside afterwards, and strolled down the garden to cool myself. The moon was full out, the sky a clear, deep periwinkle blue, the Peak white with its first coating of snow. I never smelt anything so delicious as the mingled perfumes.

It had seemed almost too much before, but now it was all pure, healing: all – who was it said it, eh? – Shelley? – that – "All exquisite."

'Yes, it was about then – oh, but what's the good of pretending to you? – it was from then, that very evening, that Tom really began to improve – steadily too.

'He pulled me down and kissed me when I went into his room to see if he was asleep. "I've been an awful brute to you all day, old thing," that's what he said. "I don't know what on earth has been wrong, but I felt – and, of course, I know I have been – absolutely poisonous. It's no excuse whatever, but there seems to have been something sort of hanging over me. Was there a storm? I must have been asleep, but that's what it feels like now – as though there had been the devil of a storm clearing the air."

'Like the house? Of course he liked it – after that; we shouldn't have bought it, spent every winter in it, if he hadn't.

'And people were so queer about it, too. They said, the people who came to call, I mean – without knowing in the very least what they meant, I'm sure of that – "there seems to be more room in it, somehow".'

9 The Villa (1924)

The Villa was tall and narrow, the cream-coloured plaster-wash which covered it blurred and patched with greenish-grey. There were small, square stone verandas to all the windows, even the smallest. The roof was covered with crinkled, dull red tiles showing a very moderate slope and wide projecting eaves, in the true Slav fashion. The long, narrow garden was terraced; at the top of the terrace, rather to the right, stood a group of sago palms, and three tall cypresses silhouetted out against the wide stretching waters of the Bay of Gravosa, the wooded slope of Lapad; those evening skies which are nowhere else quite so exquisite and bland.

Everything was thick with moss – steps, terraces and balustrades; the roses ran wild in strangling masses, fell in cataracts of bloom. At the bottom of the garden were the remnants of a decayed landing-stage, patched and re-patched, overhanging the wide and tranquil waters of the Ombla, which rises out of the flat ground – spreading almost immediately to its full width – some three kilometres further inland, and flowing in all for little more than five kilometres before it reaches the sea.

Here on the right bank there is no continuous road, and to reach Ragusa or Gravosa one must first cross the water; though there are oddments of rough cart-tracks running at devious angles away from the river and up among the hills to the scattered houses and hamlets.

All this lent an inexpressible tranquillity to the house, with its air of an elegant and somewhat faded beauty – that strange indomitableness which went with the old elegance of sloping shoulders – inclining a little forward; like a lady leaning her head upon her hand, and gazing at herself in the mirror of the river, re-living the past, watching, with aloof detachment, the sturdy peasant life, the men, women and children in their boats, crossing and re-crossing it; disturbing but never obliterating her own reflection in that stream which is so broad and, to all appearance, so steady and purposeful, that it seems as though it can have no conception of the brevity of the life before it.

And yet, begin or end as it may, the Ombla is quite complete, like a section of any long, wide river, when it passes the Villa, less than two miles from Gravosa; in the same way as the Villa was complete, sufficient unto itself; that Villa of which a chance American tourist, with an order to view, had once remarked, 'I guess I don't see that house fitting itself to anyone, adapting itself to anyone; the tenant would have to do the adapting, realize that he was there upon sufferance, and that's not the sort of colour for me.'

Some empty houses have a melancholy air of feeling the slight that is being put upon them; but this house was not like that: too indifferent for contempt, and yet not altogether indifferent, only secure in its quiet knowledge that of all those who invaded it, no one would stay very long; long enough to alter anything; superimposing their own impression upon what was, after all, a real personality.

And yet it had once been 'just a house', subservient as other houses are; that was up to 1870.

In 1869 the Chadwicks were 'doing' the Adriatic, and stayed for some weeks at Ragusa. In those days an English firm of shippers and general merchants had a business in Gravosa – which is, as you know, the port – Steven, Curtis and Co, of which young Archie Steven was the manager; and he and Daisy Chadwick fell in love with each other at their first meeting.

The Chadwicks went away at once: more properly speaking, they 'took Daisy away', with prompt decision, 'nipping the thing in the bud', as they called it. But they did not go back to America; only as far as Paris, for they were like that with her. They did not want their only child to marry an Englishman and live in Dalmatia of all places; they did not want her to marry at all, unless it were some man of their own set living quite close to them in New York, so that they might see her every day. But after this first spurt of firmness, of which Daisy herself perfectly understood the value, they were divided and weakened between their own desires and the fear that if they 'snatched her away all at once', as Mrs Chadwick put it, it might 'break the darling child's heart. Far better to go about it gradually, give her time to get over it.'

In the end – and it was always the same where Daisy was concerned; she herself had told Archie how it would be – this graduation ended in a rather shamefaced creeping back to Trieste and so on down amongst the islands to Ragusa.

That does not mean that Daisy Chadwick was in any sort of way, above all the modern way, tyrannical or over-strong-minded; but she was spoilt and they loved her, as, indeed, she deserved to be loved. There was a strain of obstinacy, too, but for all that she was very sweet and sensitive, would have been kinder – all round kinder – had she ever known what it was to come in contact with unhappiness; though there was nothing unselfish or unkind in her love for Archie – there never can be that in real, in all-absorbing love, when each finds the greatest joy in the other's happiness; when there may be, and often is, as much avidity in giving as in taking. Anyhow, she was radiant with happiness; there never was anyone so happy, unless it were Archie himself, and he ran her close.

There were a good many Americans in Ragusa just then, and the engagement was celebrated by a tea-party at the hotel; not that imposing Austrian affair of the immediately pre-war days, but a smaller and much humbler hostel, nearer to the town.

Daisy wore white – oh yes, I have a portrait of her as she was then; more, I 'feel it in my bones', as we used to say; have felt it more and yet more distinctly, ever since I came back to Ragusa – a pleated skirt, a looped polonaise preposterously bunched out at the back and decorated with flat bows of black velvet; a bodice with a multitude of small black velvet buttons running straight from the peak below the waist right up to the throat, and ending in a tight little ruffle similar to that which finished off the sleeves.

Her hair was dressed high, very elaborately, balancing her bustle, with something puffed out at the back of her head that was not quite a chignon, finished by a small square-cut fringe in front. She had a frail, slender little figure, dark-brown eyes, large and soft; a pale complexion and a small heart-shaped face. Her mouth was a little restricted, not at all shrewishly, but with that rather pathetic look of a person who feels herself weak and is yet inwardly compelled to get her own way: a something so nearly desperate that it may have justified her parents' fear of her dying, of sheer grief or chagrin, if they separated her too forcibly from her lover.

It was a gay little party. The hotel stood slightly raised above the gateway of the old town, and the window of the Chadwicks' sitting-room looked out on to the sea, the fortress with its grey feet in the water, and that enchanted isle of Lacroma, breathing romance.

Indeed, it was all romantic – the Dalmatian peasants in their pretty dresses thronging the streets immediately below the windows; the sound of strange tongues in the air; the view; the very cakes served at tea. Above all, the age itself, the young ladies with those funny little hats dipping forward on the pretty heads, those streaming veils and ribands; palpitating with excitement over the engaged couple; young ladies with their papas and mammas, no young men apart from Archie Steven, for these had to stay at home in New York occupied by 'that horrid business'.

Oddly enough, it was the lovers, with all their ecstasy of happiness, who struck the one prosaic note in the party. Mr Chadwick was obliged to return to America – that horrid business again: 'As if anyone wanted business', as someone said – and Daisy must either be married at once, or go back with them and wait until Archie should be able to come over and fetch her.

The engaged couple were both against this, as they would be now; and yet even more so, for in those days there was a sort of persistence of haste over this business of getting married, a something which was certainly not passion, and not altogether sensuality, yet nearer to that; for young people had so very little apart from sex in common; while the persistence tended to be a little harder and more fixed on the young lady's side, for the simple reason that time was short, and one lapsed so very quickly into 'an old maid', a lamentable state with nothing to it but loneliness and 'ridiculousness'.

In this case, however, the decision was mutual, and both were equally determined to get married as soon as possible. The very idea of separation – an Atlantic between them! – seemed preposterous, and, after all, there was really no need for it, no shortage of money or anything of that sort: the only difficulty being as to where they were to live when they were married.

There were a good many pleasant villas scattered about Ragusa, Gravosa, Lapad and along the shores of the Ombla in the immediate post-war days, but not as far back as 1869; and the people who had houses there then were established in them for life. They were their 'homes'; they expected them to be their children's homes, and would by no means part with them.

Daisy had a fancy for the Ombla, it was so 'sweetly pretty' and so near Gravosa that Archie would be able to return home for his midday lunch; besides, the idea of going everywhere in a boat appealed to her as very romantic, 'almost like Venice'.

At the very beginning of that afternoon she had merely felt that she 'would like' to live on the Ombla. After she had talked with her friends, and they had applauded her taste, however, it grew to seem the only place. Though, after all, it made no difference where she and Archie set their hearts, for all districts were alike in this, there was no house vacant, either to be let or sold.

'Though there is that one Villa on the Ombla which would just suit you perfectly, if only – only you could have it,' cried Amy Fuller, Daisy's 'dearest' friend, whom she had met and confided in during that very short period of probation in Paris – 'that dreadful time', as she called it – and whose parents had been induced to bring her on to Ragusa, all ready for the part of chief bridesmaid – palest pink, with those new floating panels and ruches, and Dolly Varden hat; that at least was settled. 'It's the *sweetest* place, with its garden sloping down to the river, and such roses! I never saw such roses, terribly in want of pruning though; and the dearest little balconies where Daisy could stand and watch for Mr Steven coming home in the evening, wave her handkerchief to him. A rather tall, narrow house, just opposite to that pretty little church at the first bend.'

'The Villa Carlotta,' said Steven. 'Oh yes, if we could have *that* we'd be all right; but it belongs to old Señorina Frascati, and nothing would induce her to sell or even let it.'

'Señorina – that means "Miss", doesn't it? Only fancy an old maid living in a sweet place like that!' cried someone. 'Such a sweetly romantic place, too!'

'It's belonged to her family for years: she's always lived there.'

'The more reason why she should give it up to us now,' said

Daisy, and laughed; though there was that faint tightness about her mouth. 'Archie, couldn't you persuade her?'

'Nothing would persuade her, my pet; nothing! Why, even *you* couldn't do that.'

'Is she old – really old? Because if she's really old she may die soon,' cried one of Daisy's friends, with the hard cruelty of the young.

'If you ask me, I don't know what's the use of people like that going on living,' pouted another. 'They can't be happy – they *can't*, all alone like that!'

'And the worst of it is they don't give anyone else the chance to be happy, either.'

'Well, if Archie and I have to wait until the old lady departs this life –' began Daisy, a little impatiently: upon which Archie took her hand and remarked laughingly:

'Well, my darling, we can't kill her, you know!'

'Such a lovely house!' sighed Daisy.

'And so altogether what you want!'

'It does seem a shame!'

'Oh, Daisy, it does seem a shame!'

The chorus was broken by Irene Stratton, the intellectual of the party, dark and intense: 'Listen – listen! I have an idea.' She glanced round, saw that her elders were safely out of hearing in the veranda, enjoying the sunset – a soft glow of gold and crimson – and drew her chair a little more closely in towards the others; who edged forward, so that the young heads were bent together in a circle. 'Really an idea – something too thrilling!'

'What? Oh, Irene, what? Do, do tell us!'

'Well, there's something quite new, all the rage, in New York. Rose Farquarson wrote and told me about it – people are going mad over it.'

'What? A game?'

'No, no; something much more serious. They call it "The

Power of the Will".' She paused for a moment, glancing round, giving her astounding words time to soak in.

'But – but –' They were plainly puzzled.

'The Power of the Will. They say people can do anything – make anyone else do anything – if they join together and make up their minds to do it. They just sit round in a circle and hold hands, *willing* something to happen, and it does' – triumphantly – 'it *does* happen! The most out-of-the-way things! Why, even two people can do it if their wills are strong enough, or they really want anything enough. Lena Kelly got Rose to help her will that her beau should come and see her, and he just *walked in*, five minutes later! Five minutes, exactly five minutes! – the time it took him to come from his house to Lena's. She and Rose paced it next day, with long strides like a man's, and that's what it took, to a moment.'

'He might have come anyhow,' protested young Steven, who did not care to think of his sex being so played upon.

'But he wouldn't have done; that's just it! He was dreadfully angry with Lena, because, he said, she'd been encouraging someone else; had gone off declaring that he'd never speak to her or come near her again, more than a week before. And you know how stupidly obstinate men are. Rose says that he looked quite silly when he came in, just as though he'd been walking in his sleep. Oh, of course, I'm sure it could be done; I'm sure of it. Why, I've done it myself, willing people with their backs to me to turn round, and they've always done it! Always! I just say to myself, "Turn – turn – turn", like that, very firmly and quietly.'

'Well, anyhow, you won't will the old Frascati out of her Villa, I bet you anything,' protested Archie Steven, a square-built, dark young man, capable of a sort of restive, sulky obstinacy.

Irene tossed her dark head, Leghorn hat and long drooping white feather: 'You men!' she said; while Daisy broke in, a trifle querulously, overwrought with emotion and excitement, ill-pleased that her lover should seem ordinary and unpliable, lacking in sentiment and imagination.

'Archie, how can you be so narrow and dull! I think it's all too wonderfully interesting. Oh dear, if only, only, we *could*, just put it into that old woman's head to move, think what it would mean to us – to me, anyhow. I have set my heart on that house. I know I said to Amy – didn't I, Amy? – the very first time I saw it, "Why, it's just exactly the place we want!"'

'But, my darling, she won't move, she can't move,' protested young Steven. 'It's no good thinking of it; she's practically bed-ridden. Why, you might as well wish her dead.'

'Well, I don't see why one shouldn't, if –' Daisy Chadwick broke off, turning her head aside, her lips tightening, her face a little sullen, at her lover's horrified exclamation:

'Daisy! Daisy!'

Miss Stratton glanced impatiently from one to another, determined that her chance of showing off should not be allowed to slip through any "silliness".

'Suppose we will that she shall leave the Villa – just that. No one can object to that, for the fun of the thing – as a sort of game – for once.'

She looked round at the young faces, excited and a little awestruck; drew them with something compelling in her dark eyes.

'Come, now, you take my hand, Amy, and Daisy take Amy's. – Oh, of course, Mr Steven must have the other, though he is such a dreadful unbeliever. Now you, Miss Rice – and Millicent and Laura on my left. Ssh! There must be no laughing or talking – Amy! Amy! you mustn't whisper like that; you'll spoil it all.'

Tittering a little, overcome by the imperious beauty's force of character, fearful of seeming silly or 'old-fashioned', the little party linked hands.

'Now, *will*. Will with all your might. I shall say "One – two – three", and when I say "three" you must all repeat to yourselves very firmly: "Señorina Frascati must leave the Villa Carlotta – she must – must – *must* leave it".'

There was a moment's almost breathless silence; then Miss Stratton's voice was heard: 'One – two – three,' and a little thrill ran round the circle.

The sun had dropped suddenly, the wide, bare room was full of grey shadows; tall grey ghosts from the cypresses; huddled swaying masses from the planes and fig-trees which just topped the veranda, moving uneasily, sighing, shivering with the sudden small wind of twilight through their leaves; while the air indoors grew chill. The hands which held each other, clutching tighter and tighter, were like ice, and someone broke out in a hysterical laugh; bitten off, out of sheer fright, even before Miss Stratton's impatient:

'S-s-sh!'

Then something rustled in at the open French window, across the bare polished floor – it might have been the shirr of a woman's silk gown, it might have been the Señorina herself coming to challenge them – and Amy Fuller broke into a shrill scream, cut short by her hand to her mouth.

'Oh, by Jove, I've had enough of this!' cried young Steven, and flung aside from the circle; so roughly that his fiancée, clinging to his hand, cried out: 'Oh, Archie – Archie, you hurt me!'

'You sillies! You sillies! Mr Steven, I'm surprised at you! All for this – this!' cried Irene, her voice shriller than usual, pushing at a large, dry, dead plane leaf with her foot. 'Spoiling it all – how could you! Just when I felt it coming – felt it!'

'What coming?' enquired young Steven, adding under his breath, 'What bosh!'

'Our way, of course. Oh, you men, how dense you are!'

'What's the use of being cross? It was only a game,' pleaded

Amy Fuller, clinging to one of the other girls. 'Nothing but a game.'

'Oh, was it?' cried Irene Stratton darkly. 'Oh, was it, indeed?'

'Anyhow, it gave me the creeps, just like someone pouring cold water down my back,' put in Laura Carr.

'And me!'

'And me!'

'Ugh! Horrid – but dreadfully exciting!'

'And supposing – supposing that she – Señorina Frascati – died? – if that – *that* was the way she left the Villa?' cried another, with a more daring fancy. 'What should we feel like then? How terrible it would be!'

'But why should she die, when no one willed her death?' enquired Miss Rice, more level-headed than the rest. 'No one could be so wicked as to wish for a thing like that.'

'Oh! Oh!' The interruption came from Miss Stratton, with an unusually loud laugh. 'How do you know that, may I ask? Anyhow, mark my words for it, if anyone *did* will her to die, and their will was strong enough, that's what will happen. She'll die, and then perhaps you'll believe what I –'

'Nonsense! Nonsense! Oh, what cruel nonsense!' cried Daisy Chadwick, in such a queer, hoarse voice that they all turned, staring at her through the gloom. 'Things like that are ordained by God; even if we willed and willed and willed' – she had jumped up from her chair, stood looking from one to another almost fiercely – 'it couldn't make any difference, *couldn't*!'

'Oh, couldn't it!' broke in Miss Stratton, with a harsh, offended laugh. 'Really, Daisy, that's all you know. And, after all, if it couldn't, where was the good of all our willing? Amy and Mr Steven broke the spell; but I'm sure, certain, that whatever the one of us who was most in earnest, the strongest among us, was wishing, will come to pass. And it's not always the strongest either; it's the most *intense*. That's what Rose told me. Anyhow, I don't care what Mr Steven says; mark my word for it, that old woman will find herself obliged to quit the Villa Carlotta. Why, I could feel the force of our willing running straight right up through my fingers.'

'Yes, yes; all tinglingly,' put in another girl.

'There, now! Millicent felt it too. Just you see, Daisy, the Señorina will be out of the Villa within a month. And if anyone did happen to wish she'd die –'

'No, no, no!' exclaimed Daisy Chadwick, sharply, passionately. Then again: 'No, no, no!' – her voice rising to a scream.

'Daisy! Oh, Daisy!' Amy Fuller, with her arm in her friend's, felt her sway, stiffened her slight frame against hers, and cried out: 'Mr Steven, Mr Steven, she's fainting!' as the other girl slid to the floor.

Daisy was exhausted and languid all next day. She kept in bed, by the doctor's orders, until early evening, when her insistence upon seeing her lover became such that she was allowed to dress and lie upon a sofa in the veranda, on the most sheltered side of the house; for of course it was impossible for any young lady to see a young gentleman in her own room, unless she were actually dying.

It was then, with Steven kneeling by her side, that she told him of the wish that had taken possession of her, against her own volition, without her knowledge as it seemed: 'I began to say what Irene had told us to – "Señorina Frascati must leave the Villa Carlotta – must leave the Villa Carlotta –" I never even thought of anything else – at least – oh, Archie, I'm sure, *sure* I didn't! And then it was just as though something, someone else inside me, got hold of my unspoken words and twisted them so that I heard myself – just like listening to someone else – repeating over and over again, "Señorina Frascati must die – must die – must die".'

Young Steven had one arm round her, one hand in hers; he did not relax his clasp, but something in the set expression of his face frightened her with the thought of losing him.

'Archie – Archie, you mustn't look like that! It makes me feel a murderess. It can't make any difference – it *can't*! God couldn't let the selfish wish – and it wasn't really a wish – of one silly girl …' she hesitated, not daring to put it into words; then added, 'do that,' almost under her breath.

Archie Steven groaned: 'If that was all,' he said.

'Archie – Archie!' Raising herself a little, Daisy put one hand to his face, turned it towards her, and for a moment they looked straight into each other's eyes; then she repeated, 'Archie – oh, Archie!' and, burying her face on his shoulder, began to cry. For though she was not very clever, she loved him and realized with no further telling what had happened – that her lover himself had been impelled, somehow or other, hating the whole thing as he did, to wish as she had wished; though it might have amounted to no more than this: 'I wish to goodness the old woman was dead, and there was an end to all this fuss and uncertainty.'

One is inclined to think of the early Victorian women as altogether insipid, but Daisy Chadwick must have been very far from that, for all her fragility. It is certain she loved her Archie intensely, too, for it is only a great love that can refrain from reproaches, reminders; and when the atmosphere of menace weighed too heavily upon her, she might, without blame, have assuaged her own misery and self-reproach to some extent with some such spoken words as: 'Never forget, it was you as well as me.' But, small as she was in some ways, brooding and resentful as young Steven so often showed himself with other people, they neither of them ever descended to this; never again spoke the fear that haunted them – though it might have been better if they had, dispersing it all in some small measure – not even when the Señorina Frascati died a week later, from the effect of a paralytic stroke which had fallen upon her the very evening of that ill-fated tea-party: not even when – just at the time young Steven was making up his mind to leave Dalmatia, take what of his interests he could with him to America, making a home at home for his bride – Mr Chadwick, with the air and feeling of having done a great, a magnanimous thing for the young people, announced the purchase of the Villa Carlotta as his wedding-present.

'You can be married when you like, now,' was what he said. 'There's your home practically ready for you to step into, and Mama and I can be getting back to real life again.'

'Real life!' It was strange that so prosaic a man should have uttered words so pregnant, for 'real life' was the one thing that seemed missing in the Villa Carlotta. It was all too like an uneasy dream. The young couple were not unhappy, no one could say that. They were, if anything, too happy. There was something hectic in the avidity with which they seized upon every moment and emotion; almost as though they realized that it could not last; while Daisy Steven flamed up into a beauty of which no one could have suspected quiet little Daisy Chadwick.

'She is lovely,' people said; then added, 'but she is never still for a moment; it would be dreadful to live with her.'

'She is still enough when her husband is there.'

'But how she watches him, never taking her eyes off him! A man can't like that.'

'But he watches her in the same way. Oh, I've seen him – one's as bad as the other in that.'

'As though each were a candle – puff! and it would be out.'

'There is something positively uncanny about them.'

'Something uncanny about the whole household, the house … Well, you know, they do say –'

Heads bent closer, they whispered together, more particularly the older inhabitants of the place; the story grew, beginning with some hotel servant: A spell had been cast upon the Señorina Frascati by the young American woman, and she had died.

'One may wish death into a house,' said someone, 'but it is not so easy to wish it out again.'

The tourist season passed; the summer was oppressively hot; but the old house with its thick walls was cool as a cellar when one came into it. Not that Daisy was there overmuch: anyhow, when her husband was away, for after a few months, when all her American friends had departed, and she was, on account of her health, going out far less than she had done, she spent most of her time on the little landing-stage at the edge of the Ombla; sometimes sewing tiny, intricate garments, but more often sitting with idle hands, gazing down into the water, or out along the short length of the river to the bay; her mouth restricted, her eyes strained; her face, as the sultry summer dragged on its way, growing thinner and oddly haggard, with that flame of beauty wiped out of it.

She had been there practically the whole of one day, having her light lunch, the local fare of goat's cheese, figs and coffee, brought to her, when, soon after four o'clock, she happened to drop her thimble into the water, and went up to the house to look for another; moving slowly, for it was only a few weeks until the time when she expected to be a mother.

At the top of the last terrace she paused to glance back, and seeing a boat that she believed to be her husband's, though he was before his time, hurried into the house, found another thimble, and called to her Italian servant to bring afternoon tea down to the landing-stage; for the house felt more oddly chill than usual after the warm air outside – 'As cold as death,' as someone had once said – and she hated to be in it.

Archie Steven was climbing up from his boat, as she emerged.

The landing-stage had always been rotten; they had talked and talked and talked of having it repaired, and got no further than that. Indeed, they did not want to spend money on the place, had no heart for it.

Anyhow, the steps were quite broken away; one just clambered up out of the boat as best one could. Young Steven's body and one knee were on the stage; he was kicking away from the boat, when Daisy caught the crash of breaking timber, one cry, and ran down the terrace, blinded with a mist of cold fear across her eyes.

Archie Steven was a good swimmer; but there was a swift current, and he was all tangled up with the broken planking of the landing-stage, the overturned boat. From the first moment it was hopeless; and he was out in the Bay of Gravosa before they found him, two days later.

The doctor and the local people who, at this juncture, proved themselves friends, did their best to persuade little Mrs Steven to leave the house, but she would not. Crushed by grief, incredibly aged, all her girlhood gone – though she was not yet twenty – she seemed to have fixed herself into some mood of silent, fierce determination. She would tell no one what it was, but I think I realize it; feeling it in myself with her blood: that fatalism which says, though not in words: 'If They've got to have this' – meaning the Fates, our old enemies – 'or got to have that, let them have it; nothing I can do or say will make any difference.' And something else, too, that old idea of propitiation, of an offering, to the jealous gods, which – in mid-Victorian days – took the form of a persistence in lying upon any bed which you yourself had made.

Anyhow, she stayed in the house, refused to leave it even for an hour; determined to fight it out with it; at least, that's how it seems to me. Sometimes she would go to the window and stand staring down into the Ombla for as much as an hour together, but she never moved out of doors, even into the garden.

One knows, and one can still hear something of what her days were, as she moved like an automaton through those wide, bare rooms. The old Italian servant, who was a young girl then, has told me about it, and there is that feeling in my bones: that *something* more intensely real than vision. But the nights – they are beyond me, with not so much as a hint of what they had to say to each other during those long, still hours – she and that house, robbed of its rightful owner – for, thank God! I am one of those who 'sleep o' nights'.

Anyhow, and one must be thankful for this, it did not last long, for the baby, my mother, was born three weeks later, and Daisy Steven paid the price, the double price, no doubt willingly enough, with her life.

The old Chadwicks, broken-hearted at their daughter's loss, were already on the way to Europe to fetch her, and took the child back with them; while the Villa was let to an Austrian couple, who lived there for eighteen months, at the end of which time the wife died of what seemed like a broken heart, and the husband committed suicide; these two being followed by an impecunious family of Italians who lost their two eldest children in the few months they were there.

It was empty for some years after this, until an eccentric Englishman took it, and died there. There were three or four more tenants, all equally unfortunate; and then, for a space of ten years or more, the house stood empty, intensified in that air of aloof indifference – 'Like a white-faced nun,' as someone put it – for Ragusa had dropped into disfavour as a haunt for tourists, and none of the local families, however poor – and they tried dividing it up into tenements – would so much as think of living there.

Then came a sort of revival. A new type of tourists 'discovered' the place, and it was flooded with artists. Among them a young American couple – my father and mother, Daisy Steven's daughter – who had met and married in Paris, and who, falling deeply in love with the place, took it for the season: more beautiful than ever with its cascades of roses, its air of half-wild aloofness.

Had they attempted to buy the Villa, there would have been the title-deeds to go into, and they might have realized what they were doing. As it was, they made no enquiries; to their minds it was just a delightfully romantic place to camp in and sketch from, to entertain their friends from Paris in; and nothing more. The old Chadwicks had been dead for many years, and though my mother knew that her parents had lived and died in that neighbourhood, it all seemed so immensely far away. Once she did actually say to my father: 'Why, only think that it might have been here, in this very house!' – but that was nothing more than a fanciful conjecture, and never again so much as mentioned between them, so far as anyone knew; while it seems evident that the young wife's spirits remained quite unaffected by the tragic air of the place. And yet it must, in some amazing way, have soaked past her and into her unborn child, for I can scarcely bear to think of the dreams of my childhood; the tall Villa which haunted them, the terror which overhung any walk in a strange place, lest by rounding a corner I should come upon it, be forced by my nurse to mount those terraces, enter that door; all alike ascribable to pre-natal influence alone, for I had been taken away from the place the very day that I was born; never so much as seen a photograph of it.

My father and mother must have been, superficially at least, very unlike Archie Steven and his wife; for during their short life – my mother was but twenty and her husband a couple of years older – the whole outlook upon marriage had changed, superficially – again I insist upon that word, for it is one of the states which never really change – and people no longer took for granted that almost monastical seclusion of the personal life; the jealous appropriations of two people, one for another.

In those days newly-married people were beginning to keep their own boy and girl friends, to go about in separate parties, and the Villa was livelier than it could ever have been since Señorina Frascati's girlhood – or ever had been, like enough – full of gay young voices and laughter.

People were all very certain that 'silliness' and 'fuss' were done with, buried away back in the dark ages. I know my father used to chaff my mother continually about her adorers, of whom she had a train, and she used to chaff him back, with what seemed like the greatest openness and freedom; for of course I have heard a great deal about those days, all 'so very free-and-easy'.

But were they free? – were they easy, even in the beginning? I doubt it; I doubt if there ever is, ever could be, any freedom or easiness in love, with its fierce, primitive emotions, its jealousies, still – and for ever – as persistent as in the dark ages, gloss them over as we may.

There was one young American – also an artist, and originally my father's friend – constantly at the house, though he was actually staying in the hotel at Ragusa. My father made a joke of his evident, but rather theatrical, devotion to his wife – I have met people who were staying there at the time, and it was *the joke*, they said – never betraying the faintest signs of jealousy; continually leaving my mother to the other man's care, with a – 'Oh, Teddy will take you' – 'Teddy will look after you' – 'You don't want me, you've got Teddy' – 'Tch, tch! what a wife!' for ever laughing and teasing: until one day, with no apparent reason whatever, no single word of remonstrance or warning, he walked into the long salon where they were sitting side by side upon a sofa, all the doors and windows wide open, my mother sewing, Teddy Alton reading aloud to her, and fixed his revolver at first one, then the other; finally turning it upon himself and blowing out his brains. There in the clear sunlight, in a mid-afternoon of midspring, with the rest of the party upon the terrace outside – and I insist upon this point, for it was usually in the evening that the menace of the Villa made itself most plainly felt.

Teddy Alton escaped with a grazed shoulder, the bullet shattering a mirror behind him; while my mother was hit in the breast, and died two months later, when I was born.

Somehow or other I have missed the lightheartedness of that intermediate generation. Perhaps it did not go deep enough, was never really there at all – think of the secret, brooding sense of wrong, the truly primitive suspicions and fear and passion, which must have possessed my father, despite his veneer of modernity and gaiety, to lead to such an end. And wondering over this brings one to that other wonder as to what my mother *really* thought, to affect me as I was affected; though it may have been nothing more than the fact that I was conceived and passed the months before my birth in that accursed Villa. How melodramatic it looks when one writes it, and yet that is what it was.

In the end I ferreted out the whole story. The imprint of it all had haunted me until I was a grown-up, but I had never dared to speak of it to a soul, terrified that they might put me down as a lunatic. Strange to say, I never saw any sort of an apparition in the Villa, plainly as I saw the house itself in my dreams, in my mind's eye, had no distinct impression of my mother. But I knew, I *knew* – it was like remembering – precisely how Daisy Steven – my grandmother – had felt, how she had looked, even, in the days before her marriage: her dress, the way she wore her hair, every little pose and gesture. The intervening generation seemed to be partially missed out, hurried and blurred, but it was as though she and I were moving round in a circle to meet each other; every impression growing clearer and yet more clear, as time went on; until at last, unable to bear it any longer I confided in a woman friend, who saved me by the sanest advice.

'Go to Ragusa and see the place. If necessary, buy it and pull it down. Anyhow, face it all out; bring it to book, as it were. It's the only way to shake yourself clear.'

I did that; and even going to meet it, from the very moment I left New York, I seemed to be cleaving my way through the mist. My life opened before me. For one thing, I fell in love on board ship, and though I would not let my lover come with me to Ragusa – for that must be fought out alone – the whole thing served to put me on a par with other, ordinary people. For that was all I wanted: not to be wrapt away and apart, as is the case with most girls in love.

I stayed in a little boarding-house on the edge of the bay in Gravosa, and I can never forget my first sight of the Villa. Repelled and yet drawn, I was like a woman with a mother whom she hates and fears, with whom she is yet strangely at one; whose opinion she defers to in every thought, at once cringing and defying.

Of one thing l am certain: if I had not been engaged to be married, with my lover waiting for me in Trieste, I would never have been able to get away; would have bought the house and lived in it for just so long as it allowed me to do so.

As it was, I acted at once, it was my only hope: buying the house, not to live in but to destroy, turning into it an army of house-breakers.

Even then – and this will show you – though my heart was in Trieste, something else of me, far more persistent and indestructible, was bound up with the Villa Carlotta, and I found myself unable to leave the district so long as one stone remained upon another; wrote again and again, deferring my departure.

The house had me on that, as it had meant to all along; for I could not keep away, and it knew it.

People had spoken of it as being like a 'white-faced nun', and I suppose there were nuns at the time of the Inquisition as cruel as the priests – for that was what it had grown to, out of indifference to cruelty.

And yet it just missed. I suppose that it, too, was growing old, with the spell that little Daisy Chadwick and her sweetheart had wished into it, for I escaped with nothing more than a broken ankle.

I had no business in the house; the men had warned me that it was unsafe. Later on, they insisted upon this as though I wished to dispute it, as though I cared one way or another, being free. Anyhow, I was just going out of the front door, when it awoke from an afternoon doze of senility, realized that I might escape it.

The whole fabric of the place was so loosened, it was little wonder that the heavy stone cornice over the porch fell as it did. It was my own fault; I had been warned – how they reiterated this. 'Fortunate for the American that it caught nothing more than the back of one heel as she went out; a lucky escape, that; more than she deserved.'

How lucky, no one knows; how great my escape, my sense of freedom! And yet, with it all – and is life always like this? – with all my happiness, my new lightheartedness, there is a something that I miss, a queer sense of loss and – well, yes, loneliness – with that Villa, upright and silent watcher at my bedside, gone for ever.

Notes on the stories

BY KATE MACDONALD

1 The Weakening Point (1916)

Georgian: of a temperament from the monarchs of the eighteenth century, a generation of so earlier.

mésalliance: a marriage between unequals, to an unsuitable person in terms of (lack of) wealth, class, or health.

Downs: the South Downs, a range of low hills in the south of England.

Park: not a public park but the private lands belonging to the estate, laid out for pleasure rather than agricultural production.

stud groom: one who works in the stables where racehorses are bred and trained.

hangers: slopes of beech or oak forests.

mullioned: old form of stone window-frames where the small glass panes are separated by stone uprights.

tunic days: before little Victorian boys were promoted to breeches or trousers, presumably before toilet-training had been achieved, they wore easier garments to clean, like a simple tunic and drawers.

bays: matched brown horses to draw the carriage.

one great day: 4 June is an annual celebration of Eton College, so if Bond had left school before then he would have three weeks to get past the dream.

Sandhurst: the Royal Military Academy at Sandhurst, a small town in the south of England, where the British Army's officers are trained.

funked: was unable to complete a riding exercise due to a failure of nerve, a public humiliation.

briar: a Mediterranean and North African wood most commonly used to make tobacco pipes since it is highly resistant to fire.

Michaelmas term: the first term in the university year, beginning at Cambridge on or about 1 October.

pee-wits: lapwings or crested plovers, with distinctive black and white feathers that make dramatic flights low over the fields.

warehouse clerk: the fact that his best friend's sister has taken this job accentuates most clearly the different class positions of Challice and Patterson, since the women in Challice's class do not need to work.

high tea: another class indicator (also a regional one), since the middle and lower classes would have served high tea – a large meal of a hot cooked course followed by bread and butter and cakes – as their meal at the end of the day, whereas the English upper classes would have a formal dinner of several courses later in the evening.

baccy: slang for tobacco, for pipes or roll-up cigarettes. Men of Challice's class would buy their cigarettes ready-made, and would be less likely to smoke a pipe.

first floor front: traditionally the largest and most expensive bedroom for hire in a boarding house, which may once have been a drawing-room when the house had been occupied by a single family.

morphia: now best-known as powerful pain relief, had been used also as a narcotic, similar in strength to heroin.

sent down: because Challice left Cambridge without permission, and gave no excuse, he was sent down, permanently ejected from his studies and privileges as a Member of the University.

Eternity is now: from the autobiography of the English nature writer Richard Jefferies, *The Story of my Heart* (1883).

Wherein one soul: from the Koran, Aya al-Baqarah (The Cow), 2.48.

contriving: the girls would have saved every penny they could to buy the right materials to make the right clothes so as not to shame their brother among the grand Challice family. And this would have taken money they would also have needed for winter clothes.

Nightmare Life in Death: a character in Coleridge's *The Rime of the Ancient Mariner* (1798), who wins the dice game with Death for the sailors' souls.

tiny red marks: possibly marks made by repeated injections of drugs.

Childe Roland: the wandering knight from Robert Browning's poem 'Childe Roland to the Dark Tower Came' (1855).

chariot of Israel and the horsemen thereof: from II Kings 2.12, the cry of wonder and sorrow from Elisha when the prophet Elijah is taken up to Heaven by a chariot of fire drawn by horses of fire.

a meet and hunt breakfast: the local gentry would meet to hunt foxes on horseback with hounds, starting at Challice Court, where they would have a celebratory breakfast taken on horseback with great hubbub and sociability.

2 The Country-Side (1917)

the two sons of Rizpah and the five sons of Michal: these men were killed by David to appease the Gibeonites, but Rizpah watched over their bodies for five months, keeping scavenging birds and animals away, until David relented and had the bodies buried with the bones of their father Saul. See 2 Samuel 21.

Tammuz or Adonis: Tammuz is an early form of the young male lover of the Babylonian mother goddess Ishtar, whom the Greeks transformed into Adonis.

won his blue: he had played rugby (rugby football is what his class would have played, rather than soccer) for his college at Oxford.

seignorial rights: usually this means the 'right' of the lord of the manor to sleep with any woman living on his land if he chose to; it also covers rights to a share of crops and other produce grown on the land. In this context, it suggests an unthinking expectation and sense of entitlement.

coverts: bushy areas where game birds can hide.

New Cut: a road that ran between Lambeth and Southwark in south London, two of the poorest slum districts.

to have gone wrong: to have got pregnant with no prospect of marriage.

Madeira: a fortified wine like a sweet sherry, with a much higher alcohol content than beer.

pepper-and-salt: a light speckled tweed, suitable for shooting in as it would be less visible.

St Paul: in 1 Timothy 5:23, St Paul writes 'Drink no longer water, but use a little wine for your stomach's sake and thine often infirmities.'

waxed whiter: grew whiter, in both senses of enlarging and increasing in intensity.

Honiton: thread lace handmade in the Devon village of Honiton, which was popularized after its lavish use on Queen Victoria's wedding dress.

shambles: traditional name for a slaughterhouse.

uncovered: women habitually wore hats in public in this period, so for a woman to not be wearing a hat suggested an intimacy associated with the private rooms of a house, or a state of undress, or poverty.

Did she put her nose out of doors: If she put her nose out of doors.

slumikin'; slummocking, slang for women with lazy habits and no domestic training.

dursn't: dares not.

'buses: the story is set in a period when the omnibus was being abbreviated to 'bus (and later bus).

Primrose League: an association to support the Conservative Party.

mesen: myself.

whose talk is of oxen: from Thomas De Quincey's *Confessions of an English Opium-Eater* (1821).

super: supernumary part, a part in a stage play with no lines, played by the least experienced actor.

got her mouth: she wasn't secretly drinking an illicit share of the beer.

ulster: a long belted overcoat.

tally-hoing: shouting the fox-hunting call of 'Tally-ho!'

3 The Vortex

horse-leech: from Proverbs 30.15.

domestic: servant.

4 Hodge

verger: a church officer in charge of the fabric of the church building.

waders: wading birds.

jangling keys: its seed-pods.

leaping-pole: a pole used for vaulting over streams or drainage ditches, essential for getting about a semi-flooded marshy area such as the Somerset Levels. A light person can travel as far and as quickly as a stronger but heavier person.

pent-house: a roof ridge with a downward slope in one direction.

Java: modern Indonesia. Bones from an individual later identified as *Homo erectus* were found there in 1892.

Heidelberg: the first bones from an individual of *Homo heidelbergensis* were found in Heidelberg in 1907.

Pitcairn thing: Hector may have been muddled with the names, as the Piltdown Man 'discovery' took place in 1912 (and was not revealed as a hoax until 1953, long after this story was published). There are no known 'Pitcairn man' discoveries.

frail: the basket.

Sir Ray Lankester: eminent British evolutionary biologist and Director of the Natural History Museum.

fugging: an unaired room has an atmosphere of 'fug'.

lees: the bitter particles that remain at the bottom of a bottle of wine, the unusable remainder.

5 The Fountain

change their underwear: before central heating, it was customary to wear a set of neck-to-ankle undergarments in the cold months.

wood-anenome: one of the first spring flowers, with a single white or pink flower on a slender stem.

ilex: a species of holly, casting a deep shadow.

lifted out the trays: trunks contain stacking trays to store clothes efficiently with little creasing.

motor-bonnet: in the early days of cars which had no closed compartments and drove on largely unmade roads, women passengers needed to protect their hair and clothes from the dust with special all-enveloping bonnets and dustcoats.

a Saturday to Monday: a country-house visit over what would later be called the weekend.

Daphne: a naiad from Greek myth, pursued by Apollo, and is turned into a laurel tree to escape his unwanted attentions.

Peri: from Persian mythology, spirits who have been barred from entering Paradise until they have atoned for their wickedness.

people of her stamp: Mrs Brice is a servant, and would need encouragement to voice her opinions to the class that employs her.

stavanging: similar to the Scots 'stravaiging', to roam freely.

paddy: a fit of temper.

'The Low-backed Car': a nineteenth-century ballad by Samuel Lover.

6 'Luz'

thick yellow fog: London's fogs were notorious, caused by particulates from burning coal, only disappearing after the passing of the Clean Air Act in 1956.

Parson's Green: an area in the next borough, perhaps three miles away at most.

chevaux de frise: rows of sharp poles or spikes angled in the ground as a barrier to oncomers.

Hunter's Grove: no longer in existence in central London, if it ever was.

Church St ... Oakley St: they are walking south, down Old Church Street from the Brompton Road, towards the river and then onto the Albert Bridge.

Strophe and antistrophe: formal statement and response by the Chorus in classical Greek drama. The speaker is well educated.

farthing dip: the cheapest of candle stubs, made by dipping a wick into melted tallow.

panacea: a cure-all.

B –: a place in France where the narrator did her nursing, probably Béthune.

made sure: was sure.

7 The Landlady

The Paragon: this oval square may be based on The Paragon in Blackheath, now south-east London, which is half of an oval, and somewhere from which residents would have gone to London, rather than living in it. Also convenient for Woolwich, where Denis worked.

silk rep: a furnishing fabric with a ribbed surface for durability.

Woolwich: location of the Royal Military Academy, the Royal Artillery and the Royal Arsenal, although it doesn't seem as if Denis is a serving military officer.

8 Four Wallpapers

the island: the story is set in Tenerife, one of the Canary Islands in the Atlantic. It was colonised by the Spanish and has a hot, dry climate suitable for invalids.

polonaise: a women's fashion adapted in the nineteenth century from an eighteenth-century mode, of a tailored overdress worn tucked and looped up over an elaborate underskirt.

charing: cleaning houses.

ciggara: Spanish, a cicada, large flying insect with a penetrating and incessant call.

ceindre: possibly a variant form of *cendres*, ashes, for an ash-blonde hair colour.

9 The Villa

Bay of Gravosa: a bay in the Adriatic outside Dubrovnik, Croatia, now called Gruž.

Dalmatia: historically one of the regions of Croatia, now part of the modern state of Croatia.

balancing her bustle: while the bustle stuck out behind her at the top of the skirt, Daisy's profile would have been balanced with an elaborate piled and puffed hairstyle.

post-war days: the narrator is writing in the 1920s.

Dolly Varden hat: part of an 1870s women's fashion for the modes of the 1770s, the hat was a flat oval of straw worn tipped over the eyes, trimmed with flowers to suggest country simplicity.

Leghorn hat: another eighteen-century fashion adapted by later nineteenth-century women. This is a flat straw hat with a shallow crown, with the brim slightly tilted, popularised by the self-portrait by Elisabeth Vigée Lebrun (1782).